I0675533

# This Is Not My Bathing Suit

# This Is Not My Bathing Suit

*A Novel*

# Peter Agrafiotis

HAZYLAND
PUBLISHING

Copyright © 2014 by Peter Agrafiotis

All rights reserved. No part of this book may be reproduced in any form by any electronic or mechanical means, including information storage and retrieval systems, without permission in writing from the publisher, except by a reviewer who may quote brief passages in a review.

Published by Hazyland Publishing
Cape Neddick, Maine 03902


Library of Congress Cataloging in Publication Data
Agrafiotis, Peter.
This Is Not My Bathing Suit / Peter Agrafiotis

This novel is a work of fiction. Names, characters, places, and incidents are either the product of the author's imagination or, if real, are used fictitiously.

Cover art by Edmund Ashley, Emily Larsen, Lincoln Perry & Derek Woods

Author photo by Janice Plourde

Printed in the United States of America

ISBN-13:978-0990532705 (Hazyland Publishing)
ISBN-10:0990532704

# ACKNOWLEDGEMENTS

I want to express my appreciation of the late Alexander Brook for all his advice and careful reading, and for telling me my reporter should be called Alex. And I am grateful to Alison Lurie for suggesting Alex's own voice should be the one to tell what happens. I want to thank Mark Kramer for sharing his wondrous way with words and his perspectives on pungent writing, and Lincoln Perry for his intelligent editorial and conceptual feedback, and also for his artistic contribution to the cover. I very much appreciate Sandy Agrafiotis, Carl Pehrsson, Rose Safran and Maryhop Brandon for their close readings, and Janice Plourde for her expertise at putting this whole project together. I want to thank, too, Baron Wormser and Tom Holbrook for their astute suggestions, and Jeremy Foss for telling me I should write this book in the first place.

*For Janice, the two Sandys, and Helen*

*And now, like a wolf caught in a trap, I remain
fastened, perhaps forever, to the grave of the ideal.*

– Charles Baudelaire

*When his highness sends a ship to Egypt, does
he worry about the comfort of the ship's rats?*

– Voltaire

*America makes all its children want to be famous
no matter how dull they may actually be.*

– Robert Hughes

# Northport, June 1983

"Ba, ba, BAAH! ...Ba, ba, BAAH!" At random intervals, a boy of three or four at the next table taunts his mother. She sits opposite him eating her breakfast while he ignores his. He pumps up the volume aggressively on the last syllable in each repetition, his gaze fixed on her twitchily smiling face. "Ba, ba, BAAH!"

Mommy pauses in her chewing to silently mouth the word "no."

I wonder what she should do. I don't know much about kids. But I do know she should do something to dial back her little dynamo's life force. But what? Reason with him? Of course, I don't think she should hit or scream at him.

"I'm a big BOY! I like COKE!" His final noun overemphasis reminds me of the eighties Bob Dylan doing a concert demolition of one of his formerly lovely sixties classics. Such an association does help me appreciate the vocal stylings of both a bit better – though "appreciate" isn't exactly the right word.

I'm in a coffee shop that caters to the non-affluent who live in the neighborhood's asbestos-sided, two-story "New Englanders," and to the artists who work and, in some cases, live – mostly covertly – in the renovated spaces of the hundred-year-old brick industrial buildings that were once a source of this city's prosperity. I've come to interview the painter John Hulton, an artist of some distinction decades ago, now pretty much presumed dead – presumably, that is, by any who might remember his name at all. But recently I got word that he didn't die, he'd merely disappeared into a bottle. Now word is he's come back out and set up a studio in a factory here in the provinces – in Northport, the town of his birth, and from where he strode thirty years ago in answer to the call he perceived coming from New York City, where he for a while rose high, then, when art fashions changed, fell. I stopped by that studio, a block away, as prearranged, but found it locked. He had told me on his home phone he's not bothering to get one for calls to what's only a temporary workspace. A small electrical fire put his barn studio – attached to his family homestead just outside the Northport city line where he apparently intermittently worked and drank in seclusion – out of commission. Right now electricians are hard to get, he'd said. Hard if you can't afford to pay them is what I think. I left a note on his door that he could find me here. That was almost an hour ago.

"Ba, ba, BAAH!"

I risk a questioning glance at the mother. She replies with a questioning glance of her own. Well, she's got my question wrong. I'm asking about her son, not her. Instinctively – though inconsistent with my interests at this moment – I glance at her ring finger. No ring. Unfortunately, she notices my focus there and smirks. She's okay-looking, I'm thinking. But that kid!

That's a bad attitude, I know. I'm sure I need to rethink the idea of kids in my self-centered life now that I'm single again. Angela didn't want children, and that was fine with me. But most women do want kids. A lot of attractive, age–appropriate, single women – I'm thirty-three – have kids already. I imagine some might even have four or five. The little boy perceives that his mother's attention is not 1000 per cent focused on him. He twists around and retargets – through the bars of his bow-backed chair – onto me. "Ba, ba, BAAH!" he

2

challenges the intruder to his oedipal territory.

I give him a faint smile and look away. A handsome boy, I'm thinking; soft, supple flesh over a bone-structure that, in combination with those disarmingly cool blue eyes, could easily become, soon enough, the face of a bully. Probably much the same face as the one that spent a night or two – or ten, or two hundred – then departed, leaving behind a lifelong reminder.

I glance back at mother and child. Mom is looking in my direction expectantly. But even if I found her devastatingly attractive, *and* I could immediately resolve – or conveniently forget – my fatherhood phobia, this is not the time or the place for starting. I give her a good-natured nod and turn to carefully swish and examine the remaining coffee in the bottom of my cup. I concentrate my drifty mind on why I came: a work assignment.

"Ba, ba, BAH."

Within my periphery, I see that Mommy is still side-longing in my direction. So this seems like the moment for a quick trip to the men's. Hulton, I'm getting the impression, is either casual or copeless about keeping his appointments. Alcoholic behavior, I imagine. I hear that the habits can persist after the tap has been shut off. But I doubt he'll have split-second bad timing, too, and show up in the next two minutes. I leave my bush vest on the chair.

On the way, I pass all kinds of kitschy stuff that is, or tries to be, the little restaurant's identity. A wooden sled, a plastic statue of Marilyn Monroe, a fish tank filled with frogs. Frank Sinatra's sincere voice – probably intended to be heard ironically, though – drifts softly from suspended speakers up in the corners of the black-painted, pressed tin ceiling. This place seems to be run by kids for kids – and as a challenge to adults. By kids, I mean twenty-two or twenty-four year olds.

In the bathroom, taped to the wall, a hand-lettered sign reads: "Clean Restrooms Are Up to You." I wonder how they enforce this. Maybe I missed some ticket you're supposed to take when you enter the place. And if your number comes up, that means it's your turn to

3

scrub the toilets – perhaps in exchange for free pancakes next time. A lot of artists are broke enough that that might actually be a good deal.

As I recover my seat, my attention hones right onto a striking young woman who's just entering – and then to the equally unusual-appearing young man accompanying her. She has white/blond birds-nest hair, and skin almost as white. She wears a military-drab jumpsuit and carries a black portfolio case. Her features are a bit too irregular for serious beauty, but she exudes something I like – I don't know – sexiness of an off-beat kind. Right now she seems to be pouting. I hate to admit that for me this adds to her attractiveness. Why is that? – And here I've just rebuffed an inviting smile from an over-indulgent, maternal type.

I realize I have seen this woman before. But I can't remember where or when. How would I not remember a pretty woman so strange? Her boyfriend appears no less exotic and actually is the prettier of the two. He has finer, more symmetrical features and a skin tone as rich as hers shows absence of any richness. Middle Eastern appears his ethnic heritage. The two bicker. His lilting voice tells me that he is gay, therefore not her boyfriend – just a boy *friend*. He stops the waitress and asks her something. She points to a door behind the counter. He scurries off that way. In thirty seconds he returns, and they resume arguing. Eventually she shrugs and hands him the portfolio. He opens it and removes what turns out to be a poster. Then he takes a plastic Baggie from the pocket of his billowy, elastic-ankles pants. From this he extracts pushpins. He mounts the poster on the wall behind where other arriving patrons have started seating themselves. When all at that table are down, I can see the poster's entirety. The image and text are minimal – though compelling enough. In a black bikini, the white/blond, white-skinned woman stands on one Doc Martens-shod foot, as if in frozen stride. The printed words say: "Contexts: Homage to Magritte, A Performance by Lucinda York. Blue Heron Beach, Marshland Section. June, eight" – tomorrow – "5 p.m. Be There Then." Now I place her. She's a performance artist I'd once seen – though a being transformed from a brunette, rather hippyish Lucinda York, who'd presented herself and her work several years ago in a temporary space in Boston's South End. She was probably newly graduated from art school – assuming she'd gone. She'd looked, then, early to mid-twenties. The performance was about breasts. And breasts of all sizes, presumably fashioned from foam rubber or Styrofoam, littered the stage and levitated above it. The accompanying written text denounced Western cultural fascination with the female breast. Called it regressive male hysteria. (Or something like that.) And the piece addressed a second tier complaint, too: inadequate funding for breast cancer research. At one point, the artist's own breasts became part of the performance. They were painted florescent blue, or perhaps were white and just appeared blue under the glow of the black light in the darkened theater.

When the piece ended I wasn't sure exactly what I'd gotten from it. My companion for the ride down, and roommate at the time, Stuart Cohen, didn't much help me get a handle on what Lucinda York had to say. He commented only, "Nice tits." I couldn't tell if he was being clever about all the breasts we'd seen or was just performing – or even pretending at – the requisite male/male solidarity confirmation: A man or boy almost always mutters this statement whenever two or more men or boys find themselves confronted, at a safe distance, by breasts, covered or bared, of above average size.

The artsy/new-wavy couple exits the coffee shop. And I realize that mother and son are now absent, too – their vacant table a plane of muffin crumbs and dripped pretend maple syrup. I guess she didn't like me as much as I thought. Just as well: I hadn't even noticed their departure – nor the refilling of my mug. I sip the coffee and muse that, as one of my several job titles at the paper is *reviewer*, I have a professional duty to "Be There Then" – Blue Heron Beach tomorrow, at five. That is, if I can get the boss's okay. I decide I have been here too long. Whether Hulton has had another fire or is off on a morning bender, I can't wait to see. I need to get across town to

Capt'n Tony's on the pier, to interview the man himself for his payback advertising feature. After that I've got to at least make an appearance at the paper.    And I should fit in checking on my grandmother – since her cottage is not far from Phillip's Cove. It's a shame Hulton didn't show – he would have been today's better story. Tony is about the most boring man I've ever met.

A kid in shorts and Capt'n Tony's tee-shirt tells me Tony will be late. Someday people will fear keeping a man like me waiting. But for right now, it's okay. This pier is my favorite place in town, and for a half hour, I'm a free man and the humid early June morning is wondrous. Turn off my mind, relax and float down stream.

"Hey, mate!"

Too soon the world intrudes.

A male voice rasps across twenty yards of 10:00 a.m. summer air – from a Novi-built fishing boat to where I stand slouched against a weathered piling. I know who it is. I don't want to answer. I don't want anything encroaching on this caffeine-spiked, work-avoidance reverie I'm slipping into, my mind adrift on a morphing rainbow of spilled diesel fuel that I watch shimmer on the Cove's rippling surface. Transcendence by pollution. A guilty pleasure.

Copper pulses into paisleys of teal, then into gold. Anyway, in another minute this incandescent slick will have disappeared – evaporated onto the morning breeze.

"Alex Perkins!" Fred Avery hails me again.

I give a limp wave without looking up. It's not just coffee, summer air, Tony's tardiness, and some boater's careless refueling that I have to thank for the halcyon intimations. Oblique light playing over any water – or shining on grass or creeping along a wall – could entrance me even as a kid. Lots of beautiful things can do that. I'm pretty much what you would call a "beauty addict".

"Perkins – we'll want a han at tha dock!"

Fred intermittently affects those "Down-Easter" tones. Throws in an accented word or two every few sentences. He was born in

6

Machias, Maine, maybe forty-two or -three years back, and is proud of it. But his family relocated here in Northport, Massachusetts, so his father could get a better job. I happen to know this was before Fred spoke more than a dozen words in any accent. Fred cultivates inscrutability. But, he's easier to read than he thinks. Without hope of further evading, I disengage from the remnants of drifting refined fossil fuel to try to focus on Fred Avery on his idling *Laura T,* waiting his turn about a dozen yards out while a lobstering vessel casts off from the floating dock fifteen feet or so below wharf level on the ebbing tide. But my attention is drawn to a gleaming yacht of forty or forty-five feet, still under sail on the fresh southeast breeze. It's also approaching the dock. And it's moving, it seems, much too fast.

As I try to be heard shouting, "What do you need, Fred?" above the thrub, thrub, thrub of the departing lobster boat, the sailing craft cuts my line of sight and sound to the *Laura T.* It flashes into the narrow expanse of water between the fishing boat and the dock. The skipper of this interloper consummately single-hands his quarter-million worth of racing equipment. He dumps wind by rounding up to windward at the optimum invisible point and as effectively curtails forward motion as if he'd thrown the boat's motor into reverse – which, by harbor rules, is what he really should have done anyway. The shock-absorbing white plastic fenders, dangling from his vessel's rail, only gently nudge the floating dock when he connects. I look across to the now once-again-visible *Laura T,* expecting to see Fred riled. But he only looks amused. Or he wants it to appear that way. This sailor has been lucky in randomly picking Fred Avery to cut off. An angry outburst would be a predictable reaction from most fishermen around here. One in ten might grab a deer rifle and fire it in the air. But doing anything predictable would be against Fred's code.

The skipper – tall, fifty-ish, impressively tanned in pressed, cream-colored slacks and a French vanilla jersey with its collar raised – lets his mainsail and jib flap. He waves a dismissive thank you to Fred, as though his taking Fred's turn is what is sanctioned by the coast guard's *sailboats have right of way over power*. With the breeze paralleling the leading edge of the dock, his luck holds and the boat shows only a mild inclination toward outward drift. He swoops to the deck amidships to take up the coiled half of a line, pre-positioned there, that runs to the bow. Then he steps gingerly onto the spot Fred, by all rights, should be occupying. He snugs the line around a cleat, hops back on board, paces aft, and picks up a coiled stern line. This guy's meticulous, I'm thinking. I'm a bit of a sailor, too, but I usually coil lines only after hauling a boat out in the fall. Sometimes not even then. Stepping back onto the dock, he loops this rope under a cleat at the opposite end, then shifts his weight against its tugging, listing slightly into the wind, reining in his flighty Pegasus to the public rail. He glances at his watch then frowns up to where I stand at the top of the gangway.

The muscles of his cheeks abruptly shift to project what I guess is a version of smiling, an expression usually indicating pleasure. However, his face has a grimacing quality usually associated with something like gastric distress.

"Ah!" he intones. "There you are. I'm glad to see you *can* seize the morning."

I, not fully revived from my reverie, for a second perceive he's addressing me.

"Heads, fella," I hear from immediately behind me. Someone intending to slide past onto the ramp and down to the float. He carries a cooler on his opposite shoulder and its bulk cocks his head toward me. His grinning face, only a foot or two away as he passes, exudes goodwill.

"All yours," I say, gesturing toward the ramp.

"Cheers," he says, upping the bonhomie.

Something about him is familiar – as if I'd encountered this face only yesterday. *The Big Chill*. That new movie with the overly snappy dialogue, the one that's about ex-hippies turned yuppie. Actually I reviewed it for *Currents* only a few weeks ago. This guy looks like the actor who plays the TV star – a detective, or something – who jumps into convertibles without opening the doors. Tom Berenger. Who knows? It's June in Northport and the boat is expensive enough for a Hollywood type. Maybe this guy *is* Tom Berenger.

And my Hollywood moment is further drawn-out by the demure nod and eyes-only smile I receive from the man's female companion, trailing a few paces behind. She doesn't look like any movie star I can think of. Yet, if she could only stumble through even the most pedestrian of scripts, she might still – the way her green, almond eyes project a truly gorgeous other-worldliness (India, perhaps?) – be "box office." These, I realize, are the "beautiful people." We get to see them only in summer here in the provinces. Even the captain – for all the oddity of his facial expressiveness – has a kind of beauty. The beauty that money conveys. Does my beauty tropism extend that far?

"William – where's Justin?" asks the yacht captain of his friend when he reaches the bottom of the gangway. So, he isn't Tom Berenger. I watch the woman descend the steep ramp with grace.

"Hungover," William replies. "Did you really think you could get a philosopher moving at this hour?"

The captain scrunches the corner of his mouth unpleasantly. "What hour?" he says. "It's five past ten. Well – can't be helped. At least your lovely Rebecca is here." He reconstructs the unintended near grimace of a moment before to impart his delight in offering a hand to this Rebecca stepping aboard. Rebecca's aspect is all serenity. I'm aware of having never observed three more disparate facial expressions in a twenty-second, three-person greeting.

But, this captain's smiling – or whatever it is – is short-lived. He suddenly and inexplicably scowls at the sky and comments, "Perfect day. Southeast, ten to twenty." He trades the stern line for the cooler William holds, and, nodding sideways toward the docking lines, steps aboard himself. William unfastens the bow line, but holds it under the cleat for leverage while his captain starts the diesel. At a nod from the captain, he casts off and boards. The captain puts the engine into gear and swings his vessel to starboard, out toward the harbor's mouth. When its stern finally faces me I can see the boat's name, *Pure*

9

*Conception,* painted on the transom.

*Oh.* That's who this sailor is: Arthur Dalmore, new curator of the Northport Museum of Modern Art – the NoMMA. We got a press release at the paper cataloguing his credentials – and also citing his pleasure at finding a new homeport for his J-44 of the name I see on the swiftly departing yacht. Calling his boat that, stuck in my mind.

My paper, *Currents,* is a Northport weekly tabloid, and arts stuff arriving there comes to my attention. Technically, I'm editor of the arts section – though that doesn't carry with it any extra remuneration or special distinction. I don't really have the knowledge base to deserve any, anyway. But I also write about rock concerts and, as I said, movies. And I've already divulged I write about our advertisers. Arts writing in a small city – even one where on this particular morning the artsy types seem to be coming out of the woodwork – won't pay all the bills.

So, I know that Dalmore, with much fanfare, was recruited for his Northport Museum post just a few months ago, from the Whitney in New York. And I guess this "William" sailing companion of his, would be William Kahn. Art star, not movie star. A much smaller universe of stars. But he's still a shining one right now. And he still looks like Tom Berenger. The paper received a press release about Kahn, too. He's hot. Or they want you to think he is. He'll be staring in his own show, a retrospective at the NoMMA, opening next week. He's young for that. Not quite forty, but that's the way it is today. I guess track records go into the books a lot faster now. I have a cousin, Kevin Perkins, who works as an assistant curator at the NoMMA. Coincidentally, I've been hitting him up to get me an interview with this Dalmore. It could be a hot story. Kevin has told me that his new boss would like to turn the Northport Modern into the Northport *Post*modern. Lots of strange *art* along the postmodern cutting edge in the last decade or so: artists-locking-themselves-in-boxes *art*, painting-by-vagina *art*, beauty-is-the-enemy-of-art *art*. Quite a challenge to a local Northport boy and "beauty addict." And, now having seen this imperial city art consul – *and captain,* as well – I experience a surge of under-confidence. My world, I know, is really a pretty small one.

"Alex Perkins!" Fred Avery shouts yet again. I look down and see his mate, David, jump from the *Laura T* to tie up where *Pure Conception* briefly docked just moments before. Back to reality. So finally I shift my attention to Fred. Fred lives next door to my grandmother, and, I'm embarrassed to admit, since my divorce, *me*. I let Angela keep our place. I was a gentleman. Well, it was only a rental, anyway. So, I'm thirty-three years old and I live with my grandmother. From where I stand above him, Fred, tall and broad-shouldered, with long arms and huge hands, looks apish. He's in baggy overalls even on this very warm day. Early heat wave coming, they said. His feet knead the deck that rises and falls with the remnants of *Pure Conception's* wake. As if aware that any irritation in his voice might suggest that members of the yachting set displacing him at the dock has him ruffled, Fred speaks jauntily.

"What brings a member of the press down here to visit us among the toiling classes?" he asks. Fred can be counted on to exaggerate or understate alternatively for rhetorical purposes. Whatever it takes to maintain the upper hand.

"I've got to do a business feature on Tony's." I swing an arm toward the restaurant, Capt'n Tony's Chowder House, farther down the pier. "Bonus for all the advertising he does."

David Player, Fred's lanky, wild-haired bait cutter, a young man of about drinking age hired at the beginning of spring, addresses me now, too: "You going to review Tony's photo exhibit of all his old boats?" He gives me a brief conspiratorial half smile, then looks away, his eye following a swooping gull as it skims the water. This and the sea breeze ruffling his fair curls remind me for an instant of Billy Budd. Perhaps David is "beautiful people" of a completely different kind.

"Just business today," I reply. I was never really introduced to David, but after a half dozen encounters like this, that's pretty moot. Apparently Fred has told him what I do for work. Of course, it could also be that he's read my stuff. I put my by-line on reviews and features. But not on stories like this morning's. I don't go out of my way to let most people know that I write promos for restaurants and tourist shops. It might take the heft out of my *reviewer* image. But I view image differently with the likes of Fred and David. Writing promos is white-collar grunt work: cuts the elitism associated with "writer" or "the arts." Helps me fit in as the wharf rat a part of me still wants to be. I worked half of my eighteenth summer as a cutter, like David. But it was on a party boat, so a big part of my job was butchering all the blue sharks the tourists hauled in. I quit mid-season cause I couldn't take the gore. So, member of the press or not, I'm a legitimate Northport local. Went to college in Boston, but came back unscathed, I think.

"Kindly lend us a hand heah." Fred's tone now does shift to impatient.

I look down upon the sticky chaos of the deck of the 30-year-old wooden vessel, measuring my commitment, at this moment, to solidarity with the "toiling classes." A diesel engine, starting up a few moorings out, rips the morning air. Then it idles down to a hollow thrumming. "I'm kinda not dressed for it…"

"You'll only dirty one hand," Fred insists, pointing with his boat hook, "and that ya can wash in the head over yonder."

Cut the crap, Fred, I'm thinking. Even in Maine people haven't said "yonder" in a hundred years. At least Fred *asked* for my help. Probably did because we are out in public. Nearer home, if he spots me between Gram's house and my car, he usually just says, "Stop," then shambles over and hands me some gadget or even just a very smooth piece of metal. Probably he worked all night getting it that smooth. He might instruct me, "Put your hand out. Palm up," as if offering a bush-dweller a look at the first pocket watch ever to glitter in dark regions. The upside of having him for a neighbor is that he is a genius at fixing things – like Gram's old furnace – or for replacing wiring in the attic that squirrels have been munching on. Whenever anything seems out of whack, Gram says, "Call Fred." Then, as soon as he recognizes my voice on the phone, he'll start in talking – as if he was the one who'd placed the call – about something of great technical interest only to him and perhaps a few of his cronies.

David jumps in and explains the chore at hand: "We just need some human to slide the chain from the overhead winch out to us. The horizontal action motor is fried and it takes two of us to position it to the chain girdle on the barrel. Yesterday when we came in we tried asking some of the tourists to do it. But, they just stared and backed away. They come here to look at the boats – they don't expect the boats to talk to them."

The local macho rules call for remaining deadpan in the face of a fisherman's joke. I silently comply with the request. This young guy does seem to have a sensitivity to irony. He reaches up and grabs the easy-swinging, 15-pound iron hook at the end of the chain I've sent his way. Then he jerks it down three dozen links and clips it to the chain girdling rig Fred holds in place on the barrel sitting on the open stern deck. I pick up a small metal box at the end of a galvanized conduit-encased electrical cord. I've been in on this hoisting procedure before.

"Now?" I ask. Fred nods. I push a red button and the barrel lifts off and clears the stern rail. Fred scrambles up the ramp, boat hook in hand, and pulls it laterally onto the wharf.

"I've been tellin' the harbormaster for a month, that motor was goin' ta burn out if he didn't get grease onto tha bearins. But no. Bad connection on the fog lights, too. They been goin' on and off for a week. Frank Moulton put a gouge in Sam Clark's transom because of it. That Bud Henderson just sits in the harbormaster's shack all day, a can a beer in his han. Or else he's not even around. He took awf, all dressed up, fifteen minutes ago. He shud resign or be fired. What'r we payin' taxes and moorin' fees for?"

I, too, had noticed Bud Henderson leaving. He hadn't really looked "all dressed up" to me. But with Bud, just not having his fly down could qualify for that. Likeable guy though.

Fred is clearly in a bad mood – which he normally isn't; I'll have to say that for him. Semi-rational cheerfulness is usually his manner. It almost makes up for his compulsive technical advice about how everything on the planet could be done better. Somehow I think his pique is more than just being put in his place by the yachting crowd. Then I remember. I saw him washing his truck yesterday morning – probably the first time since he bought it; and perhaps first time for any truck he's ever owned. Fred was taking the day off to go to Boston. A woman – a weekend visitor in a party of nurses that, for a spring lark, had signed on and gone deep-sea fishing on the *Laura T* a few weeks ago – had given him her number. Fred doesn't often get phone numbers handed him by women.

"Hey, Fred – how was your date?" I risk asking, probing for a connection to his sour tone.

Fred scrunches his mouth. "No date," he says. "Her old boyfriend just got back to town. She's decided to try it again with him." His Down East accent has departed.

"Too bad," I reply. I'd been rooting for him. "Not too nice of her not to tell you. Could have saved you the trip."

"Ya, well, it isn't really her fault," he starts generously. David has climbed the ramp and stands near me on the wharf now. He takes charge of the barrel. Fred tells me the story that I imagine David has already heard. "She says it's been on again, off again with that guy for five years. He's always rolling in and out of town. It's been rough on her. She knows that he meets a lot of women through his work."

Typical musician, I'm thinking. "What's he do?"

"He's a bus driver," Fred says with distaste.

I work at keeping my facial muscles under control. "A real rogue," I say.

"Yeah," says Fred, shaking his head.

David gives a grunt of support. Then he says, "When I was in Peru they were all like that." David, it seems from my encounters thus far with him, compares most of the things in this central New England coastal world – which, for all I know, he may have left only once – to Peru. Fred told me, when he hired him, that David had

14

seen a picture of Machu Picchu in high school geography class and a year after he graduated he and some pals up and went. That showed he was enterprising enough to go to sea, Fred said.

"Who were like what?" I ask David.

"The bus drivers. Always wore white shirts with two or three top buttons unbuttoned. Sleeves rolled up. Pack of cigarettes in the pocket. Real macho," he says, face glowing. "I remember one time, coming back to Cuzco on a bus, we got stopped at a one lane bridge. There were these two trucks face to face on the bridge with cars lined up behind them both ways. Neither truck driver would back off and move first. Our bus driver leans out the window and hollers something in Spanish – that's all they speak down there. But nobody moves. So our driver jumps out and goes up onto the bridge and right up to the driver's window of the truck that's coming our way. He steps up onto the running board, and he just hauls off and slugs the guy driving the truck right in the face. Then he stands down, backs up two feet, hooks his thumbs in his belt, and stares. The truck and the whole line of cars behind it back up and clear the bridge. And we go right through. – I'm thinking, 'Now there's a *bus driver*!'"

He nods in affirmation and gives me that half smile again. Is he a master of irony or just an incredible space-shot? I've observed him for over a month now and I still can't tell. Most likely he's a combination.

I let the profundity of his little hero-worship story settle for a moment. Then, wiping my hands together in a parody of brushing away any rust stains, I say, "Well, duty calls," and "See ya," and I stroll off down the wharf toward the Chowder House for my business chat with Captain Tony.

Besides the fishermen, it's mostly seniors on the dock at this time of day. But, my eye catches on a pretty young woman in a short summer skirt. No, I'm wrong. She's wearing shorts. Same amount of leg showing, but there's a big difference in the way you think about it. Where women are concerned I often see what I'm hoping for, rather than what's there – at first anyway. "Projection," I learned in Psych

101, is the term for wishful seeing like this. When I was a teenager in the late sixties and young women used to hitchhike, I could catch a glimpse of a fire hydrant or just about anything at the edge of the road far ahead and actually think I saw some free-spirited flower child in need of transportation. And, of course, I "saw" *her* as beautiful. If ever an actual female did emerge, she would lose several degrees of beauty every 50 feet closer to her I got – until she finally turned out to be a normal person as I passed by. I passed by because she, if even female, almost invariably did *not* have a thumb extended.

I think this will be the third story I've had to do about Tony in the three years I've been with *Currents*. This commerce stuff bores the pants off me. But I think my business writing duties help keep me grounded. And the art world seems too precious a place to spend most of your time. It's the eighties now and the anti-materialism of my younger years has faded away. – "It's morning in America," says Ronald Reagan. Still, I'm not likely to turn into a yuppie like *The Big Chill* crowd. But I could use some real money. I do like my job, it just doesn't pay enough. And I need real money to start construction on land I purchased a couple of years ago – bought it to build a home for Angela and me. She let me keep the land when we divorced – a nice trade-off for my having been the one to move out. She was never tight about money, anyway. Her father had enough that she didn't ever need to give it much thought. I'm going to have to start making some changes pretty soon. A guy can't expect to live with his grandmother for very long and still hope to get laid frequently. I guess *frequently* is a little misleading. It implies at least *some*. And it's going on six months since the break-up. But, aside from sexual deprivation, things are pretty much okay.

I enter Capt'n Tony's for his interview. Tony is crazy for publicity. The old guy thinks he's a celebrity of sorts; that everybody's impressed by what a popular place he owns. With his location it seems to me he'd have to serve boiled chicken instead of boiled lobster to *not* be popular. I didn't just pull this concept out of the blue. Back in my LSD days a friend of mine came back from Viet Nam and gave me his red tinted night-vision goggles. Wearing them in the daytime cancels out any red within your view. I had them on once here on the pier when I noticed Tony had the oddest of signs: *Capt'n Tony's Live Boiled Chicken*, it read – or appeared to. The words *Lobster and Barbequed* were printed IN RED between *Boiled* and *Chicken*, and it took some confused moments to figure out whether madness had come into Tony's method – or into me. The suggestion of popping into Tony's for the live-boiled chicken was the in-joke of the summer of '72. But as a grown up, when I think of Tony's, what first comes to mind is how after ten or fifteen years of my going in there, all the man ever talks to me – and, possibly everybody else – about is how business is going. Well, I remember one exception; once when I went in there as a teenager. Instead of telling me how good business was he told me how bad his hemorrhoids were. I'd heard he was gay. Well, I guess they didn't even have *gay* then. I'd heard he was *queer*. Phillips Cove and nearby Blue Heron Beach are cruising grounds for gays from Boston. Faster than going to Provincetown. I mean the travel time is less. Capt'n Tony's always had lots of young male help, in his shorts and tee-shirt uniform, that apparently certain older men liked to call "Capt'n Tony's Boys" – implying, to the gullible, that Tony had them other than as employees. Since I didn't know anything about anything then – except maybe I'd heard in eighth grade that straight young men shouldn't bend over around people of the homosexual persuasion – I'd assumed a homosexual telling a young guy like me – whom he didn't even know – *anything* about his asshole was some sort of pick-up line. So I got pretty uncomfortable. And then I embarrassed myself again later telling friends about the incident. It turned out talking about hemorrhoids wasn't a gay turn-on. I also was informed pretty emphatically that Tony isn't gay either. One of life's truths that I encounter again and again is how easy it is to embarrass yourself.

The interior of the restaurant glows butterscotch from all the shellacked knotty pine. It doesn't open until eleven. The kitchen is busy, the dining room quiet. Tony Maxwell has an office the size of a closet – I assume to allow for as much seating as possible. I think he has exhausted the planning board's generosity toward him for building decks hanging out over the water. I see him hunching over ledger books and jotting numbers with a pen. He doesn't seem to hear me, so I knock on the doorframe.

Tony looks up. "Mr. Perkins," he says.

"How are you today, Tony?" I don't ask about his hemorrhoids. It's been fifteen years, so I assume they are better.

He looks down at the desk again, trying to find his place by letting his fingers do the walking. His index finger presses a spot and he looks up and says, "Oh, I guess – I'm fine. Just not as good as I was June seven of '82. We did twenty-nine more dinners last year. I can't understand it. Do you remember what the weather was like a year ago today?" He shoves the ledger book away two inches and picks up a brass letter opener.

"Today is the sixth," I say.

"I know, I know," Tony reassures. "Until we close at ten tonight, I'm still going on figures for the sixth. This isn't the best day for me to talk about business. Can we wait until next week to do this story? Cold front's coming through on Thursday. Unsettled with showers. We always do better lunches when people can't go to the beach."

"I'm afraid not, Tony. Free story. Those go in on space available. And we've got the space now. Maybe you don't need to run the exact figures." I venture offending him. "I think you might have done that last time, anyway." Might have!

He squints at me. One of his eyes completely closes. I don't think he is trying to look like a suspicious pirate, but with the way he twirls the dagger-like implement, point on the index finger of one hand, handle in the other, this is what I can't help but see. I know I have introduced a concept spiritually alien to his whole being, and for the tiniest fraction of a second I worry this might make it seem necessary for him to take my life. The moment teeters uncertainly.

Finally he says, very slowly, "Do you think that would be all

18

right?"

I don't want to seem too enthusiastic and tell him just how all right it would be. He must be made to believe I see this as only an emergency measure. I hesitate, so as to show I'm letting the gravity of it sink in on me.

"Oh...I...think...so," I say. "Why don't we start with how nice your deck is with its incredible view...?"

In fifteen minutes, I'm out of the restaurant with a bunch of clichés and Xeroxes of sheets of this year's figures up to Memorial Day, when he was still running ahead, and those for last year and the year before. You'd think he was trying to sell stock – or the whole place – wanting that stuff in the paper. Well, it works for him. So, who am I to judge.

I go over and sit on top of a low piling in the sun. Not much chance of restarting my reverie, though. Too much pressure. The *Laura T* no longer rests at the wharf. The human *Laura T*, by the way, is Fred's ex-wife. It is traditional on this coast to name your boat for your beloved. Laura left Fred about five years ago. I still see her around occasionally in the company of a woman who looks a lot like Fred – so the attraction must have been based on something real. But it is considered bad luck, and definitely is a lot of red tape, to change a commercial boat's name. Now, unlike the old days when the boat-naming tradition originated, fishermen are often ending up divorced before their bottom paint may even be cured. Those who persevere the rigors ashore and eventually get to sea often find their vessel sporting the name of the new bride of a competitor several waves to windward. But, I assume hard feelings are rare among men of such common experience, inclination, and taste.

# 2

"Hi, Gram – I'm home." I find her in the kitchen at the stove. Not the best place, considering her bad eyes.

"Hi, darling," she says. "No work today?"

"I had a story nearby. Business story. Captain Tony's. He says, 'hi.'"

"That Tony," Gram says, waving downward with her gnarly fingers, apropos of I can't imagine what. Gram loves fried fish and Tony's is her favorite place to go out for it. "It's still morning. I'll make you some breakfast," she says.

"No, no – I'm fine. I just came to look for some negatives I think are up in my room and get right in to the paper." I run out of the kitchen and up the stairs before she can get into grand, grandmothering mode.

It smells stuffy in my room under the sun-struck eaves. I remember closing the windows when I felt chilly at four a.m. and I guess not reopening them when I got up. Now the cloying atmosphere from what's forecast to be our first heat wave has rivulets of sweat inching down the sides of my chest as I rummage through disorganized piles of photo equipment and their productions.

Got them. But I'll need a shower to get through the day.

I'm exiting the bathroom five minutes later in chinos and not-yet-buttoned shirt, toweling my hair when Gram, wringing her hands calls, "Alex – come! It's getting cold."

"So, you made me breakfast anyway," I say, trying to make my dismay sound like appreciation. One of the objectives of moving in with Gram – the one just after it being the only place I could afford while I save up for building materials – was keeping the legally blind old woman from burning down her house with – horrific to contemplate – herself in it. She's owned this winterized cottage, just off coastal 1A, for forty years. Since neither I nor my Aunt Sylvia, Grams daughter-in-law, mother of Kevin, have the heart – or the authoritarian means – to forbid her to cook, it's my job to exaggerate how much I enjoy the act of food preparation – which is not really very much, although I *can* cook. Or else try to steer Gram toward the relatively safer oven-reheating of covered dishes Sylvia might "happen" to drop off. And when all else fails, I'm to tell her I'm "just dying for" pizza or Chinese take-out.

"What did you make me?"

"I made you eggs and toast."

"Eggs – fried or scrambled?"

"Both."

Well, I'm taken aback – even though I know my grandmother's potential for novelty: one-of-a-kind recipes to utilize greatly disparate left-overs, ingenious home-improvement and repair techniques employing little other than chewing gum and bra straps. The necessities of living alone in old age can't be credited for this. She impressed the family and neighbors with her jury-rigging abilities at half her age.

"You made me both? Why did you make both scrambled and fried eggs?" I'm sure she's got a reason. And I don't want to hurt her feelings so I add, "I like them both the same."

"I made the scrambled egg first, but it didn't look like enough, and I didn't want your toast to get cold, so I fried the next one because it's faster."

Of course. I needn't have asked.

"And I made some Taster's Choice – even though I know you don't like it."

I bend down to give a pat to Rosebud, Gram's springer spaniel. That furry creature began wriggling with disproportionate joy when I entered the kitchen again. Don't know where she was when I first came home. Probably on chipmunk patrol. She clearly thinks her life has just taken a big turn for the better now that I am here — me, the god of canned dog food. I usually feed Rosebud so Gram can avoid stooping. Only two things in life get Rosebud excited: edible substances in any form and chipmunks; not to be considered edible substances because she's never caught one. If the temperature were to suddenly drop forty-five degrees and the June sky fill with snow, she would betray no surprise. But glimpse a chipmunk magically appearing from under a bush, where no chipmunk had been a second or two before, and the liver-and-white, four-legged pile of animated rags, is thunderstruck.

I open the fridge and grab for a can of Coke, drinking off half, standing inside the arc of the refrigerator door. On this sultry June morning I need cool air and a jolt of some harsh liquid before tackling Gram's creation. And at least Coke – unlike Taster's Choice – is the real thing. On the table I see a little tent of Kleenex's covering what I assume is the plate of toast and eggs. As she prefers Kleenex to any other paper product, Gram carries boxes or little packets or clumps of it in the cuffs of her sleeves at all times. I don't know whether she thinks that everyone needs Kleenex or just expects that everyone knows that she does. She might extend an upturned claw-like hand, while telling me a story, expecting, doubtless, I'll easily find a Kleenex to put there.

With some trepidation I remove the dampening and delicate paper shroud. But, except for the mildly jarring effect of seeing pure white and deep yellow, and entirely pale yellow, versions of eggs cohabitating on a bed of toast, it does look edible. Gram has by now caught up with me and sees the can of Coke in my hand.

"Alex! How can you drink that horrid stuff so early in the day. You'll have ulcers in your esophagus when you're thirty-five."

"This will be my last one." I say. But I curb my sarcasm and add, "It doesn't matter what time of day you have something. If it's good for you, it's good; if it's bad for you, it's bad." But, guilt pushes me to say, "I won't have one in the afternoon today."

"I saw them take paint off a car on TV with Coca Cola. Watching you do that makes me vomit."

Most less-than-charming things make Gram "vomit." It's her word for gagging. Watching a movie classic with Gram on PBS last night comes back to me. *Paths of Glory* – with Kirk Douglas. Very early Stanley Kubrick. World War I – the trenches in France. Insane orders to attack on foot into decimating machine-gun fire. Gram got upset, and at one point cried out: "This makes me vomit!" That reaction was not much of a surprise. But then she'd added passionately: "It would be better to be an airline pilot than to be in those trenches!" Curious alternatives, even by Gram's standards. She probably just meant air*plane* pilot. But, I didn't ask. I didn't want to spoil the movie. I'm making an effort to take her as she comes. Trying to change a 90-year-old woman – or anybody really – is a waste of time. It seems to me people change most when you don't want them to. After what I just went through with Angela, I feel a little cynical. I'd fallen into a trap with Angela. The "how-do-you-leave-the-no-batteries-necessary-freely-orgasmic-but-otherwise-totally-uptight-beauty-you-happened-upon-just-after-breaking-up-with-the-rather-nice-rather-cute-but-sexually-difficult-normal-girl?" trap. A mythic trial for any male. She was out of control in bed but controlling everywhere else. Well, I think I learned an important lesson: I'm at a distinct disadvantage around high-powered women.

But, in a way, Gram's the best roommate I've ever had – guys included. Everybody I know is pretty self-involved. I have to admit I focus on myself most of the time, too. Gram is different. She was born Georgia Peters in Cambridge and grew up in a milieu of books, ideas, and early feminist concepts. She came of college age in the early nineteen-teens, a time when few women might go to college. Though she never enrolled in a university – she eventually graduated from a business school – she regularly attended public lectures at Harvard, where her brother Henry (now deceased) was a student. She still talks fondly of the Ford Hall Forum. (Georgia came to Northport for a summer waitress job in 1915. Jim Perkins, a local college boy, cooked at the restaurant where she worked that season. And the rest is family history.)

Gram understands the broad range of human yearnings – and she finds other people's lives interesting. I don't mean in a gossipy way – though she's not above a little of that. She finds *things* interesting, too. All kinds of things. Things like art and artsy movies – wherefrom "Rosebud." Even scientific stuff. She's become the queen of public television. But her special area is poetry. Poetry is a weak point for me. I'm kind of dyslexic so I find it hard going. Maybe that's just an excuse. But Gram's got tons of it committed to memory. Old people are supposed to be apathetic, but she really gets excited. In fact, she probably gets a little too excited. Like the airline pilot thing. Most people describe Gram the same way: "she's *cute*." She doesn't seem to mind this the way some women with feminist impulses and pride of intellect feel minimized by the term. In her book, "cuteness" is one of the prime virtues. When something appears really cute she announces it like a judge at an Olympic event: "Now, *that's* cute," she'll say of an ad with a little kid on TV, or if Rosebud puts her head on Gram's knee – as if she's declaring the winner of a competition.

But her interest in people doesn't mean she's always relaxed around them. Georgia's "modern woman" aspirations have done little to inoculate her against the pressures convention exerted on females of her generation to become consummate hostesses: ready to serve and entertain any visitor—even family members—entering her home at any time. So now that she's losing some steam, vision, and balance, playing the hostess can be just too strenuous. If I tell her I'm bringing a friend by she'll try to put together a five-course meal. And if I bring someone home without telling her she might panic. She thinks people expect more of her than they really do. This can cause her a kind of stage fright.

I'm like that, too, a little, I guess. Not *exactly* stage fright. And it's probably not something I caught from Gram. It's something I guess I caught from the LSD I took when I was twenty and twenty-two. And it is fading as the years pass since my last acid trip about ten years ago. It's really more a sudden sensation of intensity to things – the other side of my blissing-out on beauty. It can be an interlude of two seconds. Or it can be minutes. Sometimes I feel like I've got *too much* self-awareness. Awareness of how I fit – or don't – into nature or the world of people.

I made the mistake of telling Angela about this kind of thing one night when she said I was being "distant." I guess I wasn't listening at the moment and didn't want to admit it. So, I attempted to blame it on something supposedly beyond my control. Well, she took this and ran with it. Called it an anxiety attack. Doing a retro cost/benefit analysis now I realize it would have been a lot *cheaper* if I'd just owned up to not listening. There's another lesson I've learned: admit and apologize. The cover-up is always worse. The same thing goes for admitting when you're wrong. A lot of people seem to think refusing to *admit* you're wrong is the same thing as *not being* wrong. It isn't. And it just ends up looking like you have an ego problem. I know. Angela picked me up on this enough times. I've come to realize that the only person in the room who doesn't notice when someone is having an ego problem is the person having it.

And then there's the fact that sometimes even a *blissed-out* interlude can be socially awkward. One time when my awareness seemed heightened and the practical world receded a little, I unconsciously followed my nose – literally, almost – into a private garden, pursuing some exotic floral scent. Roses it turned out to be. You've heard of

25

roses? After a few seconds of leaning over to inhale from a bush and exclaiming, "Mmmm," I found that I was looking down upon a naked couple, not particularly hidden behind it, lying on a blanket. Surprise and embarrassment made me blurt out something like, "I thought I smelled something... I mean my dog... I thought I smelled my dog." Well, I don't remember what I might actually have said, but whatever it was, it didn't help, so I just ran. The worst part is that I'm pretty sure I know the woman and that I've run into her at the supermarket. All I'd really seen was a tangle of male/female body parts. But she looks pretty good in the clothes she puts on to go food shopping. And she always raises her eyebrows and gives me a sort of questioning little smile. For all I know that was a one-bush stand and she might be available. But I'm too embarrassed to find out. She's not embarrassed, but I am. But as I said, such intense "interludes" – good or bad – are mostly now things of the past.

After eggs with Coke, I crave real coffee. The office is downtown and there's a French-type café-bakery I like that's within a block. I want to say a nice good-bye to Gram – and thank her for making my almost lunchtime breakfast. I step through the living room doorway and find myself suddenly immersed in an atmosphere of heightened and unnatural color. Vibrant sunlight entering through a brace of mullioned windows infuses translucent red curtains that Gram has drawn shut to spare her sensitive eyes. At first, all in the room appears muted but the curtains. The walls, ceiling, and built-in cabinets are constructed of bead board stained a deep red-brown. The many coats of varnish are crackled with age. As my eyes adjust, I can see crimson tones, reflected from the glowing drapery fabric, everywhere on the surface of the glazed wood. Damp air wafts in and out beneath randomly raised window sashes, turning the curtains into magical, pulsing forms. Across them wavy shadow bands, projections of the mullions, morph long-short, left-right. The room appears to breathe softly. What I see before me is a vision by the French painter Edouard Vuillard. His mysterious interiors, put together from patches of colored light-in-paint, transformed bourgeois sitting rooms into holy places. I realize he was painting them in Paris at about the same time this summer cottage was constructed in Northport, Mass. And if I bring my focus in close, these floating rectangles of light against the deep-toned walls become abstracts – living Mark Rothko paintings; colored shapes suffused with meaning. The beauty before me generates a humming feeling in my chest. My breathing slows and I feel an energized quiet. I have to credit acid for making my vision so much more vivid – or bringing back the vividness it had when I was a kid. But that, like the "too much self-awareness" thing, is losing its intensity, too. This, however, is something I hate to see go.

I'd like to sit down. I'd like to stay all day. But I can't. Gram isn't here. One door further on I find her in her rocker on the screened porch, perhaps asleep. Out here, the morning sunlight that she closed the living room curtains to block, bathes her from head to toe. To my presently altered senses, she appears as Vuillard's mother, his most constant model. A closed book sits on her lap. Her dog lies at her feet. But she only looks like Vuillard's mother until I realize that her face is covered by a Kleenex that she has spread out beneath her thick reading glasses. And she wears a pair of sunglasses over those, too. As I look at her, she changes position. Now I can tell she isn't asleep.

"What are you reading, Gram?" I ask her. The humid southwest airflow has those heat buzzers – what are they, some kind of insect? – trilling. But I'm sure Gram can't hear them.

"I'm reading your book about that explorer, Shackleton. But my eyes keep getting tired."

"Yes, that one's really good," I say. A few nights ago, she watched Carl Sagan – she pronounces it Say-GON, as if he were actually *from* another planet himself – and an episode of *Nova*, back to back. After they were over she complained, "I put in too much time about the universe today and now I feel sick to my stomach." So I worry about her reading Shackleton the morning after *Paths of Glory*. Shackelton's true story is one of history's most harrowing and thrilling survival narratives.

"But stop reading it if it starts to make you too excited. You know

– after that movie last night."

"That movie was horrible," she says. 'Horrible' is not necessarily completely negative to her. Perhaps like *awful* almost meaning *awesome* a few hundred years ago. She uses *horrid* to convey a completely-without-merit experience of horror.

"But was it *good?*" I press her.

"Yes," She says emphatically, "It made my skin crawl."

"I'll be back in the afternoon. There are plenty of nice leftovers to heat up, so you don't have to cook anything."

"I won't cook," she says.

# 3

*Northport, on the Agamenticus River, with its outstanding examples of colonial and Victorian architecture, its ocean beaches and historic harbor district, its charming fishing and sailing cove downriver from the deep-water harbor – with sea breezes just a few hours away from the New York City heat – has long been a cosmopolitan place. And starting in the late nineteenth century, Northport became well known for its attractiveness as a summering spot for New York artists, writers, and, with its four-decades-old summer theater, some of the finer stage actors of recent time...*

That description, as you might guess, comes right out of a Chamber of Commerce brochure. And it's basically true. But it just speaks to one side of things. Most Northport locals still go to the office or to the plant or down to the sea in commercial vessels. And, as I've indicated, having an active arts scene doesn't really generate all that much income for the community.

I guess I should tell you a bit about the paper I work for. It's a somewhat odd-ball publication. Though a weekly, its style is kind of a hybrid of a tourist tab and a city daily. My boss, Steve Towle, worked at the Boston Herald for fifteen years, until he had enough capital and credit to buy *Currents*, then a no-content advertiser, about three years ago. He wanted his newspaper to have an identity – and, like the *Herald*, an edge. And – though Steve is something of a wild man at times: drives too fast, gets into arguments with the cops who stop him – he was realistic about what a small city like Northport would put up with. So he decided on trying to associate "funny" with his paper's identity. He started with conventional stuff. Like he'd run the accident descriptions that the victims or perpetrators wrote on insurance claim forms. He'd get these from a woman he was seeing at the time – his agent's secretary. Some were good. They were usually along the lines of: "The pedestrian hit me and went under my car." Or "The guy was all over the road. I had to swerve a lot before I got him." The one I remember liking the most was: "The telephone pole was approaching fast. I tried to veer out of its way when it struck my front end."

But this kind of thing didn't satisfy Steve for long. He likes to think of himself as a satirist. And he can be pretty funny. But the truth is his humor is often forty-five-year-old-frat-boy stuff: the laugh justifies the means. Before long, he started throwing in a completely bogus story or two each week. He covers the confusion from this by running the tag line *Regional News* – *Regional Humor* in the masthead, then putting *RH Wire Service* under the headline of a bullshit piece. There's an *RH* on a story in this week's issue. It's titled "Local Businessman Hornswoggled by Unknown Assailants." Presumably, this idea evolved from Steve's threatening me a week ago that if my feature missed its deadline he'd have *me* hornswoggled. "What's that?" I'd asked. He'd said, "You know – like in all those old cowboy movies. There was always some old guy who looked like the stagecoach had rolled into town on top of him, slapping his thigh and yelling, 'I've been hornswoggled, gol dang it.' Whatever they did to him," Steve said, "I'll do to you." "Oh – got ya," I'd said and walked away. Sparked something in him, I guess, and now there's this story: "So-and-So, So-and-So, of 22 Beaver Street, a local taxidermist, was the victim of a severe hornswoggling by a gang of youths, as he walked from his office to his parked car, etc. etc." ….then continues, as I remember, something like: "Betty Such-and-Such, a hair stylist and part-time ballet dancer, who witnessed the incident, told *Currents*, 'It was terrible. I've seen hornswogglings in this neighborhood before, but never one as *severe* as this. And the worst part was that it happened just a few steps from a playground. What's wrong with teenagers today?'"

Fairly amusing, I think. But the reviewing I do has to be serious. And I've got a bit of a handicap as a reviewer – several handicaps, really – my love of beauty notwithstanding. When your job is critiquing something publicly, you should have a pretty good idea what you're talking about – even when writing in a semi-off-the-wall rag like *Currents*. You need a knowledge base. As I already said, I'm pretty ignorant of the contemporary, big-city art scene. Sure, I read *Art News* and *Art Forum*. Now and then, that is. That's my first problem. I've always had a resistance to studying. Nothing unusual in that. That described half my school friends. (The other half were top students.) But I probably got more grief for my avoidance tendencies than most of my friends. You see, a guidance counselor in the Northport School Administration called my Dad one day and told him I'd scored very high on an I.Q. test. (My mother had died about two years before this.) My Dad said the school people wouldn't tell them what "very high" was. I ended up branded *underachiever*. Today they'd probably say I had ADD. This high I.Q. thing dogged my efforts to escape pounding the books right through college. Don't get me wrong, I've always loved reading – for pleasure, that is. And I was able to get through a fairly decent school – Boston University (after I failed to get into my first and second choices). But my grades were never great. Problem was I always wanted to be outside exploring the streets of Boston. Or better yet, off hiking in the White Mountains, backpacking in Europe, or home hanging out on Northport's beaches and pier.

But, like I said, attention deficiency is pretty common. The other factors that make reviewing an odd profession for a guy like me are more unusual. I won't go into all of them now, but one is that I had no interest in the arts – other than rock and roll (and, as I've indicated, literature) – until I took those LSD trips in my college years. Acid changed me into an art-lover almost overnight. So I added an art history minor to my major, English. At twenty, I had a lot of catching up to do. At thirty-three, I still do.

Anyway, even with Steve's erratic-ness – and the limitations of staff members like me – he has created a niche for his paper. And he has been making himself enough money by now to be sailing his own classic Hinckley 34. The profits go into the boat, though, and not toward more rewarding pay levels for his staff. *Currents'* niche is just below the shelf space occupied by the Oggelvy Group daily, *The Northport Beacon.* As the oddball, we aren't much competition for the *Beacon* – so it's mostly live and let live. Oggelvy owns papers in Boston and in 12 smaller New England and New York State cities. We pretend we don't notice them. And they don't notice us at all.

# 4

Within a few minutes of leaving Gram's, my beat-up Karmann Ghia convertible sits halted by rush hour traffic – just past the entrance ramp onto I-195, which loops around most of Northport. The day is actually hot. I love convertibles, but being stopped in direct sun and exhaust fumes, proves to me that there can be a downside to anything nice. I get out of the car to stretch. The moment I do, the cars in front of mine roll a few feet forward. Immediately the ones behind me begin to honk horns. The racket continues until I get back in and also roll the available few feet to be bumper to bumper again with the car just in front. I think of the traffic jam as a living thing – like a cat that holds small prey in its claws, loosens its grip to let it free, then pounces and holds again. Caught in this one I'm not feeling kindly about modern America. That's another reason I'm into art. Art helps you rise above the daily slings and arrows. But, thinking about it, art can only make you transcend the cold, cruel world if you are already at a comfortable temperature. Being cool or being warm are luxuries on Planet Earth.

Being hot or being cold come for free.

A police car, with blue lights flashing, careens past me on the shoulder. Shit. This is more than just a normal morning slow-down. Luxury for me, in modern America, would be having freedom enough to not have to go with the flow – the flow of the traffic in this case. I'd like to be able to always be going the other way. I pride myself on my freedom from the – what's a good word? – thrall? – of the things that pull at most people in our society. But there is one thing in the contemporary world that I have to admit enthralls me. – Luckily you don't have to go anywhere and get stuck in traffic, to find it. It's everywhere you look. Images of gorgeous women. Gorgeousness in the flesh doesn't exactly clog the supermarket aisles of small American communities like Northport. – Except, for a while each summer, when the overheated "capitals of gorgeous" empty out. Then gorgeousness can be found in almost any place with a decent waterfront and a few good restaurants.

I'm equally addicted to beauty that's merely skin-deep as to beauty that's sacred. I can even confuse the two. My mother was a very beautiful woman. And I associated her lovely face with her mother-love – which seemed as sacred to me as anything could be. She died of cancer when I was twelve. I lived with my Dad until college. I was always close to Gram. She and I together did a lot of grieving for my mother. Unfortunately, the skin-deep beauty I've encountered since, brings me little peace. But I'm pretty sure fixation with beautiful female faces isn't just my problem. The likenesses of beautiful young women grace every packaging surface and are continuously transmitted through the air. Those images wouldn't be everywhere if only motherless, thirty-three year old males reacted to them. And I know it isn't just our shallow culture that's so hooked. It's planetary. I think if creatures came down from Mars – assuming Mars is "up"– they would conclude that Earthlings in general are worshippers of beautiful women. The whole planet runs more on looks than merit, and I guess I'm as guilty as anyone at perpetuating the unfair system. Someday maybe I'll have a homely daughter who I'll love like crazy and I'll rage against all the shallow people in the world like myself.

The cars start to move again a little. I'm just on the verge of breaking loose from the claw of the beast. And then suddenly I am free. I wind through the four gears of this sporty-in-appearance-only little car – as if it is a racer.

Ten minutes later, I'm downtown. I find a parking space not far from the office. As I move along the short section of sidewalk, I see a healthy enough looking woman of forty or so emerging from the ordinary license-plated vehicle she's just parked in a spot with a blue wheelchair painted on it. The license plate is ordinary, but the car isn't. It's a big, new Mercedes.

"In case you didn't notice," I declare, risking a confrontation with a stranger, "That's a 'handicapped only'." I immediately wonder if I would do this with a man. Sure I would. A small man. But she seems to take no offense and says cheerily, "Oh, that's okay. They park in our spaces, too." How can I argue with that? I'm sure there are many instances of handicapped individuals taking spaces that could go to all the equally deserving normal people in the world.

I enter our brick-fronted edifice. We occupy five rooms; formerly one big one when it was a Woolworth's. I pass the ad room on the way to my desk. Steve is alone in there leaning over the elevated layout table. Steve is his own advertising manager. Shoestring operation, like I said. Hearing footsteps, he turns and says, "Hey, Alex, how's it hanging?"

Steve's really not a bad editor. He even does a decent job correcting the arts pieces I hand in. I say "even" because he has little interest in the arts. Worse than that, he's pretty hostile to them. He likes to quote Joseph Goebbels: "Every time I hear the word culture I reach for my revolver." Steve tends to think most artists are either phonies or defectives. Like a lot of people with no aesthetic vision, he tends to believe aesthetic vision doesn't exist. This is too bad, obviously. However, I can maybe sympathize with him a little bit, in that it's probably true that only in the visual arts can almost anyone be characterized as successful, depending on how you define success. Dancers have to be graceful. Musicians can't hit sour notes. – Well, that's not exactly true with punk musicians today. But Steve defines success by money. With his attitude, it's ironic that I often see Steve at openings. He goes, he says, because he's attracted to crazy women and he believes openings are the best place to find them. I remember running into him at one and hearing him savaging the work on display to some new-wavy looking art groupie. At first, she appeared shocked and outraged. But at some point she shifted her weight from one hip to the other and cocked her head. To me this signaled a new perspective. And when she left, she took him home with her. He told me later she said she guessed that she hadn't really liked the work either. "I gave her permission to be herself," Steve said, with sarcasm obviously directed at the psycho-babblers of my generation. Steve's tall, athletic, and self-confident. Even some fairly enlightened, self-respecting females might not always be able to resist that. This is unfortunate because I think machismo can be one the most destructive forces on the planet. And my boss is loaded with it.

And Steve has very little concern for workplace impropriety. Sometimes he'll walk through the ad room where the paste-up girls bend over light tables and he'll start singing a twangy country-and-western song of his own creation, *Someone Else Is Kissing Her Other Lips Now*. So far he's only got that title/first line. But he thinks this would sell millions. All he needs are lyrics, a good melody and a handsome cowboy to record it. Bang – he'd have his first big hit!

Steve is probably more obsessed with sex than anybody I know. I took Gram to the eye doctor's recently. I read in a magazine in their rack that the average woman thinks about sex once or twice in a day. But the average man thinks about it every seventy seconds. This sounded preposterous until I realized that they might have interviewed Steve. One obsessive could really skew the sample. At forty-five he does claim to be slowing down though. He told me recently that when he was young he wanted to fuck like a wild animal. Now, though, he says, he just wants to fuck like a farm animal.

"Hey, Steve," I reply. "How you doing? He starts right in answering my greeting as though it was a true inquiry.

"Well, if you must know, right now, I'm completely pissed off. Come in. Sit down."

"Oh, yeah? What's going on?"

"See this bank double-truck I'm working on? Look at it. What do you see?"

I look at it and see a lot of bank ads. That's what I tell him.

"That's not what I mean," he says peevishly. "Who's missing?"

I'd like to impress the boss, but memorizing all the area banks is not something that I think is part of the *Arts and Leisure* editor's job description.

"I don't know – Coastal?"

"What are you blind? They're the third one down, left hand page."

"Oh right, " I say. So much for impressing the boss.

But he's more irritated with the missing bank than me, so he helps me out.

"It's Northport National. That's the bank where I have my business account. I got this idea a month ago that I could painlessly pick up a few extra bucks for the paper by putting together a full page or a double-truck bank spread. Okay, I know it's kind of bogus for banks to buy space in a paper like *Currents*. But my pitch is to tell them that all these restaurants and galleries and hotels and marina's that have *Currents* on their counters all need loans and checking accounts and mortgages and all that. Besides bankers don't know where to spend their money. They're the stupidest ones – not really businessmen at all, playing with other people's money. So I ran it by Barnes, the manager over there, and he said, 'Sounds good. Let's see who else you can get before I sign on.' Okay, so I get a quarter page from Rockingham, a half from Key, etcetera, etcetera, and pretty soon I've only got one more quarter page spot to fill page to have a two-page spread. So, every time I get another one I'm back to Barnes. – Pretending I like him and I just want to say 'hi' when I'm in to make a deposit or something. Even wasted my best banking joke on him. I ever tell you that one?"

I rack my brain a bit before I realize that from anyone other than an egomaniac this would have to be a rhetorical question. Is Steve an egomaniac? No, he's borderline. I imitate one of his gestures and give a short sharp jerk of my head while squinting. "I'm not exactly sure," it is supposed to say. He gives me a parody of the same thing back. "Don't fuck with me, I'm the boss," is what this conveys.

"The one about the guy who won the lottery?"

I try to keep it simple this time. "No," I say.

"I never told you that one?" He acts like I'm holding out on him. "Great joke," he says. "You sure I never told you?"

He starts in: "So this guy goes into a bank and gets into line at one of the tellers. He has to wait a couple minutes. Nothing serious – but he's an impatient guy. When he gets his turn the teller smiles and says 'Can I help you?' But he's irritated and he says, 'I want to open a fucking checking account'. The woman is horrified and just says, 'You can't talk that way in here, this is *a bank*. I'm going to get the manager.' She pushes a buzzer and in about fifteen seconds a man – one just like Barnes – appears. He looks at the guy who's not shaved or well dressed and asks" – Steve, cheeks drawn down, mimics a lofty tone, "'What seems to be the trouble?' The guy looks at him and says, 'No trouble, fella. I just won two million dollars in the lottery and I want to open a fucking checking account.' The manager does a double take. Then he glares at the teller. Then he says to the guy, 'I see. And this *bitch* has been giving you a hard time?'"

I laugh. It's funny. It's funny cause it's true. The best jokes are true.

"And Barnes didn't laugh, I bet?'

"No. He laughed – cracked up like regular human being."

"And?"

"And so I say, 'Hey, Tom, it's deadline time. Fish or cut bait' – Well, I didn't tell him *that*, I just said, 'deadline time.' And he says, 'No – can't do it. Budget."

"What a pain," I commiserate. "I could never sell advertising. Writing about the advertisers is bad enough."

"Yeah it sucks. But I can fill the two pages by next week and run it then. That's not what pissed me off so bad. What pissed me off so bad was, you know what he tells me after he tells me to get lost?"

"What?" I reply.

"He reaches over and puts his hand on my shoulder and you know what he says? One whole month I've been working on him. He puts his hand on my shoulder and he leans toward me – very sincere – and says – big smile – *'But I haven't forgotten you!'* Steve tries to suppress laughter that is bubbling up. When he does this, which is often, his voice gets very strangled and high. "Imagine that: 'I haven't forgotten you.' – What a humanitarian! Ha, ha, ha – What an asshole!"

I laugh, too.

Steve comes back down. "I know it's not your expertise, but can you cover a planning board meeting tomorrow at four? I've got to be in court for a speeding ticket. Three actually."

"Can't," I say. I try and fail at effecting W.C. Fields' absurd tone. "I'm going out to the beach on business." I tell Steve about Lucinda York, hoping she's a good enough excuse.

"Performance artist. Huh," he says. I can tell he is mentally trying out sexist lines, but is unprepared and too vain about his craft as a purveyor of humor to use a clichéd one.

"Check her out for me," he resorts to saying. "She cute?"

"Well, I wouldn't say 'cute.' But she is attractive."

"Get lots of pictures," he says. "If she's in a bikini, it could be your first cover story." Then he picks the act up and does a far better Fields than mine. And paraphrasing the great comedian, says, "I love artists – girl artists: 18, 20 years of age."

"I think this one may be a little old for you," I say, leaving the ad room for my own desk.

"I take them up to thirty-five, in a real pinch," he calls after me. Obviously changing the subject to sex has brightened his bad day. I also read in that ophthalmologist's magazine that a man thinking about sex can keep his hand in freezing water forty seconds longer than he can if thinking about anything else. But nobody else in the waiting room was under about 89 so it didn't seem important.

# 5

I remember walking – walking barefoot down this road. 1957, '58, '59... The dead-end cottage lane was paved then, but in spots big rocks poked up through. I remember how each time we'd jounce up to her bungalow in her station wagon, Gram would mention that the town was supposed to come and fix the road. After about twenty years it actually did. I liked it better the way it was.

This road begins as a shared driveway that runs the three or four tenths of a mile from Gram's into a wider lane that ends against the main thoroughfare paralleling the shoreline. Across that, the private drive of a stately 1900-ish summer places traverses the remaining 100 yards of sparse beach grass before the beach itself. As I walked down this road on summer mornings twenty-five and more years ago, I would jump from rock to rock, memorizing their individual shapes with my toughening sole. At the edge of the grove of trees that shaded Gram's secluded neighborhood began a concrete sidewalk. Its surface would already be hot by ten a.m. on sunny days. Every few yards I'd stop for relief on the clumps of grass that somehow managed to grow thick between the walk's frost-kiltered planes. But, about halfway to the beach, I would be paying less attention to what I was trying to avoid or step on, and start looking up for my first glimpse of it that day. A sharp pebble might call my attention back down for a moment. But when I could see it clearly it held me fascinated. The "Giant Whopper Tree" I called it; the largest tree in the known world. Merely being dappled in the penumbra of its solemn shadow would fill me with fear and wonder. Only when I was with Gram or my mother might I dare run across that neat lawn to touch the tree's massive, corrugated trunk, and crane my gaze up – for a two second dizzying glimpse into the swirl of dark limbs against the green heavens, impossibly high above me – before holy awe undid my little boy courage and drove me shrieking back to my protectors.

My pulse would gradually return to normal as I'd stumble on down the road to the barrier thoroughfare, Ocean Boulevard. There, cooling my feet by hopping left, then right, I could catch my day's first scent of maritime air. Hints of an on-shore breeze might make forays into the morning's growing warmth, chilling the sides of my bare chest while we waited for a break in the line of whizzing cars. Air currents would waft hot/cold, hot/cold, challenging a heat that would be scorching Northport proper, just a few miles inland. After the main road, there was only that short driveway left to walk.

I would stand on the beach and look. Before me a roaring, hissing monster drowned out the whirring highway noise behind and smiled a billion sparkles at my eye. It writhed past the little islands on the horizon, then stretched (I was told) across to a place called England – and from there on to coil its blue-green self around the girth of our spinning globe. Noise, sparkles, and salt haze. Mingled with the surf-noise was the noise of children. Some of them, cousins, arrived earlier with aunts carrying beach umbrellas and baskets of peaches and cherries.

That was how a day would begin – almost every sunny day of those childhood summers – with that ritual walk. I remember the road and the tree and the boulevard and the smiling, roaring sea – and the cousins and the aunts, and the peach juice running down my salty cheeks after a swim. But what I remember most was the certainty. The absolute certainty. The absolute, unshakeable, unquestionable certainty that all was right in the world.

Add time to certainty and certainty becomes uncertain. Reality enters like water into the sand castles we made on that beach. The great tree has been cut down. – Dutch elm disease, perhaps. Time comes to bear on the mightiest. I know really that I can't recapture what I feel teasing at my footsteps on this road. Recapturing is a fool's errand. All you can do is make sure things feel real in the present. You know, "Be here now." That's not always easy for me. I remind myself of that Peter Sellers movie where he's an uptight businessman in love with a dream of a hippy chick. Trying to transition to her world, he consults a guru of her prescribing, a Maharishi type who tells him he must let go of his attachments. He replies that he is trying to do that. The holy one says, "No, no, no – you must not *try*!" Sellers replies, "Well, I am *trying* not to *try*." That's me most of the time.

Right here and now, I'm sneaker-footed on this road – walking, not with the oceanic freedom of those childhood mornings, but within the boundaries of a job assignment. I am ambling the road from Gram's in the late afternoon to cover a beachfront work of performance art. Try explaining that to a kid at the beach in 1959. Try explaining that to most Northport and tourist kids *and* grown-ups at the beach, now, in 1983.

In the compromise that America has become, the three-mile length of Blue Heron Beach that, when I was a child, was one beach now has become three beaches. – Well, three *ideas* of beach. The spot I stand on right now – where I would first pay homage to the sea monster/god each summer day – appears the same; a graceful place of early twentieth century summer residences. But a thousand yards to the right of here, the homes end and a strip of busy restaurants and bars takes over. The number of businesses is limited by the beach running out – at the mouth of the little Ogunquin River. That thousand yards of ocean-front homes to the south of me can be added to fifteen hundred yards of the same to the north. North of *that* is "protected" dunes and estuary. This has not changed topographically. However, the northern-most approximately thousand feet of sand, the Marshland section, has evolved sociologically.

"Contexts: Homage to Magritte." The performance is slated for five p.m. – about two minutes from now. I took a bit of time out to fix something for Gram to eat, and a few moments more to chat with her. She seemed to have had a pretty good day – stuck in the ice at the South Pole with Ernest Shackleton. I told her I wouldn't be eating at home tonight – since I'm thinking I might get a bite with cousin Kevin, the assistant curator at the NoMMA. He said he'd be at the performance. I didn't tell her that part, though. I didn't want her to defrost a turkey and start roasting it so she could be ready for company by 3 a.m. – just in case he stopped by. If we do go back to the house, so Gram can see a different grandchild for a change, we'll have to be able to swear to her that we have eaten, so as not to activate her hostess attack-mode. I don't know if Kevin would back me up about that. He may still be enough of a boy scout that he might not agree that in some situations lies are better than truth. But, mainly, it would be nice to eat on one of the oceanfront decks tonight. Weekday night and not yet peak tourist season – we should be able to get a table at seaside pretty easily.

I called Kevin from the house to remind him about getting me that interview with Arthur Dalmore. Confidence for me ebbs and flows with the tide. Now, having let Dalmore's formidable appearance sink in, I feel up to the challenge. Also, Lucinda York, Kevin told me when I proposed he show up at the beach, is one of an anointed few locals that Dalmore has his eye on for higher things. So catching her act is good politics. Still, I guess I'm a bit intimidated: I could have a tough time not saying the wrong thing in the company of an exponent of a philosophy that *the concept* is art's first mission and beauty its second... third?... sixth? Maybe even not at all. I think most people still think art is all about beauty. But in much of the contemporary New York world, the magazines I read tell me beauty is derisively referred to as *bourgeois lushness*, an elitist thing. In the world Dalmore previously inhabited, and some say he wants to turn ours into, almost anything – accompanied by the right spoken or written edifying *text* – might be considered art. An artist locking himself in a box is called *a duration confinement body-piece*. Everything is a piece. That piece got a very favorable review in *Art Forum*. And while in the generally crazy '60's, a woman artist had only pretended to hold in her vagina (strapped it to her leg or someplace) a brush loaded with red paint (to symbolize menstruation, obviously) and painted by squatting and wiggling, in recent years, liberated creative women have actually utilized their vaginas for the dispensing of scrolls inscribed with presumably profound written content. A male body artist, named Burtrand or Burton, had an assistant shoot him – most assuredly as a statement that his dedication to his muse does not stop with the sacrifice of just half an ear the way it used to. Luckily with men, a gun can be a stand-in for the actual *male* organ. Still this is Northport and not New York. So not everyone would be happy to see artists performing with guns around here. But according to a man of Arthur Dalmore's convictions, the museum is a living thing. And life often does include guns. Museums don't have to have walls anymore. The world is the museum. Even the beach is the museum.

Magritte? Why would a feminist, identity artist name a conceptual piece in honor of a Surrealist painter? It's ironic in some way, I'm sure. You can't get anywhere in the arts today by being sincere. Well, I was never particularly interested in Surrealism, but as someone with an art history minor I've learned the basics. And the one thing anyone who knows anything about Magritte knows about him is *his pipe*. Or his *not* pipe. His painting of a pipe, which, of course, is not *really* a pipe, it's *only a painting* of a pipe. The painting is titled – and has those words writ large across the canvas – "This Is Not a Pipe."

I half walk, half run, north, sneakers in hand, my old Nikon bouncing against my chest. My bare feet make squeaking sounds sliding through the tiny crests of silvery ground quartz. Rising heat waves from sun baking on the plane of sand ahead makes distant figures on the beach appear all ripply. I love that. Loved it as a kid, and I love it still. By the time I can see Agamenticus Head I am sweating. But I need to hurry. Gallery shows and rock concerts are my usual beat and I can fake having given them adequate coverage. However I do know enough about performance art to understand a piece can be profound for its length – hours and hours sometimes (perhaps to demonstrate boredom to those who have never previously experienced it) – or for its brevity: some can be as ephemeral as a butterfly brushing your cheek or a dog lifting its leg. So my professionalism requires that I don't miss any of this one, long or short. Today, for body artist Lucinda York, all the world of Blue Heron Beach is her museum and her stage.

The south boundary of the Marshland section of Blue Heron Beach is demarcated by Agamenticus Head Rock (alternately referred to as Agamenticus Head or just, "The Rock" or "The Head"— a large granite outcropping with bumps and chunks that some people long ago thought looked (from a vantage point which I've never been able find) like the profile of a Native American male. Nude swimming and sunbathing is allowed on this Marshland stretch of sand, sanctioned by an ordinance a briefly dominant coalition of granola types and Viet Nam dissenters pushed through in the early 1970's. Though few have ever availed themselves of this right, the concept is offensive to 1983's more conservative voters and a new measure proposed for the fall ballot likely will put nudity back in the bathroom where most Americans believe it belongs.

I hurry on. A stone's throw away from the big rock, I recognize the artiste, clad in a black two-piece suit and beach-inappropriate Doc Martens boots, striding purposefully – perhaps in a parody of marching, given the deliberate swinging of her arms and the army-type foot gear – right past the big rock, in my direction. At a distance ranging from about twenty to twenty-five feet, a small group of new-wavy-looking young people follow her. They, despite the heat, wear black clothing – though mostly tee-shirts and jeans. One looks quite punky in his Mohawk and many earrings. I recognize the handsome and slender dark-skinned young man I saw bickering with Ms. York yesterday in the clean-bathrooms-are-*your*-responsibility coffee shop. He has a camera around his neck, too – one somewhat more expensive looking than mine. Close behind this group trundles a gaggle of men and boys in bathing suits. None are naked, is what I mean. Some of these men in trunks – by occasionally glancing in random directions – seem to attempt to project indifference. I get the impression they wish to appear that they were all just going that same way on unrelated business. A mass need to find a men's room, perhaps. Several of the boys giggle, though one or two have expressions of fear. Finally, I spot cousin Kevin lagging in the rear. He's just the type to assume that dibs on front row seats would always go to others.

Wearing only that smallish black garment, Lucinda York, with her straw-like, bleach-white hair and an unnaturally pale, first-time-ever-in-the-sun complexion, comes as close to being a black and white vision as a human can be without being painted that way. Some lettering over her breasts soon provides a challenge to my no-paint description. It's not quite legible at this distance. "... Is. Is," yes, "Is." "This Is..." – Her arm-swinging gait interferes with my focusing. Now at 20 yards: "This Is... Not... My... Bathing Suit." This Is Not My Bathing Suit. Okay, so what? Why isn't it? Closer. At this distance I'm realizing that details of the firm, full breasts under her black top are *too* detailed – that is, for any garment to be intervening between my eye and her flesh. The "fabric" of her bathing suit, I'm now sure, is the thinnest of all covering materials – pigment. Her text reads literally true: it isn't a bathing suit she wears, it's a painting of one. "Homage to Magritte." I understand now. I grab up my camera and start snapping.

The artist continues her arm-swinging march past me further into the more heavily populated Northport part of the beach. After a multiplicity of earlier reactions to seeing it, I now cannot help note that her behind, wearing that painting of a rather conservative style of swimwear, appears less exposed than the butts of several nearby lounging young females in fabric that is mostly smaller patches held together by strings.

This black and white theatrical vision of an artist, now apparently off-stage, stops her marching and proceeds more naturally toward a dune where an army-type knapsack lies on the sand. Bending over in a way that causes me to involuntarily clutch at my chest, she draws from the knapsack a camouflage jumpsuit. This she dons, little-girl-jumping-rope style, in a single deft maneuver. From the bag she also produces a canteen and a pack of cigarettes. She gulps some liquid that must be really quite warm, lights a cigarette, and plunks her now camouflage butt onto the sand.

The crowd that has been following her begins, like an inflatable beach toy with the plug pulled, to lose its form. Some members of the group in black – one a woman whom I recognize as the very hip arts reviewer from the *Phoenix* – now surround the artist. They're all, it appears, lavishing her with praise. The non-art worldly, bathing-suited men, now aimless, disperse – though some of the bolder and more excitable ones apparently endeavor using personal accounts of the bizarre display as an excuse to converse with some of the pretty sunbathers. Several of these young women seem aflutter with disbelief at the impropriety perpetrated in their midst by what might be a deranged fellow female. And one woman of early middle age, in a skirted one-piece costume, appeals up to a lifeguard on his nearby stand. She points at the performer engulfed by her fans. That dangerously-tanned, muscular young man scans the air to either side of his perch, presumably for a clue of what to do, seemingly hoping he won't be required to do anything. Then with a brief glance to the blue heavens, he starts climbing down.

Kevin, pushing forty, wears a khaki summer suit, necktie in place despite the heat. He stands at the back of the group of Lucinda's art-for-art's-sake admirers. Poor Kevin looks so straight.   Makes me wonder what his politics are. I don't even know what fields of art he responds to most. You'd think we'd have talked about stuff like this at family barbeques or holiday dinners. But we've never really sought each other out. There's the difference in our ages, for one thing. And he's probably as uncomfortable with my driftiness as I am with his stability. But I do think he's a good guy. And our ages are getting closer all the time. I walk over to say "hi."

"So, Alex – you made it, huh?"

"Just got here," I say. "I guess I missed it. Only saw her walking from the Head to her stuff. Anything good?"

"Well, I don't know what you might have missed – unless *walking* on one side of the Head is different from the other. – Maybe there were a few more yards of walking on the north side."

"So, no cartwheels or anything?" I ask.

Kevin blushes. "What you saw was what we got." The blush explains a lot about our divergent takes on life.

"Well, there is a difference between north of the head and south of it."

"Like what?" he asks.

"Like north of the Head it's Marshland. You know – legal."

Others apparently have made this distinction, too – very likely including the artist, herself; she who established her beachhead south of Agamenticus Head Rock. Just then the lifeguard, the woman in a skirted-suit, and a short and newly arrived overweight young woman with bottle-thick glasses wearing a police uniform – someone I'd often seen dispensing tickets at the beach parking lot – intrude on the group of agog art lovers. The policewoman speaks:

"I've had a report of a lewd display perpetrated on the beach this afternoon. Do you know anything about that?"

"No," Lucinda says simply and neutrally. Then she adds, winging it and gesturing in the direction of the string bikini crowd, "Unless you mean those sweet, young things wagging their practically bare butts at any boy on the beach that's not gay."

The policewoman, someone who, due to the realities of our beauty obsessed culture – and maybe natural world realities as well – may be deprived of much opportunity for experience in sexual matters, turns red. But she keeps on going.

"The appearance of those women complies with local ordinances which prohibit the display of breasts and genitals, but make no provision as to a particular degree of covering necessary for buttocks." Her color deepens as she runs through this formal list of sexual equipment. "Lewdity, in the form of undraped breasts and genitals, though they may be painted, is unlawful on Blue Heron Beach south of Agamenticus Head."

"Lewdity?" Lucinda jeers.

The cop ignores her. "If you can explain how painting your genitals and displaying them publicly is not a lewd act you'd better start fast, lady," she says, her own embarrassment, combined with Lucinda's dismissive attitude, has started to put the little woman on edge. And, however little she is, she is still a cop.

One of the art lovers, almost a generation older than the others – a man well over four feet tall with a bemused look – offers a legal opinion. "Ms. York is merely exercising her first amendment rights to freedom of speech. Many thousands of young Americans went to their deaths to stop the Nazis. And thousands of Russian and Eastern European artists were sent to the gulags of the Soviets. Those systems repressed all forms of advanced art. We can't have art outlawed in America. This is the USA in the 1980s, not Berlin in the 30s."

"Are you trying to tell me," the policewoman scoffs, "that those young men went to their deaths so that this lady could parade around on Blue Heron Beach with her pu...vagina hanging out?"

The lifeguard snorts. Apparently, he is thinking that a lot of those men might have believed there could be worse things to die for...

"You don't understand," the reviewer from *The Phoenix* inserts her viewpoint, attempting to shed enlightenment, "Ms. York is not *making* a sexual display. She's holding up a mirror to sexual display in our society and making a complex artistic statement about the nature of a cultural reality."

I can see she's got a better angle on what she's going to write than I have. I should be taking notes.

"Well," suddenly chimes in the lady in the skirted suit, who'd been standing, arms crossed, her bottom lip thrust up against the one on top, "just what's so great about that?"

Everyone stares at her momentarily. Was this her business? Maybe it was. If this is about the public's business, then she could be the closest thing to the general public present.

"I don't suppose you read a lot of art reviews," *The Phoenix* woman says.

"I've got three little kids and reading them fairy stories is all the time I have for things that aren't for grown-ups."

Touché, crosses my mind. While the cop and Lucinda York are for the moment letting surrogates – representatives of the art world and of an art*less* one – do their talking, I do an aside to Kevin.

"You're an agent of a major institution in this town – mayor's wife on the board and everything. Why don't you take the artist under your institutional wing. – Tell the cop this is a gray area, or something." Kevin seems to shrink an inch or so in height when I say this, but after a few seconds he, visually echoing the woman in the skirted suit, pushes his lower lip hard up into the upper in an expression that, in his case, looks like serious consideration. Perhaps he is getting a sense that an opportunity to act meaningfully is being presented.

"Perhaps I can help clear this up," he says in a grave and formal tone; laying it on a little thick. They all, including an initially suspicious Lucinda, stare at him.

"I'm Kevin Perkins from the Northport Museum of Modern Art."

"You stay out of this, fella," the policewoman cautions.

"Yeah, it's you modern art people," accuses the lady with the skirted suit, feeling her importance as the cultural ambassador of middle-America, "that are responsible for so much of the lewdity that is polluting this country."

"Lewdity!" Lucinda shrieks this time. "There's no such word. And if you ever did use a dictionary you'd know a performance piece is not

Modern Art, but *Post*modern Art."

The lifeguard, probably schooled at one of the area's finest fraternities, demonstrates his own capacity for irony by putting in, "Well, I guess that clears everything up."

So Kevin's initial attempt to acquit Lucinda by the power vested in the arts has failed. But I look at him, nodding my head rapidly in a gesture of encouragement. *Once more into the breach,* I'm trying to say. And he toughs it out, taking my suggestion about a political settlement. And Laura Eldredge, wife of Mayor Bob Eldredge, herself city comptroller, the woman who signs this policewoman's checks, is currently a NoMMA director – though it's likely she's as inactive a member there as on the nine or ten other boards on which she officially sits.

Shaking off his blow, Kevin audaciously – for him anyway – advances again. "Ms. York's consideration for a museum exhibition is currently before the board of directors, which includes Laura Eldredge. I think that even if you do not respect this artist's...uh, professional statement...you must realize that this is not a, uh, routine incident, and that it at most falls into a gray area of the beach regulations. I think it would be pretty hard to bring such a minor technical infraction before a judge in this... burg." I wince a little at the *burg* part. That is probably thicker than Kevin ever laid anything on in his life. But, even though – except for the burg – it is my script, I am still proud of my big cousin, Kevin.

The skirted-suit woman, arms still folded, her mouth open but silent, stares intently at the little policewoman. The policewoman's eyes are not fixed: they dart left and right, looking for options; more options than are apparent just in front of her. Finally, she says, "Well, if it's a gray area...if it's a gray area, we can just drop it this time. But I warn you, lady, not to try any of your art dancing on Blue Heron Beach again."

"I wasn't dancing," Lucinda exclaims, rolling her eyes heavenward. Joan d'Arc could not have been more misunderstood. "This is not a gray area. It is a matter of principle."

Everybody, or almost everyone – the cop, the lady, the lifeguard, Ms. *Phoenix,* Kevin and even I – stare at the artist with surprised foreboding. The Lucinda art groupies applaud. The small guy who spoke about fascism nods knowingly.

Does this idiot want to be arrested, I wonder. Then I realize that she likely is no idiot and very likely does. What does any person who has vision and is a lover of principle crave most in this world? Fame, of course. Most people have bad dreams of walking naked in public. Anyone who does it for a living obviously doesn't think she has any dirty underwear to try to hide. Besides, even a lot of people who have things to hide, say that in today's world there is no such thing as bad publicity. I suddenly think about how much things have changed; how different the present is from a past that existed not that far from here, in Salem, just down the road, about three hundred years ago. Then and there, female behavior a few millimeters out of the norm would have gotten a woman burned at the stake – and not for being a Joan d'Arc. The expression I see on the face of the woman in the skirted bathing suit – who, herself, might have been burned in those days for being as exposed as she is now – is a look I associate with an enthusiastic *burner*. Lucinda York, a classic *burnee*, probably wouldn't have lasted five minutes around here in the year sixteen-whatever.

"Okay, you asked for it, lady," the little cop says. But she doesn't immediately do anything. Now everybody is staring at her.

"What are you going to do – cuff me?" Lucinda suggests, like a fellow actor prompting a colleague who has forgotten a line.

The little cop looks at all the expectant faces. "That's exactly what I am going to do." But she still makes no move.

"Okay, I submit to the power of the state," the artist says, presenting her wrists, fists down.

The cop seems frozen.

"If you won't cuff her I will," the witch burner throws in, exasperated. But she doesn't make a move either.

Then, as if coming out of a trance, the cop springs into action. A well-oiled machine. My guess is that she has never handcuffed anyone, has never had to, and has never wanted to. But, except for a little tremor in her fingers, the policewoman slaps on the cuffs as if she's been doing it all her life. The acolyte with the camera jumps forward and immortalizes the moment on film.

Kevin seems to be fretting. He'd performed his bit successfully. So I'm guessing his concern is that a poor naïf will have a blot on her record. It probably hasn't occurred to Kevin, the Boy Scout, that the trade-off of "a blot for a spot" – in the newspapers – or on television, even – is one that doesn't necessarily take a lot of soul-searching for someone with a career in serious need of advancement.

"Should we go along to the station?" he asks me. I'm gratified to hear him use the first person plural about us for perhaps the first time ever. Kevin-the-Boy-Scout and Alex-Clean-Mind/Clean-Body-Take-Your-Pick.

Given Lucinda's apparent comfort with martyrdom, I am not as worried about her as Kevin appears. In fact, I'm not worried at all. The rack and the rubber truncheon have not been used by the Northport police since at least the end of the McCarthy era. Besides, I get the feeling Lucinda York can take care of herself. She seems to be doing so right now. However, I do think going to the station might be fun: I've never seen anyone booked. "Sure," I say, "why not?"

"Will they let us?" he asks.

Well, I don't know why they should let me. I haven't said a word yet – to anyone but Kevin. But Kevin would probably have to go – if this poor little cop were at the top of her game: he has basically admitted to being an accessory before and after the crime. Aiding and abetting a nudist. Nobody gets into a racket like nudism without accomplices.

"Well, if she doesn't slap the cuffs on you, too, we can just follow in your car. Mine's at Grams. Where're you parked?"

The policewoman, as it turned out, had come to work on a bicycle and has to call for backup: a cruiser to the beach for apprehending a lawbreaker. I imagine this, being a Wednesday, is probably a low crime day and the officers at the station, hearing the gravity of the offense, might all want to be present at the scene. This doesn't happen. Only three cruisers show up. While we are waiting for these civil servants, Kevin, from the beachfront phone booth, calls Dalmore, at the museum, to report. And Dalmore, enraged at the assault on the free expression of enlightened ideas, says he, too, will appear at the station. We follow the police convoy, its sirens screaming. We are in excess of the speed limit most of the way – however, I assume all the police on duty in this part of the Seacoast Region are in front of us, so I'm able to convince Kevin that driving this fast is unlikely to jeopardize his license. Besides, as an accomplice and an accomplice's accomplice, we can always say we thought it was our duty to speed *toward* the police station.

The museum is closer to the police station than the station to the beach, and, when we get there, Dalmore is already present. He is stylishly dressed. As impressive in an Armani suit as he was as a captain in whites. Kevin introduces us. I'm tempted to tell him I am the man from the gangway on the dock. But what for? Anyway, there is no spark of recognition. I don't mean just that he doesn't remember me from the harbor. He doesn't even seem to recognize that we are being introduced. But together we watch Lucinda walked up to the desk. Something seems to be bothering Dalmore. His face runs through a gamut of expressions I usually associate with exasperation – or, as I suggested the other day – abdominal cramps. I wish to ask Kevin what this is about, but Dalmore would undoubtedly hear. Dalmore has drawn a threefold piece of paper from his inside suit pocket. While Lucinda is photographed and fingerprinted, Dalmore reads remarks he has prepared. I wonder when he had time to prepare them – let alone write them down. Perhaps it is mostly boilerplate from his days at the test-the-limits Whitney. Nobody listens to it but Kevin and me – and I find it a bit too dense and art jargon-filled to easily follow. Then I realize, for the sake of my upcoming interview with this man, I should start pretending to take notes. Dalmore notices me pulling out my pad. I was a little late. He finishes in ten seconds more. When he does, he wordlessly hands me his written text.

There is no bail to pay. A hearing date will be sent in the mail. The fine will be $50, which can be mailed in before the hearing, which will only occur if the perpetrator deems it necessary to protest the fine. My guess is that this case will not go to trial. What's important here has *already* been accomplished: an artist has gotten a fabulous picture of herself.

Dalmore must leave. He is in a hurry to get to the Northport Yacht Club for the Wednesday night races. So he leaves the artist in our care. Kevin introduces me to her. I tell her that I originally came to do an interview. To my surprise, she is ready *now*. What a trooper! But she says she is just starving. Her car is at the beach. I live near there, so we decide that we will eat at a seafront place – as I originally considered doing with Kevin – and she will answer anything I want to ask. Kevin, however, can only drop us off. He has a prior engagement. I press him about it. The engagement is with a woman named Deborah. I smile, but, to my disappointment, he doesn't.

# 6

Kevin drops us at Lucinda's van. She'd parked at the north end of the beach lot. A strip of restaurants lines the south end. That means if I walk her back to her vehicle after dinner – and she doesn't offer me a ride – I'll have about a three-quarter mile walk home after dark. That's fine with me, though. An amazing early summer's night is heralded by the shimmery thickness of air, and the pastel streaks above the line of trees to the west. Sunset is about an hour away. Lucinda's van is a VW of an even earlier vintage than my Karmann Ghia. Artists, and others without money, have a harder time shedding vestiges of a hippy past – or any past, for that matter – presuming they want to. However, I'm not entirely sure Lucinda is without financial resources. There is a whiff of solid middleclass about her, whether she wants it there or not.

I feel a slight pang of separation anxiety as my cousin drives off. I sat in the back seat of his Buick for the ride from the police station. Lucinda, obviously sat up front with Kevin. He also had not met her before, but he had played the hero (at my coaching) with some success, and had therefore been officially involved in the drama. If you don't count the coaching, I'd been superfluous and therefore nearly invisible. Lucinda does not seem to hold it against Kevin that he almost ruined her plan – if plan she had – to become a martyr to the cause of free artistic expression. She talked to him like a comrade in arms as we drove here. Probably a new experience for Kevin. Then again, what artist won't be as nice as pie to almost any museum curator? Introducing yourself to an emerging woman artist as an official from the most prestigious local museum is probably a lot like telling a young female hypochondriac you are a physician at the most expensive regional medical center. It's a great basis for instant friendship.

So, suddenly I am alone – and about to dine – with an iconoclastic, apparent careerist, with whom I've only shaken hands and exchanged about thirteen words. Even as a teenager, I was never particularly shy about talking to females. But with me there's kind of a sliding scale for feeling tongue-tied: the more gorgeous the woman the more shy I become. I'd attribute this to my intense preoccupation with beauty if it didn't seem to be true for most of the guys I've ever known: even the most boorish men are beauty addicts when it comes to gorgeous women. So the infrequency of my being shy probably indicates infrequent access to *gorgeous* more than to equanimity. I don't think Lucinda York would qualify as gorgeous, though I do think few men of my acquaintance would find much that is less than gorgeous about her from her neck down. But I am a "face man" when I talk about gorgeous. Unlike a lot of guys, I don't have breasts at the top of my list. Probably I'm not good-looking enough – or rich or talented (male gorgeousness equivalent) – to attract gorgeous. Well, I'd say Angela was nearly gorgeous. But looking back on the sum total of our relationship, I guess I wish she'd looked more like Phyllis Diller and that I'd never been attracted to her. I might have put those four years into working with pygmies or something. Giving back a little. But maybe I have had more *pretty* women in my life than the average guy.

This may be related to how a number of women have told me that I'm not bad looking. – Nice blue eyes, fairly muscled build, and all that. But I think what also works for me is that I'm not very macho. More often than mentioning blue eyes women say I seem *cuddly*. My theory is it's easier for women – at least some, anyway – to let you in close if you're more like a Teddy bear than a gorilla.

How did I first describe Lucinda's physical appearance? – "An offbeat sexiness," I think I said. *Northern North American exotic* might be another way. How's that for an oxymoron? She has a bit of the quality of the women who summer here from Quebec. On the beach I've occasionally seen fairly plain ones next to perfect, all-American coeds, and the plain French girls just seem somehow *hotter*. It's some way they make themselves up. Lucinda's hot like that, I think. But she's *cool* looking, too. Whereas beauty shop girls decorate their clients and themselves to look like particular types – this or that movie star – Lucinda has made, from the raw clay of her former hippyish days, a one of a kind creation. A heavy black bar of make-up under each eye – what do they call that, *kohl?* – can add a lot of mystery. Sometimes an artificially sexy woman can seem sexier than a naturally sexy one. I'm not sure why I say that. And I know it doesn't sound too good. I mean, as an avid backpacker, I hate to admit that.

Still, all this doesn't add up to the discomfiture visited upon me by gorgeousness. So I'd probably be about a 6.5 on a scale of 10 for boy/girl nervousness – not much beyond a midpoint of five where I spend most of my waking hours – were it not for lettering on the flesh that's visible above the zipper of her army jumpsuit. That provides a cogent reminder of all that black paint in places that I can't keep my imagination from wandering into. Doubles or triples any sexual charge mere "nice tits" might put into the air. It adds a point and a half or even two to my male/female self-consciousness meter. Why am I thinking about this when I'm here on business? Well, what percentage of even non-macho, 33-year-old males, landed on a beachhead at sunset with a bleached-blond in paratrooper garb – undergarments painted over a body she uses as a psychological weapon – would be thinking *only* of business? The percentage that is gay, I guess. But just because you can't help thinking of something – even get excited about it – doesn't mean you have the wish to *do* something about it. I've recently realized that from reading that Shackleton book. Most thrilling thing I ever read. I couldn't put it down. But would I want to live that kind of excitement myself? Absolutely no way. Lots of things are exciting. – Hell, even Gram finds that survival stuff exciting. The difference between me and my grandmother is that if she were twenty years younger – 70 or so – she'd be ready to go.

I do have to admit that I can be a little compulsive about looking for sex when I'm not ensconced in a relationship. But a whole relationship is what I really want most, not just sex. *Just sex.* That's a laugh. Not quite like *just* food or *just* water. Pretty close, though. But honestly, I always need to at least try to convince myself that the woman I've just met could be suitable relationship material before I make any moves. My motto is never hold a woman's crotch, if you wouldn't hold her hand. Keep to a moral high ground. Of course, I've done a lot of Alex-what-could-you-have-been-thinking post mortems. I'm beginning to realize sex and self-delusion are inextricably linked. Even so, I don't remember ever getting cuddly with someone I could tell for sure *beforehand* was totally wrong for me. That wouldn't have been fair to either of us. And Lucinda? Regardless, of her appealing qualities, I fear Lucinda just isn't my *type*.

The numerous seafront bars and restaurants at Blue Heron cater to a range of tastes and incomes. This is good, given the thinness of my wallet. I offer to let the artist decide – though I am willing to veto – or perhaps whine about – her choice if it is too rich for my blood. Of course, I can try to get reimbursed from my boss, Steve – if it turns out the feminist in Lucinda abdicates, and she expects me to pick up *her share,* too. But I can tell you right now what Steve Towle would say. "What are you, nuts?" To my major financial relief, yet mild psychological consternation, Lucinda pauses in front of a low end saloon of uninhibitedly homosexual repute, Sons of the Sun.

"Let's go in here," she says. "I'm more comfortable around gays. You don't mind if we just have bar fare? Portions are big here. Besides what I need most is a drink. Okay?" Awash in ambivalence, I answer, "Absolutely." I can imagine she's conflicted about the appraising eyes of straight men. Why else would she be hiding in that jumpsuit on a hot day? Perhaps she only lets her body out on professional occasions.

My "nice eyes" notwithstanding, I'm probably ordinary looking enough not to draw unwanted male attention. And I'm obviously relieved that there won't be crowds of indiscriminate young females in here undressing with their eyes every man with at least one body part they like. I can live with gay men inconsequentially thinking that I might be one of them. But straight ones thinking I'm gay is something else. That can get me semi-consciously affecting a more macho bearing. One time I was walking on this very boardwalk with my friend, Stuart – the guy who made that "nice tits" comment at Lucinda's *Breast* show; not the most masculine looking straight guy you'll ever meet. A bunch of frat-boy types started whispering to each other as we passed. I actually injured a toe when I tried kicking too big a rock out of my way. I'd intuited that a demonstration of traditional, free-floating male aggression might alter their unwarranted underestimation of my virility. My screams of pain did nothing to correct their misjudgment.

Lucinda and I take a small table on the beachfront. The waiter – I think it's an *er* – sports hot pants and a halter top. He approaches with a broad grin.

"Honey," he says with surprising familiarity. I guess he's recognized Lucinda's white hair or her jumpsuit or her slightly visible "sign". "You kill me! You just kill me! I was on the beach and caught your act this afternoon. – Fabulous, just fabulous! I wish I had the balls to do something like that. Or didn't have them I should say. Put a coat of black paint on me – now that would be a performance. Well, you really showed those tight-asses."

"Thank you," Lucinda says softly; surprisingly polite. "But I'm not sure who showed who. – I got arrested."

"I know. Everyone was talking about it. I'd started work by the time the cruisers arrived. You could see the blue lights from all the way down here. You're everybody's hero at The Sons. Just fabulous."

"Thank you," Lucinda intones again.

" What can I get you?"

"I'll have a Margarita, frozen." Lucinda says. "And a menu."

The waiter's heavy-lidded eyes look sidelong at me. "And for the *gentleman?*" He says this out of a taut, twitching corner of his mouth. He's being ironic, I take it.

I reply, "A Margarita sounds good. Oh, but no salt." I'm feeling dry and if I quench my thirst on expensive drinks I'll be sorry when the credit card bill arrives. "And a glass of ice water, *before*, if you don't mind." Maybe I just can keep my credit card in my wallet.

He gives me a theatrical "daggers" glance, then smiles like we both have enjoyed his teasing me; but now that's over. "You got it," he says, then he pivots – a bit heavily – and glides off.

"He's great," Lucinda says; my agreement foreordained. "But I wish he hadn't thought I was just out to outrage public decency. I wasn't going to argue though. I feel such solidarity with the androgynous."

I find this a little perplexing, but – given her metamorphosis from the wholesome brunette of her "breasts" performance not that long ago – not *too* perplexing. I imagine she has yet to settle into a fixed identity. I can't remember if ambiguity is a tenet of identity art – or if the opposite is.

There's a silence that I don't want to become awkward. So I decide to start right in on a professional footing, I, perhaps too hastily, say, "I've seen your work before. I was in the South End in '79 for *Mammogram.* "Bringing this up was ill-considered, because now I will have to either lie or be honest about what I thought of the piece. Both options distress me. But, to my relief, she makes things easy.

"Oh, *that*. I was hoping nobody still remembered it. I was in a really different head space then." And, body space pretty much, too, I'm thinking. The only two physical things I can see about her still in that space are her breasts.

"You disavow your earlier work?"

"Pa-leese. Wouldn't you? I was… I mean…Look, my boyfriend at the time was a real shit. I moved out on him and in with some gay women, and got pretty influenced by them for a while. So I was denying any intellectual side to my art. It was all about feeling then. It was very raw. Now I only want to do cerebral things. Meditative things. More spare, more…*Eastern*."

I'm not sure there are many parts of the East where the cops wouldn't disrupt your meditations even more harshly if you sported painted genitals in public. Perhaps she should try Africa… I'm gratified, though, at her willingness for self-criticism. And, I didn't picture her as someone who'd be as *disclosive* about personal stuff. From her "spare" performance and the way she dealt with the cops, I'd expected her to be somewhat defensive – perhaps surly or remote, not self-effacing.

The drinks arrive.

"So – anything to eat…nachos…appetizers?" our waiter asks.

Maybe I'll just get two appetizers instead of an entrée, I think. "What you got for appetizers?"

"We've got a terrific dick-lovers pate today. – Oh! – listen to my potty mouth. I mean *duck livers* pate." The server pretends to correct himself. He rolls his eyes extravagantly. Everyone's a performance artist these days. Lucinda releases a snort at the joke. I find Lucinda's unforeseen, un-uptight manner appealing. She gives the server a sisterly high five and says "One of those – definitely! What else ya got?" No other humorous items enliven the menu, so Lucinda gets a bleu cheese burger. I can see from that she wants to make an easy transition into more Eastern ways. No sacred cows, yet. I, having been to the East and returned, get an order of onion rings and a salad. When her comrade in arms departs, Lucinda takes a protracted swallow of her drink. Her eyelids flutter almost imperceptibly, then close for a moment. "Mmm," she says. "I needed that." I also swallow heartily – but from my water glass. Then I take a sip of my Margarita. Ooo – it tastes good.

"I was drinking a bit too much, back when I did *Mammogram* – when I moved out on René." (Disclosiver and disclosiver.) I'm in a good space about alcohol right now. Can take it or leave it. But doing a performance always drains me. And getting arrested can add to the stress. So I think a couple of drinks would be therapeutic right now."

Genius is pain, I think privately. I don't want to ask – at least not right off – if the arrest might be therapeutic for her career. I consider whether I've ever been in the company of someone who's said *a couple* of drinks and meant *two*. I have no problem with how much she might drink – or I might, for that matter – except in relation to cost. Do I have any cash on me? I try to calculate. Let's see. I saw a twenty in with those ones at lunch. So, I'm going to lie a little in the interest of male/female equality.

"I think I've got about $25 on me." I'm implying I have no credit card. Prevaricating about my financial situation. Everybody does that, don't they? A guy I met on a train in India, whose mother was Khrishnamurti's secretary, told me that even the great man used to prevaricate – might say, "I'm carrying no money," when all he had on him was traveler's checks. If Khrishnamurti could do it….

"Well, you should be all set – I hope you don't think I expected you to pay my way." She takes another deep draft, looking fixedly at me over the top of the glass.

"Well, this is business. I mean, I am interviewing you. But my paper's pretty small and doesn't do expense accounts." Then I try to salvage my pride by saying, "But that means I can write what I want."

The corners of Lucinda's mouth turn down a hair or two as I'm saying this. I may have made a *faux pas*. I wonder if my conflation with Kevin, the *curator*, gave me some cachet that I've now lost. Maybe she doesn't even know what *Currents* is? But after my addendum, her facial muscles turn up past neutral. She says rather nicely, "Well, an art writer shouldn't have to answer to some

64

businessman."

She's cutting me slack on both financial and professional fronts. So, a lot of the harsh, *black and white* quality I'd anticipated might have been me projecting from her public pose. And with the Margarita going down nicely, this interview is starting off a good deal easier than I'd thought.

She's finished her drink – fast – and, lifting the glass toward my side of the table, says, "So, I guess you can afford one more?"

"By all means," I say.

She now swings the still aloft glass toward the server, who seems to have Lucinda out of his periphery. But by a sixth sense or long experience, he winks toward our edge of the deck. He holds up two fingers. I guess that's a question. Lucinda gives him a thumbs-up. There really does seem to be a sisterly – or just a barroom? – understanding between them. I'm not a hand signals person myself.

The tide has come in appreciably, since I last focused on the world around me, and is nearly high by now. A sultry, southwest breeze adds lift to the foam on the wave tops. The white sun, settling into the humid air, has softened to orange and it turns this white froth a soothing peach. I'm relaxing. And were it not for the presence of a hardly known – and perhaps hardly *knowable* – female entity three feet away, I might begin a drift into one of my little dream worlds. So, do I wish I were here alone? No. I've spent a lot more time within enigmatic dreams than with enigmatic women since my Angela days. Rare makes for precious.

"Do you live in Boston or Northport now?" I ask. She tells me of her move out of Massachusetts' biggest city. Boston is close enough that it is always *right there*, she says. She tells me how she needed a fresh start and how the coming of Arthur Dalmore to Northport has made this much smaller metropolis hipper, in some ways, than staid old Boston. Why not New York? I ask and she says, that it's not *for right now*. It sounds like she has a plan. The second round of drinks has arrived, but still no food – no fabled dick-lovers pate. Not even rolls.

I'm a sip or two into my second drink, telling her about getting Margaritas in Katmandu – in an Eastern version of a speakeasy. Telling her this is a show of credentials. Given her stated fascination with things Eastern, she seems to be eating it up. Though I've only had about 1.1 drinks, I suddenly, feeling how hot it is for the time of day, get a sensation of otherworldliness – a little like how I felt in Katmandu all the time. There, though you went to a speakeasy for Margaritas, you bought hashish where you bought tomatoes. Feeling that way here – and without being stoned on hashish – *and* having just had a flash of Angela, now causes me to flash on Angela's diagnosis of me as anxiety attack prone. But, it's just a flash. It passes fast.

I see that Lucinda, perhaps forty pounds lighter than I am, has already finished her second Margarita. Yet she seems still comfortably in the regular world. But she must be hot in that jumpsuit. As if reading my mind she unzips it about four inches more, exposing the pleasingly shaped tops of spheres of unpleasing black. Then again, I think: don't be uptight, Alex – black is cool.

The food arrives.

"One more round?" Lucinda asks. "Can you afford it?" The second drink is making me question the uptight logic of having a credit card and not using it. After all, you're only 33 once. And I, like her, can take it or leave it. However, I still possess enough of my wits to realize that I must make a credible explanation for the sudden appearance of an undisclosed credit card. So I prevaricate again.

"I've got a card on me that didn't go through at lunch. But I'm remembering, now, that the place seemed to have trouble with the customer before me, too. So it might have just been their equipment." I turn to our server. "Can you try running this card through your machine to see if it works?" I feel like a shit. Does it even sound plausible? If I'd known this woman was going to be as open with me I never would have started out such a dastardly prevaricator. But Lucinda and the server both take me at face value. Which, I guess, means I have an honest face. The hunger she'd spoken of over an hour ago outside the police station – along with the two drinks – has likely shorted-out her disingenuousness radar. She tears into her burger. Can I afford another drink? She'd asked. And I'd considered *afford* to mean *financially*. But can I afford it constitutionally? These things are strong. I haven't even finished my second drink. Well, just because I *ordered it* – am *paying for it* – doesn't mean that I have to *drink it*. I'll let paying for something that will go to waste be my penance for lying. I tear into my food, too. We sit silent – other than slurping and smacking – for several minutes. This time the silence isn't awkward. Attention to eating has distracted me from any concern about drunkenness and drunkenness has distracted me from any concern about silence.

"So, tell me a little about the meaning of your work?" I ask without bothering to swallow my current mouthful. I feel I will get further into my mind-altering liquid more comfortably as a listener than as a talker. I'm wondering, for the first time, if speculating about an anxiety attack actually is an anxiety attack. – Only one of infinitesimal duration.

"My work's about contexts," Lucinda answers unhesitatingly. "Zabout," I hear her say; my first verification that alcohol is at work in her systems. " – Contexts and expectations."

"Yes?" I say, lowering my brow to give the impression my mind has shifted down for lifting a heavy idea. The third round arrives. Lucinda is taking more lady-like sips by now.

"Take sex, for example."

Oh, it's just a random example – she might have said anything, of course. But she still feels inhibited enough to add a disclaimer.

"– My work isn't sexual, of course."

Furthest thing from it, I'm thinking.

"I feel that – *instead* – to the degree which I involve my own body – I'm holding up a mirror to the ridiculous over-preoccupation with sex in our culture right now." Did I hear this somewhere before? –

"But sex…," she continues, "you know – since there are so many knee-jerk associations with it – is an easy way of demonstrating my point about contexts."

I lower my eyebrows as far as they'll go. I'm now in first gear.

"How does one define *sexy*?" she asks. I know what Justice Felix Frankfurter would say. But I'm pretty sure the question right now is rhetorical. "What does *our culture* see as sexy?" There's a pause that could allow me to fall into the trap of assuming we are not still in a rhetorical realm – and of saying something regrettable.

"Boobs?" she suggests, pressing hers from both sides in a way that makes her moderately large, black-painted breasts swell into cleavage visible between the teeth of the zipper of her jumpsuit. "Ass?" She introduces Exhibit B (or should I say Exhibit "A"?) and wiggles hers, matter-of-factly, where she sits. Almost imperceptibly, she catches herself off balance on the bucking restaurant chair. Seemingly, she intends to deny any erotic quality intrinsic to a young, healthy, squirming female body. Still, in liar mode, I dutifully mouth the anticipated word "no," along with her, as she says it.

"No," she says. "In themselves, swollen flesh is pretty neutral – even maybe a little gross – right? ... It's the context in which something's presented that produces sexual energy. Or more, like, 'the inappropriateness' to the context."

I can't tell yet where she's going with this. I did a semester of logic freshman year in college and learned that even though *some*, let's say, *tits and asses*, may be gross, you can't draw conclusions about all *tits and asses* from some tits and asses. To convey that I am in a state of suspended judgment, I tilt my head, like a dog showing keen interest. When Rosebud does this, Gram says she is making a question mark. "Go on," my gesture implies.

"Those girls with the nearly bare asses on the beach," she says. "They're just not very sexy."

"No," I repeat, still tip-toeing around traps. I fear she is suddenly going to point at me, laughing, and shout "Gotcha! I Gotcha!"

"Well, like, not very, anyway." She amends the estimation, thankfully leaving me room to breathe. "My piece today was about a bathing suit. A neutral object. A bikini on a beach fits its context. It's not very sexy. It's almost natural – like the nudists. How sexy are they? – Not much. But a bikini in a restaurant – that's a different story – right?"

"That's true," I say. I'm actually impressed. My thoughts have wandered in that direction before, but I've never followed them toward a general conclusion.

She goes on, "But even in a restaurant people are relaxing and taking care of their physical selves, being, like, *sensual*…you know…like with food. So a bikini in an office is way more inappropriate – and way sexier."

I see a fundamental truth in what she is saying. So I chime in, "And a bikini in a church…"

"You got it," she says and gives me an exaggerated, approving wink.

"You know, I had a thought almost like that this afternoon when that woman in the skirted-suit was hassling you. I thought about how in other times she might have been considered whorish for wearing what looks so conservative to most people today."

"That's nothing," Lucinda says in rejoinder. "You don't have to go to other times. Her suit was two-toned. Right? – The little skirt wasn't the same color as the top. So it was only the context *beach* that told you that that was not a halter *top* and an obscenely short, plain-old *skirt*."

Hmm? I remember that I've often marveled at how much more aroused I get on the sidewalk in Boston on warm spring days – watching inappropriately *exposed* young women parade by – than I do when, twenty-five minutes later, I stop at the Golden Banana strip club on the way out of town. Okay, I've admitted I stop there. I usually need to pee or I want to get a Coke after leaving behind Boston traffic. And there's no cover charge there. So, why not? I know I could stop at a gas station. But what's the point? Why not the Golden Banana? It's like if you ask a guy, "Would you like that Coke with pussy or without?" What's he going to say? The trouble is that it's never *that* much better than *without* – not as good as the short skirt

69

on Newbury Street that gives just the swatch of bare thigh. I've never understood it. Now, thanks to Lucinda, I know why. – Bare pussy is quite appropriate to a strip club. Bare thighs are not quite appropriate to the sidewalks of Boston. For all I know that witch-burner today, walking down Newbury Street with her skirt at "c-level" (as Steve would say) might have been sexier than anything Lucinda and I have yet discussed. That would be weird. Context is magical, I realized in my inebriated state. Maybe there is more to performance art than I've ever thought possible.

But I decide not to share all this with Lucinda – the horniness epiphany, and all that, which Lucinda has stimulated. I decide to take the discussion back to art.

"It's kind of like *De'jeuner sur l' herbe,"* I say.

I see her blanche ever so slightly as she apparently starts, then thinks better of trying to repeat what I have just said. Though I know only a few words of French, most of them are the titles of French paintings, which I learned to pronounce mimicking art professors. So I am reasonably sure I am not way off in pronouncing the name of that Manet that depicts a nude woman and an underclothing clad one having a picnic with two clothed men. This composition had outraged Paris in 1863 – and probably did so somewhat more than Lucinda's performance earlier today had disturbed the sands of Blue Heron Beach.

"You know –" I'm quick to supply the translation, "Manet's *Luncheon on the Grass.*

"Right – *right,"* she says, recovering her former unruffleable demeanor, *Dejeuner – Luncheon on the Grass*. She nods sharply and beams, "Right! It was a scandal because the nude woman looked like an everyday girl. But that composition with a nude sitting right there in that pose, with men around, had been acceptable for centuries when it was painted as mythology, with some goddesses," she looks away, reaching for the association, "… by Raphael. Same nude, same pose, same proximity to the men. But they said Raphael's goddess was *a nude*, and Manet's average girl just looked *naked*. Nude isn't sexual, naked is."

So she *has* been to art school. And she's proud of herself. And I'm proud of myself, too, for hitting on such a good example. I'd feared bringing up Manet would make me seem old fartish to someone from the radical contemporary scene. Of course, she had referred to a dead master already when she conceived of today's performance. But Manet is not Magritte. Magritte was of our own century. We sit for a moment, smiling in overlapping universes of pride.

"Yes, that is an example I'd thought of using to do a performance piece. But everybody is doing something with *Luncheon* these days. I mean it was like the beginning of both modern art and postmodern art. The first painting that really winked at the viewer, and the first one to show that if the public hates it now it's going to be a big hit later on. Did you see the William Kahn, *Dejeuner with Donald Duck*, in this month's *Art Forum*? The original is going to be in his NoMMA retrospective that opens next week. That's a feather in Northport's cap."

I hadn't. I now realize how much my concern about old fartishness had been misplaced. Knowing your art history and cavalierly appropriating pieces of it for off-the-wall pieces was a way of *legitimizing*. Appropriation is the life's blood of the Postmodernist. And it helps a dad see that art school hadn't just been kindergarten for twenty-year-olds. I don't agree, though, with her implication that a work of art being reviled when it's new guarantees that it's starting down the road to inevitable, eventual greatness. I think that's just a comforting myth. Artists believe that the way the public believes an artist's work automatically grows in value when the artist dies. My logic 101 course comes back to me again: *Just because something sometimes happens, doesn't mean that it always does.* Most things called *art* by their makers probably look not so great initially and end up not looking any better. But, then again, since much art today is intended to be more about newness and – better still – *shock* than about quality, the success myth derived from *Dejeuner/Luncheon on the Grass*, that a reversal of fortune happens as public enlightenment grows, probably claims more adherents now than ever before. But, I decide not to mention any of this.

"No," I say. "But I guess I'll be seeing it soon. I'm interviewing Arthur Dalmore on Friday."

"You're interviewing Arthur Dalmore?" She is impressed. "He's *so* great."

"Kevin is setting it up."

"Who's Kevin?"

"My cousin."

She shakes her head, blinking.

"Kevin – the curator. He went to the station. He brought us here."

"Oh, *Kevin*. I didn't know he was your cousin."

I know she was told this, but I don't remind her. "Yup, he's my cousin," is all I say.

"That's great," she says unfathomably.

"Contexts," she says, hoisting her glass – as if Dalmore and Kevin hadn't come up; unless she sees them within that frame, too. She pushes it toward me for a toast.

"Contexts." I say, lofting mine.

She looks at me, eyebrows raised and sips from her drink with obvious satisfaction. The toast seems a valedictory lap or something. Well, she's right, I'm thinking. And sex and nudity are only one, as she said, handy example of the system. Of course. It can probably apply to anything. Beauty, in general – non-sexual beauty. I try to think of some art without much exposed flesh where it would work. But my mind is a blank. What about the Mona Lisa? I speculate. I'm sorry, art history minor or not, I've never found it particularly beautiful. Okay, but what if you took it out of the museum and put it in, um, a gas station? There it would it look much more beautiful, wouldn't it? Well, it doesn't seem like it. The Surrealists were always taking the Mona Lisa out for a spin somewhere, putting mustaches on her, to demystify her, not glorify her. Perhaps I've picked a bad example. And right now I can't think of another one.

But is Lucinda York's system *consistent*? (Is it even a system?)

According to what she's convincingly just explained, the paint on her naked body would make her appear more sexy rather than desexualized in the midst of nudist girls or those girls garbed in shreds and patches. And it does. I noticed a few cute ones, but the epicenter of attention from men on the beach today was on Lucinda's black ass. Yet she says her performance is not erotic. – Oh, maybe I get it: in "holding up a mirror," as she mentioned, she is being ironic – in the original sense of the word: not meaning what you seem to say. She just *appears* to be sexy. Probably none of those men would actually be able to perform an act of sexual congress if she gave them the opportunity. Because she isn't *really* sexy, they wouldn't be able to get it up. But my drink-addled intellect is not able to follow any idea, let alone hold one with certainty.

Has this been our interview? At some point I seem to have forgotten that that's what we came here for. Did she tell me this stuff *for publication?* I'm not sure. Now I realize the sunset has passed into afterglow – slipped by me without notice. I feel bad about that. But she's smiling at me. Jesus, it seems to be more than just friendly smile.

"All you say is very interesting, Lucinda," I'm vaguely aware of not having said her name before.

"Call me Luce," she says and, as if demonstrating, reclines deeply into her chair. She tosses her head back as if she had a mane and gazes at the deepening dusk above us. And then, as if several squirrels inside her are restlessly trading positions, she jerks herself upright and arches her back. Then she reclines again, this time closing her eyes. I hear a deep sigh.

"Luce," I say as requested.

She opens her eyes and focuses, a little blearily on me. Now she leans across the small table, this time somewhat further, her black breasts squashed and swelling to try to escape the confines of the jumpsuit. She seems to be scrutinizing me, as if trying to figure-out something. She nods barely noticeably and, in a kind of baby talk quite incongruous to her clothing, the heavy kohl under her eyes, and the confident lecture she just ended, and perhaps her drunken inner child emerging, says, "You know, Alex…" The first time she's used my name too. As if noticing my noticing, she says, charmingly, like a little girl, "Alex, Alex, Al-Ex. You seem like a…very…cuddly…guy."

# 7

"Look at those stars!" Lucinda marvels. And parodying a Jersey Girl, she goofs, "Mussed be unrids uvum!"

The dome of heaven swirls like Van Gogh's *Starry Night;* the moist black air thick as his painterly brushstrokes; my consciousness as nebulous as his sky. Now with an otherworldly companion, I am retracing my solo steps of earlier in the day – and of days earlier in my life – from the beach to Gram's rustic cottage. But I'm not nostalgic for my childhood now. No, there's no nostalgia at all. Why would any big boy want to be a kid again and miss this? The present moment is *it.* This is what boys dream of growing up for. The only thing causing even intermittent encumbrance to the glorious freedom I'm feeling is the bumps and tugs from the ragged dance with my summer's night nymph; clutching and letting go of my arm; hopping barefoot (Doc Martens' now backpacked), her feet attacked by swarms of pebbles – some maybe even ones that taxed my soles in boyhood – assuming pebbles don't migrate (or at least don't migrate far). We reel together, now and again, sloshed by waves from the too much drink we've consumed. – *Too much?* I don't know. Maybe it was just the right amount. Everything seems the right amount. The drink, the hundreds of stars, the woman. My only problem now is my grandmother.

"You wat?"

"You heard me,"

"You live with yer granmuthr?" Lucinda York nearly shrieks with drunken laughter. "How'd you spect to get laid living with your granmuthr?"

We are now approaching the cottage. In the high afternoon of a summer's 4:45 p.m., I'd turned on the back porch light to facilitate an unobtrusive late night return; though I'd had no idea when I left, the degree of unobtrusiveness that might come in handy five or six hours down the line. Veiled by the overlay of right-angled planes of screen, the bug-lighted, never pruned, gangly foliage behind the porch appears a jumbled jungle, atomized by a strike of yellow-green lightning. My free-floating mind fixes upon it, as if – regardless of the intensity of my current bodily preoccupations – it has greater meaning than I might be willing to give it credit for right now. Right now the demands of anticipated sex are more compelling than even lightning. Nature probably intended that.

"Shhhhhh," I hiss, not so much because I fear my dear, nearly deaf grandmother will hear, but to inhibit general, unbridled ribaldry. I have no idea what are the limits of my new friend's self-expression. Self-expressing beyond community standards seems to be a point of honor to her.  Why just this afternoon self-expressing got her arrested.

"Duz that mean yer changing yer mine?" I ask. I'm either mimicking her inebriated abbreviations or creating some on my own. I'm sure I am officially drunk.

"Changing my mine? Whoever said you were going to get laid by me tonight?"

"Well – if I remember c'rectly – you did."

"Well, mabbe I *have* change my mine. I don't know if a wummn of my backrown can sleep with a guy who lives with his granmuthr. –

But hey, I guess a promiz is a promiz. I jus haven't performed a mercy fuck in a long time."

"Oh, thank you."

"No, it's okay. I think it's cute that you live with yer granmuthra," Lucinda looses another gale of laughter.

"I don't know why," I say, "it's any funner...fun-e-er...me living with my granmothr and thinking I can bring you home, than you living with a couple of gay guys and thinking that you can't. Maybe, it's just that gays are hip this year and grandmothrs aren't. Next season gays might be out and grandsmothers in. Then we'll see who laughs at who." A part of me has trouble believing that I'm making this jaunty little speech to the black and white, naked lady from the beach only about three weeks earlier in the day.

"Who*ooom*," she corrects and presses herself against me, full frontal contact for the first time. It feels amazingly good.

"I'm sorry," she says in a fawning, maternal tone. She gives me a tequila-laced kiss, managing to say in a chewing sort of way through our locked lips, "I think granmuthrs are *way* hip." We hold the kiss for a few seconds until she snorts with laughter – blowing enough air into my mouth that some of it comes out my nose.

"Shhhhh," I say again.

"Oh, sorry," she whispers, or says in what is somehow meant to come across as a burlesque of whispering. "Have you ever had sex in your grandmuthr's house before?"

"Of course," I say, "Just not with another person."

"That's just what I thought," she shrieks.

"Shut up" I insist, *sotto voce*. I swing open the screen. "Just – shut – up."

It's dawn now. Painfully lovely, summer morning light, filtered through browning lilacs and the dew, pulses in my open window and projects peach-colored patterns on my bedroom wall. I know it's lovely because I've seen it before and it was lovely then. Right now it isn't lovely – it's only painful. I awoke just a few moments ago and opened nearly un-focusable eyes onto black shapes swimming before me. "Bath. ... Bathing...This Is Not My Bathing..." I realized: oh, shit. Oh, God - what did I do? Right – that. I did *that*...Ok, so sue me. ...But, maybe it was okay. Maybe it was great. But...but what's...what's it going to... *cost me*? What now? I closed my eyes again.

For one thing, it's already costing me the worst headache a human is ever likely to acquire. I feel like someone enduring the consequence of having attempted a good-natured jest about the virility of three or four Hell's Angel's coming out of a bar. Not only that, I have a very strange sensation in my mouth. It feels like, while I slept, Fred Avery might have surreptitiously borrowed my tongue to clean and re-varnish the working deck of his fishing boat, the *Laura T*. All my faculties – except my ego – seem impaired. I lie still for several minutes. During this time, I reason myself into believing that I will probably, eventually, recover and someday again be able to lead a normal life. – As long as... I open my eyes again, one at a time. After a quick glance to see that the bolt on the door had been conscientiously slid into the grandmother-proof position, I lift the sheet and squint down the length of my body. Nothing. I roll left and to my relief see it: stuck to my hip, a flattened, wrinkled piece of latex. Flattened, yet there is a bulbous little knob near the far end. Thank god for survival instinct. Or, at least, instinct to make sure little bastard ambassadors of the next generation don't survive.

I close my eyes again and do some calisthenics with my tongue to try to stimulate saliva secretion. No help. Something isn't normal. By that I mean strong drink alone could not account for this. I think of survival for a second time. Braving torture by natural light, I again open my eyes. There's something else I must see. I lift the sheet again and try to examine the lower central part of my bedmate's recumbent form. She is sleeping on her side facing me, but what I want a look at is chastely hidden. I try gently tickling the thigh that's on top and succeed in getting her to stir a bit – but nothing more. I slide down so my face is at the level of her belly and I blow lightly on it. Lucinda is now awake.

"Well, what are you doing down there again?"

"There's something wrong with my mouth, "I say.

"And you think that's the place to fix it?" She's playful. She naturally thinks playfulness will be appreciated.

"I'm not down here for that. My mouth is all screwed-up. Spread your legs. I just need a look."

"But, sir," she says affecting a Southern belle accent and covering her genitals with both hands. A lady's honor! Why I hardly know you, Sir. If I comply with this one rude request, what shall you ask of me next?"

I grab her wrists and gently pull them off her belly. She gives no resistance and, smiling, slowly parts her thighs.

I'm right. "You have a pink spot on the crotch of your black 'bathing suit.'"

The reason for my distress dawns on her. "Come up here and open your mouth. Hmm. And you have black all over your pink tongue."

"Oh, gross."

"You didn't seem to mind last night. But I know you men. There're a lot of things you don't mind at night that you do in the morning."

She certainly has this stuff down pat. Too pat, I think. "What do you use for body paint? My mouth has never felt like this."

"You've licked a better class of paint, you're saying? I'm mortified." Putting on the Southern belle again, she raises the back of a wrist to her forehead. "I knew it was fruitless to try to fool a man of your social rank. Oh agony!"

"I'm serious,"

"Oh, don't be a baby. It's water-soluble. It came off with spit didn't it? You think I'd take a chance on this sacred pussy. My body is a temple. Just go rinse out your mouth."

"Be right back," I say.

I grab my robe, unlock the door and peek down the stairs. From here I can see the lower left corner of Gram's doorway. Morning shadows fill the bottom of the stairwell. But I can tell her door is closed. I descend the stairs and duck into the bathroom, the doorway before Gram's. By now the wish to pee is more urgent that the wish to scrub out my mouth. Luckily the toilet and the sink almost overlap in the small cottage so I pee while using a lot of toothpaste on my toothbrush for a scrub. Then when no black is detectable I gulp about ten handfuls of water, the last of which I accompany with three aspirins that I noisily find in the medicine cabinet. Thank god hearing deteriorates with age. Several more of my symptoms begin to recede with my merely knowing that relief is on the way.

Now I'm back in bed. Lucinda is propped up on one elbow looking around the room at my stuff. She gives me a look of mock – or perhaps real – reproach.

"Aren't you hung over at all?" I ask this spiky-haired stranger.

"No, but I still feel kinda drunk. It affects me that way – the first to get high, the last to come down. But I didn't consume, like, lead paint off a way questionable surface, too. – My turn," she says, bouncing off the bed in a way that makes my temple throb. "I think I'll take this sign off my chest. The performance is over."

"What about the bathing suit."

"Maybe I'll need your help for that – all those hard to reach places. It can wait until you're recovered a little." I have to say, that sounds interesting – even to the severely debilitated.

"Take my robe," I call too late as she passes through the doorway.

I sit on the bed in a sort of lotus position. It makes my head hurt even to only think. I guess it will be quite a while before I'm in good enough condition for "hard to reach places". And now I'm feeling guilty about bringing this woman home to my grandmother's. I should spirit her out to the car immediately. Then back inside for a quick look-in on Gram and a "Be right back." That's what I should do. I put on some clothes and start down the stairs.

Lucinda, the lettering washed off her chest, is just exiting the bathroom – just as Gram is starting in. I panic and freeze six or seven steps from the bottom.

"Oh, I'm sorry, honey," Gram says, focusing as well as she can on what may be mostly a generic female form. "You a friend of Alex'? – You're here so early. I can't keep up with you kids. You two going for a swim?" Apparently the only person that "bathing suit" is going to fool at this distance is one who is legally blind. "It's Thursday, isn't it. You don't have to go to work today?"

"I'm an artist," Lucinda says.

"Oh, that's nice," says Gram. "Did he meet you through his work?"

"Uh, ya," said Lucinda. "His work."

"I'm surprised he can go swimming. Doesn't he have to go to the newspaper?"

Lucinda covers surprisingly well. "He's interviewing me about my art."

"Oh that's nice. And you can do that at the beach. You know it's just down this road."

"I know."

"Art is a good common interest. I met some of my beaus from the best families in museums. What's your name, honey?"

Lucinda tells her.

"Well, I've known several Yorks in this town. I've known Florence York since I was a teenager. First we waitressed together. Later we did volunteer work together at the Girls' Club – until we were in our 70's"

"Florence York is my grandmother," I hear Lucinda say and see her putting her hands over her "bathing suit," top and bottom.

"Isn't that nice. You tell her Georgia Perkins says hello."

"I will."

"Tell her I said she has a nice and pretty granddaughter."

"Thank you, I will," says Lucinda. Am I imagining at this distance I can see her blushing? Lucinda spots me now and gives a pleading look. It's the first time I've seen her – whether naked on the beach or handcuffed in a cruiser – showing any semblance of self-consciousness.

"Are you through in here, honey?" Gram asks.

"Yes."

"Well, you two come have some breakfast before you go to the beach." She now notices Lucinda's trying to cover herself. "Go tell Alex to give you one of his sweaters. Your bottom will be warm enough, but in this drafty house you need something on top. I always get cold around my chest."

"Okay," says Lucinda and, without a stitch on, hurries past the old woman, and up the stairs, nearly knocking me aside.

"I was afraid of that," I say, entering the room laughing to ease the young woman's distress. But I also say, assuaging my guilt with what probably comes across like petulance, "I tried to give you my robe…"

"I wasn't thinking about grandmothers just then."

"I doubt she noticed anything." I try to reassure. "She is practically blind."

"She saw my 'bathing suit' and figured I came to get you for a swim. – She's kind of cute. I think she's cooking us breakfast."

"Hmmm," I say, wondering what I should do.

" She told me she knows my Granny. They waitressed together."

"I heard that. You said you moved here from Boston."

"Moved *back*," she corrects. Do I detect a note of defensiveness? Naw. Probably just a holdover from being caught with her pants down in front of one of her Granny's friends.

Spiriting her out before her existence became known was my intent. Now what?

"You know," I say, "Gram will probably be upset if we don't at least have a piece of toast. I have to run in there anyway, to make sure she doesn't burn down the house. Can you stay for breakfast?"

Lucinda is quiet for a moment, then says just, "Okay."

I dash into the kitchen to set the stage for an entrance by Lucinda. Dark wisps are already rising from what smells like the early stages of butter burning in a pan. At my entry Rosebud wiggles in paroxysms of pleasure.

"Good morning, Gram," I blurt out as cheerily as apprehension and hangover will allow. I give the top of her head a quick kiss and jump past her to the stove to extinguish the flame.

"Good morning, darling," she replies. " I see you had a friend drop by. It's nice your boss will let you work at the beach."

A little drink – scratch that – a lot of drink and some impersonal sex makes me forget that I am a workingman. What time is it? The kitchen clock says 7:15. That's all? Phew! But I know if I call Steve to say I'm coming in late, and tell him there's a women involved, he'll enjoy it – though he'll likely dock me a few bucks. I remember once complaining to him about how a woman I ended up – after a too quick jump into the sack – having feelings for, had refrained from telling me she was married until the morning after. "What are you complaining about," he scoffed, "you got laid, didn't you?"

I wonder for a minute if the paint Gram perceived as a garment could just as likely have been taken for panties and a bra – whether Gram's reference to it as sporting apparel may have been diplomatic. Probably everyone in the world has an easier time relating to a bathing suit than panties and bra. Probably, however, a segment approaching fifty percent might prefer enduring the "underwear difficulty" if the wearer is a young, well-built female. This reminds me of Lucinda's *contexts*. Coverage defined "bathing suit" is less arousing than the same coverage defined "underwear."

"Right – to the beach," I say and squint out the window for effect. "Looks like a nice day for it. Gee, I hope you're not cooking for us…"

"That poor girl is so skinny. – I couldn't let her out of here without giving her a little something to brace herself against that cold water. Her grandmother would be very upset with me. I know her. We're of the same generation. She'd do the same for you. You're too skinny, too."

At that moment, Lucinda enters. She's wearing shorts and a tee shirt. I remember her knapsack bumping me as we staggered along. I flash whether Gram would wonder why Lucinda had on less before. But Lucinda covers that concern by saying, "I think I'll be warm enough with this on over my bathing suit, Mrs. Perkins. I think it's going to be another hot day." (Good girl.)

"Oh, call me Gram. Even the mailman calls me Gram when he has "Georgia Perkins" in writing right in front of him. You look cute in that outfit," she says. "Alex, doesn't she look cute?"

And today's prize for cuteness goes to…Ms. Lucinda York of Northport, Mass.! "Very cute," I say. Lucinda frowns at me. Well, if she'd rather look like a freedom fighter she should put on her fatigues.

"Thank you," Lucinda replies offering only Gram the pretty smile I saw once or twice last night. "Very cute," I repress saying a second time.

Cuteness begets cuteness, and Lucinda exclaims, "What a cute dog!" By a series of self-canceling arcs, Rosebud has maneuvered across the kitchen to sniff Lucinda's hand for treats.

"That's just Rosebud," Gram says. "Now I have to concentrate while I cook. I thought I'd make blueberry pancakes. We're out of Toaster Toasties."

"What are Toaster Toasties?" Lucinda asks.

"Flat blueberry muffins." I explain. "Howard Johnson Toaster Toasties. They're in the freezer section."

"And that's what they're called – Toaster Toasties?"

"That's what they're called," I say. But I've never given this any thought – I've just gone along with Gram's shopping lists. Then I back pedal, seeing Lucinda looking at me as if I'm an idiot.

"I don't know. Maybe they're just called Toasties." But my mind is on heading off Gram's production. "I don't think we have any blueberries," I say, trying to sound dejected.

"Yes, we do. I left that nice blueberry pie Harriet Weare brought over on the coffee table and after she went home, Rosebud ate all the crust. So I washed off all the blueberries and now they're in Tupperware in the refrigerator. The hot pan will kill any germs.

"Honey," Gram says, turning back toward Lucinda. "You have coffee and talk to Alex. I made Taster's Choice. It's very good."

"Thank you," Lucinda says again.

But, stating that I was just dreaming about fried eggs when I was lying in bed, I brusquely take over and start cracking some from the carton already on the counter and plopping them into the browned but still not quite unserviceable butter.

"You sit and talk to Lucinda." I gulp the Taster's choice. Any source of caffeine in a storm. In a minute I'll grind some beans for a proper pot for us youngsters. "I'm making fresh ground," I tell Lucinda. She scrunches her eyebrows.

"Do you have any herbal tea?"

"Sure," I say. "And it's only about fourteen years old."

"No Yogi tea?" She amends.

"Fresh out."

"Oh – herbal's fine then."

Where has the off-the-wall meat-eater I know so well gone to?

"Gram, tell Lucinda what you remember about her grandmother when she was young."

"Are you a painter?" Gram asks solicitously, ignoring me.

"I'm a performance artist. But I use paint in my performances. I hope to have a piece in the Northport Museum of Modern Art's exhibition, Pure Conception, in the fall."

"The curator's naming it after his boat," I interject.

"No, he's not," says Lucinda to Gram, as if conspiring with a fellow sufferer victimized by juvenile male behavior.

"Yes, he is," I say, holding my ground.

"He is?" Lucinda asks.

"Well, that's the name of his boat. I've seen him sailing it."

"Well, that's not exactly the same thing."

"That's quite an honor," Gram joins in to stop our bickering. "When I was a girl like you, men didn't get into museums until they had long beards. And women didn't get in at all."

"Well, I'm not definitely in yet."

85

"I didn't think men were still wearing beards when you were a girl," I say.

"All the *artist*s wore beards. Most of them still do," Gram asserts matter-of-factly.

Not really, I'm about to say, but another consideration supersedes: "If all the artists wore beards, and some were young, then beards didn't say how old they were when museums accepted them." Elementary freshman logic.

Lucinda smiles at my ability to run intellectual rings around my grandmother. But Gram takes the smile as more female solidarity and just says, "He's a screwball."

Lucinda laughs and solidarity is confirmed.

"Tell me about your work, honey,"

"Tell her about her grandmother," I encourage from the stove. I notice an ever so slight hint of desperation in my voice. "It would be fun," I say in what I try to put across as a merry tone. I'm relieved that Gram takes the bait.

"Florence York was Florence Stacey in my day. You knew that. Of course, you did. She was a very intelligent girl. I remember she was the only one in fourth grade who could spell Massachusetts. I don't think I can spell it even now. – Alex, can you spell Massachusetts?"

"M-a-s-s-e…" I begin, then stop abruptly, demanding, "Don't ask me now. The eggs are almost done. Do you want yours flipped, Lucinda?"

"Flipped. Right." Lucinda answers. "You were in fourth grade with my Grandmother?"

I chime in, "I thought you said you met when you waitressed together. Fourth graders don't waitress. How do you know what she could spell in fourth grade?

"She told me," Gram says as if this should have been the most obvious thing in the world.

I've succeeded perhaps never in my life in turning over four eggs without partially destroying at least two. Gram is not having eggs. Anything but toast in the morning makes her "vomit" – i.e. gag.

Perhaps from sharing some of Gram's genetic code, I don't much like morning food either. But Gram always insists that everyone has to eat to brace himself for the coming day. "What about you?" I've demanded of her. "I'm different," is what she replies.

I place the two intact eggs – though a little shredded at the edges – in front of Lucinda. "Thank you," she says yet another time. Then I put the plate with the mangled ones at what is to be my place and sit down. Lucinda says to Gram, "Aren't you having any?"

"No, honey. Eating food in the morning makes me vomit."

I think that eating just about anything else would have that effect on most other people. I'm about to clarify when Lucinda ejaculates with what sounds like true empathy. "That's just like me. Used to be, anyway – until I finally found my voice as an artist, and got more confident. Now it mostly only happens after a night when I might drink some alcohol."

"A pretty young girl like you shouldn't drink alcohol. You'll lose your looks."

"Really?" asks Lucinda. "I've heard just about everything else, but I haven't heard that one."

"It's in my Reader's Digest. It removes riboflavin from your skin."

I attempt to share an amused look with Lucinda, but she is frowning and running her fingertips down her cheeks. "That's scary – but I hardly ever drink anymore." She picks up her fork and takes a bite of egg. I watch to see if she'll vomit. But she doesn't. Perhaps she didn't drink quite heavily enough the night before.

"So you're a performance artist?" Gram asks. "That's like that Chinese art – Kabuku."

"Kabuki," I correct her, and add, "it's Japanese."

"Ok – Japanese. That's what I meant – Kabuki."

"Sort of," Lucinda says enthusiastically, perhaps glad to be on Eastern ground.

"It's exactly the same thing," Gram says. "We used to go to performances of Kabuki in Boston when I was a girl in Cambridge." Yes, but that accounts for only half the comparison. How does she know what performance art is *exactly* like?

"Well," says Lucinda, "my art is probably more political than that. It is also about gender discrimination. It's not as political as it used to be. But *political* would be a word you'd still have to use to talk about it. – One of several." *Scheming*, I'm thinking, might be on that list, too.

"So is Kabuki," Gram asserts. "They used to bind the young girl's feet so they couldn't run away from their husbands. That must be gender discrimination."

"Gee – maybe you're right, " Lucinda muses, impressed at such an insight from a little old lady. Her own grandmother, she tells me later, is in a nursing home already – though she insists her age is 25, two years younger than Lucinda.

Gram muses for a second. "What's that expression? 'Turning the tables is fair game.'"

"'*Turnabout* is fair play,'" I interject.

"Same thing," Gram says. "If it's okay for a man, it should be okay for a woman."

"That's exactly how I feel," says Lucinda.

I'd heard that expression many times without questioning it – until one of my boss Steve's jokes made me realize it's too complicated for that to be true. Steve demands interaction for many of his jokes. On this one he says, "Okay, go along with me – 'Hey, Alex – there's a great new bar in town. You get your drinks for free, free sandwiches, too, if you're hungry. Then when you've had all you want to eat and drink they take you in the back room and they get you laid'. Now you say, 'Sounds great. Have you been there yourself?'" "Sounds great, have you been there yourself?" I repeat. "No," he says, barely able to contain his mirth, "but my sister has!"

*Turnabout is fair play* will only be true when that joke stops being funny.

I decide not to mention having reservations. But I still feel a need to not be diffident. I say, "I thought it was just the Chinese who bound feet."

"They all did it," Gram affirms shaking her head, a corner of her mouth pinched.

"Who's they?" I press on.

"All of them!" Gram underscores, exasperated. "All the Orientals."

"I don't think so," I say.

"Yes they did," Gram insists with long-suffering patience. "They all oppressed the women. The Japanese women wore pillows on their backs so their husbands could use them as footstools."

I stifle a laugh, glancing at Lucinda. But she's actually nodding slowly, a deepening frown spreading across her face. I try diverting to less hostile territory – yet territory that might still provide me credentials for political correctness.

"You shouldn't call them Orientals."

"Are you going to start that again? We talked about that yesterday. About the Indians. 'Native Americans.'" She turns to Lucinda and explains, "Only I called them African-Americans instead. Isn't that funny?" Then she redirects back to me. "This is different. That area always has been called the Orient. Even Columbus wasn't wrong about that. He just didn't find it. America was in the way."

"That's not the point," I say. "They don't like being called Orientals. They want to be called 'Asians.'"

"Now look who's saying 'they,'" Gram retorts. "It's all the same thing. The gender discrimination – foot binding."

"What about Thailand?" I press on recklessly.

"Thailand is the worst," Gram frowns. "In Thailand they turn all the little girls into dance girls and prostitutes."

"You're right. The child prostitution is really terrible there," Lucinda says, continuing gender solidarity.

"*All* the little girls?" I protest. Sometimes I'm not too bright.

"Not *all the little girls*," Gram says, exasperated at all my unnecessary contrariness. "It doesn't have to be all the little girls for it to still be terrible. What if Lucinda had to dance naked to make a living?"

"No little girl should have to do that," Lucinda's affirms.

"Where did you hear this?" I ask.

"On *60 Minutes*."

"I saw it, too," Lucinda says in support, giving me an aggressive look – as if funds from this disgrace were secretly being funneled to my account at Coastal Savings.

"I don't remember that one," I say backing off. I usually watch that show with Gram – or she tells me about it in all the gory details.

"You were at the movies," Gram says dismissively. And turning back to Lucinda, she asks again, "What is the performance you hope to put on in the museum going to be like?"

Off to the beach NOW! I'm thinking. But, of course, the impression that that is where we're going was just Gram's innocent presumption. I can't guess whether this strange young woman I met on a beach about 15 or16 hours ago would have any desire to go to one again – for plain old healthy recreation; rather than for art and career advancement. What about some neutral locale like a bakery? After a first time sexual encounter with a woman I'm usually quite clear about what I want to do next. Either I want to run screaming or to dive right back in. This time is different. I'm conflicted. And – it's hard to tell – isn't Lucinda being a little distant toward me right now? – Almost like a normal girl who was drunkenly impulsive the night before and thinks maybe she needs her virtue back. Not like an artist. But Lucinda pulls herself up to her full sitting height. She clears her throat. Uh, oh.

"Gram, tell Lucinda about the Shackleton book you're reading," I say pretending to have missed Gram's question.

"Alex – Let the girl talk. She's as quiet as a mouse."

"Well," Lucinda begins, "I'm not officially in the show yet. I'm just a finalist. And my piece is still a work in progress. But, you've given me some new insights with your references to Asian repression of women. I've had a lot of conflict lately about going more *Eastern* with my work. Seemed to mean I had to back off on the polemical. But you've shown me how I can go in both directions." Her glance strays off into the distance, maybe into those two directions at the same time, and she continues talking – now apparently mostly to herself; working it out as she goes.

"I could wear one of those scarf/hood thingies they make Muslin women wear. I can make it a cross-cultural piece. Make it more – universal. And I can do body writing…"

"Alex, what's she saying. She's so soft-spoken." I'm glad Lucinda's soliloquizing is not so easy for Gram to hear – so I might be able to repeat an expurgated version if necessary.

"I could call it 'Unbind.' Underneath the – what it's called? Burkha, I think – I'm naked and barefoot – the 'universal feminine'. I cover myself with ink and I write. 'Unbind' with my whole body on a gray canvas-covered floor. … Or – no…Maybe I squat and with a Sumi brush… "She stops abruptly and seems to notice the cottage kitchen around her – and the old woman straining to listen, a young man with a forced grin of horror.

I'm not 100 percent sure what Lucinda would have said if the real world had not broken her train of thought – just ninety-nine. It seemed to be going where art had gone before – just not out here in the provinces; outside of New York, or maybe Los Angeles – on this continent anyway. That something has been done before, in another time and place, might not be an inhibition to Lucinda – if, perhaps, she thinks she can put her own spin on it; write her own text. Gram has been looking confused. But the old woman suddenly brightens as though she's solved a riddle. I'm not taking any chances. I say, "Uh – Lucinda. Uh…"

"Alex!" Gram reproves. "I asked you to let the girl talk. Can't you see what a brilliant idea she has? She's going to sit and write 'unbind' with her *feet* – did I guess it?  Honey? Unbind feet – unbind the world's women! I think it's a very creative idea. But, I think you still should wear a little something underneath: a bathing suit. You can wear the one you have on now – no one will see. And you'll need a lot of practice – it could take the whole summer – if you want it to look like real calligraphy. That takes the wrist. It swings." Gram proffers her own rather gnarled and inflexible claw of a hand, wrist high, fingers down. With it she tries in vain to make graceful passes. She doesn't notice having failed at this, though, and says, "And, it will be a lot harder with your foot."

"Yeah," I agree, relieved. "It's all in the wrist."

My sarcasm breaks what remains of Lucinda's artistic reverie. Annoyance crosses her face. Then, apparently coming to some decision, she shrugs and says, "Yeah, right – practice." And then directly to Gram, "Thanks for your...um, interest." Then brightening, adds, "And your wisdom."

"Oh, don't mention it, honey," Gram says. "I'm always glad to help."

# 8

I'm sitting at my desk. I dropped Lucinda at her van and only got here ten minutes late. No explanations necessary for Steve – although he'd love this one. I have my rescheduled interview with John Hulton for 11:00 today, about an hour and three quarters from now. He was very apologetic, but I'm not sure he actually gave an understandable reason why he didn't show. My hangover is mostly gone and my primary headache now is how I review Lucinda's performance. The one during daylight hours yesterday, I mean. Or is it not a review that's called for, given the way things turned out? I mean she was arrested. Therefore it's a news story. Doesn't news trump arts? News is about necessity, and art, basically, luxury? Of course, there are those who say things like "art *is* a necessity – people *can't live* without art." That usually comes from the kind of people who say *literally* all the time – when they almost always mean figuratively. "That guy was literally a father to me" or 'She literally crapped in my face." People don't *need* art to survive. They need meat (okay – or vegetables) and clothing and sleet-proof shelter. But we're mainly an arts and leisure newspaper. Well, maybe Lucinda is two stories. But two stories would seem like pandering. And for me, personally, it's three. There's the "Lucinda York And Alex Perkins Story," too. The Geraldo Rivera factor. I could now become a *this-is-about-me* journalist. Or maybe there's a conflict of interest and I should just recuse myself. I could get an opinion from our legal department, if we had one. I can imagine what Steve would say if I said I had to disqualify myself on the basis of having had sex with the assailant: "It's too bad you lost a day's pay. But at least you got laid."

In honesty, I admit professional issues are not what I'm most worried about. My bigger concern is I've gotten involved with another seemingly willful and difficult woman. And my first time out of the chute after Angela. – Or am I actually involved? What does it take to consider yourself *involved* these days?

Did Lucinda and I seem to have anything in common? I don't remember anything. Did I tell her what art I like best? No. Did I disagree with anything she said? No. Was I being a neutral interviewer or just a guy trying to ingratiate himself to the space between her legs? Was art all we talked about? Pretty much. Except she started out saying very personal things. René and her victory over drinking. But stopped when things got personal. So we never rose to the mid-level getting-acquainted stuff. Parents. Childhood. You know – had she always wanted a pony? Would a future identity artist ever have wanted a pony? Maybe Lady Godiva was her childhood heroine. Well, everybody was a kid sometime – even Yoko Ono. And there was that baby talk! A lot of different voices in there. Maybe she is really just an actress and doesn't know it. Maybe she's just an exhibitionist. Well, whatever – I must say I like her inappropriateness theory: sex is sexier the less appropriate the context.

But what about relationship *inappropriateness*? Could I get sucked into that again? After all, my new code supposedly is to fuck no woman with whom I wouldn't hold hands. Sounds backward, I know. In the old days in the early stage of a relationship you held hands and didn't have sex. Today you have sex and don't hold hands. If I were walking into Café Brioche with Lucinda would I take her hand?

Probably not. Too soon. Too soon, or just too strange? Can I picture us together? I mean, I already said she isn't my type.

Do I have to think of any of this? Do I have any reason to think Lucinda wants to go past one night, or beyond just sex? I mean, maybe I was just a sex object. That would be funny. But I mean, maybe Luce is just *loose*. It's lucky for her – and a lot of other women – that since the sexual revolution it's a lot harder to be called a slut. Today nice girls do most of the things that got a woman called that before the sixties came along. Now in the eighties there's all the difference in the world between a liberated woman and a slut, except for what they do on a date. Nice girls from good families in the past fifteen years have become ready to have sex on as reduced a time-frame as the sluts of fifties' America. Well, now maybe the *Moral Majority* and Ronald Reagan will turn back the clock on that. So, we may see liberated women re-redefined as sluts. But, I guess we're safe here on this liberal Northeast coast. Those reactionary moralists only don't sound ridiculous to people in the South, the Midwest, the Plains, the Mountain States, and large portions of the Southwest.

All this, I know, is just *avoidance musing*. It hasn't helped one bit with figuring how to write about Lucinda, the public property, for a work assignment. Avoidance is a long-time problem of mine that I've been doing a little better about since I moved in with Gram. She's always saying, "Doing things you don't feel like doing is a test of character." I've heard her say this since I was about two. Finally, recently, when I was procrastinating on a favor for her, she said it again, and it dawned on me that she was actually right. Unless you are born saintly, you can't be a really good person if you won't do things you *don't feel like* doing. Right now, however, I have a legitimate temporary avoidance excuse. I realize I can go to develop the roll of film I shot of the Blue Heron Beach proceedings and mull my writing options while I do that. I descend into the damp coolness of the basement darkroom under the low-tech offices of *Currents*.

In too short a while I am back at my desk with a few black and white prints of my black paint and white skin new friend. And I'm

95

thinking about Lucinda's "contexts" again. In another context it would be hard for me to think of myself as the "good person" I referred to earlier, considering that I am sitting here trying to decide which of the nude pictures I took of the woman I slept with last night to publish in a tabloid. And it's my job. And it's not even a particularly kinky job. A distance shot of Lucinda after she walked past me appears no different than the numerous girl-in-bikini pics we regularly run with articles about how great the tourist season is going. If we don't write that the bathing suit is painted on, we will get no outraged letters about corrupting Northport's children. If we do, we will. Even in liberal Massachusetts corrupting children is not cool. *It's in the mind, not the eye* is part of Lucinda's statement and I do need to give her some credit for it.

I decide to get the boss' opinion. I imagine that a normal boss' opinion would be sobering. I don't expect sobering from Steve. I decide to confine my explication to the performance itself. Well that won't work. Lucinda got arrested. That's news and this is almost a newspaper. I decide to start by taking it slow. Let it evolve. Chips fall wherever.

Steve's office door is open. He sits at his desk. I give a little knock on the door-frame.

I just walk up and drop the photo on the desk on top of the copy of today's *Beacon* that apparently he is reading. In a paranoid flash I expect to see pictures of Lucinda already in front of him, courtesy of the competition. Then the flash passes and I realize that only the reviewer from *The Phoenix*, also a weekly, was present at the beach. And they, like us, just got their current issue out yesterday. And like us, they won't go to press again for another six days. And anyway, the hard news didn't begin until after the show was over.

"This your performance artist?" Steve asks, apparently as fooled by the paint as Lucinda intended. He reacts as though I am only showing him the photo out of male camaraderie, mutual lechery. Wouldn't he love to know that I was spitting out material from that bathing suit bottom when I got up this morning. "Nice ass," he says, appreciatively. – I *am* an ass-man, you know. I guess you know me by now." He looks a little wistfully at the photo. "Have been since I was a kid."

I take the bait. "An ass-man since you were a kid?"

"Yeah," he says, "I was an ignorant little shit – deprived, I should say."

I'm having trouble seeing what this might end-up having to do with being an *ass- man*. But I assume I'm going to find out. One of my weaknesses – or *quirks* – is being willing to bolster the egos of wannabe alpha males. Humoring them. So, reflexively, I continue to take more bait. "What were you deprived *of?*"

"Pussy," my boss says.

"As a kid?" I say.

"Right," he says.

"So who wasn't?"

"You never saw a pussy as a kid?" he challenges.

"Well, I guess I saw a few."

"On grown-up women?"

"Jesus. I don't know. Yeah, I guess so."

"I'll bet you remember exactly who, where and when."

I do but I don't really want to talk about it. "So what?" I say.

"Well, I never did. No big sister – or even a little one. Prudish mother."

"You had a prudish mother?"

"Sure. She was Catholic. How do you think I got like this?"

"I don't know, testosterone?"

"Just listen – I'm *sharing* with you," he says, mocking my whole generation. "So I thought that where girls peed was about as big internally as where we peed. No room for anything to fit in there. – But I knew there were fun things that happened in girl's pants. And I'd hear the big guys say 'fuck you' and 'up your ass' like they were the same thing; holding up a middle finger while they said 'fuck you.' So I figured out that what all the guys wanted to do was to stick their middle finger up a girl's ass. – I thought that was *fucking*."

97

"Until you were how old?

"I don't know. Maybe ten. When did *Solomon and Bathsheba* come out?"

"Who?"

"*Solomon and Bathsheba*, the movie. You know, the biblical spectacular."

"What did that have to do with it?"

"That was how I learned what fucking really was."

"From seeing a biblical spectacular?"

"I didn't see it," Steve says shaking his head. "Rick Beauschesne, a couple years older than me, next door – he saw it. And he told me that Yul Brenner, or whoever it was, fucked Sophia Loren or Gina Lollobridgita or whoever in the movie. 'They show him fucking her?' I said, knowing he was shitting me. 'They did', he said. 'No way!' I said. – Well I guess we didn't say 'no way' back then. But whatever they did say. 'They showed it,' he says. This guy is really pulling my chain, I'm thinking. What does he think I am, an idiot? So I say, 'In a movie, they showed a guy sticking his finger up a girl's ass?' 'What?' he says. 'They showed Yul Brenner with his finger up Gina Lollobridgita's ass?' I say. Like I may be two years younger, but I'm not that stupid. Then he bursts out laughing and tells me what fucking really is. It broadened my interests on the spot, but I'm still an ass man. The stuff that goes into your head first usually stays there."

I can't help laughing, though there is logic to the story. I can see that, in a time that parents and schools wanted to keep kids in the dark, all you had to do was to miss a few days of playground sex education and it might be a long time before you caught up with your class – especially if the delusion you were laboring under was dirty enough to cover the gap. One thing troubled me about his story.

"Where did you think babies came from?" I ask.

"The belly button. Where else?"

"The belly button?" I query dubiously. "But why would men have belly buttons?"

"Why do men have nipples?"

"Good point," I say.

Steve looks at me for a moment to try to read my reaction. I purse my lips and nod a few nods. He seems satisfied.

"Well, I've enjoyed our little talk," he says. "I'll just save this for later. Print up another copy to go with your art review." Steve affects very clinical discernment and goes through exaggerated motions of starting to put the black and white photo into his desk drawer. "That was all you wanted – right? " he says in self-mockery.

"Not exactly," I say. "Two things to ask you about my *art review*. One, that's not a bathing suit she's wearing. It's paint. And two, she got arrested for wearing just the paint. And she got a little argumentative. How do I handle it?" – Not to mention, how do I handle fact number three. Though I continue to leave that out, I do mention my trip to the police station and the museum curator's written statement. As I go on, his eyes and grin widen. I dearly wish I'd thought to tell him that the performance piece had been of little public interest. But, assuming Steve reads the *Beacon* pretty thoroughly, there's a likelihood that he would find out that I was holding back.

"I thought there was a nude beach up that way?"

What does he mean *thought*? That's not something Steve wouldn't know for sure.

"She walked a few feet onto the not nude part. On purpose"

"What a saucy little slunt," Steve says, studying the photo more closely.

"What's that?" I ask – more to register a protest than to get an explanation of something obvious.

"Slunt? Slunt?" He says seemingly relishing the occasion for using the pseudo word. "It's a cross between the two things it sounds like. Only, maybe, not as bad as either one by itself."

"How can anyone tell it isn't supposed to be worse than both?"

"It depends on how dirty your mind is. You just flunked the test."

Not that funny, I think. At least not right now. Just then I hear some throat-clearing behind me, and, turning around I see two men in suits standing outside the door.

"Come right in, gentlemen," Steve calls past me. He hands me the photo and says, "We can discuss this later. Get to work on something else." Saved by the suits.

Back at my desk, I fuss about my quandary for a few minutes. Then I consider I may be taking the whole thing too seriously. And as Steve would have said if I'd leveled with him, at least I got laid. (I wonder if women ever say this.) It's not me, I decide, it's the culture. – There's humor in how shifting moral boundaries can throw you when you get caught outside a line that's been moved while you weren't looking. This reminds me of those sex survey articles I've read in those doctors' office magazines I've mentioned – and the ones the national tabloids put on their covers as circulation boosters. Maybe, if I gave Steve a little circulation booster like that he might be easier to dissuade about running naked pictures of my new girlfriend in his newspaper. A funny idea starts to take shape in my mind. Steve has asked me a few times to try to write something humorous when he didn't have time to come up with his much anticipated RH story of the week. "Come on, Perkins – you're not completely humorless – write some jokes about artists. It should be the easiest thing in the world." I've told him that, on the contrary, the arts were pretty much spoof-proof today. How can you make up something that would sound much different than what's really happening? I tried a couple of times but I couldn't hit on anything good. Now I think I've got something that allows me to escape doing the story that I can't decide how to do; it mirrors the progression of my Lucinda encounter from yesterday-into-today: from art-oriented to sex-based. I begin to type my banal circulation builder:

## RESULTS OF OUR READERS' SEX POLL

### A New *Currents* Feature
This is an opportunity for you, the subscriber, to tell us where you are at in relation to 1980's America's evolving cultural mores. The answers to our survey questions are enlightening both about the time and about the community in which we're living. Just consider these surprising results.

Response to Question #1.
   - *Strongly agreed...................................................29%*
   - *Occasionally agreed...............................................22%*
   - *Did not agree but could foresee circumstances
     under which I would agree...............................32%*
   - *Not if my life depended on it...............................15%*

Response to Question #2
   - *Never tried it...................................................4%*
   - *Tried it once but wouldn't do it again......................30%*
   - *Tried it but got arrested...................................22%*
   - *Any chance I can get...........................................40%*

Response to Question #3
   - *Very pleasurable response...................................24%*
   - *Mildly pleasant response.....................................14%*
   - *Unpleasant response..........................................24%*
   - *Got sick......................................................38%*

Response to Question #4
   - *Probably wouldn't be upset...................................21%*
   - *Would probably be upset but would get over it............22%*

- *Would probably never speak to her again*..................22%
- *Would probably never speak to him again*.................16%
- *Would probably never speak to anyone again*................9%
- *Would probably never speak again*.........................7%

*Well, there it is! How did your answers stack up compared to those of your sexual opponents? Our survey has a margin of error of about 3% (except in instances in which fewer than ten people replied). All answers are assumed honest since the survey is completely confidential (except, of course, in the case of the affirmative answers on the questions about exhibitionism).*

I'm no closer to deciding on an approach to my multi-dimensional Lucinda review – or is it *crime report?* – Nor to deciding anything to do with her at all. But I do feel more light-hearted. And, as the man says, at least I got laid.

I feel a cup of coffee is in order before I risk reviving my funk. I walk by Steve's door on the way out. He still sits with the suits; talks with animation. I guess these guys are not Mafia coming to sell insurance against someone setting fire to our printing press. Maybe Steve, having recalled with me the story of his determinative boyhood reproductive confusion, is now explaining it to them. No. I hear him doing an Irish accent. He's telling the joke he hit me with last week – about the American tourist who encounters a disgruntled local in a pub on the Emerald Isle. Steve does the Celtic's complaint with dripping pathos: "'Who ahm aye?' ya ask. Well, forrh a staht, I dun ahl the stone wourk forrh tha chorch ahcrahs the street. But do the cull me 'McCarthy tha Mason?' No. I dun ahl the fine carving forrh the alter of thaht chorch. But do the cull me 'McCarthy the craftsman?' No. An I dun ahl the wood wourk forrh dis luvly bar in hehr. But do the cull me 'McCarthy the woodwourker?' No! ... *But you fuck ONE GOAT..!*"

I'm suddenly less satisfied with my sex survey. It didn't go far enough. But I, unlike Steve, can think about sex just so much. I can't remember who said it – some old Brit celibate, I presume: "The costs are enormous, the rewards momentary, and the position ridiculous." Seems true right about now.

I drop my typed sheets, anyway, into the wire basket with the sign reading "for editing" on the shelf outside Steve's door. Then I head back over to the clean-the-bathroom-*yourself* café, in high hopes my expressionist painter will show.

**9**

He does. After I've sat for only about ten minutes, a tall and
gaunt, older gentleman comes through the front door. I say
*gentleman*, though grey and paint-splattered, he appears
rather shabby. This is obviously my formerly-famous subject, John
Hulton.

Though he was an exponent of New York School painting, as
Abstract Expressionism – briefly the dominant art style in the world
of the 1950's — was alternately called, John Hulton always
maintained his residence here in the provinces. And at about 75 now,
he lives on, and paints, in Northport. His style went down when Pop
Art came along in the 1960s. As I learned it in my 20th century art
history course, Pop pretty much *overthrew* Abstract Expressionism.
Seems Pop was so much easier to get. Therefore more *pop*ular. Where
Abstract Expressionist painters meant their canvases to pack a visual
wallop, Pop artists actually wrote *POW* on theirs. Where Abstract
Expressionism was difficult, Pop Art, in Andy Warhol's words, was
"about liking things." It's probably as demoralizing for an artist to be

thrown-over as for a lover or politician – and maybe a little like both. A number of the Ab-Ex greats that I know a bit about – like Mark Rothko, who cut his wrists, and Jackson Pollack, who recklessly ended his life against a Long Island tree, in a convertible with two blonds – destroyed themselves spectacularly. Hulton, the story goes, has been self-destructing slowly and conventionally for the decades since then – with booze.

But, were he successful and elegant, my enthusiasm wouldn't be greater at the chance to interview an artist of his talent. Though I am as ignorant of Hulton's current painting as anyone, I've seen his older work and been much moved. Tom Wolfe, the luminous (and overconfident) culture critic maintains that hardly anybody ever really liked abstract painting. Well, I guess that makes me "hardly anybody" because a lot of abstract painting suits me fine. Certain strong pieces – like light on spilled diesel fuel – can nudge me into acid reveries. Not always, or even often. But often enough. However, I'm not too optimistic that twenty years of being eroded by alcohol can have done much to preserve the quality of the paint John Hulton puts on his canvases. This man surveys the room, focuses on my khaki bush vest and approaches.

"Are you Alex? Your note said 'khaki.' Quite a color. I'm Hulton – I'd been painting... painting... but I was out for coffee, when you came by the other day. Not here. The other place. Down the street. You ever been there? This one's fine though. Sorry I missed you. How are you? Have you been waiting long?"

He's sorry he missed the other appointment, but only barely. I can see that he is someone for whom the usual expectations can't be too strongly enforced. He seems searching for a way to relate to a stranger. He doesn't focus on me but looks left and right and over his shoulder. I'm taken by the contrast between this diffidence and the authority I associate with his paintings of decades past. I hope this self-consciousness doesn't extend to his new work – now that he is re-emerged from his long hibernation. Next week he mounts his first exhibition in twenty years. This show, however, will hang in his

Northport factory space – not a gallery at 57<sup>th</sup> and Fifth. An announcement depicting oddly enough for an abstract painter a writhing tree, arrived at the paper, addressed, "Art's Editor, *Currents*."

"Mr. Hulton," I say, rising to shake his hand.

"Oh, don't get up," he says, jumping down into the seat opposite mine. This forces a quick end to our handshake and to whatever other formalities might have been coming. I do say – though more a part of the conversation that's starting than the greeting that's he's abruptly terminated – "I'm a great admirer of your work."

"Thank you, thank you," he says. "Yes, but my work is … changing."

"Oh?" I say. I had prepared a further opening compliment – had intended to tell him that I relate to his paintings more than the quirky cartoons or the monochrome or the striped things that predominate in the galleries today. But Hulton seems to have come here more ready to defend himself than to accept praise. – That is, if I'm not reading too much into the five or six words about his work he's spoken so far. I wonder about his being on the wagon. Whether "the old false courage," as Fred Avery calls hard drink, fueled the drive necessary to paint with the kind of power Hulton showed back when his painterly style was king.

"Yes, I'm returning to figuration, to nature – references to nature. Not doing total abstraction anymore. That is, not right now."

I've seen mysterious patterns, sinewy line, and patches of color that moved and glowed in John Hulton's older paintings. Now here is the man himself, apparently denying those works. I guess he feels the need to – and assumes I will automatically cast the cooler eye of 1983 on what he does. Well, having your school of painting closed down, your New York gallery drop you, and your work hung in open studios instead of museums could well make you start questioning yourself.

"Really?" I say. "I love abstract painting. I mean some of it. Your kind."

"Yes? Do you? Well that's a surprise. Even at the height of its popularity it was pretty much only urban types that responded to abstraction. I'm not saying you're not *urban*." He pauses, concerned that he's given offense, then continues. " – Urban types, and also those corporate types that thought abstraction didn't really say anything; was safe. And now that the cities have turned against it – long time ago now – I assume no one anywhere – except maybe decorators – likes it at all. But I shouldn't over-generalize. Shouldn't stereotype. You do like it? I didn't mean to say I had become a Realist. No, I could never do that. And I am still an Expressionist. You'll see the work. We'll go to my studio. Sorry I wasn't there."

I want to tell him that he doesn't need to justify. But I realize that I shouldn't automatically assume, because he's defensive about what he's doing now, that he might not be deeply committed to it. Depends on strength of ego – not your vision. He might be tormented alternately by lack of popularity and by worry that he might be seen as selling-out to get some.

A waitress arrived a minute or two ago. But she's been standing idling in neutral, waiting for someone to push a button. Hulton seems not to see her and continues, "I'm a painter. A painter. A painter in the sense that the paint itself is still the important thing. Paint as emotion. When Marcel Duchamp stopped painting and started producing his conceptual stuff – the stuff that's now taken over so much of the art world – he said he wasn't interested in what he called 'retinal art' anymore. But I'm retinal. It's all about the eye. *Seeing*, not thinking."

It seems this might end up the easiest interview I've ever had to do. I don't think I've asked one question yet. And, I can't remember being around anyone with more urgency to explain himself – sadly enough. I indicate the waitress with a gesture and ask Hulton, "Coffee or something?"

"No – No coffee. I've had too much coffee."

I believe him – hope that accounts for his nervousness. "I'll have a warm-up," I say, mostly as a rent payment for the restaurant space we are occupying. She shrugs. Right – I guess warm-ups are free.

I decide to try to help Hulton feel he's among friends. So, I search for a comment that might give comfort and reinforcement to this embattled old warrior. I come up with this: "I think the *sublime* that you Ab-Ex guys tried to paint – even when totally abstract – was always about awe in the face of nature. Paintings of that kind wouldn't get through to many people in a culture like ours – one that's getting more divorced from nature every day."

"Yes. Yes...Yes...That *is* how it is."

His rheumy eyes glow a bit, seemingly in appreciation of being given a good excuse. It's society's fault, I've told him. He sighs and the sigh apparently indicates I've relieved him, perhaps for just the moment, of some of his burden.

"Coffee!" he calls out to the girl who has started to move off. "I'm sorry, I will have a coffee now – after all."

# 10

"**...A**nd then we're rounding the number three mark, 6kR, off Humpback Light, off Northport Harbor. Twenty-eight knot wind, beam reach, five-foot chop. Number two spinnaker, single reef main. Still in first by two and a half. Easy jibe on the spinnaker and what do you think happens?"

I am touring the – to be grandly inaugurated as such in a week – Marion Oggelvy West Wing of the Northport Museum of Modern Art. My guide is none other than the renowned and controversial new curator of contemporary art, and – until the vacancy created by the untimely death of Director Jonathan Cutts is filled – the acting director of the museum, Arthur Dalmore, whom I met officially only a few days ago at a police station. He has made no reference to the travesty of an artist's arrest.

I'm hoping that a pose of sincere interest in whatever this man brings up will be all that's required of me. And truly, Dalmore seems to be getting enough enjoyment for both of us from his story of heroic exploits on his hi-tech sailing yacht. Unfortunately he seems to want some participation from his audience. Me. And I'm having a little trouble concentrating – what with the glorious summer morning glimpsable through the small portal in an incongruous niche in the museum wall. Didn't some great master say that the most beautiful thing in a museum is the windows? I don't know if I agree with that as a generality. But given the chaos of a new show in the early stages of installation, and my circumspect reaction to the waiting-to-be-hung, give-aesthetics-the-finger work on the floor against the walls, I agree with it right now.

The inaugural exhibition for the new wing will be a retrospective look at the oeuvre of painter William Kahn of New York *and* Northport. Kahn would be considered by many traditionalists as too young to merit a museum retrospective. But Kahn is an exception. Even at only forty, he already has many periods of his work to look back upon. This is because his technique is an ever-changing thing. His iconography, though tending toward Pop subject matter, spans the broad spectrum of two-dimensional Postmodernism. Picasso was famously quoted as having responded, "Does God have a style?" when queried about the all-over-the-placeness of his painting. And Kahn, the magazines say, regularly cites this dismissive retort by the Spanish master. He does so, though, with a humble protestation that invocations of God and Picasso are purely rhetorical.

Kahn is exceptional in another way, too. To his detractors, he is practically a creation of Arthur Dalmore. After living and working in anonymity in Germany for much of the decade of his twenties, Kahn rocketed onto the New York gallery scene, propelled by rave reviews of his submissions to several successive Whitney Biennial Exhibitions, during the time of Dalmore's residence there. I have no idea whether Dalmore really was positioned in New York to create art stars by dint of personal power. I think there are a lot of assistant curators in the big New York museums – like vice presidents in insurance companies. And Northport, comfortable as it is, probably couldn't have afforded a really major one. But a Dalmore-Kahn relationship is established in the minds of local art lovers. When the NoMMA

110

exhibition schedule for the coming year was announced months ago, a story appeared about the two men in *Boston Magazine* titled, "I'll Have What He's Having." I missed that one. In fact I missed all of the press I've just cited. I learned it on the telephone from cousin Kevin when he was kindly prepping me for this interview. It seems that to his devotees Kahn is the ultimate ironist. From what I've seen of his work, I'd just call him a *mocker*. But even given his high local profile since he bought a summer house here, and my job, I have never met him. And I only know enough to guess that we might not enjoy mocking the same things.

In the quartet of new William Kahn's before me, I see Donald Duck doing a walk-on through a number of the masterpieces of Western art – the ones everyone learns about in first year college art history. In a transcription of da Vinci's *Last Supper*, Donald sits on his savior's right, facing away, eyes demurely cast down. Next to this and in contrast, the duck is depicted throwing one of his much-beloved tantrums in Rembrandt's *The Blinding of Samson*. Then in Bruegal's, *Return of the Hunters*, only Donald's duck's ass is visible; the remainder of him is hidden behind a tree. Finally my eye comes upon the startling composition Lucinda York referred to in our warm-up chat at the beach. Donald actually floats, *like a real duck,* where the clothed female usually wades in Manet's *Le De'jeuner sur l'herbe/Luncheon on the Grass*. This painting – two males, clothed; two females, one clothed, one naked – scandalized bourgeois Paris 120 years ago. Today it is fun. These transcriptions are far superior to what I would imagine paint-by-numbers copies done by the average art student would be – but they still have a paint-by-numbers quality. This however says nothing about the paint handling competence of William Kahn. Kahn's classical training in draftsmanship is legendary. ("Legendary" could mean it has never been actually seen.) He professes to fake near ineptitude intentionally as a comment on the banality of contemporary culture. Outside of the art world, that is. He rails, within the art world itself, against the elitism of the past.

But I need to focus. Where were we? Right! The curator's

spinnaker. What happened to his spinnaker?

"I can't guess," I say, " – What happened?" I am trying to keep my responses moderate. Given the way this man's eyebrows keep ascending and descending, I'm on the verge of an inappropriate smile. I discipline myself so I won't hurt his feelings. But, then again, I probably don't have to worry. He's a big success – and he obviously didn't acquire this mannerism just yesterday. So he must have pretty good coping mechanisms.

"The sheet snapped," Arthur Dalmore says with a tone of profundity appropriate for instead saying something like, "All, all, save one, were lost."

"I never heard such a thing!" I gasp honestly. I have done some sailing – on Steve's Hinckley 34. I know that a sheet is not a sail. And I have even helped with setting a spinnaker enough times to have the tacking process almost memorized. And I know that anything can break on a boat. Especially on Steve's boat. But given the requirements for the owning and handling of a racing J-44 – and the man's perfect hair and tailored suit – I assume Dalmore runs a pretty tight ship. Having named it *Pure Conception* reinforces that he almost assuredly does.

"Can you believe it?" Dalmore presses, his eyes rapidly scanning me up and down.

"I can't believe it. The sheet *snapped*!" I say this, making some probably inadequate gesture for emphasis with my hands.

"Well, you can imagine, reefed main and runaway chute in twenty-eight knots of breeze. Our day was over. We ran up the 150 Genny to blanket the spinnaker and get it down – and did manage to finish with a third. But it was the worst day of the season so far, you can believe." A muscle in Dalmore's cheek twitches as he relives the pain. Then he smiles. I realize his expressions do not always seem consistent with what he is saying. It's like a band of rebel neurons are transmitting disinformation from a remote province in his brain. Now, as if flinging the bad memory away, he shakes his head sharply twice. Then he waxes philosophical. "But you know what they say,

112

'It's a poor craftsman who blames his tool.' And a sailboat is only a tool. Nothing ventured, nothing gained. If you'll pardon the expression."

"Yes, of course," I say, wondering why anyone would *not* pardon such an un-controversial expression. He probably really means, "Pardon the cliché," but I guess he doesn't want to suggest he might ever use one. When his features aren't moving all over the map, Dalmore is (as I've noticed from when I first saw him on the dock) an impressive looking man – trim and fit. What did I guess at? – fifty? Must be about three inches taller than me, maybe six-two. He's got a good tan and he combs his salt and pepper hair decisively straight back, like most men who believe they are alphas. But his, let's say, "animation" does not convey the coolness I associate with "cultural elite." I wonder if this is why he left New York. I imagine the museum scene is pretty tough there. Like every other scene in New York. But what do I know? Maybe it's different in the art world – what with all the famous eccentrics. And isn't celebration of diversity what the arts of the eighties are all about? If an art world can't be a tolerant one, then what world can? But all that is stupid to speculate about. Dalmore was *wooed* here.

From what Kevin has told me about internal museum politics, Dalmore's securing board of director's approval for a Kahn retrospective for the inaugural show, demonstrates he is proceeding handily with honing this institution's dull edge into something sharp and crisp. But Kevin has also told me that the votes have been close and some of the traditionalists on the board aren't entirely happy with the Dalmore intended direction. This group includes newspaper mogul Frank Oggelvy, who signed-on about ten years ago – well before the postmodern surge had overflowed Northport's shores – to donate the lion's share of the cash for the Marion Oggelvy Contemporary Wing. Oggelvy, and a few others, would like to see the museum edge a little *blunter*. Though, Kevin tells me, when the word "traditionalist" is used about Frank Oggelvy, it does not mean that he is a *traditional* traditionalist. Oggelvy is a traditional *modernist*. That

113

suggests that he still reveres Matisse and Picasso, and Jackson Pollock, Rothko, and de Kooning. He sounds more like my kind of guy – business rival to Steve Towle, my boss, though he may be.

I'm not sure how Dalmore got off on his sailing story. Perhaps it evolved naturally from my saying that it was a nice day. I don't know whether he is telling me this man-of-action stuff for publication. But, I imagine he'd enjoy seeing a picture of himself at the wheel of *Pure Conception* on our cover page, with the headline "New Man at the Helm," when he ascends to the museum directorship. Or if.

"You sail, do you?" he asks, apparently focusing for the first time more on me than on recounting the runaway spinnaker. My guess is that he's told that story before.

"Yes – a bit," I say. "Well, maybe more than a bit. My publisher has a Hinkley 34. I've crewed with him."

He scrunches up his nose as if I, or the nearby assistant on a ladder adjusting the track lighting, has just farted. "That can be a relatively quick boat – for a *classic* design." His tone when saying "classic" hints that the word has approximately the opposite meaning for him that it does for most people. "Does he race it?"

"Yes, he does. But I've never crewed with him for a race."

"Really?" He says this as if I've just declared that I have never bothered to try having sex. "Why is that?"

"Well...I don't know. I guess for me there's enough competitiveness on land. I like there being a place I can get away from all that."

"But competitiveness is human nature!" He almost booms this out. Then he tosses his head back, mouth open but silent – like a mime who has just heard a good joke.

I want to reply, "But don't you think human nature pretty much sucks?" But instead I say, "Well, I'm sure I'll try racing someday."

"Perhaps we can get you to crew with us sometime when we're shorthanded."

"Sure thing," I say, holding up and spinning my hand a little in what I hope is a "ya-never-know" gesture.

"Good... good," Dalmore says, his tone shifting between the first and second "good," from hearty fellowship to something that sounds like detached discernment. He studies me for a minute in a way that conveys uncertainty, even suspicion. Then he smiles curtly. And, with a general drawing down of his facial muscles, finally comes around to the business at hand. Speaking slowly and in a lower tonal range, Dalmore says, "I must confess I'm not a regular reader of the *Current*. So, I'm not familiar with whatever niche it is you might inhabit in this art world of ours." He rocks his head from side to side a little bit, as if he is aware he may have just been charming and amusing. "I invited you as a favor to Kevin. And I asked my assistant, Deborah, to find something under the by-line, Alex Perkins. She brought me the current issue with your article on that...second tier... or perhaps – *must be honest* – *third* tier Abstract Expressionist, John Hulton, the...local boy... who is opening a show somewhere in Northport next week." Then there is a heavy pause, indicating to me that, even though he came here from New York, Dalmore might nevertheless still have some concern for appearing polite. "It *was* interesting to read that Hulton is still in Northport painting away. And your piece was...well-written..." Another silence – and a loud unspoken, "But."

"But?" I supply for him, leaving it simple, and myself just a reporter. "You don't care for his work?"

"Well, it's not a matter of *caring for* or *not caring for*...not a matter of taste. No, not a matter of taste at all. It's just that his work...has very little *relevance* to the world of the present day." Dalmore shakes his head and sighs; the psychic burden of ministering to benighted provincials, I think, is taking its toll on this man who seems to wear his years of experience in "the imperial city" like a toga.

I didn't come here to argue art politics or defend my taste in art. And regardless of Dalmore's belief that *taste* does not apply, my guess is it almost always does.

It seems, though, that many under the big tent of contemporary art *are* looking for an argument. At least, that is the impression I get from those national arts magazines I read occasionally. *Art Forum,* especially. I actually do check in with them – so as not to be totally blind-sided. Under-educated provincial that I am. But I don't usually get too bowled-over by most of what I see there. Surprised maybe. But being surprised doesn't surprise me much. The element of surprise now seems as studied in art as it used to be in war. And I'm aware from his reputation that the *surprise* element in Postmodernism is what Dalmore loves most.

Anyway, I don't respond directly to his dismissal of John Hulton, our washed-up local boy. I wouldn't have written about him if I didn't like him – though I do have to admit he's no master of irony. Like I said, I didn't come to argue. So – passive/aggressively, maybe – I just ask, "Doesn't this museum have several John Hultons in its permanent collection?"

"Yes, yes, this institution collected Hulton in the past. It does have a great many works by artists of *historical* interest in its permanent collection." Dalmore's tone continues to sound weary and patronizing. "Some are more significant than others. But as Curator of Contemporary Art, I leave the sorting out of the past to my colleagues in the East Wing."

"But aren't you also Acting Director – in charge of the whole place?"

"Yes," says Dalmore. There's a brief flash of irritation in his eyes. Then it's gone and he bites a corner of his mouth. "It is a position with a great deal of responsibility. But – given our current board of directors – limited authority." He returns to where he was going before I introduced his dual role. He says slowly, now apparently attempting to use an appearance of being reticent as a substitute for genuine politeness, "My...question for you...*is*...if you are an enthusiast of *content-less* painting like Hulton's, do you possess the...*range*...to convey...the new *narrative*?...To educate the public to the nature of the...*paradigm shift*."

He pauses to see if I have understood. Perhaps he should wait and read my review of the fried clams at Capt'n Tony's before he jumps to any conclusions about my range.

116

"Actually, the new Hultons are not complete abstractions. They have pretty obvious content. His subject is trees – abstracted, iconic trees and forest interiors."

"Quite so, quite so. Your article pointed that out. Nature is his content. But you make my argument. Nature is no longer part of *the conversation.*"

"Do you feel," I ask, pen cocked to record his answer, "that all art today has to address the concerns of contemporary urban life?"

"Well, aren't those concerns a bit more compelling than what goes on on farms?"

With this he verges on insulting. But I keep my cool and say, "My article didn't mean to imply that painting should be only – or primarily – about nature." I know that what I wrote *didn't* imply that. "What it did mean to imply is that nature is as valid as any other subject."

Dalmore raises an eyebrow and purses his lips, but says nothing. I'm not a *hater* of Postmodernism and conceptual art. I find some of it pretty interesting. Some of the statements about war can even rival Goya's. (Though I've often wondered what percent of viewers ever are converted to peace and love just by the beholding of something gruesome.) What I do hate is that some proponents of this "new paradigm" act like their art is so goddamn superior to everything that has gone before. This new paradigm seems to me to be one in which *hip-ness* is the highest value. The *me*-times we live in have created *me*-art. (Or if art really is the leading edge, maybe it's the other way around.) Me-art is mainly about the artist – usually the artist appearing hip. Beauty art is mainly about the viewer – the viewer experiencing beauty.

"Well," he intones, dismissing my assertion, "if your man Hulton is returning to provincialism just to gain a following to replace the one he lost when he abandoned the modernists, he is not showing much courage of conviction."

I'd like to say, "Maintaining he's abandoned Modernism, just because he's not painting abstracts, is stupid. Some of the greatest modernists – Matisse, Picasso – always painted recognizable subjects. Even de Kooning depicted female body components through most of his Ab-Ex days." But, as I've indicated, I didn't come here to argue. And given our relative knowledge bases, I'd probably get creamed. So I let Dalmore's scurrilous accusation of cowardice pass and simply ask, "Have you *seen* any of Hulton's new works?"

"Well, I don't really need to see them, do I?"

I guess *you* don't, I'm thinking.

"My point is," the big man says, returning to the question of my fitness for promoting his philosophy of art, "if you believe that Hulton's retro-Modernism truly makes a valid statement today, will you be able to be...*a catalyst*...for getting the public to understand – tactfully, of course... yet persuasively – that Modernism – abstract or not – however *interesting* it was *historically*, is now quite... *over*."

I feel that probably most of Northport's museum-going public doesn't know that Modernism even started, let alone care whether it might have stopped.

I decide to do an end-run. "But this is a museum of *modern* art." I say, hiding behind the pose of an innocent, provincial reporter. – Well, I guess it isn't a pose.

Dalmore raises an eyebrow to a height I've rarely seen achieved outside of a school play. "Semantically, that's true." He says, chortling. "But 'modern' was an absolute term that became a relative one."

I'm not always very quick, but I wonder for a second if he means it the other way around.

"A term is only relevant in its temporal context," he instructs me. "'Modern' was once synonymous with 'contemporary.' When modern became an 'ism' the two... detached. This institution was founded as a 'contemporary' museum, *conceptually*, and as a museum of 'modern art'... *titularly*. The definition evolved. Don't you see? A museum is a living thing." He says this with a stab of his hand that would put a fish knife into any vestiges of Modernism still skulking around in here.

Well, he may have a point. I mean I think he has *some* point – but I'm not sure that I understand exactly what. So I defer a direct response and again ask a question.

"Do you think the museum should consider changing its name to fit with… the evolving paradigm… Become the Northport Museum of Modern *and* Contemporary Art?"

"Well, I don't think any name change is being widely contemplated," he says, with as neutral a facial expression as I've seen from him yet. Probably true. Probably not contemplated more widely than the diameter of his sailor's cap.

"Well," he says, now serene, perhaps satisfied that my question indicates he has gotten through to me. "What kinds of things would you like me to tell you?"

As we stroll through the new wing, Dalmore talks enthusiastically about Kahn's work and the work of artists chosen for up-coming shows. I feel his commentary is an attempt to mold the thick mud of my backwater mind, show me how mired I am in following the Hultons of the art world – the few remaining. He does this without once mentioning Hulton's name – or Pollock or de Kooning or any modern – among the too-numerous-to-keep-up-with contemporary names that roll off his tongue like pearls. But I am finally saved from the tedium of this – and a cramp in my note-taking hand – by the approach of two men, one of whom is my cousin Kevin.

Kevin wears the same khaki summer suit as the day on the beach – or one just like it – his conservative appearance better protective coloration here. He carries a sheaf of papers. Well, sincere devotion to art was always basic to him. Got a master's in art history from Columbia. Unlike me. – My love of art was drug induced. I doubt Kevin ever dropped acid. Could I visualize him smoking a joint? A few puffs, I guess. Maybe he'd try it a couple of times. Of course, the art scene/drug scene in Northport these days, courtesy of the pipeline from New York, revolves pretty much around cocaine. And cocaine would be way beyond the tolerance of Kevin, the Boy Scout. I mean that literally. Kevin achieved Eagle Palm status. Pride of the family.

119

As a little kid I was dragged to the induction ceremony. Erroneously, they thought I could profit from his example. Right now Kevin doesn't look so hot.

The other man is William Kahn. He is flashing that Hollywood smile I found so winning on the Northport dock the other day.

"Ah, William!" Dalmore shouts with delight, interrupting his own glowing review of the show mounted at his direction.

"Arthur," Kahn says in mild reproach, "didn't I say that the Rembrandt should go to the right of the da Vinci? Wait – I don't know – maybe it is better this way." He stares at his paintings for ten seconds and then throws up his hands. "I guess you're right. Damn – you always know." He gives the curator an appreciative smile. A mini-Hollywood. Maybe more of a *beautiful downtown Burbank*.

Then he turns to me. I came casually dressed. Next to Dalmore I must appear shabby. I hadn't given it any thought. But Kahn looks at me with the aspect of interest and respectfulness I seldom get – perhaps have never gotten. He does a quick-cut glance back to Dalmore, as if to say something like, "Arthur, don't keep me in suspense. Who is this most excellent specimen of humanity?" Then he squints as me. "I've seen you somewhere before. – No don't tell me. It was pretty recent. I never forget a face."

"I was on Phillip's Cove dock on last Tuesday morning when you and Mr. Dalmore were going for a sail."

"That's it!" he exclaims. His tone hints self-congratulation, as if he'd said it before I did.

Dalmore glares at me distrustfully. I can't tell whether it is recognizing me or not recognizing me that he might find nettlesome. But he dutifully takes his cue and introduces me as "Alec Perkins from *The Current*."

"*Currents*, you mean, Arthur." Taking my hand and forearm in a warm greeting and looking me right in the eye, he says, "How ya doing, Alec?"

It takes all the personal strength I have to risk spoiling the soaring good fellowship by correcting him. "Al-ex."

"Sorry, fella," he says, glancing at Dalmore, "Alex."

Dalmore, chastened at having made two errors in one introduction, tries out a Hollywood grin of his own. But his looks more like a Vincent Price than a Tom Berenger.

Kahn, all courtesy, controls the moment and asks me if I know Kevin.

Kevin and I say simultaneously, a Bob and Ray parody of twins, "We're cousins."

There isn't any real family resemblance. Me, tallish, him, short. I'm blondish, he's dark. Maybe we have about the same nose.

"Perkins...and Perkins..." he sorts it out. "You guys aren't lawyers?" Then turning to Dalmore and trumping Dalmore's unintentional Vincent Price with an intentional Edward G. Robinson, says, "Careful of these guys – see!"

There's a moment's silence that is broken by Kevin.

"Ah, Arthur, I've made those changes to the catalogue you specified. If you could just give them a quick look. Then I can get Deborah to type them up and mail them out today. That is if Mr. Kahn can give you two minutes before you two go to lunch."

Dalmore looks at Kahn with eyebrows raised. Kahn waves his hand and says, "I'm in no hurry." Dalmore purses his lips, gives a sharp nod and walks with Kevin toward, but not quite into, the hallway leading to the administrative offices.

Kahn, with grin and a "that's life" shake of his head, walks a few steps closer to me. "Alex Perkins? Hey aren't you the guy that wrote that piece on John Hulton?" This is a surprise. But he explains, "I was just reading it in Arthur's office. He's got it on his desk. I was thinking, 'What's he got this for?' Now I get it."

Okay, here we go again. "Right," I say but decide to leave the ball in his court.

"Yeah," he says after a pause and then pauses again. " – No, he was interesting – he had good chops as a painter – back when people thought that brushstrokes were what made a painting great. Kinda like thinking the best thing about a dog is its tail. – You've gotta admit the brushstroke thing was a little vain: My brushstroke is my signature! Come on. How many times can you sign a painting?"

"Maybe you should try doing a Hulton with Donald Duck," I suggest.

"There's an idea!" He replies, as if we are both serious. "But now you tell us that he's doing trees. So I wouldn't. Bruegal's trees or Manet's trees, maybe. But a duck in Hulton's trees – too close to naturalism."

"Even with a duck in a sailor's suit?" I suggest, as if it is an important art-philosophical distinction.

He gives me his all-embracing grin. "I'll think it over."

He changes the subject to one that I imagine is closer to his heart. "So I guess you've been looking at my new work?" Kahn says. This is a variation of the approval fishing that I've found artists almost always do. Even Hulton. But Hulton, now a has-been, deserves more reassurance. I cut artists slack for doing this, though – at least the ones that don't make big money (or any at all) from their work, the way that a William Kahn does.

Kahn's gregariousness does make a winning impression. And good looks and a great smile are such powerful things. How did Hitler get anywhere without them? I don't mean that as a reflection on Kahn – just because I don't like his work. I don't like lots of people's work – without even knowing them. Maybe I'm jealous. He's famous – art world famous, anyway. However, he doesn't seem like a snob – seems like a basically okay guy. I say *seems*, because I'm old enough to have figured out that of all the appealing traits a person can have – talent, wit, sexiness, charm, generosity, you name it – *niceness* may be the easiest to fake. Someone who seems *mean* when you first encounter him is reasonably likely to really be mean. But someone who seems *nice* – how do you know?

Though I don't really care for Kahn's new work – or any of his many previous *styles*, for that matter – I obviously can't say that to him. I like this aspect of my job the least – the need for professional dishonesty. Even privately, I seldom feel mean enough to be completely honest.

I said I was handicapped as a reviewer by a number of things – lack of knowledge, laziness. But my oddest handicap may be that I'm a *specifist*. I guess I made up the word at some point. Been using it so long I can't remember. Means I can like – or even love – individual examples of something, but can be bored by, or even hate, other samples that everyone else thinks are pretty much the same damn thing. This doesn't just apply to art. Last week I reviewed the new Talking Heads album, *Speaking in Tongues*. The lead singer David Byrne had gotten Robert Rauschenberg, the renowned painter, to do the cover. It wasn't local news, of course – except in that it was in local stores – but I figured, hey, two-for-one for the arts section. After I'd listened to the record seven or eight times to assimilate it, I found I really loved only one cut, liked a second one a lot, a few more sounded okay and the rest irritated me. But I could *tell* that *all of it* was pretty good rock music. Even the songs that I never wanted to hear again. What I mean is, I often *don't like* things I *think* are good. It's like that even with the all-time greats, like the Beatles or Dylan. Might only care about two or three cuts per album. My judgment is liberal enough – and, if I may brag, pretty good – but my taste is narrow. Sometimes I even like things I know are truly bad – like a commercial seascape or the song "Mac Arthur Park." It means I have to try extra hard to be objective, not go on my emotions. Being a specifist limits me not just professionally. It can be a drag on fun. Thankfully or sadly, Kahn's work is less problematic for me: I both don't like it *and* I don't think it's any good.

So I duck a real response to Kahn's fishing and enthusiastically say, "Yes – the quartet in the last gallery – interesting!", tossing back the adjective he'd used for Hulton. During Modernism, calling a piece of art *interesting* was a cop-out. Or even an insult. It implied *merely*. But with the advent of Postmodernism and its dominant pose of ironic detachment, *interesting* became a compliment. – Like Mr. Spock's habitual comment about any bizarre phenomenon in this universe or the one just beyond it: "Interesting, Captain."

I quickly change the subject. "I see there is a new monograph out on you. Quite a book." This kind of comment could honestly mean anything, but I've never seen an artist take a statement like this as other than a compliment.

"Yeah, right," he says, nodding and sniffing several times, as if saying "Oh that." "Where did you see it?" he asks.

"Oh," I say, "Just in a bookstore."

"Yeah, right," he says again. "Did you buy it? – Just kidding. Which bookstore?"

"Gee, I don't know," I say. "I'm in bookstores all the time. Isn't it in all of them?"

"No, no," he says. "The damn distributor is fighting with the publisher over their percentage." He says this with a big grin as if he had said something completely different. But he shakes his head and says, "Can you believe it? Art - in high quality, four-color glossy reproduction – left sitting in warehouses while people fight over half a percent."

This is really too bad, I tell him. And I do feel great sympathy for the complications and difficulties associated with being rich and famous. But I also believe one shouldn't lose sight of the problems of being poor and insignificant. It isn't necessarily that easy for those people either.

Dalmore and cousin Kevin return.

Dalmore looks at me and frowns, apparently trying to recollect the status of our interrupted interview. I smile and nod. Attempting to display a level of professional confidence I don't quite have, I say. "I think we're all set."

"Good...good," says Dalmore.

"Mr. Dalmore, – thank you very much," I say, twirling my hand a little for good measure.

"Call me 'Arthur'. – It was my pleasure," Dalmore says unconvincingly.

"Messer's Perkins," Kahn says, bowing to both of us, his hand still holding Dalmore's elbow. Then, gesturing elsewhere with his free hand and beaming his Tom Berenger, he says, "Shall we, Arthur?"

Dalmore, as he is pivoting to follow Kahn, does a half turn back. His skeptical look tells me he's wondering whether his indoctrination was successful. Then like a badly wired robot he jerks back into step with his striding, self-assured companion.

With the departure of the curator and the artist, Kevin and I are left to our own resources.

"How's it going, Kev?" I ask.

"Fine...fine," he says. "How's, uh, how's Gram."

I start to remember that tense impression I got from him when I first saw him walking up to us – before the sunshine radiating from William Kahn put everything else in the room into half-light. "Gram's great." I say. "Anything wrong?"

"Naw," he says unconvincingly, and then scrunches up his mouth.

"What?" I press.

"Ah, it's that guy."

"Kahn?"

"Yeah."

"What's the matter with him? He seemed nice as hell. Charming anyway. A little full of himself, maybe. – But what do you expect with his looks and all the attention he gets." For artists it's a blurry line between showing healthy self-esteem and plain old arrogance. If there were vanity cops, they'd just give you a warning when you go a little over the limit. If you hit a level of excess that endangered the public, they should take your artistic license away.

"He's charming all right," Kevin says, with an edge to his voice not usual within his normally narrow range.

"What – it gets old after a while? Working with him a lot... getting ready?"

"I guess."

"Something else?"

"Yeah, there's something else. There's Deborah."

Who's Deborah?

"Dalmore's new assistant."

125

"So?"

"Well, she and I had started going out – just a few times. Nothing serious. – Well not to her anyway, I guess. Then when he started being around all the time, getting ready for his show, he asked her out and she went. And – I'm not sure – but I guess she's been to bed with him. Or that's what I think."

Oh, God, I was accidentally right about Kevin, the bit part player having to compete with the star of the show.

"That's a bummer," I say. Then I realize I'm pushing his vernacular range with "bummer."

"Right," Kevin says, with a big exhale. "A bummer is just what it is."

"Well maybe they were meant for each other."

"Naw – Turns out he's got a girlfriend. Works in his gallery in New York. She's just moved up here to be the director of the Northport branch. Rebecca Sharma – beautiful. And now he just acts very polite and distant to Deborah."

Ah! The wondrous Rebecca. And it's Sharma. I was right. India. My favorite sub-continent for women. But I say, "Did Deborah tell you all this?"

"No, just some of it. Dalmore told me the 'beautiful Rebecca' part – and that she was Kahn's girlfriend right along. Dalmore said he hated to see Deborah hurt. But I doubt he cares much about that. Half the time he snaps at Deborah and talks to her as if he thinks she's an airhead. And she's a really smart girl. What Deborah told me was that Kahn said, 'my ex wants to try again – and since she's willing to leave New York to do it, I think I owe it to her.' And Deborah believed him. Told me that she was going to 'wait and see.'"

He's silent for a moment again. Then he says, "What did he need Deborah for anyway? If Rebecca Sharma is as beautiful as Dalmore says, Kahn couldn't have just forgotten all about her."

"He didn't have to forget. With a lot of guys it's not just about quality – they need quantity, too."

"That's stupid…and not very…decent."

Of course I agree, but we all know by now that men are smartest and most decent when they lack the opportunity to act some other way. I've never been good-looking or successful enough to experience the full-on availability-offers that a guy like Kahn must have to endure several times a day. So I don't know how I might handle the pressure. I'm no monk, but still I've been pretty much a one-woman-at-a-time man. I have to admit, though, that I've always found it a little humorous to hear people (usually female) say that so-and-so has a wonderful woman at home so why does he chase around? That strikes me like asking a hunter to give it up because his wife has plenty of venison in the freezer. It isn't just about the consumption. But even if it is, freshness isn't nothing. But the last thing I want to do is sound like I'm defending William Kahn.

"Yeah, that's true," I say. "But my guess is that Deborah will wise up soon" – I, of course, have no reason to think this – "and you'll be able to pick up the pieces."

"Maybe. But I wish I didn't have to spend time with the guy. I'm in his studio practically every day."

"Yeah – that's a bummer," I say. I pause for a few seconds so as to seem adequately sympathetic. Then I say, "I've gotta get back to the office." I lean in and give him a hug, realizing I probably have never hugged him before. Another thing my generation feels comfortable about that his doesn't. Well, "comfortable" may be too strong a word. Many guys my own age do the same three quick slaps on the back that Kevin responds with now.

"Say 'hi' to Gram," he says.

"Sure thing," I say. And I go.

# 11

I let the screen door slam and I am immediately sorry that I did – since it provokes the dreaded, "Mornin' naybah." Not this morning Fred, please. It's Sunday. AND oddly enough, I'm heading to Jack's Cove, to Arthur Dalmore's waterfront home. As you can imagine, I'm rather non-plussed. Kevin called last night and said Dalmore'd invited me for a sail. On a quarter million dollar boat. And I'd thought I hadn't made a particularly good impression on him.

I can't see Fred. And sadly I can't see any other living creature – Rosebud, a member of the Weare family whose house is on the other side of Fred's, or even the Weares' orange cat, Sydney – that I could pretend Fred was addressing instead of me; some being hopefully more willing to indulge him by listening for an hour to the kind of information he always imposes on whomever is handy. I've never been particularly fascinated by mechanical things. And I've told that politely to Fred perhaps 1000 times. I imagine any animal that wouldn't bite him would be as good an audience for his obsessive data-dispensing as I am. I assume Sydney would be adequately attentive; wouldn't swish his tail in an insulting manner. I've never seen such a patient cat! But I know Fred's morning will be ruined if he isn't given the chance to impress me with whatever he's just invented or reinvented – banging away during his long night of the soul. Saturday night, no less. But I try to affect a pose of self-absorption, anyway – give the appearance of someone whose psyche, like Fred's when he is fixated on technical stuff, might be totally sealed-off to overtures from the world outside.

A few steps further and I can see him standing – legs wide – just inside his open-fronted garage. He has a welder's mask in the "up" position on his head and he is extending a big right index finger in the direction of the workshop's interior, while waving his left hand back and forth – the international gesture for "go there." The self-congratulatory grin on his face tells me he's in a better mood; isn't thinking about his rival, the bus driver. Well, nurses come and go, but gadgets are eternal.

I did pad in some extra time for a coffee stop, but I say, "I'm running a little late," and point at my wrist – another international signal. But mine lacks the authority of his. I don't mean there's a hierarchy to sign language. I mean *I* lack the authority. I could impress him into backing off, perhaps, by mentioning the J-44, but that doesn't seem wise. Probably get his competitive instincts going. Then I hear David Player's voice – talking to Fred, to himself, or to some unseen party – perhaps to the Weares' orange cat, Sydney – and I relax a little; thinking I will be able to escape Fred more quickly with another human present. Three or more is a social group – offering a buffer against the enforced attentiveness required by "one-to-one." There's less risk, too, of getting down to a *feelings* level. What I'm saying is that, regardless of Fred's overbearing personality, I'm somewhat concerned about hurting his feelings. Before I moved in with Gram and got to know him a whole lot better, I'd wondered if he was impervious to hurt feelings. I'd thought only a person who assumed he had the boundless adoration of everyone he encountered could believe random other individuals might care enough to give him immediate and limitless attention. Well, I've yet to see Fred publicly adored. Still, out of the blue, he might hold forth, from his tied-up boat, to an old lady tourist standing within hailing distance on the Philip's Cove wharf, on the gallons-per-hour flow rate of some newly installed pump. Perhaps he adores himself *enough* that he doesn't ever consider that his obtrusive information-sharing could sometimes be unwelcome to even the most diffident. My guess is he would intuit my repeatedly striking him with one of the heavier metal objects in his workshop as some kind of disapproval. But anything more subtle – like perhaps my screaming at close quarters, "I don't want any lesson in any fucking popular mechanics right now, okay?"– probably wouldn't cause him to be even a bit more circumspect. Anyway, I – now sensitive to the wounded child that a little Angela-mandated therapy taught me everyone (except possibly Leona Helmsley) carries within – am unwilling to take the chance that Fred is incapable of feelings other than self-delight. His reaction to that nurse from Boston is a case in point. So, I pretend to listen, regardless of my own inner child's desire to scream or run.

I enter his garage and pretend to marvel at the big, odd wood and metal contraption sitting there on two of those roller things that mechanics use to scoot under your jacked-up car. Actually, I do marvel. The machine combines a large reel – either found at the dump or stolen from the power company – and an engine that looks like it could have been lifted from my Karmann Ghia. I panic for a moment, then, glancing over my shoulder to see my car sitting where I left it, figure, "*Naw*". Aluminum tubes, stainless steel cables, and two apparently swingable arms extending at oblique angles like horns augment the original apparatus. I don't take the bait, though, by foolishly asking, "What is it?" Asking even one question would play right into Fred's hands. I would get answers to fifteen questions I hadn't asked nor wanted answered. And each of those answers would come packaged within terms he'd know I didn't understand. Therefore, I'd need to ask further questions – like "what's a jasco"? – or just look stupid. I think Fred's greatest satisfaction comes from a listener both asking and looking stupid, too. So, I just say, "Hey, that's fantastic." It's pretty much true. Fantastical it is. And I imagine it is quite useful *for something.*

Fred just smiles, looking back and forth from me to the thing, the thing to me. The sin of pride is upon him in spades today.

David, tweaking away lovingly with a pair of channel-lock pliers, says, "I call it 'the Gorgon.'"

I can't remember what a gorgon, or *the Gorgon,* was. Something from mythology. I violate my own injunction and find myself asking – David, though not Fred – "What's a gorgon, now?"

"I got it from this book I read, *Oroso Foroso,*" David says proudly. "Gorgons are monsters. They look like women – only more horrible."

I repress a laugh and just say, "I see."

Then I add, " – Um, do you mean *Orlando Furioso?*"

"Yeah – that's it." David says.

"You read *Orlando Furioso?*" I ask.

He doesn't take my incredulity as insulting. With luck I've avoided another mine in the field of human feelings. He says, "Sure have. I read it twice. An American girl I met in Peru gave it to me. Best book I've ever read."

"Hey – that's great," I say, unable to think of anything else.

"Hey," David says in a friendly appeal to intellectual rapport, "I can lend it to you. I want to read it again but not till fall. Maybe around Halloween."

"That would be great," I say.

"I've got it in the car," David says, taking me at my word. He carefully places the channel locks on top of the Gorgon – an additional set of horns – and walks out through the open front of the garage into the dazzling June light. I see Fred take a big in-breath, as if he has a lot to say, and, using David's book as my letter of transit, I quickly pivot to follow.

"I'm converting over to a dragger," Fred says, starting after me. "No more putting up with tourists." See – the nurse *is* still bothering him. He's over-reacting normally. But I jump to preempt him.

"Fred, you can explain it all to me when I get home. I've really got

131

to run now." I decide not to tell him that I'm running to hop on the yacht that stole his spot on the dock a few days ago. And without waiting for him to formally release me from my duty as listener, I exit. He takes an in-breath. I know my running off is breaking the rules.

David leans into the back seat of his multi-colored Chevelle. It is multi-colored from having a door and a fender "donated" from other vehicles. "I think it's in here," he calls out.

I need to act fast. I don't wish to insult the young man by bolting when he is making a gesture of friendship. But if I don't, Fred will start rolling this way and I can't risk being caught in his clutches again right now. My solution is to hurry over the line onto Gram's property, like a kid touching *goals*. Thinking fast, I frown at the grass and shake my head. Fred watches me uncomprehending. His lecturing was stymied by the certainty I would jump in my car and drive right off. He doesn't know I'm ensnared within range of his grasp for as long as it takes David to dig to the bottom of the second home that is his backseat.

But David comes up for air waving a thick paper parcel surrounded by duct tape. "Got it," he says. He sees me now twenty-five feet off and moves over toward where I'm standing. To cover my odd behavior I say, loud enough for Fred to hear, "I guess this grass really needs mowing."

David is puzzled and does a survey of Gram's lawn. In a better neighborhood it would indeed be time for a mowing. But around here it looks pretty normal. David puts a hand on my shoulder in what seems like a consoling gesture.

"You know," he says, looking me right in the eye, "I don't even worry about things like that anymore."

I take his ragged book. "Thanks, a lot," I say, tossing it onto the passenger seat of my car.

"Wait," shouts Fred.

Instinctively I freeze.

"You don't expect us," he chastens, "to lift that thing alone?"

# 12

"Look lively, mate!" Arthur Dalmore shouts as if he owns my ass. After a half dozen comings-about I still don't have his self-tailing winches down. And we have probably sacrificed a total of ten or twelve seconds through my ineptitude. Enough to lose a close race. If we were in one. However, we're not. Today *Pure Conception* is a party boat. And, oddly enough – only three days after my hardly simpatico meeting and interview with Dalmore – I'm invited to the party. Lucinda York – whom my slightly old-fashioned cousin Kevin referred to as my girlfriend – has been invited too. The other guests are Kevin, William Kahn and his lovely Rebecca Sharma, Deborah Irvine, and the little guy I saw at Lucinda's beach performance. His name is Justin Bollard. Though he doesn't look like a Northporter, I'd assumed he was merely an acolyte of Lucinda's. But I have gathered from his chumminess with Dalmore and Kahn that he has some sort of greater significance to the arts in general. I know your first adjective about any man shouldn't be that he's *little*. But I am pleased for Kevin's sake that there is someone on board whom he can tower over.

I must say this is a helluva boat. And I must say, too, I feel a guilty pleasure – guilty, since I've bragged of nautical non-competitiveness – in flying past bigger sailing vessels. The design of this craft proves that the axiom, *waterline is destiny* – the length of the wet part of a boat determines the top speed of its hull – is a relative term. It's relative to the technology. Now I understand where Dalmore gets his disdain for "classic" designs. I don't agree, but I understand. Relative, too, is the word *flying* when talking of sailboats. It can take your boat, modern marvel though it may be, several minutes to "fly" past one of classic design. This is because single hull, fossil-fuel-combustion-less travel on water happens at not much more than a walk. A run at best. Factoring this in, though, you can legitimately gasp at your velocity when you've humbled a slower boat.

Dalmore, of course, has a regular race crew, but they are not hired or indentured in any way, so they might not be cajole-able for a Sunday sail. They likely are fanatics who sign on at the beginning of a season to race one evening each week. *Pure Conception's* crew, Dalmore tells us, consists of two middle-aged lawyers, two college boys, a fireman, and a gynecologist. When he mentioned this last sailor, Dalmore sniffed hard, tossed his head and laughed. I myself have never thought of gynecology as funny – except when considering how a male gynecologist tells his mother he's decided on it for a specialty. Race crew members might be just about anyone who doesn't associate an interlude on the water with peace and harmony.

So, eight are aboard Dalmore's boat, but the crew is just three. Kahn, apparently used to expensive boats, is displaying consummate sailing skills. Deborah seems quite a competent sailor. I, so far, am proving less than competent. Kevin admits to ignorance of the boat's functioning. I guess he skipped a sailing merit badge. Lucinda and Rebecca are passengers. And Justin has not revealed himself one way or the other. So I can't guess the extent of his manual abilities. He does seem like he'd be good at operating a corkscrew, though.

Kevin sits in the cockpit. He seems a bit lost. Rebecca, next to him, looks serenely lovely. By "serene" I may be stereotyping her — that is, because she is of "Eastern" origin. I mean, I assume from her last name, her olive skin and coal black hair, that she's at least part Indian. Could be Pakistani. She could even be Nepali, or part, I mean — though I've never met a Nepali outside of Nepal. Anyway, it might be better for my equanimity if Kevin were the one who looked serene and Rebecca looked lost. Make it easier not to stare at her. She is a true test for a beauty addict. I don't think she remembers me. But why should she?

Kahn is on the winch opposite my station. He gives me patient, supportive looks each time I screw up. That's nice. Kahn is looking even more supportively at Deborah — when she does things right. But I also read some apology and wistfulness in his expression. And she's having none of it. She doesn't look at him angrily. She seems stoic enough to not appear hurt. She just looks away. Kevin watches Kahn with suspicion. Right now Deborah is at the helm. I'm surprised that Dalmore put her there. I wouldn't have guessed he'd give away the wheel. Maybe he's doing it to bolster her. But he doesn't seem the bolstering type, especially after what Kevin told me about their boss's tone with her at work. Perhaps he's just enjoying calling out commands and watching the boat perform elegantly.

Lucinda, oddly enough — given her trademark personal whiteness — is *sunbathing*. Or, maybe, not so oddly — given her penchant for personal exposure. Well, I think she needs a sunbathing context: otherwise what excuse would she have for taking off all her clothes? Perhaps a protest piece about the bourgeois obsession with couture? No matter. All present are grown-ups, all have backgrounds in the arts — no firemen or college boys on board today; and any gynecologist's presence in the crew would have been moot. She probably would have thought it bourgeois, given the sophisticated milieu, to *ask* if anyone aboard would be offended in any way if she disrobed. So she just disrobed. She did it matter-of-factly. Like going skinny-dipping. Nothing sexy about that. She did not remove her sneakers, though. I don't know if she kept them for traction or —

aware of contexts as she is – because she knows a woman is *nakeder* with shoes. Unfortunately she forgot a hat. Hats make women really naked. After removing her clothes, she just as matter-of-factly slapped a white tanning lotion all over herself. No – I can read the plastic bottle now and it says *sun block*. I've seen ads for that stuff on TV lately. Skin cancer is suddenly a big item in the news. More likely than preserving her health, Lucinda is trying to preserve her whiteness. Of course she wouldn't be trying to *tan*. Well, there goes the sunbathing excuse. Unless she can make a case that a body can soak up vitamin D without any visible sign of having been in the sun, she is naked against charges of having no reason for being naked. She now lies on the varnished deck like a knocked over doll – Artsy Barbie, let's say – arms stiffly at her side, head-above-feet, feet-above head, alternating as the heeling angle of the vessel reverses with each successive tack.

Among those who seem to approve of what Lucinda is doing are Dalmore, Bollard and Kahn. The ambivalent ones are me and, perhaps, conservative Kevin. And the not-too-happy-but-trying-to-seem-as-blasé-about-a-naked-woman-as-she-is-about-a-faithless-Kahn is Deborah. Rebecca is inscrutable on the subject. There I go again. But – what the hell – India is a thousand miles west of the part of Asia that generated that cliché. Whether she has the serenity or equanimity of the East – something I detected only in pockets when I was there – or, by merely being beautiful, is protected against anything untoward in her vicinity, I can't tell. Seeing both Rebecca and Lucinda in one view, I am torn between my tropism for beauty – an ethereal thing – and earthy lust. Right now, this lust for Lucinda goes somewhat beyond what I felt at any time during the drunken night we spent together. – When was that, four nights ago? The intensity is probably another context thing. That, and *loss anticipation* – fear I may never sleep with her again. Not a normal concern for me. I've dumped but never *been* dumped after only one night. (I suppose I sound a bit proud of that.) But nothing seems normal where Lucinda is concerned. She's seemed friendly enough on the phone when I've called. (Twice.) Not cool. Not cute. Not seductive. She said she has been secluding herself in her studio. She's *working-with* Gram's insights, she says. "I know she's a little kooky. – You know, the ninety-year-old thing," Lucinda said when on the phone. "But Gram has a real understanding of what it means to be a woman." This makes me wish that my grandfather Jim Perkins, Gram's husband, were still around. He might be able to give me some idea of what it means to be a man. I could use that right now. I assume that in Lucinda's view *gender* is something you can't figure out on your own. I hadn't seen her again until this morning when I picked her up for this outing. I got only a polite peck on the cheek. So, given that our beachfront dinner was an interview, this could actually be considered our first date.

I'm quite impressed by Dalmore's yacht. But, even more impressed by Dalmore's harbor-front home. My admiration of it, though, is primarily from a how-much-does-a-place-like-this-cost angle. I wouldn't exactly call it cozy. Kevin and I now sit together on the rail of the heeling boat, feet dangling high above the sea. *Pure Conception* currently cruises on a long tack – a close reach, headed for the Isles of Shoals off Portsmouth. All that is required of me as a crewman on this point of sail is that I exert 165 lbs. of gravity to counter wind leverage on the mast. Highlanders are as useful for this as old salts. So Dalmore has ordered everyone to sit inboard of the life-line on the surging windward rail opposite the leeward rail that correspondingly occasionally dips a few inches beneath the churning surface. Everyone except Lucinda. She is performing a vital function – charging the onboard air – for which neither of the other women on board has the requisite qualification – willingness. I take the opportunity to furtively ask Kevin about Dalmore's finances.

"You weren't thinking he pays for all this on a curator's salary?" Kevin answers my question with a question. The breeze seems to blow the sound immediately inboard, but the noise of the wind itself and the roiling water insures our privacy.

'What else?" I reply.

"Not much of a Scotch drinker, are you?"

"Huh?"

"*Dalmore* – twenty-two year old single malt?"

"Uh, I only drink cheap stuff. – So, you're saying, family money?"

"Well, that's one way to put it."

"But he doesn't have a brogue, or whatever – or even any Anglo-type accent."

"Well, neither do we and we're Anglos."

"Yeah, right – but we don't get any royalty checks from *back home*. If we did you can bet I'd be talking like a BBC announcer – except, maybe if you woke me at 3 a.m. – then I'd probably still say, "Who dat?" like a regular person. Any successful Perkins' in the old country you know about that I don't?"

"*Sorry*," says Kevin, respectably aping a Brit. This is the loosest he's been all day.

"Dalmore is a first-generation-*and-a-half* American," Kevin says. "His father was the family brown sheep and they sent him to the colonies to supervise American distribution or something. He married a beautiful actress, Dalmore told me, but she got bored with him and left. So the old man went from distribution to consumption."

"Dalmore stay with the father or leave with the mother?"

"Stayed with the father."

"So he was abandoned by his mother and raised by a drunk? That's pretty tough. Where does his boundless self-assurance come from?"

"I don't know – the money? Over-compensating? And there was an aunt or older cousin – he was a little vague about her – who came over to the States to fill in for the straying mom. "

"A *sort-of* aunt," I say trying to do a Brit myself.

"What do you mean, 'sort-of?'"

"Private joke. There's this wealthy Brit artist I interviewed once who has homes in Northport and in London, too. Goes back and forth. Paints the ships leaving the harbors there – like South Hampton or someplace – then arriving here. Or maybe that's just how it seems. He mentioned he had a dog back home, and I asked him who took care of it when he wasn't there. He said there was 'a sort-of Swedish Girl.'"

Kevin smiles a little. "Maybe like that." His class bemusement seems to mirror mine – "Maybe a 'sort of' aunt. Wouldn't want him to commit himself."

"I'm surprised Dalmore'd tell you all that."

"Why?"

"Well, it's very personal. And you know – a bit embarrassing."

"It's the times – and New Yorker chauvinism. *And* an art world thing. It's not like around here. My guess is that nobody in that scene gets embarrassed about anything anymore. – Except, maybe, getting caught with a white bag coming out of some MacDonald's."

"I don't know," I say. "It might be hip today to admit to anything. But…"

"But what?"

"But I think someone – a man anyway – always has to give the impression that whatever it was that happened didn't bother him. Not show weakness. Weakness has still got to be embarrassing. Maybe a*dmitting weaknesses* can be hip. But not *showing weakness*… Well, Dalmore sure doesn't show any weakness the way he runs this boat."

"You're right," Kevin says, "or the museum."

I'm getting a nice feeling from connecting with Kevin a little. I've never been that big on family-for-family's-sake. At thirty-three I haven't been hit yet by any urge to produce a little Alex or Alexandra to carry the Perkins' flag into the twenty-first century. I'm more into the Kurt Vonnegut thing that your *real* family is whomever you connect with most. He had a word for this kind of group. *Karass?* I think. But, I have had a few stupefying "family fights" with one or two karass members – so that's no guarantee either. Now I feel like I have to address a question I've had in my mind since I failed to ask it when Kevin called me last night about sailing today.

"Hey, Kevin – how come I'm here?"

"Didn't you tell Dalmore you could sail?"

"Right. But lots of guys can sail."

"Well, you're in the arts and you sail."

"I've got one foot in the arts and it's pretty much in a rival arts camp. And being from a rival camp is probably worse than being a gynecologist."

"Well, maybe he likes to get all points of view." Kevin's expression indicates that he knows that this is bullshit.

I just smile. "Did you mention to him Lucinda having spent the night at Gram's"?

"Uh…" He pauses, then starts slowly. "Well, you remember he came to the police station? You know how he took a great deal of interest in everything that surrounded her arrest."

"Right?" I say, but I mean, "*So?*"

"Well, he thought the three of us were going to dinner, right? But, you remember, I couldn't?

"I remember it well," I say, sensing that Kevin is starting to feel boxed in. So I decide to cut him some slack.

"Yeah, yeah – I get it," I say, implying that his not having considered whether Dalmore might have a big mouth could be a problem.

My bragging – kind-of *admitting* – to a not very arm-twisting Kevin that I slept with Lucinda that night, makes me as guilty as he is – though it was my own life I was, in pop psych terminology, *being disclosive* about. However, though I didn't tell him to keep it under his hat, I assumed conservative Kevin wouldn't blab. His blabbery of what, even now, post sexual revolution, some still consider *a conquest*, could explain why I've sensed a more positive appraisal, a clear-eyed nod, in the looks I got from Dalmore and Kahn when Lucinda and I arrived this a.m. They both seem conquest-oriented types. I'm not used to getting clear-eyed nods.

I change the subject and ask Kevin, "So how's things going with Deborah?"

Kevin looks pained.

"I don't know where I am with Deborah." he says and pauses as if wrestling with how much embarrassment – *showing weakness* – he can take just to get some sympathy. Like I've said, he's kind of an old fashioned guy. Doesn't disclose just to be hip, like people in the New York arts – or like his bragging asshole cousin would do. Maybe if he had something to brag about he might. But I don't think so. I think our being related is the only motivation he might have for opening up to another male about something embarrassing. That and the fact that anybody who lives with his grandmother – and also who lives with *his* grandmother – must be someone who'd be unlikely to shoot you down just for competition's sake. Living with your grandmother, like wearing sweatpants when you're not just out for a run, is a sign of having given up.

He offers more. "Well, we had a talk that night you...that I dropped you at the beach." With the wind and the surging bow wake under our sneakers, amidships, he's hard to hear. I lean in closer. "She said that she wasn't looking for a relationship with anybody right now." The politest way, I'm thinking, to tell someone, *you lose*. "But she says she really likes me." I wonder to myself in which order she said these two things.

He continues, "She arrived first at Dalmore's this morning. Then I did. Then Kahn came with Rebecca. I saw his Porsche pull up before Deborah saw it. When he and Rebecca got out of the car he took her hand. But when he saw Deborah on the terrace he pulled his hand away. Pretended he had to swat a mosquito. Phony bastard. Deborah didn't see the handholding. But, I do think seeing him with Rebecca Sharma – hand-holding or not – probably stung her quite a bit. "He says again, "Phony bastard."

Well, I guess it's nice to feel some energy coming from Kevin, though I can't say that negative energy is in every case better than none. I think maybe – for the sake of the day at sea and his need to deal with Kahn at the museum – I should encourage him to cut Kahn a little slack.

"You're probably right. But he might not be quite as bad as that. Maybe there was some truth in the story he told Deborah. Leaving one woman for another doesn't exactly make him a total phony."

"Oh, he's a phony, all right."

There's a conviction in his voice that hints at something I haven't heard.

"What do you mean?" I ask.

"Well, I'm curating his retrospective, right? And when the assistants were bringing all his stuff over to see what goes best next to what in that space, they brought in this old crate from Germany by mistake. I opened it and you wouldn't believe what was inside..."

"Ready to come about," Dalmore shouts, giving me ten seconds to abandon my spot on the rail and again go wrestle with his high tech winches. As soon as I'm gripping the downwind Genny sheet, he orders, "Helm hard a' lee." This time I've got it. Smooth as silk. I was acting instinctively: my conscious mind is busy considering what Kevin has just told me he'd seen in that crate – and what that says about William Kahn, the hip and ironic art star.

We've just passed White Island Light and are about to round into Gosport Harbor. Dalmore has mentioned the accessible-from-the-water-only take-out shack that offers only lobster rolls – excellent ones. I can attest to the quality. I've come here with Steve. Dalmore retakes the helm.

"Thank you, Deborah. Nicely done," he says.

Maybe, knowing his ethnic origin, I'm projecting, but for the first time I hear in his voice: *Scotland.* With his facial aberrations I can't help thinking of Long John Silver. But, a Long John Silver dressed in Ralph Lauren.

"I think it's time for a little libation," Dalmore says. "Perkins – start your sail." I feel a little uneasy that all the *Perkinses* shouted out today have been for me and not my older cousin. But there's nothing I can do about that.

We've been on a broad reach the last ten minutes. I ease off on the jib as Dalmore does with the main and we sail slowly between the other sailboats and a fishing vessel or two moored in the close harbor.

"William – to the bow with your boathook, please. We'll grab that big white mooring ball off port." Dalmore rounds-up, a perfect approach on the first try – no auxiliary power necessary – and lets the sails flap. Kahn, deft with the boathook, sweeps up the green-slime-covered, inch-thick, half-submerged mooring line hanging from the floating plastic ball. We are now attached to the planet again, as Fred Avery would say.

"Perkins, kindly help me catch the main." Dalmore and I drop and sail-tie the mainsail. Kahn drops and bunches the jib. No roller-furling on a racing boat.

"Deborah, Justin – you'll find a rum punch in the icebox below," Dalmore declares, stepping off the cabin roof into the cockpit. I guess we don't eat quite yet. I'm starving. Boats always do that to me. Probably it's the idea of being cut-off from all source of nourishment – except raw fish. I've even panicked on fifteen-minute ferry rides – if there are no candy bars for sale on the ticket counter. Looks like Dalmore's another individual that drinks on an empty stomach. And before the sun is below the yardarm. But I'm most surprised it's rum and not single malt scotch. I guess seafaring traditions take precedence over family ones.

This boat sits for the first time since we left the dock in a fixed and fully upright position. I don't know if it is this or the word "rum" that causes Lucinda to stir. I – and perhaps everyone else on board – am wondering what context is about to emerge. Clothing for drink time? Or is that just too bourgeois, too. I think it is a close call. Personally, I favor her considering it *too bourgeois* and remaining unclothed – but only if I will be allowed to have sex with her at some later point, hopefully later today. But I would instead vote for *it would be just plain tacky to sit naked with others fully clothed* – as felt the bourgeoisie of 19th century France about *De'jeuner sur l' herbe* – if I am to be left to die of erotic thirst.

But Dalmore is way ahead of me. He calls out, "Lucinda – '*De'jeuner sur* la Mer'" – Luncheon on *the Sea* – practically challenging her to prove that an American woman in 1983 is at least as psychologically free as her French counterpart more than a century before. Kahn, perhaps apprehensive that Lucinda will not get the reference, springs to reinforce Dalmore's challenge, "If it was good enough for Manet, it's good enough for us." Where's Donald Duck when we need him? Deborah scrunches her face a bit. I look at Rebecca who has been the least expressive *active* presence on the boat. *Passively*, she's been outstanding. She is Mona Lisa now. Western inscrutable. Is she thinking, "Come-on, girl, it's a dare?" Or, "God, what an asshole my boyfriend is?"

Lucinda rises on her left elbow, shading her eyes with her right hand, surveying the harbor and islands that nearly touch each other. The pink-flecked, electric green of beach-rose bushes and the sun-bleached white of cottages and a seasonal hotel from summers long passed must be a shock to eyes that remained mostly closed for more than an hour, or else took in nothing but blue water and sky. She appears to consider only the land and seascape. The eyes of her shipmates have adjusted focus to the rocky strips that grew slowly in vividness while Lucinda has slept or meditated – or worked-out a performance piece or contemplated changes to her curriculum vita. Now everyone on deck is focusing on her. To quote my favorite line from J.R.R. Tolkien, "Time seems poised in uncertainty." Lucinda rises to a sitting position and glances at her little pile of garments, then briefly at the humans in the cockpit – very briefly. Then she sweeps the island again as if the eyes watching her were no more intrusive to her boundaries of self than the distant cottage windows.

"De'jeuner sur la Mer," she says, deftly turning the dare into contextual justification. "Oui, Merci," And as if hardly interested at all – French languor being the order of the day – she comes as she is into the cockpit. All the world's an art gallery and all of us but artists.

Except during, and for a short while after an acid trip, I was never too fixated on *the energy* or *vibe* of a situation. I guess I always think there is some of that, but that it's seldom a critical factor. Well, right now the cockpit feels like a parking lot full of psychic cars revving in neutral. You can almost hear the energy.

"Here comes the rum punch!" Deborah says from the companionway. She has an ice bucket in one hand and a cylinder made up of clear plastic cups in the other. "Hey, great! – rum punch!" I think almost everyone – but Mona Lisa – says in near perfect, tension-breaking unison.

Justin, who'd been in the galley and, along with Deborah, not privy to the drama on deck – he who might have the least interest in it, as he is assumedly gay (though that of course is a meaningless consideration since nakedness in this artsy situation has no sexual component) – emerges from the companionway with a large plastic cooler. He takes in Lucinda sitting chastely on a cushion, removes his round, wire-framed glasses, rotates them a half turn and holds a lens over one eye, looking the young woman up and down appraisingly. In a parody of an academician, he says, "Ah – *'De'jeuner sur l'herbe* – no, *'La MER!'* " He corrects himself too late. The poor man had missed Dalmore's smoother pronouncement of this witticism moments before. To his surprise he gets only a few polite laughs for what he believed to be a 10-carat art joke. He covers by saying, "Oh, well. I keep telling you – all is replicum."

I suddenly place him. *Justin Bollard.* I could say "the Justin Bollard." The guy who writes those articles in *Art Forum* about something like how, thanks to the dominance of mass media, we now have more "signs than referents." Things like that. "Nothing is real anymore. Everything is *replicum.* Everything is a copy." Well, this is an honor. A genuine philosopher.

"Never mind that now, Justin," Dalmore demands, scowling what would be perceived as *deeply* for anyone else, but for him as barely expressive at all. "Pour us some drinks."

Through the magic of alcohol we are all more or less comfortable in a few minutes. – Except perhaps Lucinda. The southwest wind that brought us here from Northport Harbor has become a sea breeze, and I can see goose bumps and rigid nipples. I think of gallantly offering her my sweatshirt. But that would make her naked only from the waist down. It might be hard for even Lucinda to shift to a new context in which a clothing configuration like that could be tolerably considered art. My knowledge of art history, at least, isn't broad enough to suggest one.

With a few rums under his designer belt, Dalmore departs in the Zodiac for lobster rolls.

Justin had good-humoredly been shut down, but having already downed several glasses – *plastics,* that is (replicums of glasses) of Dalmore's strong, tasty concoction, he tries again to invest artistic – as opposed, I imagine, to *existential* – meaning into our sitting and drinking. Or else tries possibly to show that nothing – anymore – has meaning at all, now that it is all mediated, is all *replicum.*

"Before the media age," he says mock-wistfully, "people sat on real boats, drank real drinks, and thought about real reality. So, they could be at peace. Now we sit on replications of boats and feel self-conscious."

This is the world of my bad trips – the downside of my acid experiences. There is a kind of silence in apparent homage to the totality of his truth. I think it is no more than 50 percent true and the degree between 0 and 50 of truth in his conception rests in the degree to which he is being metaphorical, *and* in the degree to which he can be sure that lots of people might not have felt socially alienated or uncomfortable in the past – before there existed media other than newspapers. My guess is that in the *Crucible* era of hidebound self-restraint, people felt uncomfortable all the time; as opposed to most of the time, like in the present. And then, too, perhaps there are a few people who don't feel too alienated in 1983. I, right now, am feeling pretty real.

"That, in a nutshell, is what I am trying to say in my painting," Kahn chimes in.

"I draw like a cartoonist, and not like Titian, not because I can't draw like Titian. But because Titian's world has ceased to be. I paint people as flat because that's what people have become." For the first time, I realize Kahn's Donald Duck is his symbol of himself mocking

146

his way through the great art of the past.

I glance over at Kevin, who is in the process of glancing over at me. We roll our eyes simultaneously. I project that Kevin is also thinking if someone broke the looking glass and we were suddenly back in Titian's world, William Kahn would not suddenly become a great draftsman.

Somebody has to put a few obstacles in Bollard's road to a flat earth, but once again alcohol is an inhibition to my ability to be thoughtful and verbalize competently. So I just ask, "What about regular people?"

"Regular people?" asks Bollard, with a tilt of his head.

"You know, people who don't know much about art, but if they saw a Titian they'd think he sure could make things look real."

"Those people all watch TV. More people have seen Titians on TV than have seen them in museums."

I again glance at Kevin – this time for help, realizing how I've never inquired about his specific interests within the fields of art. He went to work at the NoMMA, about the time I was first appreciating painting. I guess I assumed he worked there because Modernism was his love. But Northport doesn't have a pre-modern fine arts museum. And, even if Kevin had been willing to commute to Boston maybe he couldn't have gotten a job at the prestigious Museum of Fine Arts. So I don't know how into classical art he is. But, I assume that as an art historian he would probably be the closest thing to an onboard Titian expert.

Kevin, can of Coke in hand, just looks a little glum. (He'll never get the girl that way.)

"I've never seen a Titian on TV," Deborah joins in.

"I meant it metaphorically," Bollard says. "What I mean is, everybody looks at TV. Everyone sees replicum.'

"What about somebody who's off the grid?" I press.

"Off the grid?" It didn't occur to me that, as a city fella, Bollard might never have heard the term.

"You, know – built his own house in the trees, heats with wood, home-schools his kids? Can't he have an authentic experience?"

"My dear boy," says Justin Bollard, "he is the original replicum – the copy of the American pioneer surrounded by urban America. How could he be authentic? He's the most self-conscious of all."

"What if he's not trying to be an authentic pioneer. Just trying to have some authentic experiences before he dies."

"He's wasting his time. He grew up on television.'

"What about his kids?"

"What *about* his kids?"

"Can't they have authentic experiences?"

"They've never seen TV?"

"Never seen TV," I say. How did I get myself into this?

"Well, that's an interesting question. But it is so far-fetched as to have little real significance."

My instincts finally find a footing in the slosh of alcohol. And I think of rebutting the philosopher on less frivolous grounds. I bring up the so uncool *T–word.*

"What about a person of vision – or just a person with a healthy sense of things – *transcending* all that?" I see-saw back to the good side of my acid trips; the side without his replicum. Things often seemed quite, quite *real.* Astoundingly real.

"*Transcending?* Isn't that a bit naive?"

"I don't know," I say, feeling juice in my veins. "Not compared to the *Invasion of the Body Snatchers.* Maybe both are naïve."

Bollard is glaring at me with a kind of disdain I haven't seen since my fifth grade teacher, Miss Kilgore, caught me peeking into the girl's bathroom. We are like two punchy fighters; the alcohol seeming to have debilitated both of us. I am waiting for an answer. But I am getting the idea that Bollard has decided my suggestion is beneath comment – my question can be taken as rhetorical.

This "replicum" thing isn't really that bad a theory, though. Most stuff today is pretty much a hollow replica of something that's gone before. What he is talking about is basically why I stopped taking acid. The seesaw of the LSD experience was such that I could go from seeing all the things in my room in their exquisite, infinite singularity one minute, to believing them all exact duplicates, replaced by some malevolent force while I was briefly in the bathroom. The trouble, I think, with Bollard's "All is replicum" is the *all* part. "All" takes in *too much territory*. I mean this as W.C. Fields used the phrase. In – I can't remember which movie – the stout, aging Fields character is about to demonstrate a wrestling hold on a policeman. But the bath-robed Fields pauses first to ask the uniformed cop where he's from. "Toronto," the cop says. So Fields brags that there isn't a man in the United States *or Canada* who can get out of his hold. As Fields demonstrates it, the cop picks him up and tosses him on his head. After a moment in pate-rubbing ignominy, the Fields character – the reason why he's sprawled on the sidewalk dawning on him – says, "I guess I took in *too much territory*." A lot of being sprawled on the sidewalks of life, I think, comes from taking in too much territory.

Kevin has moved over to my side again.

"Nice try," he says to me.

I shrug. Then I tell him about Field's unbreakable wrestling hold.

His bottom lip pushes the upper one up. Then he smiles and nods slowly. "Good to know," he says. "'Too much territory.' Might come in handy sometime."

At this moment I hear the whine of the returning Zodiac's little outboard. Lucinda, having apparently gotten nothing but cold and a few discreet, non-Berengerish smiles from Kahn, scurries up onto the cabin roof toward the foredeck to grab her clothes. This makes everyone remember that she is there and naked. (Not nude. Don't forget the sneakers.) All eyes follow her progress. When she returns, dressed, I do offer her my sweatshirt. She declines at first, then accepts. The sea breeze is getting stronger.

The lobster roll tasted great, but having been ravenous before the drinks – and before the twenty-five minute or so wait – I am about as hungry as before we moored. I should have pressed my wallet on Dalmore and ordered six. As we are casting off, using the unspoken pretext of finding the head, I go below to scrounge. Getting underway again – the cranking of halyards on winches – provides me covering sound. So I risk the noise of opening cabinets and lockers. I'm looking for anything edible. This clearly is a racing boat. Stripped to the essentials. Nothing on board to eat. Except…*a jar of caviar*. I've never been a great lover of caviar. But I've probably had only cheap stuff. This doesn't look cheap. And it's still sealed. But I cannot help myself. I tear the paper seal with my fingernail, twist the top, and, with a quick look-round for a utensil or a human observer, insert two fingers, then plop a glob into my mouth. I hear a click and look around to behold Rebecca exiting the head. I'd missed her going below before me. I still have my fingers in my mouth. She stares for a moment, as surprised to see me as I am her. Then, wonder of wonders, she says. "Ouu – can I have some of that. I'm completely starved. That lobster roll barely made a dent. – Something about the salt air."

I hand her the jar wordlessly.

"No fork or anything?" she asks.

"I don't know, I think a fork would be extra weight in a race. Anyway, I didn't want to risk the time looking."

She follows my lead and dips in two fingers. "Don't you just love this stuff," she says, like some kind of regular girl. Well, some rich regular girl.

"I do now," I say. She smiles and digs in again.

"*Perkins!*" I hear Dalmore shout.

I lurch in the direction of the companionway ladder, but halt a second and look back at what may be the most beautiful woman I have ever seen off television. She misunderstands and holds out the jar in my direction. I run two steps back and do the two finger lunge one last time. "Thanks," I say.

"It's almost empty," she says, guiltily, a question implied.

"Finish it and toss the jar overboard, I guess."

"*Perkins!*"

"Coming," I shout upwards.

150

"Oh… Perkins," Rebecca calls after me as I step onto the ladder. "I mean, Alex."

"Yes?"

"I liked what you said to Justin. He can be a bully sometimes – I mean, intellectually."

"Kind of a sado-intellectual, you mean?"

She smiles. "Well, maybe I should just say he's a little high-strung."

"Well, he should be," I say in support.

Her smile waxes irrepressibly. I breathe in her beauty for a few heartbeats, then I bolt up the steps.

On deck I feel a change in the atmosphere. Though Bollard is still sitting with a drink – seems drunk – or lost in thought – or both, there is a lot of activity. The wind has picked-up several notches and Deborah is helping Dalmore, it looks like, to put a reef in the main. Kahn is at the bow un-hanking the Genny.

"Perkins – good," Dalmore tells me when I finally appear. "Go back below to the sail locker forward and grab the 130 jib, the bag with a big '2' on it."

I jump again to the short ladder, this time to descend. But I have to wait for Rebecca to get clear of the companionway coming up. Her expression is entirely neutral – as if we'd never shared a fish egg in our whole lives. For some reason this gives me more pleasure than a conspiratorial smile.

With Dalmore at the helm, single-reefed main, and a still good-sized jib, we are making perhaps nine knots in perhaps a twenty-knot breeze; beam reach – heading in. Northport grows more distinct by the minute. It feels wonderful. I stand at the stern rail surveying our odd crew. I either want to or feel I should, sit with Lucinda. I can't tell which. But she – in my sweatshirt – is in animated conversation with William Kahn. He reclines on his elbows, long legs stretched across the width of the cockpit. Kevin, across from them, sits quietly next to Deborah. She is smiling – but I think the smile is due to the glory of a beam reach on a fast boat. Rebecca, comforted by a lobster roll and a half a jar of caviar, sits on Kevin's other side. She again projects that "Eastern serenity." I certainly have not seen her interacting much with Kahn today. I realize I'd VERY much like to go sit next to her. I could perhaps tell her about the dog I had as a boy, my visit to Khajuraho, and my visions of a world at peace. But I don't. A bolder man would. But my gorgeousness/nervousness meter is at about a nine.

Justin is emerging from the companionway, presumably after a much-needed trip to the head. The volume of the alcohol he consumed in relation to his almost nonexistent body weight must have produced a great deal of pressure. On a beam reach the degree of heeling is not extreme but the wind is building up some good-sized swells, so there is something of a roll. This can be as pleasant to a sailor as a cradle in the tree-tops. To a highlander it can be nauseating. Justin focuses on me and scowls, apparently having remembered or figured out something he wanted to impart. He approaches. "I just want you to know…" he begins to say as he stumbles over Kahn's extended legs. He flails for a moment. Kevin rises to steady him, but his grasp is two inches short. A swell tosses the boat to leeward – and Justin Bollard out of the cockpit onto the lifeline.

"I just want to say…" he tries to continue his thought, unable to conceive that he is in jeopardy. He is pivoting vertically on the plastic-coated horizontal wire that surrounds the deck. Now he notices the inevitable ocean below. What he does say, as he falls over board is, "I can't swim…"

Kevin, already standing, hesitates not a second. He dives into our roiling wake.

"Perkins – the throwable!" Dalmore shouts.

This activity seems like a dream – happening both instantly and in slow-motion. So I don't know how long it takes me to get to the stern rail, detach the horseshoe-shaped life preserver and throw it as hard as I can in the direction of the two bobbing figures. Dalmore has already come up into the wind to end our motion away from the two castaways. The main is flapping wildly, but the jib is back-winding.

This is good. And it may be not an accident, but excellent seamanship on the part of the captain: the headway – or sternway, actually – that it provides allows us to drift broadside slowly in the direction of our quarry. Now, I can make out that Kevin has reached Justin and, from behind, has gotten an arm under one of Justin's and across his chest. With his free arm he is grabbing handfuls of water in a moderately successful attempt to swim toward the life preserver. Then, he has it.

When we are almost on top of them, Dalmore calls to Kahn to luff the jib and when he has done so, the boat pretty much sits in place in the swells; the men in the water just off its stern.

Not waiting for instruction, I grab the line on the trailing Zodiac, haul it in and jump aboard. It is as close as any part of the boat to the two struggling men and it will clearly be easier to drag them over a foot of inflated rubber than up four feet of fiberglass freeboard. Kahn climbs into the inflatable right behind me. I lean out and touch Kevin. He is breathless, but surprisingly calm, saying, "Get him. Get him."

We haul a coughing Bollard into the rubber dingy. Then we pull Kevin, who is part way in on his own, in all the way, too.

"Put him on his chest against the…you know, the side," Kevin says with an exhausted exhale.

We do as he says. Kevin reaches around the prostrate, choking Bollard and does a kind of Heimlich thing. There's a loud burp followed by a lot of coughing and spewing of seawater – and probably rum punch.

"Justin!" Dalmore calls from above. Looking up at him, I can distinguish at least four different expressions on his face in about three seconds. "Are you *all right?*"

After perhaps five more seconds, Justin, voice high pitched and raspy, emits a nevertheless comforting, "Yes." And after another pause, adds, "I guess I drank too much."

I turn to my shivering cousin. I'm overcome with admiration.

"Where did you learn all that?" I ask.

Kevin exhales heavily again. "Boy Scouts," he says, softly. "Just Boy Scouts."

# 13

I have my sweatshirt back. And a pair of jeans I brought along, knowing the vicissitudes of temperature encountered during a day on northern waters, replace my pretty-much soaked shorts. The cockpit seems like a sanctuary. That water was cold. Lucinda now wears her jumpsuit over cutoffs and tee. And she is sitting beside me. Actually, she's not in her trademark, artist/freedom-fighter, jumpsuit. This one is orange. I guess, now since she came afoul of the law she has gone from mocking militarism to mocking the penal system. Who was it – Eugene Debs – who said, "wherever there is a man in jail, I am there with him?" Could he really have believed everything was *society's* fault? And therefore no individual should ever pay? Though I wouldn't say she exactly *snuggles* against me, her body language indicates that she leans my way. A parallel reality seems to exist for my cousin Kevin. Deborah, by her posture, shows a similar tropism to his physical presence. This is probably the best moment the Perkins family has had since it came to the New World. Kevin looks funny, though. His Boy Scout rescue training – the part that wasn't taught to him in the First Congregational Church basement – was all imparted at lakefront. So he was unprepared for the weather on the North Atlantic – especially if you include having been fully clothed while under it. Like a lot of more cerebral denizens of cold-water coastlines, he's actually spent little time on or in the ocean. So he brought no warm-up clothes. Why should he have? It said 89 degrees on the bank thermometer, I – and likely he – passed on his way to Dalmore's dock. A better cousin than I am might have called to tell him what was what. I had thought about it. But, *one*: I, at seven years younger, didn't want to suggest to him that he might be less prepared than me. And, *two*: I had no idea that he, six hours from when I might have made that call, would have become a soaking wet hero. Kevin looks funny because he is in a pair of Dalmore's crew's foul weather pants and a yellow slicker; both items three sizes too big. He looks about as heroic as Frodo Baggins or Sam Gamgee might have in dead orc clothes. But Frodo and Sam were still heroes – even in their baggies. And so is Kevin. It's all relative. Justin Bollard is sitting in clothes *five* sizes too big. But then no one expects him to look like a hero.

Justin is apparently not playing a victim either, he is not letting his drunken mishap and near-death experience get him down. I think he's in denial. He even is acting strangely empowered. He started babbling – while still coughing and disoriented, as he was lifted into the cockpit – that he was now a peer of Pascal. Blaise Pascal was a French philosopher whose world and world-view were powerfully altered in a single moment. He *almost* fell out of a speeding carriage – the door of which opened of its own accord at the edge of a precipice – *into the void*.

"The *authenticity!*" he kept exclaiming for the first several minutes. – Bollard, not Pascal. Although I don't really know, Pascal may well have said the same thing in French at the time of his own near miss. It seems likely, in fact. Justin – though suddenly a convert to *authenticity* – is not necessarily ready to acknowledge the possibility of *originality* in the world of 1983. If he did though, applying it to himself might be characterized in the philosophical community as a win/win: *He is a man authentic and original.* But some might say it is a lose/lose: *Isn't he the guy that made his reputation on the conviction that nothing is original?* And therefore not authentic – depending on how convincingly he might be able to put it. My question is whether he is still too close to the authentic state he was just rescued from, to *realize* anything? Or is it that, in being what strikes me as a quintessential inauthentic creature of hip society, he might still be denying with his last breath on earth? – Provided that his windpipe is not too filled with seawater. But perhaps I am being too harsh. And, I don't know – I always thought the philosopher in the coach was Descartes. But that was because Descartes is the only French philosopher I would have been able to name – before Bollard reminded me there even *was* a Pascal.

I have my own view of what Bollard is experiencing. I think he is feeling *relieved* and doesn't quite know it. And in my philosophical opinion, *relief* is the most powerful feeling a person can have. The greatest sensation there is. I've never heard anybody else say this, though. I got this idea when I had a bad head cold a few years ago. Both nostrils were blocked and I could breathe only through my mouth for days. – Well, it seemed like days; maybe it was just hours. – Not really torture, compared to some of the things nature and the mind of man can dream up. But it was unpleasant enough to make a non-stoic like me pretty miserable. Well, suddenly one nostril seemed to give a tiny "pop" and a little cool-seeming air streamed through. It was better than an orgasm. I now had maybe 20% of normal nose breathing capacity. But by comparison to zero it was heaven. Anyway, the first thing that occurred to me was a question: If 20% is this good why am I not dancing in ecstasy all the time that I am breathing normally? Well, I know why: human perversity – we feel what we feel *relatively* rather than *absolutely*, and that means *we get used to things.* Anyway, I told my little theory about the primacy of relief in the pantheon of emotions to a woman at the first party I attended after I got well. And though she smiled, she slowly shook her head all the time I was talking. And when I finished she said, "Oh, no. I'm a

156

dancer. And when I'm performing on stage – getting applause – nothing could even come close to *that* feeling." Then, apparently bored with me, she moved off. So I wrote down on a paper cocktail napkin, *anybody who thinks glory and ecstasy are better feelings than relief should be asked about it again with a loaded gun pointed at her head.* Then I went and found her and put the napkin in her hand. She looked at it a few seconds, puzzled, and then gave a snort and said, "Okay – you got me!"

So I say to Bollard, trying to sound as much the banal provincial as I can, "Relief is the greatest sensation there is." He just gives me a mini-glance like those jabs that Mohammed Ali would throw that nobody could see until the slow motion replay. And he continues on as if he hasn't heard at all.

"What happened and why it happened was a perfect manifestation of the union of sufficiencies at a particular moment. Had the wind been, perhaps, one – what do you call it? – knot less, I would never have fallen," Bollard says, apparently beginning what I imagine will be the first of at least several postmortems. I, as you might imagine, have a slightly different analysis. I believe that even if the wind had been five or even ten knots less he still would have fallen. However, if he had had five or ten *fewer* plastic cups of rum punch, even if the wind had been several knots stronger, he probably would have stayed below hunting for the caviar that Rebecca and I removed from the boat's stores. But he continues with certainty, "Had the wind been a knot greater, caution would have ruled. And I would have remained in the – what do you call it? – gangway?"

"Companionway," say three or four of his helpful listeners.

Bollard smiles, assuming their attention to him – which I think is a symptom of *relief* of their own that he is able to talk at all – comes from fascination with what he is saying. I, myself, am fascinated at how resilient *in-authenticity* can be.

Rebecca, perhaps hoping to shift the conversation on to a more general philosophical area – while still humoring the salvaged Bollard – says, "I've often thought about how very different life on this planet might be if some of the factors of nature were only of a tiny degree changed from what they are now." I notice that she has very nice diction.

"Like what?" asks Kahn.

"Well," she says. "What if the wind were always higher than it is – say an average of 10 knots – or miles – per hour more; I don't know what a knot is – which is greater?"

"Knots," says Kahn. Then he says, "So?"

"Well, if it were always very windy, would more boats have been lost as a matter of course? I mean, would going to sea have been a lot riskier? And, therefore, would the discovery of the New World have been later in human history? Or perhaps some of the northernmost cities – Leningrad, *St. Petersburg*, when it was founded (I can't think of another one right now) maybe they would have stayed just towns or villages if the wind chill had made it seem like a less pleasant place to build palaces for czars and czarinas." Justin, I see, has an authentic expression on his face: the look of a person afraid he is being cheated. But Rebecca continues and he brightens when he hears his name, "How much wind would have been *sufficient*, to use Justin's word, to make the use of a sail something no one would ever consider? Therefore perhaps no New World discovered at all. Or maybe, not discovered *yet*?"

Dalmore takes up the theme. "Yes," he says, jutting chin and lips up and moving eyebrows down, "And what if the tides had a greater range – a range that is still reasonable to imagine for thousands of miles of water, miles deep, on a sphere spinning at 1000 miles an hour through the void of space? The tidal range in front of my house averages about eight and a half feet. What if that eight or nine thousand miles of tide that comes up from the tip of Africa were to slouch a hundred feet rather than eight? Seems not unreasonable, given the eight thousand miles. The tide would probably come in faster than a man could run. Then no one might ever go to the ocean except at high tide – for fear of being swamped."

"I wonder if anyone would ever have taken a boat onto the sea in that case at all," Kevin says, joining in. His current hero stature does not inhibit Dalmore's implying that Kevin is condoning wimpishness.

"Of course, we would have." He says as if his manhood has just been challenged.

"I grant fewer would 'go down to the sea in ships.'" A corner of his mouth rises as if he is pleased with himself for having gone biblical. "But many of us would still go. Men adapt."

"Perhaps," says Justin, trying to retake the floor – or the deck. "But there would be a *sufficiency*, a level beyond which certain things would become impossible." He seems to be trying to make it sound like this all is what he had been getting at when he introduced the term "sufficiency" to the group. – But related *not* to the concept, for example, of a person being sufficiently drunk to fall overboard. Hadn't having had too much to drink been his initial – *authentic* – explanation for his presence in the North Atlantic? That's what he called out ignominiously from his prone position in the rubber boat. Like a good Postmodernist, Bollard *appropriates* as necessary: in this case, Rebecca's novel conversation piece. But she, either out of insensitivity to his needs or out of healthy needs of her own, says,

"Well, that's not exactly my point – though it does follow from it, I guess. I was only thinking about how different things might be if physical facts were only *slightly* different. It could even be about things to do with the human body."

"Like what?" Deborah asks, cocking her head a little.

"Oh, I don't know," says Rebecca. "I can't think of anything right off."

Do I detect a blush on that almost too lovely face? What if some women were so lovely men couldn't stand it? Well, I guess that's already true.

"I've got something," Lucinda jumps in for the first time. "What if men got erections whenever they were around women they were attracted to? – Attracted, even just a little. I mean got them *uncontrollably* and *immediately*. How would that change things?"

Kahn claps his hands and slouches deeply, apparently delighted with Lucinda's creative style.

"Or *men* who attracted them," Bollard says brightening. The whole idea is intriguing enough that he doesn't need authorship. "That would be the end of a man being able to hide his desires in the closet."

"Unless he did it literally," Dalmore says dryly, raising one eyebrow. I can't tell if he is making a funny face to go with his funny idea.

"Well, *you* wouldn't have to worry about that," I say directly to Bollard. He looks daggers at me. Everyone else stares too. "I mean," I say, "in all that foul weather gear nobody would be able to detect anything…I mean…unless you …" I start to realize that, in addition to my having perhaps driven this man to drink earlier in the day – almost resulting in his death – I am now implying that his penis is probably quite small. "…Unless we all went around in foul weather gear." The looks I'm getting say that I am digging a deeper hole for myself. I glance at Lucinda – *my date* – the one who put us all on this slippery slope with her seemingly habitual sexualizing. She's no help. I remember that I first encountered Justin in the role of a Lucinda groupie. Kevin looks uncomfortable. Already yesterday's hero. I see that Rebecca is giving me a smirk that I suppose could be taken either way. But, now is not the moment to weigh the relative likelihoods. I quickly add – though it seems like minutes – "I mean, probably men would be the ones wearing skirts."

Luckily this sparks some ethnic pride in Dalmore and he says "Maybe that is why we Scotsmen do wear the skirts." He throws his head back in exaggerated self-congratulation. – Another of his "laughing-mimes" impersonations. Since he is our captain – and later to be our host (his wife will have "a little something" waiting for us to eat upon our return) – all the assembled force varying degrees of hardy laughter. This ends my awkward moment satisfactorily – except for eye contact from Justin lingering after everyone else having moved on to individual small talk, related and not related to a world of stronger winds and harder men.

About a mile and a half off Northport on the return leg of the voyage to the Shoals, the sea breeze finally drops and the southwesterly wind of earlier in the day resumes. This means we "have it on the nose." But the breeze is light, and after several tacks a vote is taken to drop the sails and motor into homeport. The air surrounding us is again fat with humidity – as on each day of this enfolding early mid-summerish heat. Everyone but Kevin and Justin has stripped back to summer wear. Their bodies have dried, but their clothes haven't quite. And both over-dressed men have drops of sweat running down their foreheads – taking the place of the seawater that was streaming from their soaked heads of hair two hours ago. The sunset that's underway, though not one to have risked death for, would be worth the excursion by itself. A band of sky at 30 degrees above the horizon glows subtropical azure blue. Just under that a swatch of violet hangs in smoky peach. Conversation pretty much dies as the sky comes alive. Each person appears wrapped in a transparent shell – singular, but seemingly without the self-consciousness that Justin asserted was inevitable for beings of our time and culture. This is why I love sailing.

Near total darkness covers us as we enter the main harbor. Tiny red and green port and starboard lights flit across the water – color-echoes of the luminous orbs of tinted humidity on our bow. Two sets of these red and green dots, traveling at oblique angles from opposite sides of the waterway, converge with our course. They are heading for the center of the channel. I can hear distant laughter and the pop of snap can tabs. Then we leave the channel, veer to port, and head for Jack's Cove – away from average-Joe motor-boaters putting to sea for a cold beer on the third or fourth warm early season night. We weave through a group of moored yachts, but no fishing boats, inside the Jack's Cove jetty on our way to Dalmore's private dock. As we approach, I can see what looks like all the lights in his incongruously modern and angular harbor-front home shining. He told us proudly, when we all assembled on the lawn there at noon, how he had

161

succeeded in constructing a 90 percent new edifice on only a remodeling permit from the building commission. It had been necessary to keep intact only the back wall of the rambling, weathered cottage that had stood on the spot for 110 years. Well, I had always liked that old house. But it was no match for this structure – except to the mawkishly sentimental. Old is bad. However, I must admit to mawkish sentimentality.

I balance on the port bow, line in hand. As is customary when approaching a dock, especially in the dark, the diesel inboard is at idle; we are creeping at a toddler's pace. We round into what little is left of the breeze, at an oblique angle so we can skim the wooden structure and bump along ineffectually on the inflated plastic fenders that we've hung out along our port rail. But we feel a jolt, and the boat, abruptly and unfathomably ceasing forward motion, pretty much bounces to starboard – perhaps ten feet away from its destination.

"What the Christ?" calls Dalmore. "Perkins, what did you miss? What did we hit?" Well, I suppose it is my fault. But nothing was or is visible. And nothing was expected.

"Perkins!"

After a pause I say, "I don't... see anything. Can I get a flashlight and boathook up here."

Kahn is ahead of the curve and is already approaching with both. But Dalmore is impatient and says, "I'm going around to come in on starboard. – Deborah! Fenders to the starboard rail."

Kahn is raking the water's surface with the light but we are now far off the spot where we encountered the obstruction. He and I move to starboard as we make the second approach. Eight or ten feet out from our new landing point, thirty feet west of the first one, we "bounce" again.

"What the Christ?" Dalmore shouts again, bellowing this time.

I notice a faint but unpleasant scent creeping into what had been fragrant early summer evening air. Kahn's flashlight reflects off of something dark and bulbous on the black water's surface. He looks at me for confirmation. "Hmm," I say.

Kahn turns toward the cockpit and says matter-of-factly to his captain at the helm, "I think we've got a whale."

"What?" says Dalmore. "What did you say?"

"I said, 'I think we've got a whale.'"

# 14

My hard-to-read female friend – not quite or not yet *girl*friend – is right now giving signals of girlfriendship. For most of today's cruise on the *Pure Conception* she acted indifferent to me. Right now – about ten p.m. – I'm driving Lucinda home from Arthur Dalmore's deck party – an event that, subverted by a demise on a very large-scale, ended early. Although I'm listening solicitously, ambivalence – perhaps mirroring her own – remains my interior mode regarding Lucinda. This young woman is recounting her impressions of a rather eventful day – one of fun, near death, and death. But she seems most interested in feedback about her role as Ship's Muse, her performance in the impromptu *De'jeuner sur la Mer*. This is gratifying. She's displaying feet of clay – her real feet being the only part of her anatomy that she didn't already display. "You don't think anybody had a problem with that, do you?" She phrases the inquiry in a way that assumes the answer she wants. But asking, regardless of semantic form, implies self-consciousness. I've wondered about this. This may be the first time she's asked my opinion of anything. So here's a little breakthrough. Perhaps it is again the result of drink. She consumed quite a bit, by my informal reckoning tonight. Drink sure seemed to shatter barriers the night of the day we met. Of course there are other ways to look at it. One happy alternative might be that this is the first time we've been alone since that first night. Translation: although Lucinda seems so *public,* she requires privacy for intimacy. That wouldn't be unusual. But I'm afraid her distance from me in public hinges more on her perhaps perceiving that a relationship with me would not be a career enhancer. Another happy explanation for her interest in my opinion – and in my person, which she touches now and then to emphasize her commitment to the various things she's talking about – may be that I acquitted myself reasonably well today. Alex, handler of the Zodiac and fisher of men – pulling Lucinda's mentor, Justin Bollard, from the pull of the drink. Both kinds of drink. And I may even have gotten a few points as a fisher of fishermen: In fairly short order I set up the pending rescue of the Dalmore household from the aroma of rotting blubber. The cavalry arrives at dawn and I will ride with it. Tomorrow morning I will be assisting Fred Avery, my fisherman neighbor, in disposing of the dead whale that has bobbed in and deposited itself under Arthur Dalmore's dock. I'm fearful of what *helping* might mean in this case. But I have ended a long day – which began with me as a peripheral player – pretty much in the center of things. I hope I know better than to let that status-boost go to my head.

Lucinda lives in one of the many renovated, brick, former factory buildings that line the Agamenticus River. (Northport had a textile-producing, as well as a sea-going, past.) The coffee shop where I met John Hulton sits two factory blocks away, and the next building houses Hulton's studio. I've learned from attending open studios in one of those adjacent buildings that some of the loft spaces are pretty nice. Lucinda lives one of those. Lucinda's family has money. Well, Northport-level money, anyway. Gram told me that, the day after Lucinda's visit. Florence Stacey, Lucinda's grandmother, married one of the five York boys. The York family has owned dry-cleaning establishments all over the North Shore for three generations, and the Northport Cadillac dealership for two. Clean clothes and a clean car. The perfect heritage for a rebel daughter to challenge. This makes her desire for arrest even more loaded. And what turns up in the paper more problematic. I guess I could tell that Lucinda, for all her freedom-fighter proclivities – or because of them – was at least comfortably middle class. Her sense of entitlement, in the face of Middle America's assault at Blue Heron Beach, bespoke the background of someone either raised on the streets or else sheltered from them. The cost of art school gave the nod to the latter.

This will be my first time past Lucinda's door, or even to it. I picked her up in her building's small parking lot this morning. Parking seems to be a problem here – one that Lucinda wants me to address *spiritually*.

"We have to be open to finding a parking space," she says when we are within a few blocks of her place.

"Okay, I'm open to it," I reply cheerily; though I've got a caution light flashing about where she may be going with this. I assume that a 1980's American being "open to" something means he or she is deeply conversant with the wisdom of the East.

"I mean really open," she says. "From your center. Open – but not *attached*."

Right – not attached. Jeez! How could I be such a silly? I was stupidly attached to finding a parking space so I could forget about my car quickly and go have sex. Zen is sooo simple and I am sooo thick. Okay – I do some fast mental calisthenics; now I'm no longer attached. I'm clear. I'm so attachment-proof right now that I could drive around this block for the next ten hours and still not get reattached to the concept of finding a place to leave the damn car and go climb on this girl. Concepts are just sooo bogus. Imagine, for example, becoming attached to a concept like doubting the probability of a previous concept just because it sounded *far-fetched*. (There's a word you won't find in the New Age Gospel: Far-fetched.)

I actually went along with things like this for a while in my post-LSD, let's-go-to-India phase. – It's pretty hard not to get soft-headed after acid has made you see things seem to melt and flow. You think: The real world of atomic energy has been revealed. – Rather than: I have temporarily fucked-up my nerve synapses. It's – again – the difference between *figuratively* and *literally*. Maybe after you die things really actually do *flow*. But in the material world they really don't. And atomic energy doesn't overwhelm the law of averages.

"I'm not attached," I say docilely. It's true, I'm not. I'm just pretty fucking *hopeful*. But hopefulness is sooo Western. I'm in touch enough with the universe to tell that in the vortex of dark air feeding into and out of my little convertible on a hot early summer night Lucinda is scrutinizing me for unwanted irony. That's funny because she loves irony. After her body, it's her main thing. Well, I guess, irony is as irony does. (I have no idea what I mean by that.)

"There! There's one," she says. "See – works every time." I whip into a space a pickup truck with teenagers in the back is vacating. They wave madly at the cute little convertible.

"Every time?" I ask, trying to project sincere discernment – to morph skepticism into something that isn't going to prevent me from getting laid tonight.

"Well, not *every* time," she says, falling for my disingenuousness, thank Krishna. "Non-attachment is hard to achieve."

"That's true," I say. I'd like to add, "So is non-mechanical flight for those who aren't birds." But I don't.

We stop on the third floor landing and Lucinda says, "I forgot my key. But Avrum is always home." What if he isn't, I wonder? "Who's Avrum?" I ask.

"Avrum's great," Lucinda non-answers. "And there's Bruce, too. But they're just friends now. Avrum is why Justin is here." *Justin?* I think. Did she mean Justin is *here?* My look conveys adequately. "Justin is probably at his hotel," she says.

"I got the idea he was staying with Dalmore?"

"He is," she explains. "But the jets in Dalmore's hot tub are broken. So he has a hotel room too."

"Aah," I say. Amazing how fearless this man still is around water.

There is an incongruous Victorian lion's-head knocker. Lucinda gives it a rap.

"Who is it?" I hear through the door – or through the light-emitting inch and a half of gap beneath it.

"The Spanish Inquisition," Lucinda says in a BBC accent.

"We were just expecting you," the gap replies.

There are a number of different kinds of clicks, then the door swings open. The very slender figure on the other side of the door is the young man who bickered with Lucinda in the coffee shop where I went to meet Hulton – and who wielded the camera at her performance on the beach. Avrum is a very beautiful boy. Boy, I say, but he's perhaps twenty-two or twenty-three.

Avrum gives me an eyelash-bat that is, nevertheless, dismissive. Not that easy to do. He says "Hi," so softly I am not sure he did say it. Then running – or almost skipping – across the high-sheen hardwood floor, says, louder than necessary, "We're playing *Mad Libs*. Come *play*."

"We're playing *Dirty* Mad Libs," says a slightly overweight man closer to my age. Three or four years younger, maybe.

"What's 'Mad Libs'?" I ask, trying to seem as though I'm feeling right at home. It is one of those moments where I'm paranoid everyone will act as if they haven't heard my question just to show me how unimportant I am. Maybe I shouldn't admit I have those moments.

"Lucinda, who *is* this *guy*?" Avrum demands with theatrical shock.

"You've never played Mad Libs?" She echoes his amazement.

"No, I…"

"Mad Libs is a poetic Ouija board," Avrum says. "It reveals your true nature."

Lucinda decides to help: "It's a children's word game. Little stories in a book – just paragraphs – with words left out. You fill in one blank when it's your turn. – *Out of context* though. – You don't know the story, just the subject. You supply what you're thinking."

"We're thinking about *sex*," says Avrum, batting those long lashes again. "But here," he says, "have a toot first. It's more fun that way." Evidently these young men have been tooting away for a while.

On the coffee table is a gilt framed little mirror – probably courtesy of whoever picked out the doorknocker. And appearing to float on it are a razor blade, a little cocktail straw, and a smattering of white powder. I've tried cocaine exactly twice before. I scored it from Jeff, *Currents'* photographer. I'd heard from him how it enhances sex. He'd said this quietly, glancing around the paper's basement photo shop – looking out for Steve, I imagine. It was hard to tell if he was more worried about the boss finding him selling a bit of coke on company property or his hearing a mention of something that enhances sex – without his having any of it offered.

I smoked pot for a while but have stopped. Pot was good for sex, eating, and sleeping, usually in that order – if I was lucky. All three of those might occur within about 15 minutes. But the head stuff with pot got to be not worth it. I'd be too aware of other people's *otherness*. Not too pleasant. Of course the alien nature of a woman's body when I was stoned is probably what made the sex more exciting. Like I'd just met her and it was our first time. But eventually, if the scene was not conducive to going to bed with anybody there, I would turn down the joint when it was passed. This was not a good social move. In those days being *uptight* was as bad as being pro-war. And turning down a joint unquestionably meant you were uptight. So I adopted a pose – I'm embarrassed to admit – of putting the joint to my lips and making hissing intake sounds. I didn't inhale, but I tried to appear to. Inhaling was a kind of affirmation of group solidarity – like forcing myself to eat a few of Naomi Dalmore's anchovies earlier tonight instead of saying "Yeck," when the tray came my way. Well, not exactly the same; anchovies aren't considered a sacrament in any subculture I know.

"Ooo, it's nice to be home after a hard day at sea," Lucinda says as she picks up the razor and straw. In a few deft moves, she has caused about a third of the white powder to disappear into her sinuses. She passes the implements to me. Seeing that cocaine is a solid – and not a gas, like marijuana's delivery system: smoke – I can't *pretend* to consume it. So, I'll just consume a moderate amount. A phrase pops into my head: *moderation is the soul of mediocrity*. Where did I hear that? Aren't I here for the lived life? Today has been something of an adventure. And the day is not over. Besides, in my two imbibings of coke, I didn't feel the alienation I associate with being high on pot. So does coke make sex better? Didn't have the opportunity to find out. What I noticed from coke was a *general* excitedness, an apprehensiveness – a pleasant sensation that I was *about to* feel like something was *about to* happen. Then it would start to pass without anything happening really. No *peaking* – like with acid. Coke seemed like heading up the slope and then rolling back down without ever making it over the top. This implied to me, if you went just a little further – snorted just a little more – you might just make it. But both times I'd been too moderate to find out.

"Oh, that's *right!*" says Avrum. "Your *boat ride*. Where's *Justin?* How did he like his first time in a *boat?*"

"First time in a boat..." I mumble.

"You'd better ask him," Lucinda says.

"Where *is* he?" Avrum presses.

"Try his hotel," says Lucinda. " But let it ring. He's probably in the tub."

"But it's so hot out *already*. I had to put on the air conditioning," Avrum objects.

"Give him a call," Lucinda repeats.

"We're going over there later, anyway," Roger says. "After one more game. Come on, everybody, time to play. Everybody sit over here." There is a couch on either side of a coffee table. Avrum and Bruce appear to have been occupying the farther one. Avrum picks up a book that is more of a pad. "Mad Libs" is written in explosive, psychedelic lettering on its cover.

"O*kay*," he says. He flips through the pad. "Oh, good-*dee*," he says. "Here's one for young lov-*vers*." He gives us a saccharine smile and his eyelash-bat. Very sarcastic. "Okay," he says again. 'A Letter From An Admirer.' Me first; then Bruce; then – what's-his-name? Then Lucinda."

I realize we haven't been introduced. Somehow I don't take that personally. In a world where you're offered illegal drugs by strangers, names are not critical. Not knowing may even be preferable. But I say, "Alex."

"Nice *name*!" says Avrum. "Al – *ex*," he says, like a twelve year old girl. Cute, I think. "O-*kay*! For your first blank we need a person in the room. I vote: *Lucinda*." He stretches elegantly to reach a pen on the coffee table and writes, apparently this, on the pad. Then he says, "Bruce, we need a noun. It doesn't have to be funny as long as it's dirty. After each turn – if I like your word – you get to do a line." He takes an envelope from his shirt pocket and sprinkles more white powder on the mirror. I can't tell if he gets to make the rules because he has the cocaine or just *because*.

"Dildo," says Bruce.

"Excellent start," Avrum says, and writes this down. "Do your line.

"Alex? – We need an adjective."

"Compound words okay?" I ask.

"Say what?"

"Hyphenated words?"

"Try me," Avrum says.

"Fucked-up," I say.

"Very good," Avrum congratulates. "Compound words are *very* admissible." He gestures elegantly to the gilted mirror, "Have a snort." Nobody seems to take my adjective as a comment on the proceedings. "Lucinda – another adjective?"

"Sex-addicted," she says. She obviously has hyphens in her quiver, too.

"A little clinical, but I'll allow it. My turn again. Another person in the room," he reads from the pad. "Let's see, I'll say, 'Bruce.' Now

Bruce: your turn. Another adjective. What a lot of *adjective*s."

"Throbbing," says Bruce. He hasn't seemed to catch on that hyphenated words give you more bang for the buck.

"Not dirty enough – no coke for you," Avrum says. "Alex?"

"Well-hung," I say. Avrum smiles as if I had said this just for him.

"Lucinda – a noun?"

"White-trash," she says.

"I'm going to allow it. It's the wrong kind of dirty, but it has possibilities."

Avrum the munificent says. "My turn again. I like these *hyphens*. Humm. Okay ass-licking."

"Bruce – another adjective for you."

"Doggie-style," says Bruce, catching on, but with an exaggerated yawn. Perhaps cocaine has a paradoxical effect on him.

"Good – take a snort." He points the pen at me. "Adjective?"

"Cum-filled," I say.

Avrum squints at me. "Lucinda, do we have a ringer here? Take a snort," he says.

"He's a writer," Lucinda says.

"That *explains* it. Lucinda – your word?"

"What?"

"Your turn."

"What part of speech?"

"Oh, *pardonnez-moi*! – Adjective."

"Ball-busting ," she says.

"Good one. My turn. I need an adjective. I'll say 'disgusting.' It's not strictly dirty, so no coke for me. But disgust is part of being human.

"Bruce – adjective?"

"Grotesque," says Bruce.

"Not dirty. I'll allow it, but no coke."

"Al-ex. An adjective from you."

"Pig-fucking," I say, going for broke.

"Touché. Lucinda, I think you've found a keeper. Adjective,

Lucinda."

"Reaming," she says.

"Not particularly creative, but nice, I guess. I'll allow it. Do your line. My turn. A noun. Let's see. I think, 'pelvic exam.' Is that a compound word or just two words? It's clinical, too – but it's not *merely* clinical. Bruce – a hard one: the rounds first *adverb*?"

I'm wondering about Bruce's age. How long has he been out of school? Does he even remember what an adverb is?

"Sadistically," Bruce says.

"Just passes," says Avrum. "– Alex? Person in the room?"

"Alex Perkins," I say, laying it all on the line.

"I'm going to allow it. But you hardly get cocaine for saying your own name – no matter how highly I prize vanity in a man.

"Well, it seems that brings us to the end of our love letter. And our secret admirer of the obscure object, Lucinda, is none other than our newest player, Alex. I'm sure Alex Perkins would like to thank you all for playing Cyrano to his Christian." Avrum pauses theatrically. I'm impressed. I couldn't have told you whom Cyrano wrote for. Maybe he's bullshitting. But he's got the tone of authority.

Well, I'm not sure how I'm feeling. I think I had three *earned* lines after the initial free one. I skipped one intentionally in a cocaine version of not inhaling, and no one seemed to notice. Or if they did maybe they thought my loss would be their gain. So how am I feeling? Well – alert, nervous, kind of excited. I feel a nice hum. How high am I? Strong pot high – but without feeling like my head is filled with smoke. I can feel a big grin is frozen on my face. Avrum clears his throat elaborately.

"The envelope please." Another pause during which he looks each of us in the face like a sergeant-major testing the metal of his men. "Okay. Here it is – our letter from Lucinda's covert admirer. It reads: 'Dear Lucinda, You may not remember me. I was the one with the stylish *dildo* at the socially *fucked-up* party thrown by our *sex-addicted* friend, *Bruce*. When we talked we were in *throbbing* agreement about *well-hung white trash*, and I was impressed by your *ass-licking* level of conversation and your enthusiastic reaction to the *doggie-style* intermingling of people of different ages and social backgrounds. Also, I was very attracted to your *cum-filled* little nose and your *ball-busting* eyes. If you'll pardon me for being *disgusting*, I'll say I was really fascinated by your *grotesque* walk and your *pig-fucking* figure. I hope I made a *reaming* impression and that we can get together for a nice *pelvic exam* sometime next week. *Sadistically* yours, Alex Perkins."'

Avrum claps his long, slender hands together and throws back his head.

"Oh, it's sooo true." He says, "Mad Libs never lies. Alex Perkins, we've read your mind."

Lucinda and Bruce are laughing through frozen grins similar to the one I imagine covers my face. – We're a lascivious tableau from an Italian fountain, transplanted to a factory in Northport, Massachusetts. This is probably what fun was like in ancient Rome. Or at that other factory – Warhol's – fifteen years ago in Soho. All three denizens of this loft are looking at me now as though I had planned and composed the lecherous and perverse "admiring" letter all on my own. I can't tell if this beautiful boy control-freak has succeeded in convincing his stoned-out friends that his inane analysis of the game is reality, or if they are all of a single mind in making a goat of me, the interloper? I actually feel myself blushing, as if I am a sexual predator who has just been publicly exposed – but to an oddly enthusiastic citizenry. And, what do you know, folks? I realize I'm extraordinarily horny. This may be the legendary cocaine effect. However, right now the dirty words seem to be somewhat like post-hypnotic suggestions. I've considered the potential of talking dirty enhancing a sexual moment, but it always seemed a little forced. As usual, I was too moderate. I do have to admit – drugged or not – Avrum's little word game has had a liberating effect on me.

And in my very stoned state, I contemplate this provocative and willful young man whom I have already acknowledged as "beautiful." I study him as a strictly academic inquiry to judge whether all his sexualizing – his stock in trade, I imagine – is contributing to my excitement. Put simply, I'm wondering, *does he turn me on*? Men never have before. But I am really stoned, and Avrum is really something. Well, I…guess…really…*not*. Sure, I find something sensual, when I study his fine features. But it's just not for me. Right now, all I want is to get to be alone with Lucinda and explore my heterosexuality. But I don't know exactly how to get from here to there.

It turns out it's not my job to make that happen. Glances are exchanged between Lucinda and Avrum. They have an understanding. Lucinda's drugged-up grin melts quickly into a smirk, and Avrum, doing a saucy shoulder shake says, "Well, Bruce, shall we go see our benefactor?" I'm at a loss for a second. Then I remember that heading for Justin's hotel had been introduced "for later" when we first arrived. I get a quick picture of the kind of Northport sensual scene that could tear Justin Bollard away from New York: *Sex and cocaine at factory outlet prices – courtesy of a world-class, dirty-minded, olive-skinned pretty boy, as pretty as any you'll find on Broadway.* Well, anyway, I'm delighted they're going.

They slip out quietly, as though decorum was finally, at long last, expected.

Lucinda smiles.

Without getting into all the details, I'll say that when it was all over and my head started to clear – and you come down from this stuff pretty fast – I remembered one of my favorite sex scenes in any movie: the after-opera encounter in Woody Allen's *Love and Death*. The Russian Countess and the hero, Boris, finally find themselves alone in her lavish bedroom. She wears a grand gown. He, a high-buttoned uniform. They stare wantonly at each other. A grandfather clock is shown striking midnight. The scene dissolves. Then, in a moment, it reappears; now in turmoil. Furniture has been overturned and broken. Drapes are down and twisted – and these hide the privates of the now naked, exhausted couple on the floor. The clock strikes 12:02. Lucinda's and my bout wasn't exactly like that, but it probably came as close as I'll ever manage without special effects.

But talk about *post-coital letdown*…

What now I wonder?

I – not wanting to betray the distance I'm feeling – avoid an abrupt disengagement with the nevertheless still pleasant warmth of Lucinda's body, sleeping in the now too cool conditioned air of the loft. How can she sleep on that much cocaine? But, as with alcohol, perhaps she has a tolerance level that I don't. I feel I need to ask her about this. But first I want to get my bearings a little. I try to look around with only a minimal turning of my head. I've focused only on the people, since I got here. The interpersonal stuff all happened too fast for me to really take the place in – other than an impression that this is not like the lofts of artists I've visited before. It's really quite nice. Comfortable. There's the air conditioning, first of all – something I doubt many artists in their twenties – or any age, for that matter – can afford. All the wood surfaces shine with the rich butterscotch of many layers of polyurethane. The lighting is low. Little track spots glow in rows. I realize Avrum must have rheostat-ed them down as he and Roger departed. Thoughtful little bastard. My guess is he's enough of a master of matters sexual to know ambiance can be critical. In this case, it's critical to cushioning post-coital let-down. I wonder if he assumed it likely. I was far too goal-obsessed to notice the lighting before or during the actual sex act. "Sex act." "Sex act." The words ring in my ears, though no one has spoken them. I realize I've not come down. I'm still quite high.

Well, back to my survey. A flashing and elaborate-looking espresso maker sits on the floral-tiled counter. I guess those are Mexican tiles. Angela and I went to Mexico on our honeymoon. I get a pang of nostalgia, then remember the amoebic dysentery, and am glad to be here-now rather than there-then. More to look at. The stove is that black cast iron kind that I know costs a lot. Several nearly life-sized photos of Lucinda in the garb – or lack of garb – of past performances decorate the walls. One picture shows Lucinda, Avrum, and Bollard scrunched together, mugging for the camera. What about poor Bruce? There he is: in a photo wherein he's dressed ironically – or perhaps *sincerely* – as a stockbroker. Maybe he *is* a stockbroker.

Then I spot a couple paragraphs of just type, large enough to read at this distance, printed out on a sheet the size of *Currents*. It says:

*Be Drunken*

*Be always drunken. Nothing else matters: that is the only question.*
*If you would not feel the horrible weight of Time weighing on your shoulders and crushing you to the earth, be drunken continually.*

*Drunken with what? With wine, with poetry, or with virtue, as you will. But be drunken.*

*And if sometimes, on the stairs of a palace, or the green side of a ditch, or in the dreary solitude of your own room, you should awake and the drunkenness be half or wholly slipped away from you, ask of the wind, or of the wave, or of the star, or of the bird, or of whatever flies, or sighs, or rocks, or sings, or speaks, ask what hour it is: and the wind, wave, star, bird, clock, will answer you: "It is the hour to be drunken! Be drunken, if you would not be martyred slaves of time, be drunken continually! With wine, with poetry, or with virtue, as you will."*

*Baudelaire*

Wow. Except for the poems my mother taught me, poetry is one of my weaker points. I'm too dyslexic to get it without a great deal of effort. But this is fantastic. ... *the stairs of a palace, or the green side of a ditch*... It doesn't get any better than that. But I'm coming down from being drunken. Drunken on a drug. And though there's the desire to imbibe more to continue to be drunken to avoid or postpone the coming down, I don't think it's a good idea. Maybe I think that because I'm not a poet – or an artist. I know I'm taking a metaphor too literally, but who could sustain drunkenness like that. Lucinda? Avrum? Baudelaire himself? And we all know how insufferable people "drunken with virtue" can be: televangelists, Lucinda's tormentor in the skirted bathing suit. I'm even too judgmental sometimes to want to be around myself. But this doesn't stop me from wanting to read more Baudelaire.

Though I am coming off a stimulant, I'm certainly not ready to think of sleep. I feel that Lucinda and I need to talk. I realize that I have yet to be really sincere with this young woman. I don't know if it is the drugs that want to do the talking, but I feel like it *is* time to talk. I'm still holding her in my arms – but from behind. She's wearing only a blouse that I seem to remember recently lost a few of its buttons. I have stayed in one position as long as I can. I stretch out of our left-over spoon configuration. Lucinda stirs and says, "Hi."

"Hi," I say.

"How did you like my roommates?" she asks.

What? I'm thinking – no, "Wow, that was great!"?

But, "Fun" is what I say.

"They're great," she says.

It confounds me that she proposes for postmortem something not between her and me but between me and them. This seems like a *male* distancing device. But I want to talk about more than superficials. I want to ask her about alcohol and drug consumption. But I realize that that only matters to me if we have some basic attitudes in common – a foundation for caring what the other one does. So instead I ask, "Do you really believe that stuff about finding a parking space by visualizing one?" Of course, I know she does, so this is really just me giving her shit. My doing this is the down side of drugs. The *coming down* side.

"You mean, you don't?" Lucinda says, attempting to shift her position to one not of classic submissiveness.

"Well, what do you think could make it work?" I ask, trying to back off from outright confrontation.

"Energy fields," she says matter-of-factly.

"I know that," I say, trying to inject the sound of genuine inquisitiveness into my trashing of something quite important to her. "But how do you think energy fields *work*?"

"I don't know," she says, "Everything is energy. It's just being open and feeling the currents."

"But how does energy change the *physical reality* – create the parking space?"

"What do you mean, 'create'? It's always there."

"Right," I say. "But the space has two thousand pounds of metal in it."

"So? Cars come and go all the time."

"Right," I say again. "But if everybody is home in that part of town and people are having dinner in the restaurants – and all the parking spaces are full – what makes someone leave just before you arrive?"

"What do you mean, 'what makes them leave?' I just said, 'people leave all the time.'"

"But you're saying they leave because of you?"

"Not *because* of me. In harmony *with* me."

"How's that different?"

"It's very different," Lucinda insists.

"You mean somebody, eating pasta in the restaurant with the checkered table cloths, decides that he and his wife are full and want to be out of there, when you are four blocks away because you start to *visualize* a parking space – *their* parking space. They skip dessert, pay the check fast, and pull out in the nick of time, so that you can pull in?"

"You're twisting it," this woman, possibly in the process at this very moment of conceiving my child, says helplessly.

"Well, you tell me how it works then," I say, trying to sound magnanimous and folding my arms like Mussolini.

"Well," Lucinda, still assuming I am open-minded, says, "it's all karma." She truly believes that dropping this venerable word will silence a naïve critic. Karma is both Hindu *and* Buddhist. Who would be so foolish as to argue with two of the greatest ancient traditions of the Eastern world – and over a parking space?

"So you're saying, because you're a good person, God will give you a parking space?"

"Not God!"

"What then?"

"The energy fields."

"The energy fields don't do what God wants?"

"Wait a minute," she says, "who said I even believe in God?"

179

"Well, you believe in *moral* energy fields."

"Why moral?"

"Why moral? The good get parking spaces. – Excuse me the *non-attached* good get parking spaces."

"Well, why not? I'm not being greedy. All I want is a fucking parking space."

"Why not? Why doesn't the positive energy field make sure that little black kids in Africa get food? Or medicine? Or even water? Do you actually think that an energy field that can't or won't provide the nourishment that anyone born onto this planet has the right to expect, would spend time trying to make sure that a pretty woman in the high rent part of the world should be able to abandon her two thousand pound metal transportation unit close enough to her shelter so that she doesn't have to get tired – or raped – walking a long way home?" Where is my heat coming from? I'm having a hard time not sounding contemptuous. I like to think of myself as *Mr. Tolerant.* I'll blame it on the coke.

"You're twisting *everything,*" Lucinda says. "The energy is different all over the world. It's a beautiful system and you make it sound racist – or worse – *elitist.*"

I want to sarcastically apologize for suggesting that this planet – where life is based on survival of the fittest, and one life form devouring another to achieve that – is *elitist.* But I look down and am surprised to see that I have put all my clothes on. I must have gotten dressed unconsciously as I pursued my argument. I have to try to be nicer.

"Of course," I say, truly speculating, "if there are local gods – spirits around the waterhole or something – and they like you – it could work the way you say. So maybe my problem isn't with the energy thing, but with monotheism. If Gods have favorites and compete, just like humans do – and the Greeks thought the gods did – then it could really work." But, I'm thinking that the only forces I ever see intervening on the part of *goodness* on planet Earth are *accident* and, as brutal or indifferent as people can be much of the time, *human compassion.* For all I know – for all its faults – the human mind may be the highest – or even *the only* – moral force in the universe.

Lucinda seems to teeter on the edge of believing me sincere, in speculating that one has to throw monotheism overboard to dependably find a place to park, or believing me a sarcastic shit. The trouble is I AM sincere – that is if I try to accept there is an invisible power that helps certain people, regardless of affluence or pitiableness – and not others. Certainly any grand power that might have created anthrax and supernovas could not also be attending to parking cars. Too – dare I say? – far-fetched.

By now I'm so uncomfortable that I feel that this pitiful little attempt to redeem myself in her eyes will have to suffice. I decide to rely on a clichéd, archetypal male excuse for post-coital disappearing.

" Well, I have a very big animal to dispose of first thing in the morning," I say, leaning over and giving her a peck on the cheek.

She doesn't look happy. Looks confused. But what woman can argue with a statement like that?

The door gives a very loud *click* behind me.

I oafishly clamber into my little car and I think about, and then dismiss thinking about, whether I'm fully capable of driving successfully. Curiously, the engine starts exactly as it's supposed to. I realize that putting the transmission into reverse is my next step back to my grandmother's house. So I do that. Headlights shine in my rearview mirror, though. But not blocking my exit. I realize someone is awaiting my leaving. Someone with excellent parking-karma, no doubt. Also, good enough money-karma to afford a Porsche. I pull out and when I am alongside my replacement I see that the driver is William Kahn. I feel a flush. *My replacement.* Is that why he is here? Why *is* he here? Could Lucinda – unclothed (a common state for her, though) when I left her five minutes ago – be *receptive* to another male visitor *now?* Perhaps one who's more opportunistically tactful than me? Well, who am I to be judgmental about opportunism?

"Alex!" he says, taken aback, and adds a bit too quickly, "I'm just looking for Justin. They said he'd be here…here with somebody named Avrum. I mean Lucinda said… Avrum's her roommate…I guess you know that." He is the last person I'd ever expect to see appearing sheepish. And he is sheepish enough that he almost neglects to flash his transforming smile. Nope. There it is. "How you doin," he asks. "Poor Justin had quite a scare. You all dried off yet?"

"I may still be a little wet behind the ears," I supply.

"Good one," he says, acknowledging my mistrust. Regretting having done so he pushes the smile to an extent that even he seems to have difficulty sustaining.

"*They* say that Justin is at his hotel. Avrum went there with one Roger Something an hour ago." An hour? – how long did the fuck, the "Be Drunken," and the karma battle take? I look at my watch. More like two. Huh.

"Lucinda there, too?"

If she is, why am I here? I don't say this to him. "Gone to bed," is what I do say.

His smile disappears. He looks at his watch, too. "Yeah, it's late. I guess I'll just leave a note under the knocker.

He's been here before, I see.

"Let 'r down easy." I say.

"What?" He says.

"The knocker. Don't want to wake anybody up."

"Right," he allows with a nod. "Right!" he says a second time, stuffing enthusiasm into it and turning the smile back up. He fumbles around in the car and holds up an envelope and a pen. Then he stares blankly at me.

"Right," I say. "I guess you want my spot."

"Right – tough finding parking spaces around here."

"You should try visualizing them."

"Oh – ya? Zat work?"

"Only if you're not attached to it," I say and drive off.

Anxiety at losing any attractive woman – even one I'm not sure I really want – *and* tepid macho competitiveness, makes me stop my car just beyond the corner of the adjacent brick building. I'm intending to get out and time how long it takes him to "leave his note." But as soon as my fingers touch the key to de-ignite the engine I change my mind. Do I want to stoop to that? No, I'm better than that. I turn the key and get a revolting rasp. I'd not turned the car off. Grating. Sounds about how I feel.

# 15

There have only been two so far, but the mornings following evenings with Lucinda suggest a pattern: if I keep this up – I'll wake up messed-up. I wonder if she awoke feeling damaged too – not by what she consumed through her nose, which she seems to handle easily, but by what I put in her ear: a generous dose of negative energy. But likely she's still asleep. Or maybe she is *still awake*. Who knows how long her coke-fueled night might have continued if William Kahn's facile hand made it to her readily accessible knocker? (Pun intended.) Well, after my cynical rejection of things she holds quite dear – and allowing for the probability of succor available from a more alpha and artsy male (though one endowed with a seeming plethora of female companionship) – there may not be another chance for me to find out about any patterns. A pang of guilt for my trashing her quasi-religious parking beliefs complements my physical discomfort. The smell of diesel fuel and the rocking motion of the *Laura T*, Fred Avery's fishing boat, convey a greater comprehension of seasickness than I've ever known. Never having been truly seasick, I understood it only by analogies – one of which might be to the aftermath of the kinds of things I do nights with Lucinda. And, analogous to the anticipation of imminent climax from continued consuming of cocaine, I feel seasickness roiling just over the next swell. I pray that a motion-induced altered state remains as elusive as the one that that drug fails to deliver. Focus on the horizon, isn't that what they say?

Fred Avery, David Player, and I – Nikon camera dangling from my neck – are motoring the half-mile from Fred's mooring in Phillip's Cove to Arthur Dalmore's private dock at Jack's. Jack's Cove is a mostly manmade geographic feature. The pre-existing land formation – created by nature and running north-south – was known as Jack's Point for about 250 years – presumably from when some Jack named it. But in the 1930's, great granite chunks were craned from barges, courtesy of the WPA, and dropped at a right angle to the point, to form a breakwater. This closed off exposure to the open sea for the west side of Jack's and added sheltered anchorage for a very few favored Northporters. Arthur Dalmore is one of those individuals wealthy enough to afford a piece of this peninsula-ed waterfront property: waves breaking from the east onto ledge and pebbles, and from the south against the granite. Bay water laps from the west onto rocks at the edges of lawns.

The Agamenticus River, which begins its fresh water flow somewhere in New Hampshire, becomes brackish upstream of the city in Great Bay, a fifty square mile tidal lake. On an outgoing tide, a six-knot current pushes onto the breakwater at Jack's a significant percentage of everything that has washed down from the sites of careless picnics or negligent industry along the bay. Natural and manmade objects that have drifted inland from the open sea on the last incoming tide collect here when it turns around and flows out. So the enjoyment of nature and of higher social status conveyed by property ownership at Jack's Cove is mitigated by a significant mess of crap. At Jack's, brightly-colored plastic containers, beer cans, flip flops and fish heads all end up tangled in the seaweed that's attached to rocks on Jack's western side like chunks of meat or shrimp in a bed of pasta. This happens because the construction of the jetty created an unforeseen back-eddying. Natural flushing has been impaired. Therefore, the appearance of a dead whale here causes little surprise. I don't mean that dead whales are as common as beer cans – there probably hasn't been one noticed in the region in ten years. It's just that if there has to be a dead whale somewhere on this coast, you'd expect Jack's to be the place.

I'd managed only about three or four hours sleep after my night of word games, drugs, debauchery, and theological speculation. It seemed like I had only just dropped off when at about 6 a.m., Fred's voice rasped agonizingly up to my open bedroom window.

"Mornin' naybah. Time, tide, and dead cetaceans wait for no man" – or some similar nonsense. " Not even for those who didn't get ta bed 'til afta two."

*God – the dead whale thing,* flooded my returning consciousness. How did I get myself into that? What business is it of mine? Why did I open my big mouth? Then, unbidden, the face of Rebecca Sharma drifted in front of my blinking eyes. I must have been trying to be Menachem Begin invading Lebanon to impress my own Jody Foster – or some damn thing. I don't have a chance with Rebecca Sharma, is what I quite rationally thought this morning at 6. And yet I found myself committed to giving up precious sleep and go off with my dear friend Fred Avery, for the benefit of my dear friend, Arthur Dalmore. How could I have offered to help either of them?

But, as I woke up a bit, I understood how easily I could have. I've done foolhardy things to impress unattainable attractive females before – sometimes even strangers; women who may not have been aware I was even there; women I could assume I'd probably never even get to meet. The reality of this first came home to me when I was hiking in the White Mountains on a hot day, when I was about twenty. I saw guys clamoring to the top of a waterfall and jumping from a twenty-five-foot height into a small, mid-stream pool. Wetting my feet in that pool, I thought it looked wide and deep enough; the jump fairly sane fun. Until I got to the top. From there the pool appeared pitifully small. Life-threateningly small. My knees shook when I rose to my full height. I was about to make discretion the better part of valor and climb back down when a young woman in a bikini, sunbathing on a large rock at stream's edge, sat up on one elbow. She shaded her eyes with the palm of her other hand and squinted upward to where I stood. A well-built, well-tanned young man dozed beside her. The chances of my diving gracefully enough to make her want me more than him, swimming over and fighting him to the death, and then passing on my genetic code to a new generation given life by her fertile young body, were not high – all things considered. Yet, as a compulsively heterosexual male, unlucky enough – in this case – to have attracted notice, I had *no choice* but to jump. So I did. Obviously I survived.

Fred couldn't have had much sleep himself if he'd been able to keep tabs on the lateness of my return. But then I remember his habit of taking a several hour nap in his kitchen recliner after dinner – before he hits his workshop and slams and bangs, sometimes until dawn.

I was feeling really quite odd, but not really that sleepy – perhaps because I'd been snorting cocaine instead of drinking alcohol. But I nevertheless didn't want to get up. Or at least didn't want to go out on Fred's damn *Laura T.* It was a workday anyway, I realized, so how could I be expected to go boating? Then I remembered my call to my boss, Steve's recorder, telling it I had a story with some nice visuals to pursue and I wouldn't be in until afternoon. I realized that my convoluted hope for a chance with an unattainable woman no longer was my driving motivation. I'd boxed myself in. I'd told three uncompromising *men* – Dalmore, Fred, and Steve Towle – that I'd be there.

"Naybah! Shake a leg," Fred browbeat my open window. "Things to load."

I staggered to the screen and yelled down, "I'll make some coffee and be out in twenty minutes."

"We're stoppin' at Connie's. Always plenty of coffee theya."

Oh, God – Connie's. There's always plenty of coffee at Connie's because they about quadruple the water to grounds ratio and end up with extra beans at the end of each day. At the end of the month they have more beans than they started with on the first. But if I'd argued with him I'd have awakened Gram. And that might have been the result anyway if I'd crashed around in the kitchen making coffee of my own. She can't hear, but she has some sort of autonomic motion detector somewhere in the back of her brain. So after peeing and brushing my teeth, I grabbed my camera and appeared outside – five minutes after Fred's last shout.

I helped Fred load several boxes of ropes and wires and pointy metal things and long pieces of two inch PVC pipe with oblique angles cut in the ends. Then we climbed in and headed to Connie's, the greasy grill of Fred's heart. There he consumed an irritatingly leisurely breakfast. I had a high-caffeine coffee substitute – tea made with three bags. After a night in which I'd indulged in an excess of everything but sleep, I could understand Gram's dislike of eating *food* in the morning. I also could understand hating people who chasten you to hop to it while they take their own sweet, goddamn time. Fred availed himself of the opportunity to chat-up Connie and twelve or so skeptical patrons about his need to "swing by" the new curator's place at Jack's, to haul off a misplaced leviathan. His use of the word, *we* – while nodding in my direction in an unprecedented attempt to include me in a story – allowed it to sound like he'd been at my side last night, too: one of whose enjoyment of cocktails and canapés had been sullied by an unfortunate cetacean that was now adding its own haunting song to the choir invisible. Fred asked a smiling Connie for as many empty plastic milk jugs as her dishwasher could give us. About a dozen were offered. Fred said a dozen would do. Do for what, I'd asked. "For the blasting wire," he said. "You think I'd let it sink?"

I hated to think that Fred thought that I'd think he'd let blasting wire sink. So once in the truck again I queried Fred about the subject.

"What blasting wire?"

"Standard procedure," Fred replied.

"What is?" I asked.

"Dynamitin' the whale."

"Dynamiting the whale? Dynamiting a dead whale is standard procedure?"

"Well, if it isn't exactly standard procedure, it should be."

"Have you ever done it?"

"I've never had my own whale before. But I've heard tell of it being done. It's a safety issue. Dynamitin' a whale *should be* standard procedure.

"Let me get this straight," I said. "*Not* dynamiting a whale is not safe?"

"A course not. We can't leave such a large hazard to navigation just floating around out there in the boating and shipping lanes. We're not dragging that thing that far out – cost of diesel bein' what it is. I don't want to go out more than five miles. Can't afford the time."

Well, I was at least relieved that he was not going to dynamite it under Dalmore's dock. I asked, " What about all the whales that die at sea?" The vast majority, I assumed, did that. Where else? "Aren't they hazards to navigation?"

"They aren't my responsibility," Fred said.

I didn't think this was worth arguing. And, I have to say, the little boy inside who likes to see things go boom was intrigued. This did not quite overwhelm my primary concern of not looking like a fool to my new wealthy, artsy friends – especially Rebecca Sharma. And avoiding unpleasant associations for Dalmore with the name "Perkins" was a consideration, too: that could affect cousin Kevin's livelihood. But I knew there would be no deterring Fred from any course once he'd chosen it. Might as well try to stop this truck by dragging my foot.

"Dynamite in one of those boxes?"

"Nope, I don't keep it around. It's dangerous stuff."

Well, that reassured me of something – like, maybe, my

grandmother's continued longevity – and perhaps my own.

"Where do we get it?"

"Young David's."

"David Player – he has dynamite?"

"Yessa."

"What's a young guy like him doing with dynamite?" I knew that he was odd. But I still wasn't sure what kind of odd.

"His father is superintendent of roads in Marshland. David was working grading roads when I hired him away. He can get pretty creative with the stuff."

"What's that mean?"

"Place where he lives – a few miles out, toward Marshland – has a junkyard behind it. Sometimes he takes little pieces of a stick and blows up old cars, bathtubs, washers, dryers."

"Why's he do that?"

"To see what they look like after."

That should have been obvious.


David had been waiting for us – sitting deep, a mug in one hand, in the product of two large wooden boxes that he'd united obliquely to form a primitive recliner. Next to him on the grass sat a thin case, marked *explosives*. His place didn't appear so much as one with a junkyard behind it as it did a junkyard with a living place *in* it. His apparent domicile was an unfinished geodesic dome. It was sheathed by a variety of materials, some of which I assumed were temporary and some permanent. The structure gave the feeling of its having had a previous lifetime giving shelter on some other piece of land to some other form of life.

David gave us a wave as we neared. He wore a clean white tee-shirt and jeans. When he picked up the smallish box it appeared heavy from the way his muscles bulged as he hefted it. He approached the truck to get in beside me, but I jumped out and said, "Let's see some of the stuff Fred tells me you've blown up."

Fred pounced to assert control, "No time for that now. We've got a schedule ta keep."

At 7:45 a.m., I was already tired of him. I whined back over my shoulder, "Come on, Fred. We had time for you to have three cups of that piss coffee of Connie's. I think we can spare a minute here."

"All right," he said, tilting his head to show deep skepticism. "It's your friends I'm helpin'. Just figured you wouldn't want to get 'em all anxious. Dead whale and all. You say they come from New York."

"Back here," David directed happily.

Behind a stand of still late spring-green saplings glowing in the morning light, a third of an arc of vertical metal objects – apparently refrigerators, now deformed, with ragged-edged, large and small gaping holes – brought to mind weird associations of sites of standing stones I'd seen in Ireland. In some of the former appliances, there was more *hole* than remaining metal. And those wrecked boxes appeared barely able to stand on their own. Their vestiges of "skin" varied from small expanses of white or 1950's baked enamel green, to burnt black or lacy rust. The sense of speeded-up decay time was unsettling. It certainly was a collection of junk. But an aura of otherness hung over the place. "Huh," I said. Then I was concerned about where the missing metal had blown to – concerned with David's safety, I mean. David saw me avert my gaze from the relics themselves to survey his working space. Silently he pointed at a curtain of woven black pneumatic rubber hanging from tree limbs. A pile of the same material lay nearby. And beyond, stood a freestanding, mortarless wall of cinder block, about six feet high and four feet wide. A *River Kwai*-like detonator was sitting on a neat stack of cinder blocks behind this wall.

"Oh no!" said David, "Can't forget this." He went over to his mission control, and picked up the plunger. "You got that reel of wire, Captain?" he asked Fred.

"In the truck, matey," Fred said. "Let's go."

I grab David by his elbow. "What's this all about?"

"I don't know," he says. "It's just my way of riding the decline."

"'Riding the decline?'"

"Yeah. You know. We all have to have some way to ride the decline."

"The decline of what?"

"Aw – you know. Of everything."

"Ride the decline."

"Right. Ride the decline."

Last night on the dock I'd thought the whale gave off barely any aroma. However, Naomi Dalmore had expressed certainty that her nice little after-sailing party was "ruined, just ruined – by *that sickening smell.*" Women, I believe, have a far more sensitive olfactory apparatus than men; sometimes being able to detect odors that I'm sure aren't even there.

Arthur Dalmore, a man who seems to value order and cleanliness – or should I say, *cleanness* – more perhaps than anyone I've ever met (though this may say more about me than him), had seemed befuddled by the marine interloper. A sorry condition for a man of action. In addition to finding the messiness challenging, Dalmore had been disconcerted by the results of phone calls he'd placed to the harbormaster, the Coast Guard, and – due to frustrated efforts with those two entities – his lawyer. He'd gotten only a recording on the harbormaster's line. The Coast Guard, which always answers, told him that since the whale was not a hindrance to navigation it was not their problem – any more than a driftwood log on his hundred foot private beach would be. Dalmore did not think the analogy apt. Anyone just watching the calisthenics performed by his facial features as he listened to what was coming from the receiver could see that. The only positive input he received was from his attorney – someone well paid to be positive. On hanging up, Dalmore told us, his guests, that this man was willing to initiate legal action against the Coast Guard the following morning. And, the attorney encouraged, there should be a positive finding quite quickly – even by the Fourth of July. Well, last night was the twelfth of June. The whale would probably smell bad even to me within a day or two, let alone next

192

month. At least decaying blubber doesn't have a smell with a lot of bad associations for people in the twentieth century. To us it is a new bad smell. But to Arthur Dalmore's petite and anxious wife, Naomi – the hostess who'd had a varied and delicious spread awaiting us when we returned from the sea – she who'd said many times, "Now nobody will be able to eat anything" (which wasn't true in my case) – even a day's wait would be intolerable.

So after Dalmore's calls to "the authorities" had proved fruitless, and after my look round at each member of our group told me that none appeared likely to come up with any realistic suggestions, I – a wave of compassion for my hosts engulfing me – recommended Fred Avery. He was the right man for the job of removing a deceased cetacean. Obviously, I'd had some trepidation – though I was not a bit concerned about Fred's technical qualifications. He had the tools and the talent. In fact, one of the varieties of professional capacities for which Fred had employed the *Laura T.* had been as a floating platform for whale watchers. (Fred had gotten bored with that pretty quick and moved on.) The newest incarnation-to-be for his boat is "dragger," a hauler of nets filled with fish. This transformation is not quite completed. The outriggers for the stabilizing *doors*, slabs of wood dropped from either side of the vessel to keep the net open, are still in pieces in Fred's yard – and, I think, overlapping onto my Grandmother's. But the *Gorgon*, as David Player named it, the Volkswagen engine, that I learned was for activating a spool for reeling in heavy line or wire is by now bolted in place. Some of the grunt work for this conversion was done with the complaining help of yours truly. The levitating of that heavy object, from garage floor to truck bed, with only a tripod and block and tackle, almost made me miss the boat for my Sunday sail. And about the worst part was Fred constantly giving inflexibly specific instructions like, "Stand here with your hands 14 inches apart." He can be mercilessly punctilious when he's impressed you into helping him. So it remains Fred's manner of relating to people – pretty much as though they had no minds of their own – that caused the catch in my voice as I heard myself starting to suggest Dalmore consult him. For a moment I thought I should elaborate, lay a foundation for a preemptive defense by referring to Fred as a "lovable eccentric" *before* he turned out to be an infuriating one. But I dismissed the thought, guessing that the New York sophisticates surrounding me might not be as charmed by *loveable eccentric* as normal people would. I could perchance have mentioned that Fred had failed to fire his deer rifle in the air when Dalmore stole his spot on the dock as a sign of good character. But I let that one go, too.

Dalmore scrutinized me, evincing more than his usual aura of suspicion, when it happened that I knew Fred's number by heart. Did he think it was a setup – that I'd had the whale planted there to get a little work for my friend – and maybe a kickback for myself? Well, suspicious people don't always know what they are suspicious *of.* That can be why they are suspicious in the first place. "Fred Avery lives next door to my grandmother," I explained. This to my surprise didn't cause Dalmore's dubious expression to relax. I guess in New York you are no more likely to know your neighbor's phone number than anybody else's. Then I realized that it had not been established that I live with my grandmother, and I almost blurted out that *I* lived next to Fred, *too.* But I thought better of it and, considering the sophisticates present, said, "He's somebody I call when I'm worried if the 90 year-old woman doesn't answer her phone. – He's been a lifesaver at times." I almost went even further than that and added: "She's Kevin's grandmother, too, Isn't that true, Kevin?" feeling oddly pressured by the disapproval on Dalmore's face to bolster what in any other circumstance would not be considered an outlandish claim. But Dalmore and his wife both said, "Ah," while nodding affirmatively. Having someone to check up on your grandmother – or mother or aunt – *so you don't have to do it yourself,* is something I imagine every middle-aged, upwardly mobile narcissist can understand. The "Ah" implied that I was one with them as regards mitigating any guilt-inducing duty to a previous generation.

A cordless phone was sitting on a table on the oceanfront deck, and I was encouraged – though Dalmore's post-"Ah" scowl still indicated reservation – to dial up Fred. When Fred answered, he launched, as usual, into telling me everything about the specific thing he was preoccupied with at the exact moment the phone rang – before I could say anything but "Hello, Fred?" I – fearing Dalmore's impatience – God knows why I should care. Or care more than hurting Fred's feelings by cutting him off (God knows why I should care about that either?) – *did* cut him off by saying, "I'm visiting friends out at Jack's Cove, and they may have a little job for you." "Jack's Cove" and "job" got Fred's attention – as my using the word "friends" got Dalmore's. He clearly had yet to decide if he wanted to own me as a friend, no matter how much he'd felt he'd owned me as a crewmember earlier in the day. "There seems to be this whale part way under his dock," I said. "I'll give him the phone – his name is Arthur Dalmore." I noticed Rebecca looking at me expressionlessly from the far end of the deck. As on the boat earlier – fool that I am – I valued a neutral look from her more than I would have a smile from anyone else. That's why I am up at this hour after having had a quite interesting sexual encounter with a perfectly suitable alternate woman. I'm not serious. Lucinda, however desirable she may be, isn't "perfectly suitable" – that is, she isn't for me. And she isn't for reasons unrelated to sex. And, even if she were *somewhat more* "suitable," to a beauty addict great beauty close at hand makes all else *less than* "suitable."

Today is Monday and the NoMMA, though situated on the edge of the provinces, keeps to an urban museum schedule. So it's closed today. And the West Wing would be closed regardless, as the installation, though according to Kevin almost complete, is still in progress. The opening will be Wednesday, for members and the press, and Saturday for the riff-raff. Apparently Dalmore is comfortable that preparations at the museum are proceeding satisfactorily; that Kevin, the rest of the crew, and Kahn, himself, can take care of things without him. So he is here to deal with his whale.

The day is hot already and David, at the wheel of Fred's boat, is now bare-chested. He looks at me, and, nodding twice, as one who sees something presumed obscure clearly, says, "Jack's Cove." I guess this is his way of saying *rich people*. I'm not one for talking in code, but in camaraderie I reply in kind: "Jack's Cove."

As we approach Jack's, I can see Dalmore standing on his dock. My guess is Fred didn't have a good line of sight to Dalmore when he grabbed Fred's place on the wharf the other day. I've withheld any mention that this client is that asshole. With Dalmore are Naomi, and to my surprise, Justin Bollard. I would have guessed Bollard wouldn't want to be near even a fish tank after yesterday. Seeing him, I tense up a bit. The roll of the boat when it slows and its own wake catches up with it, as David briefly reverses the engine to stop at dockside, renews in me intimations of motion sickness. Naomi has her hand to her nose, and though I still don't smell anything, the idea that I might, causes another ripple of nausea. With the day already hot at nine a.m., if the whale doesn't smell now, it probably will soon – when the tide goes out and leaves more than the topside of the creature exposed to the summer sun. Well, the tide still has a few hours.

Fred and I disembark leaving David to tie up to the bit of Dalmore's dock that the whale hasn't obstructed. *Pure Conception*, riding on her mooring, catches Fred's eye. He smiles slowly and long. "We know that boat, don't we?" he asks. "Right," I say.

I attempt to make introductions. But Fred walks past everyone. His only acknowledgement of people there – as he looks momentarily in Naomi's direction – is his touching the brim of his long-billed fisherman's cap. His *modus operandi* – as long as I've known him – is to befuddle all comers; and he has many ways of doing that. This morning – or at least at this moment on this morning – his persona is *the taciturn Mainer* – which he actually isn't.' Silently, he begins to survey the situation.

Dalmore and wife glance at each other and then at me. I now wish I'd introduced the "lovable eccentric" concept last night, regardless. Bollard gives me a smile. *That's funny*. And it doesn't seem a mocking one either – not even one that might be legitimately mocking Fred. It's a smile that could be construed as *friendly*. He starts to say something. But his attention is caught, and he looks past me to where shirtless David – impressively tanned – is stooping to fasten a docking line to a cleat. David then stands to his full height, pivots our way, and gives us both his shy grin. I am momentarily again reminded of Billy Budd.

Bollard gives him an appraising look, and a smile even friendlier than the one he had for me. Young David likely appears of junior rank in the scheme of this operation. But I am egalitarian enough to feel it is socially incumbent upon me to introduce everyone to everyone else. I don't mean in just this situation. I always do. Liberal guilt, or something. And Bollard's having focused on him implies that David is not insignificant to at least one of the individuals on the moneyed end of the dock. However, I feel a bit protective of my naïve young Billy Budd – around the likes of Bollard. No Claggart, Bollard, but who knows? But David Player shows the opposite of a need for protection. He – as I am getting to understand little by little – is someone for whom confounding easy stereotyping is as salient to his persona – and perhaps less self-consciously so – as that is to his boss. He nods to Bollard pleasantly enough, but steps past him right up to Dalmore – obviously the kingfish of the dock. David affects exaggerated sociability – in marked contrast to his captain's perfunctory manner. He leans in toward Dalmore and, unnecessarily and vigorously, pumps the reticent hand of the natty and well-combed museum curator, the wealthy Jack's Cove-er. As he does this he intones, nature documentary style: "The whale, the largest creature in the seas, is not really a fish. It's an insect."

Dalmore apparently doesn't find this funny at all and pulls back. His face says he fears he's found a madman. This may be the first expression of his I've found appropriate. Bollard, on the other hand, laughs heartily. What's up with Bollard, I wonder? He's not the guy he was yesterday – *and* I got the impression that the guy he was yesterday is the guy he's always been. Dalmore summons the composure to ignore David and moves over toward the affectedly preoccupied Fred. But Fred moves, too – paces slowly back and forth across the width of the dock, up and down the length; tries to peer under it. He looks for some reason out to *Pure Conception*. He looks at the sun. He looks at his watch. He begins humming softly. The melody issuing from him sounds like a combination of "Good Night, Irene" and "The Night They Drove Old Dixie Down" – or a medley of the two, if two can be a medley.

"What do you think?" Dalmore asks. Fred does not reply. Dalmore idles half a minute more, then repeats the question. Waiting, he draws down the corners of his mouth. Cords in his neck are taut halyards.

Fred remains silent – but for his humming. He continues to walk the dock, looking and considering. Arthur Dalmore, captain of *Pure Conception*, and a man who has been known to crush full-grown artists between his eyebrows, is very likely not used to being ignored. I'm guessing – and hoping – that he takes Fred's manner as incompetent – an estimation I believe Fred likely to soon belie – rather than as insulting. Dalmore's hands move from his hips to his chin and back. But, as if seeing himself through the eyes of others on the dock, he suddenly masters this fidgeting and pulls himself up to his full height. He's perhaps two inches taller than Fred – though with his massive shoulders and long arms, Fred appears the bigger man. Fred stops humming.

I'm relieved. He's as intimidated by Dalmore as the rest of us.

But, no! Now Fred starts singing. "*... It's a time I remember oh so well.*" Unable to hit the approaching high notes and unwilling to change key. Fred shifts to whistling.

Dalmore gives me an accusatory glance. It says: "I took you out on my fancy yacht and gave you rum punch and stuffed artichokes (and you are probably the one who stole my Russian caviar) and this is how you repay me?" I'm not happy that Fred is making me look bad. Of course, I tell myself, it's natural that Fred, a fisherman, would seem a little bizarre to a New Yorker. But then again I guess he seems a little bizarre to other fishermen, too. However, I don't really have much to gain or lose in this situation. It's not like the Northport Museum of Modern Art is *Currents'* biggest advertiser.

But Fred, though basically incapable of adjusting his thoughts or actions to the needs of others, is, it seems, *of his own accord*, ready to share his thoughts.

"She's a humpback – about 35 feet – a small one for her breed, probly not full grown. They go about a ton a foot. Died young – died recently – a day or two ago. Bumped, probly, by a barge on a thousand foot cable, dragged off the stern of a tug heading into Northport. One like that come in the day before yesterday. Barges run pretty silent. That gouge on the poor creature's head tells that story. She never knew what hit 'er, She's pretty well jammed up under there."

Oddly, as he comes to the last line of this, he, as if still surveying the situation, glances sideways past me and winks almost imperceptibly. What does that mean?

So when he finally spoke Fred sounded like the voice of authority. However, it seems to me – and perhaps the wink corroborates it – that he is exaggerating about difficulty of the whale's extrication – at least for the next hour or so until the tide drops another foot. Right now, she seemed to slosh pretty easily from just the force of the *Laura T's* wake. But I don't think Dalmore is considering such details. Pleasure boaters – *racers* especially – probably don't.

"Well, can you get her – it – out?" Dalmore asks flatly; unsure this is what the long wait was for.

"I can," says Fred.

"How much will it cost?"

Fred doesn't reply immediately. He strokes his chin and looks from the planks beneath his feet – with rubbery black visible between and beneath them – to his boat, and then over to *Pure Conception* once again. Last, he looks up at Dalmore's impressive home before he refocuses on the planks he's standing on.

"I'd say – with the dynamite – $600 would do."

This is the first time the word "dynamite" has been brought to Dalmore's attention. My guess is that putting that word before the cost of the service was intended as a way to get Dalmore to react initially to something other than the price. Probably Fred calculated that a client's hearing something more outrageous than the price would make the price seem less outrageous.

"The *dynamite*?"

"Dynamite is standard procedure. You wouldn't want to hit something that big at 10 knots on a spinnaker run in your $200,000 sailboat."

Dalmore actually gives this some thought. Then he chuckles derisively:

"The odds of me encountering the same dead whale twice don't seem particularly significant."

"Did you per chance call the Coast Guard about this whale?" Fred asks. He cocks his head to give the impression of bringing his ear closer – as if to make sure he doesn't hear the man wrong.

Dalmore glances at me. "Did you tell him?" his look says. I try to appear unconcerned – and as if I have not made any connection. "Yes," Dalmore admits.

"Well, the Coast Guard's goin' ta want ta know where you put your whale. They'd probly be happiest if you put it out by the curb and let some other bureaucracy worry about it. And if you give your whale to me they are goin' ta come ask me where I put it. And if I say I just left it bobbin' off Northport Harbor and then somebody else's J-Boat rams it at 10 knots and somebody spills a drink – or falls in the drink – I might just end up getting sued."

"$500," Dalmore says.

"You see that nice Volkswagen engine bolted to my deck. My cutter, David here, likes to call it "The Gorgon". That whale isn't coming outta there on just propeller power. Perhaps you should find one of the other fisherman with a hauling rig as strong as that and see if he would do it for $500."

Dalmore thinks he sees an opening. "That rig isn't going to do you much good if your propeller can't keep your boat from slipping."

"That's true," says Fred: "But I mean ta be attached to the planet. I mean ta have your sailboat's moorin' holding me stationary. How big a block you got on that?"

Dalmore looks at his beautiful boat and says, "You're not thinking of tying this old thing alongside my J-44?"

"Course not. You can go for a nice little motor around the Cove while I use her mooring. Won't take long." Fred drops his "g's" as intermittently as a congressman campaigning in the wards. "The moorin' block – what's it weigh?

"12,000 pounds"

"Good. Mud bottom or ledge?"

"Mud."

"Good. Shouldn't be any trouble then."

Dalmore glances at his wife. Naomi gives him a pleading look. He scrunches one side of his mouth, rolls his eyes, and breathes deeply.

"Okay - 600," he says. "What's first?"

"First somebody needs to get into a bathing suit and go under the dock to get some of that 3/4-inch nylon line, running offa that spool, secured to the tail of the beast. She went in between the pilings tail first, as you can see. Don't know why she did that, but she did. Tail's the only place we could tie onto. Rope's gotta go in the way she did. Going in we can do from up here. But the tail's too far under to reach for tyin' on ta. So for tying on somebody's gotta be in the water."

Dalmore stares blankly. "Well," he says. His eyes go to David and all other eyes follow.

"My cutter has sustained an injury that wouldn't take well to soakin'."

David grabs the cuff of his pants and raises it a few inches to reveal a wad of gauze wrapped round several times with white tape. "Took some shrapnel," he says. All assume he is continuing with his earlier theatrics. However, after visiting his place, I know that for David shrapnel might be just what he took.

"Don't you ever do anything but joke?" Dalmore scorns.

201

"I'm not joking now. If I was joking I'd say: a horse goes into a bar and the bartender says, 'Why the long face?'"

Dalmore spins onto Fred. "What's wrong with you?" he lashes out. I assume you knew somebody would have to go into the water when we talked last night – when you agreed to take the job."

"*Consider*," corrects Fred. "I agreed to consider the job. Said 'I'll have a look and be *ready* to go.' Didn't say I *would* go. Didn't know how she was under there. I never agree to a job I haven't looked at."

Fred is probably the only person in the world that could make me feel sorry for Arthur Dalmore. He seems to be enjoying punishing these New Yorkers for the various sins of all New York.

Fred continues: "I wouldn't have made the trip over if I thought I'd have to get wet. I haven't been in the North Atlantic myself since I was 17. – Without a wetsuit, that is. Perhaps if this whale washed up in a lake..."

"Well, why don't you have a wetsuit – a man in your trade," Dalmore presses, exasperated.

"I do have one," Fred says.

"Well, why don't you put it on?" Dalmore's volume is increasing and his face is getting red.

"Can't put it on. It doesn't fit. Hasn't fit in ten years."

Dalmore's features resume the I'm-dealing-with-a-madman expression. But he can't resist getting drawn in. "Why don't you buy yourself a new one then? I imagine you could buy five from the proceeds of this one job and still have money for dynamite and paying this boy."

"That wouldn't work. It would destroy my incentive."

"What incentive?"

"Incentive to lose weight. Doctor's orders. My blood pressure runs fifteen points too high as is. Then there's diabetes to worry about. Runs in the family."

Dalmore looks incredulous. But then he so often looks that way. He turns on me and snaps, "What about you?"

"Me? What do I have to do with this?"

"What do you have to do with this?" Naomi jumps. "You started all this."

"Huh?" I say.

"You found these people. Or your grandmother did. How do we even know you have a grandmother?" I may have been right when I considered using Kevin for grandmother backup. Naomi apparently is another one who's high-strung. And, as I'd thought appropriate for Bollard yesterday, I think she should be, too.

"Naomi – stay out of this," Dalmore orders. Then he stares into me. "Will you do it?'

"I – I don't have a bathing suit."

"Got the wetsuit below, " Fred says. "Slim fella like you should go in easy."

I have a wet suit at home that I use mostly for whitewater kayaking. I find it most comfortable with nothing on under it. But the one Fred gives me is so funky – even I can smell it – from sitting below, absorbing diesel fumes since Fred was twenty-five pounds lighter, that I'd like to keep everything on under it. Though the rubber is dry and cracked, the suit still seems big enough for me to get into over my clothes. But if I left clothes on I'd have nothing dry to wear after my errand. I came unprepared for the North Atlantic today. I leave on only my Jockey shorts. After I'm out of the wetsuit, I can live through the day without them.

I get the suit on easily, but I can't get the zipper – that I reach by a foot long lanyard over my shoulder – to move more than a few inches. It stops at about the middle of my back. That's not good. But look on the bright side: it's like a dream that, after sitting for a third of my lifetime, this zipper moves at all.

By the time I emerge from below, David has fed the line around the inside of the pilings and is holding it for me at the point where I should enter the water. He seems to be speaking with animation to an apparently quite receptive Bollard. Probably Bollard has been to Peru. Dalmore and Naomi stare at me expectantly. Fred stands at the far end of the dock looking out to sea.

There is a ladder of nailed two-by-fours that disappears beneath the briny surface one piling away from where I need to enter. I start my climb down. I have no booties. I know it is going to be unpleasant. The sharp cold stabs my ankle as I submerge one foot. It takes all the fear of social disapproval I can muster, for me to keep me from crying out. My anticipatory mental calisthenics failed to remove the element of surprise. I pull that foot back up to the dry rung. I'm certain that, though my feet are out of the line of sight, everyone can tell I'm cowering. I forge ahead – or downward – now that I know what I'm up against; no surprise this time. My foot stays down and the other follows. I concentrate on fighting an overt reaction to the cold wetness rising to my balls. The wetsuit, though loose, does its intended thing in protecting them. However, since the suit is baggy, cold water enters, as I descend, at the point where the zipper is frozen. A trickle down my back tenses me. And that reminds me how, as a kid, I used to jump into the sea around Memorial Day – in just a bathing suit. (Now I seldom bathe in the ocean before the middle of July.) Of course, that was mostly running, then diving into surf. Immersion into stagnant water is a different thing. It certainly didn't feel this cold yesterday in the heat of the moment of pulling out Bollard. But surface water is always warmer on a hot day out to sea than near the shore where waves mix surface water with colder water deeper down.

The sting begins to pass. I breaststroke over to the spot below where David waits with the line. And it occurs to me, for the first time since we reached Jack's, that I am on an assignment for my paper. I should be taking pictures of myself – if I am at this juncture *the* story. (I realize this is my second Geraldo Rivera/*me journalism* moment in a week.) Or else I should stop being the story. I understand alternatively though, that I, as the reporter not the player in the story, have it easy. I know all the story's characters and will be, in real time, watching as the story unfolds. I'll need to interview no one; take no notes. I don't even have to mention that there is a story.

No one need be inhibited by the presence of a member of the press. I should use my camera casually – tourist-style. Snapshots for my grandmother.

David has put about a 30-inch loop in the end of the line that I gather is to go over my head and shoulder, so as to leave my two hands free. Barely encumbered, I swim under the dock. As soon as I am moving beneath the wooden structure – with morning light strobing my eyes through the spaces between the planks above –all color is lost and I'm advancing down a black and white tunnel. Right then the enormity of the rubbery black *thing* beside me hits me full force for the first time. I realize that I, too, right now, am a rubbery black creature. And of all things, a tenuously connected memory comes to me – perhaps the saddest thing I've ever seen in my life. A dog lying in the road beside his little boy – a boy who'd been riding his bicycle, his dog romping beside. The dog had romped a little too far, or a car's driver had shifted his hand on the wheel – an inch perhaps. And in no measurable time, the dog that had been filled with play and love for his boy became a thing. And the boy who loved his dog more than anything, jumped from his bike and hugged and hugged the thing that had been his dog; the two-way love now going only one way. This creature, the whale, maybe at play itself at the moment it died, struck by another one of man's ubiquitous contrivances, became a *thing* in an instant, too. The dog and the whale, innocent-natured victims, seem as one for me right now. Endlessly lovable. Endlessly sad. Now I realize that I will, too – probably not today or soon, but *possibly today or soon* – become a *thing*. One day, anyway. But I *will* become a *thing*.

Alone with my thoughts under the pier, I feel I could panic. Or I could just as easily drift into one of my water reveries. Screams, sobs, even *om* – each or all of them – stand a chance of emanating from me and reaching the ears of those above.

"How ya doin'," I hear Fred call down.

Once again, social self-consciousness gets me moving forward. "Fine," I shout. I breaststroke on and find the end of the carcass –

205

the dead animal's tail. And, to my relief, it, though inclined slightly downward, mostly floats.

The toughest moment psychologically seems to have passed. But diving under the tail, wrapping the rope a few times, and tying a good bowline will tax me not just physically. But I get it done and swim out.

As I climb the ladder, I see Fred proceeding slowly with ferrying Dalmore out to *Pure Conception* – which is riding about 40 yards away – for the temporary swapping of the mooring. The white line I tied to the whale plays out from the reel and trails behind the fishing boat. David pulls in when slack develops, then lets it go when tension returns. Dalmore will idle aboard his sloop until the whale is yanked free. Then the *Laura T* can head for open water, and the sailboat can reattach to the planet.

The fishing boat comes abeam of the sloop and Dalmore jumps aboard. In a half minute, I hear its inboard diesel thrum. He moves briskly to the bow and casts off, handing the tall-buoy to Fred whose boat bobs two feet away. Dalmore motors off and, in a minute, Fred is moored, stern toward the dock.

"Are you ready?" he shouts to his mate on the pier.

David puts a thumb in the air.

We hear the VW engine, the Gorgon, start. Then we see an advancing little fountain of water as the submerged rope becomes taut and progressively breaks the surface. This phenomenon suddenly evaporates at the point where the straight line of tightening rope, running from the top of the spool at an oblique angle to the whale's tail two feet below the water, intersects the flat of the cove's surface. I see the stern of the *Laura T* drop about two inches as rope and Gorgon both strain against the whale weight. Then the boat's transom comes back up a bit and my eye catches movement under the dock. For a heartbeat, I feel a primitive, apprehensive thrill as it appears that the great creature has come alive to swish its tail. This swipes unnaturally around to become almost parallel to the bulk of the body. My emotional reaction shifts from fear to compassion – at the pain the creature would have felt at being thus jerked around in life. The reel continues to wind. Some effect of the water displaced by the sideways pulling causes the whale's head, which is slowly being turned our way, to rise above the surface. All of us on the dock – David, Justin, Naomi, and I – let out little cries and jump backwards. The tail flaps – as the retained strength of the beast's massive muscles brings the streamlined body back toward natural alignment – and we cry out a second time.

Fred puts the Gorgon into neutral. "What?" he calls to the dock.

David gives a flat wave that ends in a thumbs-up, indicating "Nothing." The Gorgon goes back into gear. The great bulk of the head continues to roll and turn. For a moment I see the ugly laceration that killed this beast. Then a giant, milky vacant eye down low behind the jaw turns to look directly into mine. It says, "Your kind did this."

Then the turning is complete and the creature backs away from the dock for all time to come. I now understand Fred's wink. "She come out real slick," I can imagine Fred saying. Is Dalmore going to feel taken? But he wasn't here to witness. Perhaps that's why Fred wanted him off shore bobbing away.

With the whale clearly floating free, Fred stops reeling. The leviathan's slow backward motion halts against the outgoing tide. Fred shuts off the *Gorgon* and starts his boat's engine. He revs sharply, and then lets it idle down. He walks to the bow, casts off the hawser, but retains the tall-buoy and waves it at the sloop. Dalmore has been drifting and regaining, drifting and regaining about 25 to 50 yards further out. He cuts the wheel and creeps alongside the fishing boat to receive the tall-buoy. After the hand-off, he moors his sloop and then swings himself onto the *Laura T*. The fishing boat makes a wide arc around the whale and the slack rope floating off its stern, and returns to the dock to pick up its crew.

Fred doesn't tie up there, but idles. The inflated white plastic fenders chafe against the float at the end of the dock. Dalmore jumps off.

"Aren't you comin'?" Fred taunts. "Once in a lifetime experience. How many people ever get ta see a whale explode?"

After my brief but heartfelt bonding with the dead cetacean I am not very enthused about this myself. And I imagine I have earned the right to a ride home from Dalmore. But I am still in the wetsuit and the day is hot. I'm going to be pretty funky when I peel it off. I'm not sure I'm deemed heroic enough to merit a spot in Dalmore's Mercedes, smelling of essence of Alex Perkins and diesel fuel. In any case, the cold water seems to have cured my hangover. So I decide to file my sensitive feelings in the place I'd put the boy and the dead dog, long ago, and intentionally deny them until *perhaps* the death of my grandmother – when I may suddenly, irrationally think of the milky eye of a dead whale looking into mine.

"I'd like to come," Justin Bollard says with surprising enthusiasm.

Naomi is scandalized. "Justin!" is all she says.

But he hops aboard.

"Naomi," Dalmore says to his wife, "if Justin is going, I'd better go, too."

# 16

I sit sideways on the transom, watching the whale dragging tail-first behind us. Cacophonous seagulls, sensing a meal to come, follow in wheeling flocks. The reverse of the whale's natural hydrodynamics is probably even more efficient for gliding through water than head on. But still the going is slow. Thirty-five tons of dead weight is taxing to a vessel about the length of its burden. This slowness is something that probably no one but Fred anticipated – part of why he had little enthusiasm for heading to deep water. But I am enjoying that things have slowed down – after yesterday, last night and this morning. And the hour is not yet 11. The suggestion of nausea having passed, and the surging of the straining boat – overtaken continually by a southwesterly following sea – produces some of the sensation of rocking in a cradle. And for the second time this morning I feel intimations of water–reverie. A mood of peace is not exactly consistent with blowing something up, though. Especially something with eyes as big as dinner plates, one of which looked accusatorily into my own not long before. Of course, until the advent of motors, everything done on the sea was slower than just about anything on dry land – except maybe building stonewalls. And everyone who went down to sea in ships knew a big change of pace was in the cards. Perhaps that is why many went. Thinking this reminds me of the story about the two New England fishermen who meet up, with only a nod, as the sun rises on their cove, and row out in a dory to fish. About a mile from land, they put down their oars and – each crossing a leg over a knee – drop in their hooks. After twenty minutes without any nibbles, one of them uncrosses his right leg, then lifts the right to cross his left. His comrade, looking him up and down, squints in scrutiny. "So," this second fisherman chides, "ya heah ta *fish* or just ta *dance*?"

But though there is serenity in the slowness, we are dragging somberness along too. I've sensed that all aboard have thought of this disposing of a whale as a combination of nuisance and lark. I, myself, only began to consider its demise a minor tragedy when I "entered an animal's space", i.e. splashed into the water beside the massive dead *thing* under the dock.

It seems to me a fishing boat is a place of death that horrifies no one. Unmoved, we witness animals, the size of chickens or pigs, suffocate – dozens, even hundreds, at a time – in the air we breathe. If genteel individuals, which all of us onboard presume we are, were to visit a slaughter house and there see pigs and chickens thrown live into water-filled vats to slowly drown while clawing at the surface for oxygen – as the first step in the process of bringing them to the dinner table – we likely would feel some discomfort. But sea fauna drowning in the air we humans cherish is something we don't comprehend as torture. I've mentioned my party-boat job ended halfway through the summer of my eighteenth year. I'd been hired as the cutter on Captain Dick Bruce's *Island Prince*: cutter of bait for the hooks of the tourists, but also as an eviscerator of nuisance fish – mostly dogfish and blue sharks. My captain-oh-captain would likely not be called a sadist, given the prevailing attitude that fish have no feelings. But I knew he was. He had taught me that landing a dogfish was displeasing to a customer and "trash fish" should be removed and the line re-baited as quickly as possible. The way to do this, he showed me, was to skewer the underbelly of the small shark with a gaff – a barb-less hook on a pole – pull it aboard to where you could grab it by the snout, and then, with your fish knife slice through its jaw to cut out the hook for reuse. During this time the shark's eye – unlike our whale's, still a living window into the animal's being – would stare into mine, and the body would writhe powerfully; intestines squirting out of the half-inch hole gouged by the curved spike. When I'd saved the precious 35-cent fishhook, I'd been instructed to toss the live mutilated creature back to the eager mouths of its brothers and sisters. Dogfish and blue sharks are the piranhas of Gulf of Maine clean-up. One day, after several weeks and an untold number of deaths, a grandfatherly tourist aboard that morning informed me that it was faster and easier to eliminate the gaff and, after pulling the fish aboard by the line, grab it by its snout and just bend the snout back until it snapped. The animal died instantly, and the hook pretty much popped away. At the end of that day I confronted Captain Bruce about the inferior and inhumane method he'd taught me. "I thought you'd enjoy it," was his reply. That was my last day as cutter on the *Island Prince*.

But that captain would not be considered a sadist because we do not think of fish as our cousins – in the way we do animals with lungs. The dead creature being dragged ignominiously backward behind us, though, is an air breather, a fellow mammal. And one who does us no harm – a peaceful eater of seaweed, krill, and shrimp. At least I think *she* – as Fred refers to *it* – is that. What do I know about whales? Not much, but enough to have heard that every so often one of these water mammals grabs a cousin of its own, a porpoise or a seal, to snack on. Sounds bad, but I'm a meat eater myself, so I can't point fingers. And I'm not implying that humpbacks are expected to be the saints of the sea. Everyone has a right to a little change of pace. This reminds me of vegetarian Nora, one of the ad reps at the paper. We go out to lunch together from time to time. And when we do, she

211

almost always grabs my burger or pastrami sandwich for a quick bite
– while I pause to say something without my mouth full. But, she's a
married woman, and maybe biting some other man's sandwich is
more a way of having extramarital fun.

"I think I may owe you an apology." Justin Bollard snaps me out
of my psychic drift.

I turn and see him feeling his way across the undulating deck, hand
extended. Though I thought he seemed somehow different today, this
still comes as a shock. Instinctively, I proffer my own hand in reply.

He says, "You were part of saving my life yesterday, and I didn't
thank you."

"I didn't do much," I say. "My cousin Kevin did all the dangerous
work."

"Yes, I know – and I was kind of a shit to him, too. When we get
back in today I'm going to buy him the best bottle of champagne they
sell in Northport."

I'm tempted to tell him Kevin won't drink it, but since he won't, I
might get to, so I keep my mouth shut. Besides, it's the thought that
counts.

"I want to say…," he starts a little haltingly, "… I was
stunned…and pretty drunk…when I came out of that cold sea. It all
didn't seem real. It was like something happening to someone else. I
swallowed some water and choked. And that felt real enough. But I
had no idea what had actually happened. I hadn't caught up with it.
And before I did catch up with it, somebody was holding my head
above the surface. And I just felt like other people were taking care of
everything. Like when I was a little kid and I didn't have to worry
about life. And – I have to admit – I was embarrassed. Embarrassed
as hell. And instead of thinking about what had happened – my *Pascal
moment,* that I bragged about so foolishly – I talked and
talked…babbled. I was being a bad philosopher…"

He seems *authentically* contrite.

"Well, don't be too hard on yourself," I say. What am I talking about? I'm delighted as can be that he's being hard on himself. But I'm distrustful when people give me what I want. I assume there will be a price to pay. So I help them off the hook when they put themselves on one. I quickly glance over at Dalmore, wondering if he can hear – and wondering if Justin's embarrassing himself with Dalmore would be part of his penance; would he be willing to let the big man hear what he's saying? I realize I don't know the hierarchy: is an art critic above or below a curator? They didn't teach me this in art history class. Dalmore, I notice, is looking sullen. Since this boat has no cockpit, one can sit on the rail or one can stand. Fred did, I must say, an admirable job of hosing down the *Laura T* at the Phillip's Cove dock. But a hose does not a scrub-brush replace, and my guess is that Fred's rail is not quite a fitting perch for Dalmore's white slacks. So he stands under the boat's flying roof between a now chatty Fred and a silent David at the wheel. Captain and mate have done the persona change I guessed could take place. The bits of conversation – monologue, really – I can hear from the stern, reveal that Fred is lecturing Dalmore about insulation, the "R factor" desirable for his oceanfront home. Fred thinks everybody has too little insulation.

Though Bollard doesn't show concern for privacy, I think we've got some anyway. And he is masochistic – or something – enough to want to stay on the hook for a few more flagellations.

"Do you mind me talking about this?" he asks humbly.

"Of course not," I say.

"I was a bad philosopher because I was letting my embarrassment – my ego – govern my interpretation of phenomenon. – I mean, what had just *happened*. But it was only last night – in the quiet of my room – a person's room is where Descartes said the most important things occur – that the authenticity that had been thrust upon me...that I'd stumbled into – literally stumbled into – took over. And I trembled. I started to feel myself going under. Going under, knowing it was all over. Everything: art, my reputation, my mother, the boys and men that I've loved, Pascal, sunlight, air. I felt what it was to know that all is ending. I didn't know that feeling yesterday.

213

But I knew it last night. Ending in perhaps just two more minutes. Two minutes that I could claw at a liquid world to try to make last five seconds more – while at the same time wanting it to end as fast as it could end. Mother, time, my beautiful apartment in New York, everything. To stop the agony of what it is like to breathe water instead of air." This small, intense man's eyes are welling up and his voice is choked. But he goes on.

"And I sobbed and sobbed. A boy I know came to my door. But I sent him away. – I don't even know if I want to see him again. Finally I relaxed and took a deep breath of wonderful sweet air. And then felt as light as the air. I realized what I was feeling was just what you said: '*Relief! Relief is the greatest sensation there is.*' I'd never even considered that. Never had to. Haven't been sick much. Never been mugged. I'm something of a hedonist, I have to admit. I like my pleasures. But last night I realized what you said was true. *Relief.* Sweet *relief!* I realized that the greatest positive there can be is very simply being delivered from a terrible negative. So then the relieving of pain has to be the greatest pleasure there is. The ending of fear, the greatest joy."

Bollard has gotten pretty worked-up and I think he realizes it, and he comes back down a bit.

"I mean, I'm not sure if that is what you meant. But what you said opened my eyes to seeing that that is *true*, regardless"

Gay or not – him, I mean – I feel like I could kiss him. It's seldom that anyone believably affirms to you that they really know what you mean. And it's almost never that anyone who actually might do this is a person who has invested much of his life in proselytizing about something entirely different. This could be an exception to what I thought was an inflexible rule: "Never argue with a man whose job depends on not being convinced." Of course, arguing with a man may not be enough: probably you need to nearly drown him. But I'm getting ahead of myself. He hasn't said that he is renouncing his whole *replicum* theory. Oddly, it seems he experienced replicum in the moment of crisis and reality after the fact. Well, denial of death works in strange ways.

"That is about what I meant to say," I reply. "Had an experience once myself that made me realize that's how things are." I guess I won't tell him the experience was a head-cold. Anyway, this is gratifying – and enough so that I don't ask him whether it is incompatible with the worldview he was expounding only 20 hours ago. "I'm surprised you came today. After a night like that, I mean. There are some moments when I wonder if going out on the sea is really all that sane."

"Well, then call me crazy, but today I feel like I'm not afraid of anything – except maybe drinking too much and getting into stupid arguments. I feel like George Bailey in *It's A Wonderful Life*. Scrooge on Christmas morning. Also, I came because I wanted the chance to talk to you."

"I appreciate it, I really appreciate it," I say. Well, he may be a philosopher, but I think I know a little bit about relief – that it fades. I do hope that he can ride this horse he's on for at least a few more laps around the track – before the horse ambles back to the barn.

There is an awkward silence as apparently neither one of us has anything further to say on the meaning of life and death. We both look back at the churning water and the dragging whale.

After a minute Bollard finds a new subject that's close to his heart. "Your young friend – David, is it?" So much for leaving hedonism behind. And authenticity, for that matter. We both know that he knows that David's name is David. But this is a different kind of disingenuousness. Everyone has a right to a little bit of cover for hedonistic proclivities. Or for plain old shyness.

"What's his work like?" Bollard asks.

"His work?"

"Yes, he told me about his metal sculpture. Sounds like quite a vision."

"He did?" I say, surprised. "He told you he did metal sculpture?"

Bollard seems puzzled. "You're saying he's pretty private about it, I guess?"

That isn't what I'm saying. But I can see where he is going and

215

decide to humor him. "I've never known David to talk about it."

"But you've seen it?"

"Oh, yes," I say – not adding that I've been aware of David's *vision* about two hours longer than Bollard has.

"And?"

I don't know what to say. So I say the all-purpose: "It's pretty ironic."

"I'm sure it is. He has quite an enigmatic manner. His wild jokes. I'd love to know what's going on in that head."

"Yes. He's an enigma, all right," I say.


"Put her in neutral, laddy," Fred says to David. "Time to get to work."

Fred flips the top of a wooden box on the deck and removes a large hunting knife, some heavy twine, and a roll of electrical tape. He picks up a wooden pole that has been lying on the deck in the niche between this big box and the gunwale. The pole is about six feet long and I suppose it could have once been a curtain rod. Fred places the knife handle against the end of the pole and wraps tightly first twine then tape around the overlap of both – so it creates what could be nothing else but a spear. Then he starts up the Gorgon, puts it in gear and winches boat and whale toward each other. When the two bump, he takes the winch out of gear, goes to the helm and cranks the wheel hard to starboard. Then he puts the boat's engine in gear so that we creep up along the length of the whale. With a boat hook he gathers the slackening line from the whale's tail and pulls it on board to keep it away from the boat's propeller. When boat and whale are side by side – with the midpoint of Fred's work deck at about the midpoint of the whale – Fred goes to the rail and leans his head and shoulders out above the carcass. With the spear he's made he attempts to cut into the tough hide. This appears not so easy. When he does get through, and then succeeds in burying the blade into blubber, he begins a circular sawing motion, apparently attempting to make an opening large enough to allow the thickness of the union of the blade and pole to penetrate. Regardless of my feeling for the whale, his activity compels my attention. Even more interested — I'm surprised to see — is Dalmore. He is practically leaning over Fred. Bollard is close behind him. Fascinated though I am, I remember my camera and duck below to get it. By the time I'm back, the necessary enlargement has been accomplished. I'm clicking my first frames just as Fred pushes hard on the pole.

As the lump of the handle disappears into the wound a *whoosh* of a gas escapes and sprays into Fred's face with enough force to blow his skipper's cap off his head. He snaps upright, brushing Dalmore aside, and staggers backwards from the rail toward amidships. Then he reels, first left then right, and crumples onto the deck. Even from the 10-foot distance away that I stand, I'm revolted by the fumes. I can't vouch for the cumulative experience of the lifetimes of those on board, however my guess is that none of us has ever smelled anything so bad.

Dalmore got the second worst of the whooshing. His eyes are rolled back revealing mostly whites, as he digs at the air in front of his face. Reflexively, he moves backward, away from the source of misery, and encounters passed-out Fred's large, up-pointing rubber boots. This causes him to sit down hard onto sprawled-out Fred's midsection. That revives Fred, and reflexively he doubles ups, head-butting Dalmore right between the shoulder blades. Dalmore's own head whiplashes back onto the top of Fred's now hatless pate, and Fred falls backwards again.

David, far enough away at the helm, appears unaffected by the noxious vapor. Justin is coughing. But his exposure was mostly blocked by Dalmore. Though nauseated myself, sympathy for the afflicted is my strongest reaction. But I can't contain a smile at having witnessed the best slapstick I've ever encountered in real life. All but David are too distressed to notice my "schadenfreude-istic" amusement. And David, noticing, smiles too.

"Methane," Fred manages to choke out as he rolls to the right away from Dalmore and regains his wind.

Dalmore, doubly victimized, gets up and staggers in a circle, jutting his elbows backward and tilting his head up and down, apparently trying to remove a head-butt-induced kink from his neck. To me his movements look like a very credible Funky Chicken dance stepping. I've been snapping away, not really cognizant of how many pictures I've actually shot. But in the debilitation and commotion, I don't think anyone but David is aware that the scene is being recorded. And David is not one to volunteer much. Too enigmatic.

Fred shakes his head a few times and manages to stand. "I guess that should be deep enough," he says. "I'll get the dynamite." He has apparently recovered rapidly from his disorientation and unsteadiness – at least to the minimal level required to handle dynamite. He staggers toward the covered wooden box – pausing as he coughs a few times – opens it and takes out a spool of wire. Under the rail, sit the plastic milk bottles we got at Connie's. Fred unrolls several yards of wire and threads it through the molded handles of the containers. Then he picks up a piece of the rigid PVC water pipe with the sharply cut ends that we'd loaded into his truck. He feeds the wire down the length of the pipe until it protrudes from the pointy end. Then he lays the pipe on the rail. The two-inch combing prevents its rolling into the sea. He goes back to the big box and removes the small, heavy case David had supplied. From that, he takes out an explosive stick about a foot long and an inch in diameter. A metal tab extends from one end. Fred goes back to the rail, pinches hold of the black plastic-coated wire protruding from the plastic pipe and pulls more out. Taking up his jack knife, which hangs from a string on his belt, he bares two inches of copper at the wire's end. He pushes this through a hole in the tab on the dynamite. Then he removes needle-nose pliers from a pocket of his rubber overalls and with them crimps and twists the copper wire to make it fast. Next, he pulls on the wire at the other end of the pipe and the dynamite recedes until only about two inches of it protrudes at the sharpened end. It's a close fit. I speculate that this is good. He instructs me to hold the end of the pipe with the wire extending so that the relationship of the two stays as is. Then he reaches into his pocket again and withdraws the electrical tape he used earlier. He tightly wraps tape around the bit of dynamite still showing so that it's affixed at that spot inside the pipe.

It occurs to me that David, the dynamite expert, is instead in charge of running the boat. I wander over to him.

"How come you aren't doing this?"

David looks at me blankly and says, "He's the captain."

We stand together watching this captain continue with his rigging. Then I change the subject with young David, "When did you start calling your refrigerators sculpture?"

"Huh?" he says.

"Justin Bollard said you told him about your metal sculpture."

"I didn't say they were sculpture."

"What did you say? "

"Said they were somethin' I liked to do. He asked me if I was devoted to the sea and I said, 'not particularly.' – It didn't give me time to be creative. And he asked 'How do you express your creativity?' So I told him I blew things up. I thought it was funny— *blowing things up to be creative*. But I guess he took me seriously – said he wanted to see what I did. I didn't realize he thought they were sculpture. Do you think they might be worth some money? That would be nice. Who'd want one though? Where would they put it? In the kitchen? That would be funny."

It would be very funny, I think. And I think about how as a New Yorker – New York being a place where your waiter or plumber also maintains an art career – Bollard would assume David likely to consider his fun his *work*.

"You know Justin Bollard's a big art critic in New York."

"No. I didn't ask what he did. I guess I should have. Big Apple, huh? That might have told me whether he'd get a joke. I knew the big guy was the museum director or curator or whatever. Art critic, huh? So you think I could get money for my stuff?"

"I don't know," I say. "But good luck."

I turn and watch as Fred goes to the rail. Boat and cetacean are bobbing only about three feet apart. Fred can reach his incision adequately with a good stretch and the length of PVC. It still smells bad. But now methane is just *wafting.* Any fisherman can deal with that. But Fred's audience shows less interest this time. Dalmore, leaning against the cabin, head inclined skyward, doesn't even watch. I move to the rail to try to get a shot of the dynamite entering the carcass.

Fred pushes the pointy plastic pipe into the incision. Then pausing to remove a handkerchief from his shirt pocket and putting it over his nose, he orders. "Everyone back."

We all cringe.

Then he pushes hard. But a second pressurized emission fails to occur.

Fred shoves the electrical tape into my hand.

"Every time a length of wire the width of the boat is played out into the water you wrap a piece of tape around the wire *here.*" He says this, handing me a plastic milk container with his index finger on the handle where the blasting wire runs through it. "Gotta do it fast." I now remember the milk jug is to keep the wire on the surface. I'd found the statement unfathomable when Fred made it this morning. Obviously, we will distance ourselves from the whale when it's plunger-pushing time. So I guess we can't take any chances of catching the wire on the prop when we maneuver. Should have figured that out.

"Helmsman!" he calls out affectedly to David. "To the wheel."

David is already standing at the wheel – has never left it. He just raises his eyebrows and looks left and right. "What?" he says flatly.

Fred orders, "Helm hard to port. Put her in gear at idle speed. Perkins – your floatation devices – overboard now!"

I feel a tug on the wire coming from deep in the whale as we creep away from the dead creature.

"Helmsman, take 'er outta gear and let 'er drift." I keep on with the taping until six plastic bottles are bobbing in the water. The momentum of the boat has slowed to almost a stop. David puts the engine into gear just long enough to remove successive slack, to keep the wire fairly taut. When it seems that some strain may be developing, Fred reels out a few more feet of wire and throws it overboard. The whale is now about twenty yards off our rail. Fred quickly takes out his knife, severs the wire from the spool and bares an inch of copper on the end coming from the sea.

"Mr. Perkins," he says. He holds the wire in front of my face. I take it. Then he reaches into the box again and pulls out the detonator. He puts this on the rail and pulls up on the handle. He grabs the wire from my hand and feeds it into a slot under the plunger. Then he turns a thumbscrew. He looks into each face on the boat. Even Dalmore, composure regained, watches now.

"Are we ready?" he asks his audience. No one replies. All eyes are on the whale, about seventy feet off. "Five," he says, "four…three…two…one – *ignition*!"

The plunger goes down. And, yes, there is ignition. There is a boom. And there is definitely a reaction in the body of the whale. But the boom is muffled and the whale reacts with little more than a shudder. My first thought is of those shock-absorbing blankets made from old tires that I'd seen at David's. They are probably not that different from the blubber and hide of a whale. I look over at David. He shrugs and looks out to sea over the opposite rail.

I glance at Fred and he either isn't surprised or does a good job of hiding it. Perhaps realizing everyone is looking in his direction for a chance to disapprove, he nods sagely.

A challenging stare comes from Dalmore. Dalmore is paying for the dynamite – and for this whole unsatisfactory boat trip as well.

"'Standard procedure?'" he asks. Disdain drips from his lower lip like hot pudding off a spoon.

If Fred is daunted – and my guess is he is – he doesn't let it show. I speculate now that he has never done anything of this kind before. This is just his latest science experiment. But I reevaluate: he probably isn't the least bit daunted. He has plenty of dynamite, doesn't he? He says, "You always start with a *test stick*."

"A test stick?" Dalmore mutters, shaking his head.

"The test stick," Fred explains, "tells us that this operation is about a five-stick job."

Dalmore sniffs hard and tosses his nose in the air. This normally innocuous calisthenics move apparently causes discomfort now, after his fall. He throws a hand up and over his shoulder like a soldier who has been shot. The pain in the neck of dealing with Fred is not merely metaphorical. He goes back into a couple of Funky Chicken shrugs, seemingly to no avail. Wincing he asks, "How much longer is this *operation* supposed to take?"

"Just the same amount of time as the first time took – with about a minute added on for wiring four more sticks. We do the whole five in one blast. And we've got a nice big cavity for five sticks now." For Fred it may well be that everything is proceeding like clockwork. My guess is that he has already forgotten that a few minutes ago he was sprawled on the deck with his antagonist on top of him. I imagine that what he can't pretend is *standard procedure,* he'll just ignore.

So we repeat the steps: approaching the whale, inserting explosives, milk jugs, drifting off sixty–five feet – everything.

I move over to young David. "Five sticks sound right to you?"

"Not sure. Depends on what the first stick did. Just because she didn't open up don't mean it didn't do some real damage."

Fred does his, *Are we ready? Three...two...one.* I raise my camera on *one* and snap on *ignition.*

The boom this time is thunder. And the reaction sixty-five feet away at sea is as startling as close-up lightning. A dome of pink matter and blue smoke arcs forty or fifty feet high. Then it separates into falling pink and ascending blue. Some pieces of exceptional mass travel a greater distance than the perimeter of the arc and splatter the boat, its passengers and crew. This time I'm not spared contact with essence of whale. A black and white and red chunk lands on my shoulder. Justin, next to me, takes a hit, too. "Oh, gross," I say. But I can't help laughing. And I think I hear Justin exclaim, "Now that's authentic!" and laugh, too – at the same moment that a surge of seawater radiating from the epicenter of the blast lifts the boat and lists it dramatically toward Europe. All of us but David, who's clutching the wheel, end up sprawled this time. But – what – do you –know? – *everyone*, Dalmore included – is laughing. And not just laughing, but *whooping*. Suddenly we are band of brothers – that is, while our chests still reverberate and our ears continue to ring. Something basic has brought us together: men and boys whether cultured or cultureless – love a bomb. The sensation is one of – what? Maybe victory? Perhaps it's a primal reflex imprinted by a few million years of facing larger animals with only pointed sticks. "We can do it – and we just did!" *Authentic*, perhaps – though, in truth, it was all pretty contrived. For the second time today – the first, when David accosted him on the dock – I see Dalmore, now with his summer whites splattered with pink and red, wearing an expression appropriate to his situation; in harmony with his environment. He's grinning like a naughty boy of twelve.

The euphoria lasts about as long as the smoke. When we can see the spot where the whale was, we see that it still *is*. I didn't poll my comrades but my guess is that we all thought such a thunderous blow would have reduced the whale to fine particles. But two pink continents of flesh – landing platforms for seabirds now – float in a sea of red; where a rubbery black animal had, a minute ago, floated on blue-green. Meat islands of various sizes bob just off shore of the two great masses. What it seems we have done is to make a disgusting mess. Hardly a reason for euphoria. Dalmore, touching his shirt, now seems aware of being sartorially compromised. I recognize a blush suffusing his sailor's tan. He succumbed to the thrill of destruction. I imagine his realization of this bothers him more than the state of his clothes – though, of everyone I know, Dalmore is the one that I believe would most find personal funkiness insupportable. His expression morphs from embarrassed to vexed, as he observes Fred nodding in self-satisfaction.

I'm revolted by the scene, too, but I think it is exactly what we all should have envisioned – that is, when we signed on back at the dock.

"Have you finished?" Dalmore asks in a tone appropriate for confronting Joseph McCarthy about decency.

Fred doesn't answer. Back to persona number one, I'm thinking.

"Some of us have obligations," Dalmore snipes. "We would like to head in now."

"Just a moment," Fred says crisply, straight-arming in Dalmore's direction. "It's starting."

I follow Fred's gaze. Afternoon sun glares off the wreckage we've wrought. But I can see that one of the big meat masses seems to be *wriggling.* And some of the smaller chunks submerge and come back up. And they are smaller still when they do. The surface of the water, calm since the circular, blast-generated wave passed away, breaks up into chop.

"Dogfish," I say. "Dogfish and blue sharks."

Fred says, "Young David – put 'er in gear and coast over that way."

Within a minute we are at the edge of the islands of flesh that float in our man-made sea of red. We bump into chunks and get thumped by blue sharks deranged by the blood that is part of nature's terrible "bounty." Everything is moving. Shark bites shark. Sharks, in frenzy, even bite at diving seagulls.

I hear Bollard softly intone, "The horror."

I can't tell whether he is quoting Joseph Conrad or Marlon Brando, or saying this on his own. I might just contribute in the vernacular, "Yes, the system sucks." I might ask what kind of supreme being – or random process, for that matter – would come up with a system in which one life form can survive only by feeding on the life of another? I think of just the herbivores I've consumed – the flocks of lambs and herds of steers. And then there are the dozens of coops-full of chickens that I have devoured in just my life so far. If they were all still walking the planet and were living alongside the chickens, lambs, and steers my fellow men have consumed in the same time, there might be no place left for anyone to comfortably stand. Eating each other is an efficient, nutritious, and tasty method of controlling population. Makes war without cannibalism seem civilized to the point of being wasteful.

But what about the pain that comes with all that death and devouring? What is it that makes all the pain necessary? Yes, pain tells us to keep our weight off a broken ankle. Well, how brilliant! Pain is *useful.* Serves a purpose. But why pain of the *degree* we are created to feel – and the *duration*? Why are the heights and duration of pleasure always limited. While the depths and breadths of pain limitless? Why? Because the world is out of joint. That's *why.* That broken ankle will torment until it is attended to, if attention can be had – and then, long after the attention, the pain persists. And in the animal kingdom a broken ankle means pain unto death – and being devoured.

"The horror," Bollard, watching, intones again.

Yes, the system sucks. But it can be shamefully fascinating to watch.

And Dalmore is watching. He looks troubled, looks confused. But he smiles a little, too. He also looks like he might want to retract the demand that we immediately depart.

Then the Captain speaks: "I guess that does it."

Fred addresses his mate at the helm, "Come over to a heading of 275, and we'll call it a day."

David turns the wheel to starboard and the *Laura T*, unburdened, heads for the comforts of shore.

# 17

As I enter the house I see Gram asleep on the living room couch in front of the TV. She has closed the red curtains again. But now they are just lifeless fabric. No breeze stirs them and the afternoon sun has traveled far away from entry through those windows. Rosebud jumps up from the rug beside the couch and in her characteristic reversing arcs scurries toward me for a head scratching. The television glows with President Reagan fielding questions. I can't hear him, though. The TV's speaker is all the way down and the old stereo tuner – with headphone jack – that I wired to the television, has its volume control knob way up. Headphones sit a bit askew on Gram's head. So, though unconscious, she is being blasted. She's hot and cold about our President. One day she'll say, "I think he's a great man," and the next she'll say, "President Reagan is not a great man." I'm not sure if she believes Ronald Reagan shifts or if it's that her criteria for greatness shift. But some men, in her opinion, are continually great. Men like Phil Donahue, Professor

Jacob Bronowski, Peter Ustinov, and the already noted, Carl Sagan. I don't know if Reagan is up or down today in her book. But she is watching – or was – because she considers it her duty as a citizen to keep up with what is going on.

Nevertheless, I turn the TV off. The sudden absence of sound wakes her with a jolt. She looks a little flustered. I bend down and remove the headphones, giving her a peck on the forehead.

She leans up on an elbow. "Is he gone?" she asks.

"Is who gone?"

"The president," she says. "I've been trying to get up for the last ten minutes and I couldn't. He was giving a speech right here. He was practically sitting on my chest. Boy can he talk. He wouldn't stop."

"Gram, it was a dream." Gram has vivid dreams. Sometimes talks aloud during them. A few weeks ago I heard her saying from her sleep, "What a beautiful baby. Don't bring him near me. I have a cold." (Actually, she didn't have one.) "I said 'Don't bring him near me – I have a cold.' Is he sick? No? Good. What a beautiful baby!"

She looks confused. I say again, "It was a dream."

"It wasn't a dream. Reagan was right here. I told him, 'Will you shut up? I have to go to the bathroom.'" Gram pulls herself to a sitting position and looks around. Only now is she fully awake. "Oh. I'm being silly. It must have been a dream. But it was so real."

"He was on TV. You fell asleep with your headphones on. He's on right now."

"How do you know that?"

"Well, he was on one minute ago when I came in. I turned it off."

"Why did you do that? I was watching. Turn it back on."

"I thought you had to go to the bathroom."

"I do. I'll watch the end when I get back."

So, while she manages to achieve a standing position and trundle off, I turn the news conference back on – sound up – only to hear, "Mr. President, Mr. President...This 'welfare queen', you talked about – Can you give us her name?..." Reagan cups his hand to his ear for a split second, looking uncomprehending, then gives a wave, swings away, and disappears down the hall. So I turn it off again.

I sit down in the rocker opposite the couch. Gram reappears.

"Alex – put the TV back on. I have to know what's happening in the world."

"It's over. He ducked out."

"You made me miss it," she says.

"I didn't make you miss it. You fell asleep on your own."

"Oh. I guess you're right. I'm sorry I blamed you. He wasn't saying anything anyway." She goes from recriminating to apologizing and back to recriminating. "Where have you been? You haven't been home for days."

"I slept in my bed last night and was out early. I left you a note."

"Oh. That's right. You said you were helping Fred. I thought you worked on Mondays. Did you go fishing?"

"Fred blew up a whale. I'm surprised you can't smell it. I'm writing a story about it for the paper."

"That Fred," she says, waving her hand, "he's a screwball. Show me the story when it gets printed. Did you eat? I made the beans."

Gram staggers a bit as she winds around to now sit in her wicker TV chair.

"I wish you'd use your cane," I say.

"I am using it."

"Well, I can't see it."

"That's because I'm not using it right now. But I know where it is."

"So if you have a fall you can crawl over to it to help yourself back up?"

"I have to walk without it. It's the only way my body will know to keep its equilibrium."

"You promised me you'd use it after you fell off the front porch throwing out the dead flowers."

She changes the subject. "I'm almost finished with your Shackleton book. He is one of history's great men. – And those men he took with him to the South Pole! They had to eat their favorite

228

dogs. Imagine eating Rosebud?"

She looks down with an expression of unconditional affection for the canine I am unselfconsciously scratching under her floppy, liver-colored ears. Suddenly I'm self-conscious: I think about my fingers and give them a sniff. Springer ears are infection prone. Not too bad right now. But I'll shower as soon as I leave the room.

"I'd rather starve than eat Rosebud," she says with deep feeling. Then moves right on. "And they put on minstrel shows on the ice at the South Pole. Imagine: minstrel shows at the South Pole. I've never heard of such a thing."

"They didn't quite make it to the South Pole," I correct needlessly.

"It doesn't matter. I froze to death last night with my windows open. And this is June!"

Her mention of Rosebud reminds me. "Hey, Gram — I've got a joke for you."

"What is it?" she asks.

"Okay. You need to help. I say, 'My dog has no nose.' And you ask me, 'How does it smell?' Okay?"

"Okay. 'How does he smell?'"

"Wait for me. Okay? — My dog has no nose."

"How can it smell?"

"Not 'How can it smell,' how does it smell?'"

"What's the difference?"

"There's a difference. Just say it."

"Okay, 'How – "

"Wait for me. My dog has no nose."

"How does it smell?"

"Awful!"

"That's not very funny."

"Well it would have been if you hadn't called all that attention to the wording."

She waves me away with a down-flick of an up-turned palm.

"I've got a better one than that."

"Really?"

"Yes, but you don't have to say anything – so there won't be any mix-up. I say: 'When I die I want to go peacefully in my sleep, like Grandpa – not screaming like all the passengers in his car.'"

I crack up and she does too, repeating the punch line she'd enjoyed delivering so much.

"That's pretty good," I say. "Where did you hear it?"

"At the nursing home, when I went with Harriet to visit Mildred Weare. One of the CNAs told Harriet – they're friends – and Harriet told me. I think the CNA would have been afraid to tell it to someone my age."

"You might be right. Might hit too close to home. Could get her fired."

Gram changes the subject. "I told you I made the beans. Did you eat?" She means a lima bean soup. And that means the pressure cooker – an instrument of destruction, designated by my Aunt Sylvia and me as strictly off-limits. My blood runs cold at a mental picture of her and the big pot wrestling for dominance. Full, the thing almost outweighs her. And it's probably full – she always makes enough of the beans for a month. I consider the effect of scolding her after the fact – rather than just putting the pressure cooker on too high a shelf for her to get it when I'm not home – something I thought I'd already done. I wonder how she got up there? But I just say, "Yes, the house smells good. I'll get some."

"Well, have them while they're hot. They taste like chestnuts. And they're very nutritious. They're good cold, too. Your grandfather and I used to take them on picnics with your father and your uncle Jimmy. They're a great invention. They're healthy, portable, and long lasting."

Gram congratulates herself on the good qualities of her "invention" every time she makes the beans. "The beans" is the invention's official name. I'm not passionate about beans of any kind, but hers make the best of a bad legume. And they do taste a bit like chestnuts. I'm big on chestnuts. The beans are Perkins family comfort food. My mother used to make them Gram's way, too. Sometimes she'd give them to me cold for a snack when I'd come home from school. What had been a combination of solid and liquid elements when hot, congealed into a porridge-like mass in the refrigerator. It sounds awful now, I know, but I remember gobbling them up – I mean "it" up – many times before running out to play.

"Okay," I say. "Can I get some for you?"

"No, it's too early. They won't go down yet. They'll make me vomit."

"Vomit" again. I can't stop myself from another futile correction. "You mean 'gag,'"

"It means the same thing."

"No, it doesn't, Gram. It has to go down first if you're going to vomit it. If it won't go down yet, it's just gagging. You should say 'gag'. The other night when the McCarthys brought over that pizza you said, 'No thank you, it makes me vomit,' and I think everyone was pretty grossed out."

"They knew what I meant. Pizza has always made me vomit." With barely a pause – the subject having perhaps stimulated her appetite – she now says, "Get me a little bowl of the beans, too." She makes a nest of gnarled fingers from both hands woven tightly to indicate a small container. "And make sure that they're really hot. They're best when they're hot."

"Do you want your teeth first?" I ask. Dentures irritate Gram's mouth. She employs them like a fourth utensil. Just during a meal. Or wears them cosmetically, like putting on lipstick for guests – though she isn't particularly concerned about being caught by visitors without them. No shame in that – not like being caught by visitors without food on hand to offer.

"No. This book has me discombobulated. I need something stronger. Bring me a Scotch."

"I said 'teeth' not 'tea.'"

"No, the beans, I can eat without teeth."

"And you do want the Scotch? – It's only 4:30."

"Yes. Bring it to me. I won't have one tonight. I need it to settle my stomach. I'll take it like medicine."

"Okay," I say.

Later, while Gram watches excerpts of the press conference on the evening news, I take the cordless phone and go out to the porch. The early summer late afternoon is a warm, translucent blue and green. Birds of a variety of feather chirp or sing together. A cardinal trills a call my mother always used to tell me was, "be-a-hero, be-a-hero."

Not feeling like a hero, I remove a scrap of paper from my wallet. On it is the number for Lucinda York. I sit down on the daybed to call. I feel guilty and ambivalent. Guilty, because I tried to make her feel like a fool for believing in something I think is childish and stupid. Ambivalent because, though I'm attracted to her crazy energy and love having sex with her, I am enough of an intolerant type that I'm not sure I want to be with someone who believes in things I think are childish and stupid.

So I feel guilty. But I'm not sure how much guilt I *should* feel in this situation. Goes with my questioning trusting instincts. How do we know when the supposed instinct comes from some beautiful, deeper, more spiritual source, or from something neurotic, conditioned at a very early age – and our not being able to remember its origins makes it seems just as primal? I'm actually a bit guilt-prone. I called an ugly girl ugly once in seventh grade and I still feel bad about it. That kind of guilt. And the trouble with guilt is the type of person who readily feels it may be – or even probably is – less likely to do things he should feel guilty about. And the type of person who seldom feels guilt has less inhibition for doing something bad. So, it may be that more often than not the wrong people feel the most guilt. This set up may be exacerbated by the new age/pop psych value that guilt is entirely unhealthy – repressive of the human spirit. It's true – it is repressive of the human spirit. Guilt, though, I believe, is a humanizing part of the human spirit, represses some bad parts. (Like, I wonder, when did the first caveman feel guilty about clubbing his neighbor for no good reason?) Think of how much more mayhem there'd be if the guilt-prone were as uninhibited as the don't-guilt-trip-me types. It's true that guilt-tripping often isn't pretty. But I'd venture to guess that more guilt-trips are somewhat legitimate than are bogus. The trouble is they usually only succeed on the already guilt-receptive.

But all this rationalizing doesn't quite do the trick. I do feel guilty. I attacked Lucinda's beliefs. I even was sneaky in setting her up. And even though I feel guilty, I'm still not sure that I'm sorry that I did it.

I let Lucinda's phone ring many times. And just as I am about to hang up it's answered.

"Dog pound."

I recognize Avrum's voice. It can even be melodious on just two syllables.

"Hi, Avrum," I say, trying to sound like an old pal. This is Alex Perkins." There's no reaction. " – From last night," I add.

"Oh – right. The admirer who wrote Lucinda that naughty love letter."

"Right – that's the guy. How you doin'?"

"Good."

"Lucinda there?"

"Luce? No, she's gone out. She and William."

Uggah – I feel a stab.

"Right," I say.

"Shall I tell her you called?"

"Uhh – sure – I guess. It isn't important."

"Well, that's not how it so*wunds*. Affairs of the heart are always important. My paramour is off with someone else, too. I'm just like you tonight. Ditched for an artist."

A wild thought crosses my mind. Is his paramour, Justin and David, the *artist*? Another thing that would have been inconceivable twenty-four hours ago when *Pure Conception* was just about to bounce off some black rubbery thing under Arthur Dalmore's dock.

"So you want to come over and get high? We can lick our wounds together."

Well, it is flattering when anybody exceptionally pretty takes an interest in you. But I say, "Can't. I'm babysitting my Grandmother.

233

Maybe next time. Bye."

I put down the phone. Suddenly I'm no longer ambivalent. I'm sorry. I'm very sorry. I want my Lucinda. I've been a jerk! And now I'm going to pay.

# 18

"Hey, these are good! Who're the people?"

I've just come up from the darkroom and handed Steve my photos from the whale disposal expedition. I've also submitted my story about Dalmore and the NoMMA – a puff piece I wrote with one hand tied behind my back for political reasons. But, no Lucinda performance story.

"The guy in the overalls is my neighbor, Fred. He owns the boat. The other two are the new curator at the NoMMA – name of Dalmore – remember I went out there to interview him last week? – and an art critic visiting from New York."

"Oou – nice" my boss says. "Strange boat-fellows sell papers. Which one is the curator – tall or short?"

"Tall," I say. "Aren't we a freebee?"

"You know what I mean. – Hey, this one's great!" He almost wheezes. Steve's face contorts as he merges laughter and strangled, high-pitched, barely intelligible syllables. He can hardly talk when he is attacked by mirth. "Why the hell is a museum curator doing the

Funky Chicken? What's he, a performance artist, too?"

"Everybody at the rail got gassed – methane – when Fred opened up the whale for the first time. Fred fell over backwards and the curator fell on top of him. Pulled something in his neck, I guess. In that shot I guess he's trying to work out the kink. It'll be in the story. I can't get it done by deadline. It's for next week."

"So, what's the story you've got here?"

"It's the one I just mentioned: 'New Curator Comes to Northport.'"

"I don't get it. What's the whale got to do with the museum story?"

"Just a coincidence."

"Just a coincidence?" Steve is dumbfounded. "What do you mean just a coincidence?"

"That's what I mean. I interview him at the museum and then a whale washed up under his dock. Just a coincidence."

"What's a museum curator doing with a dock?"

"He's rich. He's got a dock."

"So a whale washes up under his dock and he calls you?"

"I was there at the time."

"You go by the NoMMA curator's house and a whale washes up?"

"No – I was on the bow of his boat, with a line in my hand and we kept bouncing off something when we tried to dock. It turned out to be a whale."

"What's he got for a boat?"

"J-44."

"Ooo – nice. What the hell were you doing there?"

"I'm not sure. But I wanted to talk to you about it. I think it has to do with the performance artist – the one with the painted-on bathing suit – I covered last week."

"Right – I guess – where's that story anyway?" So the moment I've been avoiding has arrived. I certainly have considered giving Steve any number of lame excuses. But working for him has helped me eliminate lame excuses from my repertoire. Steve will just say, "What kind of bullshit is that?" If you give most people a lame excuse they will likely let you *think* you got away with it. Steve has helped me realize how transparent I am – and most people, I now believe, are too. Reminds me of when I was a tiny kid and I'd put up my hands in front of my eyes and say, "You can't see me." Worst example of this I ever saw was a guy, maybe 16, I worked with at a ski shop during a high school February vacation. One time the phone lines got iced-up and we couldn't hear the person calling but they could hear us. So this kid enjoyed answering the phone with obscenities. Of course, everyone, including the boss, his father, who called in to see if the phones were fixed yet, knew who it was. The guy was a complete idiot, so this is an extreme case, but I do think most people believe they get away with more than they really do.

"I can't do that story," I simply say.

"Can't do that story? Why the hell not? You've got pictures of a cute nudist getting slapped into cuffs – I've never had a story like that in my life – why the hell can't you do the story? Maybe your job depends on it?" Steve makes this last comment as if he is trying out a threat.

"Conflict of interest."

"Conflict of interest? This is a tabloid. What are you her pimp?"

"It's a little more direct than that."

"What the hell does that mean?"

"I'm sleeping with her. Or was. I think I hurt her feelings"

Steve dismisses the second part of my statement. "Well, touché." he says, "but what's the conflict of interest?"

"That's it."

"That's it? You're sleeping with her so you can't put a story about her getting naked and getting arrested in *your own* newspaper? I'd find it very exciting to have the chance to do that. Think about your image. Like Roger Vadim."

"Who's Roger Vadim?

"Bridget Bardot's husband. French film director. Put her in his movies. *Directed* her. Come to think of it, he did the same thing with

Jane Fonda, a later wife. Some guys have all the luck."

I ignore the implications of this.

"Can't do it. I can't write the story."

"What if I tell you your job is on the line?"

"I can't do it."

I return to my desk and try Lucinda's number for about the fourth time this morning. Just a recording again. I haven't left a message because I wouldn't know how to interpret it if I didn't get a quick call-back. Wanted to make sure I got a chance to make the charm offensive that I think is necessary. Now I realize that if there are four hang-ups on her machine, and then *me,* when someone finally answers, I will look desperate. So I vow to quit calling Lucinda for at least an hour or two. Besides, Avrum might answer and I'm definitely not desperate enough to need him.

John Hulton's opening is tonight. I was planning to ask Lucinda to accompany me. It might be reinforcing to our threatened relationship if I took her on a date. But maybe I'm just being old-fashioned. Besides, I can be pretty sure that she would not have much interest in John Hulton's work. It might instead emphasize the artistic and spiritual gulf between us. The feeling – brought on by Avrum's revelation about Lucinda keeping time with William Kahn – of wanting a woman that I may not actually want, is maddening. It's probably just jealousy and competitiveness making me needy. *Just –* that's a laugh. If there were a law that people had to say "really," every time they say "just," the world would be a better place. That's if a more honest world would be a better place.

And Kahn! What does he want with Lucinda when he's got the great beauty, Rebecca? – Okay. I know. I know. And I know I sound just like Kevin when Kahn was buzzing round Kevin's Deborah. Maybe I'm not really jealous – just righteously indignant at Kahn getting all the women, just because he's richer, better looking, and more talented than I am. There I go again with the *justs.* Sure Kahn is rich and good-looking. But maybe I shouldn't think Kahn has any talent at all – after what Kevin told me on the boat Sunday: seeing that kitschy painting from that crate from Germany. That woodland and lake with deer and eagles. Kevin said they looked like the stuff Fred Avery's father used to paint when he was recovering from his stroke. I'd like to see what the critics – and Lucinda, Rebecca, and Deborah – would think of *that* "work of art".

This makes me think about Kevin. Hey, maybe I should call him and see if he wants to come with me to Hulton's show. Might give me a chance to find out what Kevin thinks of Hulton's painting. Give me an opportunity to talk to Kevin for a first time about what he actually likes. And Hulton might appreciate it if I brought Kevin along. Having a museum curator attend might make up for the come-down of having to show in an "open studio"– after the Venice Biennale, and all other *triumphs* from his glory days twenty-five years ago.

# 19

"Alex!"

"Hey, Kevin – Glad you could make it; short notice and all that."

I'm sitting on granite steps, worn an inch lower at the center by hundreds of textile workers entering and exiting for perhaps 30,000 days. This building is two factory blocks away from where Lucinda hangs her jumpsuits. It has been converted to house about 25 artist's studios. These are open to the public for three hours this lovely early summer evening. Mostly young people enter and exit. Nobody that looks like a buyer. But there is about an hour left of festivity. Anything could happen. But it probably won't. Kevin worked late at the museum in preparation for its far grander opening tomorrow night. So I had dinner at home with Gram.

"So, how's it going?"

"Fine!" he says.

*Fine?* Kevin never says, "fine" – at least not sounding like he means it.

"Yeah?" I say. He seems to understand the question in my tone.

"Deborah's coming."

"Great," I say.

"Well, I mean at least she said she'd drop by. Things are going a lot better between us. – I mean it's only been two days. So who knows? I mean two days since the boat."

Since you became a hero, I'm thinking.

"I mean she was planning to see Hulton's show anyway. When I told her I was meeting you and asked her to come, she said an uncle was taking her to dinner and then they'd stop by here. – Here's something interesting for you – she said this uncle read your article about Hulton. And that's how he knew about the show and that he'd want to come. Old fan of the old Hulton, it turns out. Pretty neat, huh"

"Somebody read something I wrote?" I say. "Yeah, that is pretty neat. Who's her uncle?"

"I don't know. I didn't ask. How do you ask somebody who their uncle is? – Like: 'what's he do for a living?' Figured we'd meet him anyway. Wanna go inside?

We enter a vestibule with a wide staircase and ascend to the second level. Hulton's space is toward the back. Chattering people are bunched here and there in the hall. We pass the studios of a weaver, a photographer, two young painters, and someone who makes bow-back chairs. There are come-hither looks and gentle entreaties from inside each doorway. From a glance in at these I can see that I respond most to the weaver's work. A certain sheen. Colors morphing into their adjacent relatives and complements. Resembles what I like about floating diesel fuel.

Hulton's studio, I know from my interview visit, is large with decent natural light. But arriving now at summer twilight I notice that those $3.00 aluminum utility spot lamps from hardware stores provide the illumination – rather than track lighting. Hulton could use an electrician here as well as at his barn. The artist, coffee mug in hand, is talking to three young people. One looks bored, but the other two seem to be listening with sincere attention. One of them, a girl –

young woman, that is – utters complimentary exclamations at irregular intervals. I think we should let him continue with his audience. What man of 75 doesn't appreciate a young woman gushing over him? So I nod Kevin toward the paintings on display. As if we'd agreed to separate reconnaissance, we head – I making a short detour to a punch bowl (the two bottles of cheap white are empty) – toward different ends of the wall of the studio opposite where Hulton stands.

When it isn't hitting you in the eyes, the lighting isn't that bad. I sip my punch and look. Strong – I mean the beverage. Vodka and cranberry and orange juice, I think. Makes me wonder about Hulton and the metaphoric wagon. – Whether the artist had to jump off it and acquire some of the old false courage before, at 75, getting back into the game.

The paintings, most of which I recognize from last week, begin to call to my senses. Trees. But not particularly great old stately ones. Second growth trees, even spindly ones. Some of the images, however, look only vaguely familiar. Then I remember Hulton's increased distraction as our interview had progressed. Every few minutes – or less – he would rocket up, grab a brush from a jar of turpentine, and stab it into paints arrayed on his pallet. Then he would slash at an area of an unsuspecting canvas. As he did so he would mutter things like, "No no, no" or "There, that works." The smell of the turpentine lingers in the air right now and almost stings. I'm pretty sure the artist has continued to retouch most of these pieces – during and even after hanging them – many times.

As I focus on the paintings my respiration seems to slow. I guess that my pulse and blood pressure are going south, too. I can't be sure about blood pressure, though. They say you can't feel your blood pressure. Bonnard slows me down like that. Cezanne, of course. The "water-lilies". Rothko, too. I can get that physical hum when I look at the work of any of those greats who demonstrated the power of the brushstroke. (Cezanne even famously said: "Painting that attempts to hide the painters tools earns the admiration of imbeciles.") I'm getting that sunlight-on-water hum. Or sunlight on a wall. Same kind of feeling. Almost, anyway. Art just doesn't do it as dependably. There isn't that much art that brings me peace as readily as sunlight on water or sunlight through stained glass or sunlight onto a pitted stucco or stonewall. Maybe some.

A phrase from the piece I did on Hulton's work floats through my head: "In these iconic paintings of trees overwhelming their large canvases, Hulton offers us nature as a portal for transcending our contemporary lives and for experiencing the timeless." Sounds a little effete. I can see why Arthur Dalmore would object. If quick-cut, high action simplicity *works* for you, you wouldn't want things any other way. Postmodernism is crisp. Nature is fuzzy.

So, John Hulton's paintings evoke the floaty sense of peace I crave, while at the same time emanating a certain "spookiness." They betoken violence held at bay. Those opposites, I think, are rarely addressed together in contemporary art. The light that suffuses his canvases, or plays over them, seems almost to come from another world. In this new work about nature, Hulton, for the first time as far as I know, employs chiaroscuro – light entering a dark atmosphere. In most of the canvases the atmosphere is a vibrating field of intense color – all reds or all blues or reds and golds – and black. In some paintings, this light strikes like lightening. Branches or tree trunks are lit as if in negative. They seem to reference the high key *stab*s in a Clifford Still, the Abstract Expressionist whose paintings evoked volcanoes or earthquakes. Mostly, however, chiaroscuro is classical, not modernist. So I guess using it breaks Modernist rules. Perhaps this brings Hulton to the edge of Postmodernism. Whatever the definitions or politics, his control of light forcefully conveys the ungovernable power of nature. As I look at his show, I run through my memory of the rest of my review. "Hulton," I remember writing, "though now addressing landscape in a manner that harkens back to earlier pantheistic traditions – those of Turner and of the Monet of the "water-lilies" – and of the philosophy of Emerson – is nevertheless a modernist because he is not copying nature. His canvases are *emblems* of nature not depictions. His first concern is, as

243

ever, with the abstract qualities in a painting. 'The painter's tools,' as Cezanne said. Skies aren't voids. They are edged in dark to make them come forward rather than recede. Images hover. The resulting painting then reminds you more of a tablet or tapestry than a window. And by dint of his modulated stroke and calligraphic line – a tablet that breathes and emits light."

Seeing the paintings again, I'm pretty dissatisfied with what I wrote. The facts are there, but it's just words, a bit academic. As usual, I wish I could paint so I wouldn't have to try to translate sensations to paper. I'm not nearly enough of a poet to do that.

I downed my first glass of punch unselfconsciously during my detached "looking". And at some point I got a refill and am now halfway through that one. So I'd have to say – no slight intended to Hulton – that the primary source of my intoxication has shifted from the paintings to the punch.

People have streamed in, around, and out in ones, twos, and threes since Kevin and I arrived. None have seemed thrilled. One woman exclaimed to another, "Ooo – what colors!" That was okay. But an artist would rather hear "What color – singular." Colors come out of a tube. Color comes out of an artist.

Kevin seems to have been paying considerable attention to each piece. A few times he's looked over at me and nodded and smiled. A quiet statement of respect, I think. I finish my second punch and go for a third. Hulton's young people seem to be saying their good-byes. He spotted me a while ago. His face lit up. Then his glance returned to his audience. Now the youngsters are gliding out through the door.

I haven't heard from Hulton since the interview. He isn't the type for thank you notes. But he comes toward me with his arms raised for an embrace. The mug is still in his hand. I wonder – given his ebullient demeanor – if he has been drinking coffee or larger doses of punch than available from little plastic throwaway cups. Well, his walk is steady enough.

"Here is the esteemed art critic," he says.

I look behind me. I know I'm not esteemed for anything. But he doesn't sound sarcastic. He approaches and does give me a hug. At the same time he states: "You're a terrific writer. What a shame you don't have a wider forum for your work." From anyone else I'd assume the desire for a more extensive readership would accrue to the greater glory of the painter, not the writer. But he seems sincere enough that I wonder if he is thinking selfishly at all. And I'm surprised at the embrace. In fact, it is hard to recognize the man I interviewed. His diffidence is gone. Maybe he's just not a morning person.

I do enjoy the hug and the praise. But it embarrasses me a bit, too. So I do that male/male slap-slap-slap on the back and break to introduce Kevin. I decide to hold back on Kevin's credentials, lest he think that Kevin has some power to improve Hulton's lot in the art world. Kevin, no stranger to sincerity, gives Hulton intelligent and believable compliments. Hulton appreciates this mightily. I think he may be drunk after all. It takes one to know one.

At that moment, seeing a certain figure in the doorway, I feel the blood draining from my face. Rebecca Sharma enters the studio. She does a gratifying double-take when she sees me. Behind her by four or five steps is William Kahn, talking over his shoulder to someone left behind in the hall; an admirer of the great artist, no doubt – of Kahn, I mean.

Rebecca smiles and extends a hand. My heart starts pumping harder to drive the lost blood back to my face. I do feel my face warming. Sometimes I hate loving beauty so much; at least beauty in women. Maybe there is actually more downside than up. Like with anything you want that you can't have. And then, of course there's the pitiful unfairness of the whole thing. To all the unbeautiful of the world, that is. We know nature has no mercy.

"Hello, Alex," she says. Then she spots Kevin and greets him, "Hello Kevin." She extends her hand to him, too.

Kahn, catching up, says, "Hey look, it's the lawyers, Perkins and Perkins."

Kahn, I sense is another one under the influence at the moment.

"Hey – did you get rid of that whale?" Kahn asks. Rebecca puts on the serious face of one who should have thought to inquire about such a thing herself.

"Piece of cake," I say, not wishing to elaborate.

None of us seems to know what to say next. I try to remind myself this is not about any of us. It's about Hulton.

"John," I say – I realize I am dropping the "Mr. Hulton" for the first time; probably in the interests of trying to seem less beta-male to Rebecca – "have you met Rebecca Sharma?" I leave Kahn out of the introductions for the moment. How I wish something sudden and unexpected might take his life.

Hulton reaches out his hand for Rebecca's as if she were a normal person. I can see not a trace of intimidation from her gorgeousness – if he's noticed it. Well, more power to him, if he has. (But how could he not?)

I can't snub – or assault, for that matter – Kahn. But as I'm about to introduce him, he steps forward with his facial muscles set on ten.

"William Kahn," he says, pretending to be clueless to the reality that everyone already knows who he is.

But I'm wrong.

"Ah," says Hulton, straining to place him. He squints and asks, "Are you a painter?"

"Yes," Kahn says, unaffected by lack of universal recognition except for a few chips of marble splintering off his smiling cheeks.

"I'm sorry," says Hulton. "You have the advantage on me. I'm not too up on the contemporary scene."

Kahn gives a quick glance at the far wall and says, "I can imagine."

Hulton doesn't take this as a slight – seems, rather, to interpret it as a compliment. Something like, "I can see how you must be too busy." A corner of Rebecca's mouth twitches, though.

"He paints Donald Duck." I say, tossing down the last of my punch and then gently placing the plastic cup on the serving table beside us. No, I won't have a fourth. Yes, I will.

Kahn maintains his smile, minus a few more chips.

"You're a cartoonist?" Hulton asks.

Kahn looks at me to explain and redeem myself. And then he glances at Kevin who has been assisting him with organizing a retrospective at a small but not insignificant museum of art. Kevin just smiles pleasantly.

"Not exactly," says Kahn, forced to speak for himself. "Our friend, Alex, is teasing. I use cartoons and other frivolous things to make serious statements."

"Oh" Hulton says. Though he leaves a question mark off the *Oh*, I think he implies adequately that he can't imagine how this might be done.

Probably unable to endure, in Hulton's words, "having the advantage on Hulton" – in other words, being in the rare position of not having an advantage – he explains: "My retrospective at the NoMMA opens on Friday."

Hulton is embarrassed. "I'm so sorry," he says. "You see I don't get out very much..." He suddenly seems ten years older. His confidence – or false courage – seems to have drained away. He falls into self-deprecation: "Well, I'm sure my work wouldn't be your cup of tea."

"No. That's not true. I find it very, hmm? ... lush," Kahn says, winking at Rebecca. The wink underscores that the chances that Kahn means this in a positive sense are slim. "Bourgeois lushness" being one of the current hip put-downs of art that aspires to beauty. Next thing you know William Kahn will be calling John Hulton an elitist. There is also the chance that Kahn was reaching all the way for a double entendre with his choice of the word *lush*: Hulton is well-known for alcohol consumption.

Hulton doesn't realize the possibility of either of these interpretations. But Rebecca does and so she steps forward and takes Hulton's elbow. "Tell me about your work." she says as she whisks him from the range of Kahn's wit.

I have my fourth in my hand and take a hard swallow. The old false courage.

"Why don't you tell us what you really think?" I say as firmly as four glasses of 50 per cent vodka will allow.

"You may write about this stuff, but I think I know a bit about it, too," Kahn says dismissively.

"Ya, well, you may be a kangaroo, but I think I know a little bit about marsupials," I riposte, just as dismissively. Kevin has been silent. He has a professional relationship with Kahn that needs to run smoothly, at least through the opening on Friday. But he is old-fashioned. There is Deborah to think of. Kahn's seducing and abandoning her during his idle time in Northport, before Rebecca arrived, is unlikely a small matter to Kevin. I imagine he would disapprove of what I conjecture is Kahn's philosophy – that sex is something sacred to be indulged in by a man and several women. But Kevin, not having been drinking, chooses tact. He just laughs. This is ambiguous. It could just as easily mean, "What an idiot my cousin is" as "What a shit you are, Kahn." Kahn, his smile reduced to about 32 percent intact, just shakes his head.

I am about drunk enough to delicately change the conversation to: "What were you and Lucinda up to last night?" in tones loud enough for Rebecca and people in every other studio on the floor to hear. But more people enter. Those people are Deborah and a man I've never met nor seen in person, though I recognize him from the papers and the TV. The man is the publisher of *Currents'* rival, the Northport Beacon. *And* the owner of the newspaper chain, the Oggelvy Group. *And* the donator of the Marion Oggelvy Wing of the Northport Museum – *and* board of directors member thereof – Frank Oggelvy.

"Oh, there you are Kevin – sorry we're late. Oh, William. I didn't expect… Hello, Alex. Oh, hello, Rebecca. Hi, everybody. Everybody – this is my Uncle Frank."

248

# 20

"No, I'll stay here and chat with John," I say.

And Kevin says, "And I'll stay with my cousin, Alex."

Hulton, with Frank Oggelvy's business card in his hand, has politely declined to go out for a drink with Oggelvy and his niece, Deborah. In doing so he also said no to Rebecca Sharma, and to William Kahn, who's idea the get-together had been. Hulton escaped by citing the need to keep his open studio open twenty minutes more – until 9:00 – and by then he would be too tired. His age allowed this to stand without offense.

His opening was not a great success – by a measure of the art lovers attending and exclaiming, and by the number of paintings sold. There were few of the first and none of the second. But throw in the offer to Hulton of a museum exhibition – for which Frank Oggelvy would lobby the board of directors – then it wasn't a half bad night. In fact, it was a stellar night.

I didn't go along for the drink because I was afraid. I feared making a very great fool of myself – vis-à-vis William Kahn. That is,

I feared my *wanting* to make a fool of *him* could easily backfire. But it would have seemed a point of honor that making a fool of him was something I should at least have tried, had I remained in his presence.

Just as inhibiting to my sociability was my believing I could not comfortably sit across from William Kahn and Rebecca Sharma tonight – given my feelings for Rebecca, and also for Lucinda – whatever they may be for her – and given Kahn's dismissive treatment of an accomplished and rather kindly older painter, John Hulton.

But what right do I have to *feelings for Rebecca*? I mean, am I the mirror of Kahn: wanting my territorial rights to Lucinda respected while – at the very least – *imagining* infringing on his to Rebecca? Well, yes. But also, no. It's apples and pineapples. The difference, you could say, is I'm neurotic and he's character-disordered. Our motivations are not the same – though the *objects* are the same. I am in lust, but not in love, with Lucinda. My agitation caused by her abandoning me before I got the chance to abandon her is neurotic. It's childish. I admit it.

And I assume that my craving for Rebecca is also childish. But in a different way. I *do* feel like I am in love with *her*. And not in lust. And as a judgmental person, I assume that character-disordered Kahn (my diagnosis) feels lust for all the women that he and I both know – who are three – and probably hundreds of others I haven't yet met.

What I am trying to convey – though it sounds like I'm lying through my teeth – is that I am not conscious of a strong *sexual* attraction to Rebecca. As yet, anyway. As an obscure object, her beauty has something sanctified about it. Like the quality Marcello Mastroianni perceived in Claudia Cardinale in a couple of movies: *8-1/2*, the greatest film ever made, I believe, and that minor one, *Bell' Antonio*, where all he wanted to do was push "Cloud-ia" on a swing. Antonio was an Italian Mamma's boy. I might be kind of an Anglo version.

I've mentioned that I perceived my mother as beautiful from when I was a small child. Family and community affirmed this. My love of her beauty and my loss of her may be the main cause of my becoming a beauty junkie. There were other reasons for it too, but the others came indirectly from her as well. In addition to her being born with physical loveliness – of which she never seemed particularly aware – she was something of a beauty addict herself. She was in love with the beauty that could be found in all kinds of things, in all kinds of places – in art, in poetry, in music, in nature. I still remember the time she held me up for my first heavenly inhale of lilac, to a branch sagging with the weight of fat purple blossoms. That may have been my initial experience of *the romantic* – whatever the romantic was or seemed. The spring after she died, my Dad, with Sylvia, Gram, and me standing-by, planted a lilac bush in Gram's yard. We each put a handful of my mother's ashes into the soil. I feel a quiet joy each year when it blooms and a bit of anguish ten days later when the flowers start to turn brown. Another magic season – wherein my mother's spirit arrived and then departed – passing. As a child in love with my mother's loveliness, I felt only affection – regardless of what Freud says may have lurked below. And though sexual sensations from random sources did begin to show up by the time I was ten, and take over by my mid-teens, there exists still a small part of me that wants to love beautiful women innocently. *Romantically.* Neurotically. Neurotically, because I know that being in love *spiritually* with physical appearance is a contradiction.

But the illusion of that haunts me still. It's a love that contradicts my animal nature. I'm like a horny schoolboy, who nevertheless has a chaste crush on the distant goddess of the other sixth grade. A girl he'd be afraid to talk to if she ever came near, while at the same time he's obsessed with trying to steal a glimpse of white cotton from the merely cute – and no less innocent – little girl at a desk in the next row.

So what I have right now is a *crush* on Rebecca. I'm sure grown-up feelings would take over quickly enough were I to help her off the pedestal I'm putting her on. I saw her briefly off it when she ate caviar with her fingers. But for the moment, given this probably dubious self-perception, I can *claim* that Kahn and I are not the same.

Why did Kevin decline to accompany his own "other-sixth-grade" goddess – whom he'd just learned is gold-plated, by the way? My guess is that he'd have endured as much discomfort sitting across from William Kahn and Deborah Irvine as I would William Kahn and Rebecca Sharma. We are both in about the same boat. No, that's not true. He has no Lucinda for contrast and perspective – perhaps never has.

And about that *gold-plated* thing: Kevin appeared taken aback to learn that Deborah was the niece of a rich and influential member of the board of the institution that writes his paychecks. This likely activated Kevin's "confidence issues." Deborah, however, did seem to be metaphorically leaning his way.

Well, I imagine Oggelvy can easily handle a drink with Kahn. Oggelvy's reputed an "up-for-it" guy. Steve talks about him that way. They're about as friendly as their different social and professional stations might allow. Steve tells me he plays poker with Oggelvy. And Oggelvy owns racehorses. Things like that show he's got some spirit. If Steve, a minor league competitor to Oggelvy in the Massachusetts publishing world, says Oggelvy's an all right guy – and Steve thinks most businessmen are assholes – it likely means something. (Steve, by the way, calls himself a businessman when it suits him, a writer when it doesn't.) Ultimately, anybody willing to pal around with Steve for even five minutes would have to have an ability to roll with the punches. My guess is that a fun-loving spirit – and the self-confidence that comes with great wealth – means Oggelvy can handle whatever Kahn might dish out.

"So, you had no idea she was related to him?" I ask Kevin, while Hulton puts away glasses, bottles and things.

"None at all."

"Why do you think she's kept it a secret?"

"Who says it was a secret? Maybe nobody asked. She came here with him, didn't she? If it were a secret, why would she do that? She's a good girl. – I mean… I mean, maybe she just didn't want anybody to think there was nepotism in her getting her job. Wanted to make it on her own."

"Do you think that Dalmore knows? Didn't you say he doesn't treat her that well?"

"Right. He probably wouldn't show irritation if he knew who she was. At least I don't think he would. I don't know. Maybe that's backwards – maybe that's what gets him irritated."

I see Hulton has finished his chores. He is now just standing by the drinks table, staring at Oggelvy's card. I'm aware that our ignoring him might appear impolite. As I realized once earlier tonight, this evening is meant to be his. Watching him so intently focused on that business card, I realize this Oggelvy/museum melodrama that Kevin and I have chattered about in his studio probably affects him too – now that he has that card. (Certainly affects him more than it does me.) I give a jerk of my head toward the painter and Kevin lifts his in a half nod.

"Well, John," I say, in keeping with the familiarity I embarked on earlier. Nine o'clock. Can we take you out for a drink? – Or coffee?" I add, thinking of his best interests – and my own. I have had a lot to drink already. Kahn had mentioned where they would go – in case we changed our minds – so all we had to do to be Kahn-free and socially correct would be to find someplace else.

"Yes. A drink would be nice," he says.

"You'll come – right, Kevin?"

"Yeah, I'll come."

Hulton and I each hold a Cape Codder in hand. No sense in jarring the system with major change. Vodka seems Hulton's drink. And Kevin is drinking! He holds a beer. The place I suggested we go is rough-hewn, a former warehouse. The building sits on the riverfront but the bar doesn't. It occupies the back (formerly the front) of the structure. That means the drinks go cheaper, no tourists, and no Kahns. The lighting feels better than in most low-toned * establishments. Meaning there's less. Usually, the cheaper the drinks, the higher the electric bills.

While we waited for our beverages I revealed Kevin's association with the museum. Hulton appears a little stunned by this – on top of carrying Oggelvy's business card in his shirt pocket. He looks at me with what seems like awe and gratitude – as if I am responsible for all his good fortune. And for the first time I realize that maybe I am. I remember Kevin's disclosure of Deborah's disclosure – that Oggelvy would attend *because of my story*. And I did bring Kevin – out of boundless compassion – when I couldn't get my little sex machine to answer her phone. So now I am starting to think of myself as a jolly good fellow. Helluva writer, too.

Unfortunately, Hulton now acts deferential to Kevin. I'm sure Kevin doesn't want him to. First of all, Kevin knows it overstates his possible influence. Dalmore casts a giant shadow at the NoMMA. He would veto any attempt at freelancing by Kevin. More importantly, in my opinion, Kevin would find being deferred to incompatible with his nature. He's diffident enough to never believe himself capable of *greasing skids* or *opening doors*. So, in an attempt to humble himself – *assert his diffidence* – he adopts what is my usual role: interviewer. He asks Hulton about his heady New York years, inquires about some of the *greats* Hulton used to hang with – at the legendary Cedar Bar in Greenwich Village. And Kevin knows all the names; many I've never heard. The arrivals at the open studio – both expected and unexpected – prevented my intended questioning of Kevin about his basic artistic proclivities. So, I don't know whether this knowledge of 1950's New York School painting that he displays hints at a preference or just betokens professionalism. (That would contrast with my specifist motivations: when I know more than a very little about something you can be pretty sure it's something I really like.) An art historian can choose a specialty – which I believe Kevin didn't do – but he needs to know about other fields as well. Hulton's reminiscences fascinate me. His manner of story-telling too. Fueled by successive Cape Codders, he's gone from halting to vibrant as he starts to *relive* incidents from long ago glory days.

Then Kevin answers my question about his preferred niche in the art world by bringing up something I'd noticed too in Hulton's paintings.

He says: "About your own work, Mr. Hulton, I was particularly struck by your using chiaroscuro in an abstract way – and in a shallow space. I'm a Rembrandt man myself – I did my dissertation on Rembrandt, by the way – and, of course, your stuff is Modernist. But it links up to him, I think, in a way… in a way I admire."

"Oh, well. Rembrandt is my main guy," Hulton says. "I mean I love Caravaggio for that too. But Rembrandt was a little subtler about it. I look more at those guys – all of them – than anything else when I'm in New York. "

This surprises me. And it gives me a chance to sound like I know more than nothing. Something I do know relates to a painter named Barnett Newman who created large canvases whereon he painted a ground of a single color, then he painted one, two, or three vertical stripes and that's all. Interestingly, I first learned about his style not in college, but from the novel, *Breakfast of Champions*, by Kurt Vonnegut. Vonnegut's much maligned character, Rabo Karabekian, was a stand in for Newman. In the book, he won over a hostile crowd with a simple explanation of his work. But in real life, Newman was known for bombast.

I ask Hulton, "What do you think of Barnett Newman's famous statement about Abstract Expressionism versus the old masters: 'Our quarrel is with Michelangelo?'"

"Well," he says, "I was there when he said it. Or repeated it. Or said something like it. It hit me at the time as pretentious. I think he was milking the outrage he expected he'd get. He was a guy who liked a quarrel. I guess that's well known. But I thought it was silly. You can't argue with Michelangelo. What's the point? The way I see it, we were all descended from those guys – at least all of us who loved pushing paint around and making even a little bit of space. Newman was different – with his flat fields and zips. How anyone ever put him in the same *style* – Ab-Ex, I mean – as Pollock or de Kooning is beyond me. That doesn't mean I didn't think he was great. He was. But his work was more a part of what came after us than what the rest of us were doing. And I don't think any of the minimalists ever improved on Newman."

Somehow I don't want art and the past to constitute all that Hulton – and whatever relationship I might have with him – is supposed to be about. I'd like to get to know *him*. (Assuming he is not just a painting robot.) But the prevailing impression is he now only paints and drinks. And what little he has to say about his own paintings he already has said – and that's now part of the public record. (If a story in *Currents* constitutes that.) So I decide to ask him about his childhood. Though I see a kind of *dignity*, even with a glass in his hand, I don't suspect elitist beginnings – despite Kahn's imprecation about "bourgeois lushness".

"Where did you grow up, John?" I ask.

"Somerset County, Maine."

"I can't exactly picture it," I say, though I think I can. "Nice country?"

"Let's say there's not a lot of... charm. I didn't..." He pauses and stares at shadows where the wall and massive ceiling beams meet. Then he smiles. A twinkle seems to burn through the light glaze over his eyes. He begins again, this time in the persona of a Down Easter.

"Din't get ta see much a tha countryside frum tha house. And we din't have none of what yud call tha amenaties of life – video games and TVs and such thet kids have taday... I can still remembah when we gut ar fust windah."

He looks quizzically at us for validation of his whimsical detour. The "tales of Maine" aesthetic that trickles down the coast requires a listener as deadpan as the storyteller. Though I know this, I don't know if Kevin does. But, cognizant of my greater familiarity with the old man, Kevin watches my expressionless face and reveals only edges of a smile.

"Weren't that a big day at ar house. All twelva us young'ns braught tha stools that we slept on outa tha bedruhm and put um in a little hahf cehcle in front ta tha hole in tha wall where Pa and Uncle Ned was workin' away…'"

He pauses. Kevin eyes me again. We don't know how long the old man can keep this up. But I'm taking no chance with stepping on his shtick.

"…Naught that it were a new windah! …Mama was embarrassed thet ar windah come from tha Littlefield's cow bahn thet they tore down when tha last cow up and died a hoof-n-mouth dahzeez. … But thet din't matter ta us kids. Just ta be able ta watch tha rain stop and staht…withut goin' utside n gettin' all wet wus treat enough for alla us."

He's really pretty damn good at it. Makes me wonder if he's reenacting something performed many times for the denizens of the Cedar Bar thirty years ago.

"Don't' mean ta plead pahvaty. We din't have it bahd as some. What with Pa's manure business pickin' up all tha tahm, why it wehrn't long before we had a windah in evreh ruhm. Ceptin' course tha outhouse. Ma thought that'd be puttin' on ayas…and it'd incite some of tha yung'uns ta take more tahm en theyah then theh needed. …Besides with one 'r nuthah of my sistahs comin' up over pube-tee every yeaah 'r so… 'n tha outhouse bein' more on tha Littlefield's prop-tee then it achly wus on ar own…and tha Littlefield kids all bein' boys – and them bein' too poor for Mama ta consida any a them able ta be any husbin patential, Mama thought thet a windah in tha outhouse might be tha cause ah trouble…not ta mention tha expense."

I decide to contribute. I take out my pen and my wallet and pick up a paper napkin and, using my wallet as backing, I pretend to be taking notes.

"I guess I missed some of this when I interviewed you. What was it like being the little artist of the family in that household?"

"Weren't tha little ahtist," he says, shaking his head emphatically. The gesture jars him and that helps me determine his level of inebriation. I'd give him about a seven – that's a three for *sobriety*. "All twelva us kids had talent. Hahd ta keep us with enough aht materials, though. Pa use ta have ta baah-tah manure for aht supplies."

Hulton's riffing off my lead tells me this story is at least somewhat extemporaneous.

"Sometahms when manure praduction wus slow and weed nothin' ta tread for brushes, we would have ta use chickun feathehs ta paint. Din't raise chickuns ahrselves. Littlefields did tho. Got ar feathahs frum them. Many tahms I remembah hearin' Mrs. Littlefield shoutin' 'Getya shotgun, Henri – tha ahtists are afta tha chickuns again!'"

This is almost too much for my required straight face. And Kevin does actually, unselfconsciously, crack up. That's good. Seems I seldom see him really laugh.

"Mustn't enjoy the travails of others," I say in Kevin's direction. "Didn't our common grandmother say we should never laugh at the less fortunate?"

Suddenly Hulton turns bright red. I don't know if he's flushed with excitement, alcohol or embarrassment. Damn, I hope it isn't embarrassment. No way he needs to be embarrassed for that.

"Well, enough about me," he says in southern New England English. "Tell me about you guys."

Neither of us could top, or even maintain Hulton's bravura level of performance – even if we use politeness as an excuse to avoid trying.

"Aw, we're just typical Northport boys. Nothing too unusual," Kevin says. Considering his age and scholarly leanings, this is a relatively odd thing to say. But he adds, "I did hear a joke today, though."

I've never heard Kevin tell a joke.

"I can't tell if it's really funny or not," he disclaims.

"Well, try us, " I say – helping him. I'm a little frustrated with his reticence.

"Okay. You don't have to laugh. Just analyze it or something. Tell me if you think it's funny at all."

"Okay, okay – just tell the joke," I say. Hulton smiles.

As Kevin is about to begin he surprises himself and his audience by emitting a fairly significant belch. He reddens slightly, pounds his chest with the topside of his right fist, says, "Pardon," and starts his delivery.

"This guy goes to see a psychiatrist and the psychiatrist asks him why he came. 'My wife said I had to. She thinks I'm crazy.' 'Why does she think you're crazy?' the psychiatrist inquires. 'Because I love pancakes.' 'Because you love pancakes? – There's nothing crazy about that. I love pancakes too.' 'Well, then you should come over to my house,' the guy says, 'because I've got a whole closet full of them.'"

Hulton snorts with approval. I like the joke too.

"You guys think it's funny?"

"You don't?" I ask.

"I don't know," Kevin says. But he does smile. Reminds me of David Player right now. Never know whether that guy's putting me on. I assume Kevin isn't, but who knows.

I feel it's time to change the subject again.

"What did you think of William Kahn?" I ask Hulton.

I immediately regret it. Kevin's smile fades. Hulton appears much more sober. And I have re-immersed myself in my Kahn-obsession. Hulton's routine had lifted me from it handily.

"Well, he seemed pleasant enough. Good-looking fellow. Looks like a movie star. His wife looks like a movie star too. I wish I knew his work. That was embarrassing – with his having a solo museum show right here in Northport."

"Retrospective," Kevin corrects.

"Girlfriend," I add a correction of mine to Kevin's.

"Retrospective? A retrospective? How old is he?"

"It's not his age," I say. "It's his temperature. He's hot."

"Well, more power to him," Hulton says.

"What!" I ask, my fifth drink of the night sliding down my throat quite a bit too easily, "no resentment for an up-start like him?" I probably don't know Hulton well enough to delve into areas – like

259

resentments – where even best friends usually don't stray. At least – if I end up playing the fool tonight – after all – it won't be in front of Rebecca. But why play it for poor Hulton?

"Well, it's not like he is standing in my way."

I'm thinking that that is what it is exactly like. But I don't say so.

Kevin, perhaps more of a twin than a cousin in my feelings about Kahn, says, "Don't you think he seemed pretty vain?"

"Oh, that. No. – I mean, maybe he is. But vanity doesn't bother me. We're all vain."

"We're all vain," I chime in, "but most of us try not to be."

Hulton takes a large swallow of his Cape Codder. I can see *relief* in his eyes as the liquid goes down.

"Try not to *be* – or just not to let it show?"

"Well, both – I guess. Isn't it one of the seven sins?"

"Well, that's what they say. But I think vanity is really one of life's great consolations."

"I've never considered that," Kevin says. "I'd be embarrassed to admit that that was true."

"Well, forgive my saying so, my young friend, but if that's the case, then it's vanity that stops you from admitting it. What's embarrassment but wounded vanity? Think of all the things you might admit to if you didn't care about embarrassing yourself."

"Hmm," says Kevin. He waves to the waiter for another beer.

"You talk about 'sins.' Well, there's probably at least some vanity in most of the things we consider virtues. Courage must have a large vanity component. 'I wanted to show those sons of bitches bla, bla, bla…' Doesn't the stoic feel superior to the rest of us who are indulging all the time? If all the saints who are proud of themselves for all their good works were disqualified, there wouldn't be too many religious holidays."

And I was afraid *he* couldn't handle too much honesty.

Hulton continues: "I think that vanity is a survival instinct. We know we are going to die. We don't want to. We're actually, privately, all terrified of dying. Maybe even the risk takers who laugh in the face

260

of danger. I had a friend who was in the war with me. Two Purple Hearts – wounded twice. Second time, he got a bayonet cut in hand-to-hand fighting in the Solomons. He was right next to me. I killed the guy who cut him. Jay. – His name was Jay. I don't think he really believed his time was near. So he was fearless. But he was terrified of needles. He slugged the medic that came to sew him up. Said he'd sew himself up. And he did. When we got out of the service he got a motorcycle. Drove real fast. Cracked up his bike a few times. Sewed himself up again when he needed it. He was always 'tempting fate.' Said he didn't give a shit about dying. Drank a lot. One day he told me his doctor said he was killing his liver and his liver would kill him. I asked him, 'Ya gonna stop?' He said, 'John – you know me. You know I'm not afraid to die.' 'Okay,' I said. 'But what if you don't die – or don't die fast. What if you just get really fucked up?' He laughed and said, 'Hey – I still got a gun. I'd shoot myself before I'd put up with any of that shit.'

"Well, I pretty much left it at that and forgot about it. He'd become a biker. I'd become a painter. We didn't see each other that much. But one day a few months later, I hear a knock on my studio door. I look out the window and there's Jay. I didn't hear any motorcycle. I see a blue pickup. I open the door. Jay throws himself into my arms. *Throws himself into my arms.* I don't know if in the twenty years we'd known each other we'd ever touched, but for shaking hands. He says: 'John, I'm dying!' 'Your liver?' I ask. 'No cancer.' And he starts to cry. He hides his face behind his hand in shame. But his eyes look at me through his fingers.

"Bone cancer. And he went through a lot of the kind of shit he said he'd never put up with – to try to stay alive. He let them core into him with needles. The guy who hated needles more than death."

Hulton's voice is cracking. The going is slow. But he goes on.

"He wanted every treatment they could give him. Hopeless, but he wouldn't accept that it was hopeless. He lost weight. Went to under a hundred pounds. But he kept fighting. I'd go to see him. He wasn't in a hospital. He was at home. He'd married a nurse. Jay earned his living as a carpenter. He was a good one. Did fine finish work. Had all the tools. But he lived in a shack. Don't know how his wife put up with it. There was hardly a place to sit down. A deer rifle leaned in the corner two feet from the bed. Jay was in a daze the last time I saw him. Morphine. Or else he was polluted from his bad liver. He recognized me though. He told me – making a spiral in the air over his chest with one skeletal hand, one finger extended – 'Sometimes I get up to about here,' he said with his arm almost fully extended. Then he drops it under its own weight – 'then I can't go any further.'

"His wife and I go outside. The snow is melting fast exposing the sand backfill around his house. It's a warm March day – almost sixty. She says (she was a Catholic girl), 'I keep asking Jay if should I get a priest.' Jay was Catholic, too – but he hated the church. Hated it. It let him down, I guess. He'd been a real believer as a kid. Even was an altar boy. ...Funny that he married a Catholic girl when he hated the church. But not really so funny. 'He keeps saying, "No,"' she says.

"She called me two days later to say Jay'd died. ...Told me she asked him about calling a priest again the next day after I was there. This time he said, 'Yes.'

"She told me, when the priest came, Jay told him he was afraid to die, afraid of going to hell – because he had killed people in the war. The priest said, 'All is forgiven,' and Jay died. Just like that." Hulton chokes down a sob.

I don't know what to say. Kevin doesn't know what to say. Why do people ever say ninety percent of what they do? Why do I? Afraid of silence. Shoring up the foundations of my own little world by *talking them* up.

"Jay's...bravura?...on the battlefield...," Hulton says more to himself than to Kevin and me. "Jay's laughing in the face of uncertain death by motorcycle....it was the *vanity of the hero*. It was thinking: 'if I can just be a hero I will get special dispensation,' as his church would have put it. God will spare me. Jay just had yet to encounter a war of attrition against his body. Didn't ever think it could happen to him. Or if he said he did, he didn't believe it. Didn't believe it – but deep down he *knew*. Like we all know. Deep down. We know we are going to die sometime and we are afraid. So we all want to be heroes. And vanity helps us think we're succeeding."

The waiter puts down Kevin's beer and leaves.

"A waiter," Hulton says, "wants to be a hero waiter. A hero lives forever, we think."

I think about *relief* again. It gets its power from fear of death. The call is always so close. The difference between "yes" and "no." Five letters total in the two words. "No, your test results were negative – it isn't cancer." "Yes, your daughter was the little girl who was found dead in the park." "No, I don't love you anymore. I want to leave." Salvation or damnation. Every call can go either way. Most of the time they go with the law of averages. The law of averages may be the thing we can count on most. But in our three a.m. hearts, we know that nothing is certain; little is within our control. We live in the steady flow of our everyday world. But we know that that world is separated from a frozen or evaporating looking-glass world – and that that pane of glass can be shattered at any time and the two worlds will flood into one another. It may be only when we are snatched out of that flood – like Kevin snatched Justin Bollard – that the preciousness of life becomes fully real.

But Kevin, to my surprise, has reservations.

"I know what you are saying about not being honest with ourselves. But it's hard for me to believe that everyone is walking around unconsciously afraid of dying. I don't go to church every Sunday, but my religion tells me that I have nothing to fear from death. I'm not sure I believe it. Or that primal instinct isn't even more basic than religion. But I'll bet that many of the people in my church are more worried about making a living than about their lives just stopping."

Though I *instinctively* agree with Hulton, I try to give Kevin's reservation some credit. After all, just two days ago he broke the pane of glass and threw himself into the flood.

Though Hulton has no reason to assume Kevin operates on any

263

higher plane relative to mortality, he is circumspect.

"Well, perhaps I shouldn't over-generalize," he says. (*Take in too much territory.* I'm thinking.) "I guess there are waiters who don't want to be hero waiters – or heroes at anything else in their heart of hearts. But I think they are the exceptions. Most people seem to me to be anxious about something – losing something, not having enough – and I wouldn't be surprised that it is tied to being afraid of the biggest loss of all."

"Maybe so. Maybe so," Kevin says, perhaps as much out of politeness as true conviction. "Maybe people do want to be heroes to prove that when they died they had been alive for a reason. Their life had had meaning. We are social creatures and, even if we don't know why we are here, if we do something that our fellow men value, it can give us a reason that we won't have to think about much."

Then Kevin is self-conscious: "But I guess that doesn't speak to your friend, Jay. His religion made him more fearful, rather than less. Sorry." Kevin puts down his bottle and slides it about five inches away – while a recognizable quantity of useful alcohol remains inside. He will drink no more tonight, I can tell.

For a second time Hulton has subverted polite conversation; first with a flight of comedy, second with a flight of tragedy. The first time he feared he'd embarrassed himself. – Turned red, though he was, in fact, due an ovation. This time he says, "Well – sorry to bring everybody down. How did I get started on this anyway? Oh right – William Kahn. Vanity. But I guess seeing some of the things I've seen are the reasons I find it hard to condemn a guy for vanity."

Well, it should be me who is embarrassed. But even after the story of Jay, I am still Alex Perkins, am still drunk, and am still obsessed with William Kahn. I can't stand hearing Hulton defend him. I'll have to give some sober thought to what he said about vanity and heroism and all that. I think I agree about the heroism part. Sure, I'd like to be a hero. But vanity is a thing of degree. Narcissism. There's a point of no return with too much of it. Wasn't I already thinking about this? Vanity cops revoking artistic licenses for going too far over the limit.

But I'm not quite up to making distinctions right now. So I say, "Well, then, what about *smugness*? I'll buy it that vanity is complicated. That I'm vain, you're vain, we're all vain. – But smugness" – and the knowledge a smug guy is fucking your girlfriend, *and* behind the back of someone else who you wish was *your* girlfriend – "is irritating. Don't Kahn's Donald Ducks seem a little smug?"

"Well, I don't know. How could I say? I haven't seen them?"

This reminds me of Dalmore's "Well, I really don't need to see them, do I?" – He'd said it about Hulton's trees. Reminds me in reverse, I mean. Hulton needs information before he disrespects. Dalmore needs none to be disrespectful.

He continues, "I'm a *pluralist*. I certainly don't think everybody needs to be painting trees – or nature – or abstracts. I'll move on from trees. Maybe I'll paint figures too. Any painting about anything – painted in anyway – *could* be good. It's not like if I paint trees I can't like Warhol."

"You like Warhol?" Kevin asks this with a tone that betrays more of his personal taste or opinion than usual.

"Sure. He's an important artist. I don't really care for his soup cans. But I like his electric chairs and his car wrecks. Pretty devastating. I like his dark stuff. He's uneven. But, we're all uneven. Well, maybe Michelangelo was even. But nobody expected him to do something new every time."

I feel a bit odd. Me – a guy who writes about Capt'n Tony's clams and Lucinda's anatomically correct body paint – trying to talk a colleague of some of the most esteemed American painters of all time into being angry at charlatans. And he doesn't want to be – or else he's resistant to believing charlatans are what they are. Am I wrong? Am I just *uptight*? Does this mean I have to take Kahn's paintings seriously? No, damn it. Unlike Hulton, I have seen them. You can't defend something you haven't seen any more than you can condemn it. I've seen them. They can't really be good. They just can't.

"What about *sincerity* in art?" Kevin chimes in, looking for another opening.

265

"I'm afraid sincerity doesn't guarantee much," Hulton says. "Igor Stravinsky said 'most sincere art is bad art.'"

"Wait a minute," I say, dueling quotes with him. "Didn't Rothko say 'the cartoonists were out to kill us?'" – You know, when he walked into his dealer's on 57th street and found paintings that he'd turned himself inside out to do, had been put away, and jokey, hip things were now hung instead. You want to be a pluralist, but it isn't a *live and let live* world – or art world."

"Well, that's something else. It's true," Hulton says. "There's only just so much wall space – whether it's in museums or galleries, offices or people's homes. There's probably too much art being produced for more than a small portion to find someplace to hang. Too many artists, practically speaking – sad to say. I think if art were carpentry, there'd probably be twenty-five workmen in every bathroom being remodeled. And if art were medicine, there'd be more doctors than patients. You're talking Darwinism in the arts. Only the dominant species gets to carry on. But not necessarily *the strong*. I may like art that comes from the lion's claw better than art batted-out ... by a ...kitten's paw. But the lions are gone for now and we can't wish them back. It's now the age of the kitten. The mighty kitten."

"And we have to ride the decline?"

"What?"

"Ride the decline. I have a young friend who says that. Apparently he thinks it's all downhill from here."

"Well, maybe he's right," Hulton says.

"But do we have to put up with it," I say. "Do we have to put up with it in art? I can see it for the things we can't control – or have a hard time controlling – like overpopulation or pollution. But art is art because we can make it be what we want it to be. This isn't about natural inevitability. This is about promotion. Promotion and taste – bad taste. Not all of it. Sure, Warhol could be amazing. But there's always crap in any era. And apparently more in this one than is usual. Do you have to validate every bit of it because you're a pluralist? Or because you are afraid of being called an elitist?"

I feel myself getting very heated. Kevin, who has been quiet, but attentive, during all this, looks at me with concern. He seems surprised. Well, I'm surprised too. Beauty addict or not, I've never been particularly militant about the things I find *not* beautiful. It may be that the subject boils down to the name *William Kahn* a bit too much for my own good.

Hulton seems to be giving serious consideration to what I'm saying, but his facial muscles remain relaxed. I start to wonder if this man's equanimity comes from a kind of enlightenment I'm too shallow to achieve, or just from being beaten down; from acceptance of his obsolescence. God, I don't know. Isn't enlightenment just accepting things? Yes. Or so *they* say. – But no! There has to be some right and wrong. Just because something wins doesn't mean it's right.

"You're saying – kitten or not – that *might* is right?"

Hulton is quiet for a minute. So is Kevin. Kevin looks squinted-eyed at me. I'm wondering if I have ended up tormenting someone whom I was bragging to myself, just an hour ago, about how much I'd helped.

Hulton raises an eyebrow and says, "Well, maybe you have a point."

I look at Kevin for confirmation of the rightness of what I'm about to say. He looks confused. How could he know what I'm about to say? So I just say it. I tell Hulton about Kahn's *German Lake With Deer and Eagles*; our unofficial name.

He takes it in and is silent for a minute. Then he says with a smile, "What a shame an important historical reference piece like that can't go into the man's big show."

# 21

"Alex. It's your boss. He says to tell you, it's *Steve.*"

"You came all the way up, Gram?" Every morning after I've been drinking, somebody needs me at dawn. "I don't want you climbing those stairs. I could have called him back."

"He's you're boss. Bosses don't like to wait."

Gram hands me the cordless phone. I slap my face fast three times.

"Hi, Steve."

"Sorry I disturbed your grandmother."

Yeah, right – I'm about to say. But he actually doesn't sound sarcastic. Didn't snicker. Maybe he's going to fire me for refusing to write the Lucinda York story.

"Can you drop into my office first thing?"

"Sure," I say.

"Before you look at a paper."

"Before I look at a paper. A *Currents*?"

"That's right. Like if you stop at Brioche. Don't look at a paper until you come by my office."

This is ominous.

"Okay," I say.


Within an hour I'm entering his doorway.

Steve launches right in: "You remember that bank double-truck I told you about last week?" He's studying me.

"Sure," I say. "*Barnes* – the asshole at Northport National."

"Right. Right. Well, Barnes came through, the spread was filled, and we ran it this week."

"Good," I say. I try – as newspaper writers are chided for not doing – to think from the ad sales perspective. "You put in a lot of time on it. Pays the bills, right?"

"Well, ya. – But I had to buy a whole four more pages just to get those two."

"Right," I say. "I know how it works. But paper's cheap compared to what advertising brings in."

"Right. Right." Steve says. "But then you've suddenly got two new pages to fill – right at the last minute."

"Right," I say. "House ads and stock photos. Wire stories."

"Right. And I had some good photos. Good photos I didn't have to buy. That I'd *already bought* – when I paid the salaries of my employees."

"So what are you saying?"

Steve picks up a copy of *Currents* that's on his desk – presumably the one that's just hit the stands. He opens it and pushes it my way.

I see a banner headline reading: "CONCEPTUAL ART COMES TO NORTHPORT." I see my interview with Dalmore. And next to that I see a photo I took of the dignified curator at his desk. Fine. But next to that is the shot of him in Funky Chicken mode with Bollard and Fred at the moment of the gas release. It's caption reads. "*Even death on the high seas can be a performance.* " (See next week's paper.) Then, I focus on my photo of Lucinda striding toward the camera, painted lettering: *This Is Not My Bathing Suit,* fully visible. The caption reads: "Not Her Bathing Suit?   No, It's her birthday suit!" Black bars cover her nipples and her pubic region.

I stare at this backstabbing son-of-a-bitch of a boss of mine and remember the old saying, "He has no enemies, but all his friends dislike him intensely."

Steve is fiddling with papers on his desk. He doesn't look up but he says, "Jeff and Nora and I were here until midnight. We were all tired... trying to fill up that last extra half page. We'd had a few beers. I guess we were a little punchy from the long day. And we started to cut-up a little – tossing out captions for your pictures. You should be glad we didn't use some of the other ones we came up with. Some of those were *really* bad. And Nora – you know what a little minx she can be – she dares me to run the feature like that. And I figure if I leave your bi-line off you can tell your artsy friends that you didn't have anything to do with it – which you didn't. And then..."

# 22

"Hello?"

"Hi, Kevin."

"Alex?"

"Yeah, it's me – how you doing?"

"Okay, okay. Hey, that was fun last night. You coming to the opening here later?"

"I wanted to talk to you about that. I've got a little proposition for you. You still feeling brave?"

"Still brave – what do you mean by that? Why *still*?"

"I mean after your unplanned swim on Sunday."

"Oh that. No big deal. Why? What do you have in mind that might scare me?"

"Oh, nothing dangerous. It's really an 'only thing to fear is fear itself' kind of concept."

"Yeah. Well, I like Franklin Roosevelt, all right. But I always thought that statement was just rhetoric. When he said those words, there was lots of the bad stuff all over the place that people were *really* afraid of: poverty, bombs from Japanese planes, losing wars to fascists, death camps…"

"What are *you* really afraid of?" I ask this to prepare him for what I'm about to suggest – make it seem innocuous by comparison.

"I don't know – clowns?"

"*Clowns?*"

"Yeah. I was always afraid of clowns when I was little."

"Why?"

"I don't know. I guessed they always seemed so out of control, you never knew what they were going to do next. And those weird red rubber noses."

I'm glad to see he's in a kidding mood. Actually, I've never seen this side of him. Still I say, "Seriously, though."

"Well," he says thoughtfully, "maybe conscience. – You know, Hamlet said, 'Conscience doth make cowards of us all.'"

This isn't the direction I want the conversation to go.

"Well, if you can take issue with my FDR, I can do that with your Shakespeare. And I think that was one of Shakespeare's more bogus statements. The things you mention are a lot more powerful than conscience for turning us all cowardly."

"Yeah, I admit Shakespeare could be a real idiot a lot of the time," he says. "But in this case I don't think he was. He was considering conscience by itself. He wasn't trying to be categorical. You know – like 'Conscience doth be *one of the seven or eight things* that doth make us all cowards.' Or maybe, 'Fear itself doth make cowards of us all' – like if he'd been talking about what was worrying Roosevelt."

"Hey, that last one's good – it covers the 1600's, The Depression, and the Second World War, all at the same time."

"Maybe. But I think it might sound a little dogmatic today. As you yourself would say, 'Takes in too much territory.' Maybe 'Fear itself doth make cowards of *most of us,*' would fit better in these relativist times."

"Yeah, that would be a safer way to go, all right – but it completely leaves out the clowns. I think, 'Fear itself doth make *clowns* of most of us,' would hit all the scary notes and still not sound too arrogant."

"Okay, okay – I can't keep this up. What's the frightening proposition you called me about?"

"Well, remember, last night, how John Hulton said it was a shame that *German Lake* wasn't going to be in William Kahn's definitive, 'life's-work' show? Well, I was just thinking, that, maybe, you and I might…find a way to…"

# 23

I'm usually pretty law-abiding. My traffic record is good – though driving a Karmann Ghia, an automobile barely capable of what is commonly known as acceleration, discourages speeding. Of course, there is a petty criminal thing I did a very long time ago. Nothing significant, but I guess since I did it repeatedly, I probably shouldn't just brush it off. One spring when I was in my early 20's, I bought a pair of cheap corduroy slippers at a department store called Marshall's. I wore them outside as moccasins that summer, so they deteriorated pretty fast. Well, in September, I walked back into the store with them on my feet and, when the coast was clear, took the dirty, holey pair off, grabbed a new pair the same size from the rack – they didn't ever box slippers this cheap – and put them on. Then I replaced the missing ones on the shelf with my disgusting ones. For some reason I found this gratifying enough that I repeated it over the next three or four summers – until I either felt too guilty or just grew up too much to continue something so tacky.

Other than *that* crime, just using illegal drugs when everyone else is and driving while intoxicated comprise the few times I've broken the law. And I rationalize the latter offense by the consideration that driving and drinking are both legal *individually*. Still, I know I should cut out driving under the influence. But for that I'll wait until tomorrow. I'm a little nervous right now. It's probably just fear of fear. I doubt my curatorial input to the Kahn show actually breaks any laws. But I think I'll need to drink pretty heavily tonight – before I eventually have to drive myself home. To tell the truth, I'm *very* nervous. If I can't keep it together this may be the moment I make the biggest fool of myself in my whole life. Well, fear itself doth make clowns of most of us. Right?

Currently I'm wishing I possessed a temperament more like Kevin's – however much I've disparaged his steadiness as "boring" over the course of our lives (before last Sunday, anyway). And at the bar with Hulton last night, I was surprised to see that even Kevin can push the envelope. His own envelope, I mean. Everybody's got his own. He ascended from being a consumer of just lemonade at family barbeques, to a man capable of downing two and a half beers in an hour and a half. Then, of course, he reverted to his innate stoical form when he pushed away the bottle before emptying it. I read this as a kind of methodical decision-making. That kind of thing usually escapes me.

Well, I guess I showed myself a bit more decisive than usual – at the irresponsible end of the spectrum, unfortunately – by suggesting Kevin and I bend a few unwritten museum rules for the sake of artistic justice. But while it was my idea – in truth, actually John Hulton's idea – most of the burden of my decisiveness will probably be Kevin's to bear. At worst, for me, I might succeed in getting Kahn, someone I don't like anyway – and who probably doesn't like me – to not like me a great deal more than he probably already doesn't. As for me and the subject of responsibility, I'm now responsible, innocently, of course – thanks to Steve Towle's irresponsibility – for three other people, who don't really deserve it, being heaped with public ridicule:

275

Lucinda, Dalmore and Justin Bollard. I assume they will assume that I am the reason. And though I didn't really do anything except shoot, develop, and hand in to a member of the press uncomplimentary pictures of them, I do feel bad. But, oddly enough, I *feel bad for* only Bollard, as opposed to *feel guilty toward,* which I do feel toward Lucinda and Dalmore. I've come to like Bollard. And at least he wasn't humiliated personally by Steve's flippant captioning – or worse wasn't humiliating himself with strange gyrations at the moment of being photographed for the paper. Bollard was just an innocent bystander. Humiliation by association. Courtesy of yours truly.

So, though I could probably get away with telling people I thought Kevin wouldn't take me seriously and wouldn't actually go ahead and put a stupid painting from Kahn's Berlin days in his grand retrospective, *ethically* I should instead insist to the assembled multitudes: "He's innocent. I goaded him. I threatened. I deceived. I told him *Lake, Deer and Eagles* was my favorite of all that great artist's work. I pleaded: 'If you have any cousinly love for me, you'll put that painting in his show.'" But I'll probably do neither. I'll let the chips fall.

And actually, Kevin's compliance took no goading at all. Conscience didn't make him a coward. After I told him about the newspaper, and how unfortunate it was that everyone but Kahn was getting trashed by me, and that, in the interest of fairness, we had to do something to trash Kahn, too, Kevin just said, "Okay." This surprised me. I'd expected I'd need to employ a lot of persuasion. But, if you're a man willing to jump out of a speeding yacht into a cold, churning sea, two hundred feet deep, just taking a painting – signed by the artist, no less – out of the store room and putting it into that artist's very own show, maybe isn't that brave. Sure you might risk your job. But risking your job is tiny compared to risking your life.

I park the car.

I have arrived at the members and press preview celebration of the opening of the Northport Museum of Modern Art's just completed

West Wing – and, inside the wing's new galleries, the exhibition honoring the life's work – thus far – of maestro William Kahn. The sky is clear, the evening softly humid with enough haze to put pastel streaks around the fuzzy setting sun. But the air is not so thick that it will obscure the stars that will be floating above when I head back, in who knows how long. Still, I may not remember to look up then, as looking up is not an easy thing to do with your tail between your legs. Not physically difficult, but spiritually. Who knows? I may be run out of this place before it's even dark. That I consider the evening sky right now demonstrates my ambivalence about being here at all. Were I not a fool, I would be content with walking the road from Gram's to the beach and sitting quietly in the dunes. But, as Captain Kirk said when he rejected the peace-inducing spores on Omicron Seti 3: "Man wasn't meant to be contented." As a social animal, I am condemned to play the fool. Human endeavor too often is a pretty tacky thing.

The first figure I recognize in the crowd – corralled in the East Wing until the ribbon cordoning off the West Wing is cut – is Justin Bollard. I'm sorry to admit that he is recognizable mainly because of his height – or almost total lack of any. Kevin has told me that Justin made good on the pledge to buy him the bottle of Dom Perignon. Justin converses, head craned up, with a tall young man in a black silk jacket and slicked-back blond hair. I approach intending to return the apology Bollard gave me on Fred's boat, i.e., to apologize for my involvement in his likely becoming a local laughing-stock. But before I get the chance for even *"Sorry"* to pass my lips, my mouth instead involuntarily ejaculates, *"David!"*

"Hi, Alex," says David Player. "Everybody's here, huh? I've never been in this place before. Pretty eleganza."

"David…you're…here?" I imagine my eyes are cartoon versions of their former selves. I'm rendered speechless, in the sense that too many questions compete for exiting my brain simultaneously. (A minor one might be, what does *he* mean by *everybody*?) But I strain to appear non-nonplussed and just say, "Yeah, it's a cool place." David helps me a bit by misinterpreting my surprise.

"I called in sick for fishing today," he explains, drawing down one corner of his mouth in a stage-wince self-rebuke. "Actually, I'm taking a week off. You see, Justin…" David gestures at Bollard's shoulder-high face, "says I should bring some of my pieces into the City for a little reaction. He knows a few people there who could…"

I drift off: *Pieces? The City?* – "The City" from *David Player?* A few days ago the only cities I imagine he'd ever contemplated were Boston and Lima, Peru.

So I guess I get the basic picture. But since I can't truly assimilate it right now, I just give David a thumbs-up and say "good luck". I pull myself together enough to approach Justin about the pictures in *Currents.*

Well, he hasn't seen the paper. Why should he have? So I describe it. He's incredulous. – But incredulous that I am concerned that he might mind! I realize that I am talking Northport to him. And, to him, anything *Northport* is a lark. – It's that, or else that his *relief syndrome* is still in active mode. Or maybe he's in love. (What happened to Avrum? Maybe there's no desire for a male bimbo right now – after Justin's long-night-of-the-soul, that is.) So, Justin actually laughs, and says: "Oh, that's funny. Dalmore is going to be so upset. You naughty man. That's so funny."

David is smiling, both on his own, and in support of his – what? mentor? He says, "That's pretty cool. I saw you snapping that very shot. When I get a copy of the paper I want you to autograph it." Bollard looks at David with something like pride. I assume he's seldom seen anything as authentic as David Player. – Though authentically *what?* – Probably no one knows. And if he does prize authenticity, why does Justin want to see David in this inauthentic uniform? I ninety-nine percent assume Bollard provided the uniform. Well, attraction and objectification might be inseparable. Like plumage to horny birds. Why else would I like seeing sane, healthy women dress themselves like sluts? You know my opinion: sex *is* pretty stupid. Of course there may not even be anything sexual here. At least not for David Player – no matter how willingly he seems to play dress-up. And who knows? This conjecture – and I've probably been doing way too much of that lately – may be just a product of my own dirty mind. Maybe David's sculpture is really something great. I mean *I* was moved by it. At least, I think I was. I just didn't take myself seriously. Seems like with postmodern stuff you're never sure. I just assumed that I was wrong for liking exploded fridges. I grab three champagne glasses from a passing tray. They are all for me.

Bollard continues: "I doubt that much could bother Arthur tonight though. See that fellow with the goatee and the horn-rimmed glasses. That's Christopher Vine from *The Times*. He doesn't often review on the road. Just getting him here is a coup for Arthur – and for your little provincial city."

"Oh boy!" I think. *The New York Times*. Maybe this wasn't such a good idea after all.

A local punk/jazz group, the Lymph Notes, is dispensing music. They do moderate volume, free-form, contemporary. So not really punk at all. I saw them booed at a high-energy club called Nowhere, here in town, when its house band, the Insertions, was opening for The Clash in Boston. The only thing really punk about the Lymph Notes is spiked hair, black tee shirts, and frightening tattoos. The word is that they are just opportunistic former members of the Northport Central High marching band. But to the 90 percent unhip individuals among the press and local museum patrons here, their presence increases the sensation that the evening is at the leading edge of what's *really going on.*

Through the leaves and the blades of the Calder mobile that hangs from the skylight over the foyer by the East Wing entrance I can see the stars of the show: Kahn and Dalmore. Dalmore wears grey. Kahn wears white linen – a shawl-collar evening jacket and matching pants. Actually, I have on about the same white jacket. But mine is vintage and I wear it over jeans. Both of these alpha men wear their hair slicked back. Mine doesn't go in any particular direction. I'm always a little ambivalent about dressing up. I like looking good – but I'm leery of standing out too much. I see the paradox in nature, which gives the creatures that stand out a better chance of getting mates, but also affords them a greater danger of being eaten. Dalmore is smoking a cigar. *The Times* critic has moved in close. Dalmore looks relatively jovial for Dalmore. He's either telling a joke or doing an imitation of Sir Winston Churchill. The critic slaps him on the back. So much for press objectivity.

The plan for the gala, according to Kevin, is to wait until the presumed majority of those likely to attend has arrived – entering via this the old main entrance – and then, after a brief talk by Dalmore, parade the crowd en masse through the new connecting corridor, lights rheostating up from "dim to full" as the transition is affected.

I scan for Rebecca. No luck. But there's Naomi Dalmore at the canapés table. She's in a white spaghetti-strap gown. She cleans up good. Looks five or six years younger with make-up. I wonder if she is still mad at me; I thought the whaling adventure ended pretty well – though a good set of her spouse's summer whites became a casualty. I don't suppose she would have seen today's *Currents* yet (or if she has *ever* seen one) – unless Arthur's attention was directed to it, and he handed it off to her. Pretty humiliating, as I think I've stated. I don't get a clear enough picture of the Dalmore marriage to be able to tell if he would try to shield her from the sight of her husband doing the Funky Chicken, or if he would go to her for comfort and commiseration after learning that the public in their newly adopted community had beheld such a vision. I usually tank-up on cheese at these things. A bite or two might settle my nerves. But I think I'll keep my distance until Naomi has had her fill and departs. Now she's talking to that gallery owner, Sally Nissan. I've attended more than a few openings at Nissan Gallery. Sally sees me watching them. She points at the cheese wheel with one hand and with the other makes a circling motion over her midriff, licking her lips. I guess I've got a reputation for grazing. Naomi notices the direction of Sally Nissan's sarcasm and glares at me. I casually look away – back toward the main action.

And there she is: Rebecca Sharma. She wears red and black; a black dress – I guess the official term is *a little* black dress – with a red scarf over her left shoulder. Her hair is up. This is formalness I don't usually like. But when she moves her head to speak to the *Times* guy I see a great, full shock of shining black tumbling down the right side of her face, swishing onto her bare right shoulder. This may be the best of both worlds. The pleasure of looking at her competes with the pain.

And now I see Kevin. And I catch his eye. He nods. There are maybe three hundred people in here. Most are patrons, but Boston and local press seem to be well represented – as well as the aforementioned *New York Times*. Yes, there's Steve, my loose cannon employer. The artist-dismisser – except for susceptible female artists. I don't know why I put up with him. The same reason everyone puts up with his boss. Not much alternative. What's the old saying? "Any alternative is preferable to a worse one." A lousy paycheck is better than no paycheck at all. And between his lousy pay and proprietarily subverting of my stories, I'm particularly unhappy with him right now. I assume that he's attended just to enjoy the fruits of having offended the art community – and, of course, to try to get laid. Steve stands with his back toward Rebecca. The reason for this could only be that he has not seen her yet. And look – Steve's chatting up Oggelvy. Steve has no shame. He's ridiculed the museum and now he's drinking its wine. It appears Steve is ogling Deborah – though she is on Oggelvy's arm. Double no shame. I certainly hope she isn't one of those good girls who goes for outlaw charm. Well, it seems she did with Kahn. Unless good looks alone was all it took. What is wrong with women? I know: pot calling the kettle… Well, Oggelvy appears content enough. Oggelvy is a newspaperman. And I know they are all compulsive about checking out the competition. So my guess is that he has seen the new *Currents* – and that it's impugning of the direction taken within a museum wing with his name on it, doesn't faze him. Well, he was a dissenter over-ruled. I wonder if he might be happy to see Dalmore taken down a peg.

Kahn seems to be soaking up all the love in the room. His smile glows about a dignified seven. Then I see him focus on the museum entrance and briefly dial the smile up to a nine. I follow his gaze, as do several admirers, including Rebecca. And I watch Lucinda enter. It's the first time I've seen her since I left her disheveled on her couch. She never returned my calls. Her appearance is as different tonight from then as it was different from her brunette hippy days to when I first saw her again last week. She wears a little black dress of her own. So much for the girl freedom fighter. – And her little black dress is somewhat littler than Rebecca's. The minimal yardage of black fabric – minimal yardage being less than one – assuming it isn't paint – against her skin as white as marble, underscores the erotic presentation. And there's something else. Perhaps in black she looks *longer.* No, that's not it. – She *is* longer. Lucinda, the feminist, wears heels. Tiny, three inch stilettos replace her signature combat boots. For a terrorist attack of a different kind, I guess, a different uniform is required. It flashes in my brain that William may have stated blandly – or whispered in her ear – that heels are cool. Realizing that I will likely never hold Lucinda against my savage breast again (and remembering that it was her back that I held to my breast last time), and also most likely never hold Rebecca at all, restores my sense of the justice of taking vengeance upon Kahn. Minions Avrum and Roger accompany Lucinda. She glances in the direction of where I stand – but *seems* to not see me. Then Roger recognizes me – recognizes me as someone he doesn't recognize. That's a good trick. It makes me wonder briefly, "who am I anyway?" Only Avrum makes true eye contact. He scrunches the left corner of his mouth and shrugs. I think he is implying solidarity. We've both been sidelined by great artists. I'd like to tell him that appearances can be deceiving. That I don't think David is looking for love. But, once again: *what do I know?* I wonder how Avrum would feel if he knew I was the conduit for Justin to David. With that, all solidarity would likely depart. Then, I have a paranoid flash. A rewrite of these entrance dynamics might be that Lucinda has seen the newspaper and thinks it my doing and that I took revenge on her for a body art performance with Kahn.

Whereas, in fact, I am innocent of vengefulness toward her, but am about to take revenge on Kahn – for myself, for Kevin, for Hulton, and for Deborah – and even for Rebecca, who, for all I know, may not want it; may be perfectly capable of taking care of herself. I do a quick glance at her. Concern for her situation is my excuse for looking.

If I am going to share responsibility with Kevin I must get closer to him. I make disengagement mumbles in the direction of David and Justin. Though David, oddly enough, doesn't appear uncomfortable – as a fisherman out of water might be supposed to – he follows me, the only person he knows, as if he's naturally expected to move as I move (unbeknownst to him, toward the eye of the coming storm). David, of course, does know the king of this hill: Dalmore. But Dalmore likely still thinks him a madman. Unless Bollard has had a few words in Dalmore's ear. Perhaps Bollard's sponsorship – and I presume he's a man of influence – can transform the quality: *madman* – into an indispensable component of David's artistic genius. Since competence is no longer a symptom of greatness, I am out of my depth to judge with current criteria. Wildly my mind fantasizes an arts magazine a few months hence whereon David Player, a former provincial space-shot, now an urban conquistador, graces the cover – and John Hulton, a master of his medium, is nowhere inside. I'd be righteously indignant. But I guess I would be happy for David. If anyone has to be the beneficiary of unmerited art world success, it might as well be a Northport fisherman. And I'm touched by the naive respect David showed when he asked for my autograph. – And that he has shown such deference to me previously – me, someone who gets a byline in a tiny newspaper every week or so. What will happen if and when he sees his own name in print?

David glances at Bollard politely and, without deference to him, tips his head in my direction. As David and I move, Bollard follows us both.

Lucinda and company arrive at the center of things – that is. approximately where Kahn and Dalmore and Rebecca and Steve and

Oggelvy and Deborah and *The Times* critic stand clumped. Kevin hovers only a few bodies away, unfortunately. The spot under the Calder is the black hole of a tiny galaxy I gravitated into just over a week ago. I'm afraid that when I enter that energy field – with David and Justin sucked in right behind me – critical mass will have been achieved and I will either be knocked flat or ejected into another universe.

Now, Dalmore focuses on me. Lucinda does too. Both squint vehemently. I've never imagined the two might be capable of producing the same facial expression. But before words-to-match-the-looks issue from their mouths, the band's non-melody abruptly stops. Dalmore, for one, shakes off his squint. This loud silence apparently cues his speech. He pulls himself up to his great height and beams out, upon the multitude, the Vincent Price smile I'd first seen not far from this spot. He begins to speak. He thanks everyone effusively and after extravagant praise for the tradition of this museum, and of Modernism itself, he launches into an easy explanation of why Modernism and other elitist notions of art suck so badly. This is followed with a version of the *new paradigm* polemic he laid out when I interviewed him. The way he – now surrounded by representatives of mainstream media and people with money – puts it this time goes: "We are all making a great and historic cultural journey,…blah, blah, blah…together… into a brave new world…" I admire at how fearlessly he maintains composure in the face of likely charges of flagrant predictability and tediousness. But I realize that one of my most common judgmental reactions is activated when somebody uses "journey" to mean something other than geographic travel. I know this is smug of me – me, the smugness hater. I'm guilty, I know. I even remind myself of a paraphrase of Steve's Joseph Goebbels imitation: "Whenever I hear the word journey…" I imagine I'm on much firmer ground as a snob when I'm dismissing less metaphorical manifestations of "new age" thought – like the astral projection of cars into parking spaces made vacant by divine intervention.

Dalmore's *journey* segues into an introduction of Kahn – "a man

284

for whom there is no adequate single metaphor." Kahn, "the bold adventurer"... "striving to challenge the canons of Western Art that were inviolable for five centuries."... "Kahn the prankster."... "The Jonathan Swift of visual arts."... "The delighter of children."... "The bane of the academics."... "Kahn the chameleon – as ever changing as pop culture itself."

"...And without further ado"... Dalmore concludes, swinging his open hand grandly but gracelessly – like an older matador a little stiff from the years of goring – toward the new wing; illumination, as if emanating from the curator's palm, grows along the foot-lighted hallway from the old wing. "Shall we?" he asks, striding into the breach where previously there had been a wall.

We shall. The black hole is moving – its gravity carrying me along.

Dalmore leads us in a respectfully hushed walk-through of the exhibition. At the end we will be on our own – free to return and linger as long as we like before pieces that are our favorites. I notice with suppressed rage that Lucinda and Kahn exchange more than a friendly greeting. Perhaps I delude myself that I'm not vengeful toward her. Lucinda and her friends join the procession flowing into the new wing. She walks just four or five feet behind Kahn and three or four behind Rebecca. The dress Lucinda wears is not quite revealing enough for me to be sure I have glimpsed a dorsal fin just beneath its surface. But I intuit there is one there.

The retrospective hangs chronologically. We approach, first, the "early" Kahns. These date back as far as 1972 – when he was only about 75 percent as old as he is now – the year of his return from Germany and his first Whitney Biennial submission and acceptance. That Biennial painting is actually here – on loan from the collection of actor, Jack Nicholson. This seminal work is entitled, *This Buds for You*, and is from Kahn's political period, the wall text informs us. It depicts George Washington raising a glued-on Budweiser can to Abraham Lincoln. Lincoln, in black-face, appears pensive. After several works of similar presidential iconography, the paintings evolve to cultural-political. In one a muscle-builder, with an appropriated

Warhol JFK head superimposed, holds in his arms a bathing beauty with a stuck on Warhol *Jackie*. Raising the ante to dizzying heights, a Warhol *Marilyn* floats above and between the president and first lady. The words "I am a jelly doughnut" emanate, via cartoon balloon, from Marilyn's glossy, green lips. This triple appropriation, and its being visited upon an artist only a few years Kahn's senior, was bold even for that era. That Andy Warhol himself, as the text informs us, stopped by Kahn's studio and did the lip-gloss, reinforces the celebrity status of this work. The piece hangs here courtesy of its owner, AT&T. A series of three paintings depicts Richard Nixon and Pablo Picasso walking into a children's book sunset, paddling a canoe, and standing on a street corner in trench coats under a theater marquis emblazoned with "All Nude Review." In each painting, balloons over Nixon's and Picasso's heads say, respectively, "I am not a crook" and "I am not a crook, either." These works were the signal pieces for Kahn's transition from political art to art about art itself – arguably considered his greatest contribution to date.

In the period that followed, the references became more obscure; more truly "art insider." The continuing text tells us Kahn, the iconoclast, briefly battled unfair charges of elitism himself related to these. The most significant example cited for the erroneous epithet "elitist" is a painting called *Prostate Problem*." As I read the narrative, a bald figure, representing Jackson Pollock, pisses paint that lands in a multicolored splatter on the head of a heavy-set middle-aged woman in a merry widow and fishnet stockings. On the corset she wears a Pizza Hut nametag reading, "Peggy". This refers satirically to the gossiped-about artist/patron relationship Pollock had with Peggy Guggenheim – into whose fireplace Pollock famously once pissed. "The noted critic and philosopher, Justin Bollard," the wall text states, "came to Kahn's defense." Writing in *Art Forum*, he explained that Kahn, in this and similar urination works of the era, "was boldly raising a mirror to elitism – not indulging in it." That, we're told, put the charge to rest. If I may be allowed to insert my opinion, I would say that I also find nothing elitist here. This is very far from an elitist painting.

This gallery also notably contains a version of *The Last Supper* on black velvet, with Elvis in the chair normally occupied by Lord Jesus. The twelve apostles are represented by five Elvis impersonators and Snow White's seven dwarfs. Snow White is absent, as she also was from the da Vinci version of this same subject. (This Kahn piece is a progenitor of the definitive *Last Supper*, to be seen in the show's climactic Donald Duck's eye-view series.) In this earlier Last Supper – actual title, *Dinner with the King* – a balloon over the Jesus/Elvis head reads, "Ah – thank ya. Thank ya very much." Next to this hangs another religious piece. Herein, Andy Warhol wears white robes and stands on "The Mount." A balloon above his head reads, "I can't remember what I was going to say."

Eventually we come to the room containing the new art canon-demolishing Donald Ducks – the works that impressed me so the day of my interview with Arthur Dalmore. I am honored to have been one of the very first art lovers ever to have viewed these pieces in the flesh. It would not be an exaggeration to say that they may be as good as anything Kahn has ever produced. I need not describe them again.

This gallery has an alcove with a small window for natural light. That window, though, has been covered over with a large unframed canvas: the afore-discussed "lost" Kahn; the signature product of his German odyssey (his actual signature, "W. Kahn", writ bombastically large in the lower right corner); his grand monument to the power of the popular, the sentimental, and the primitive eye and heart: *German Lake with Deer and Eagles* (as we decided it had to be called). Where the title and text card usually stick to the wall, a small hand-printed (in crayon) sign – small, but still perhaps five times the size of the standard text card – reads: "Who knows what's next?" Unfortunately, the "next" is anachronistic – out of keeping with retrospection. And, there is no date to inform the public that this may have been painted *before*. The public may assume what it likes. And the sign may be merely asking, "Could the artist return to this cornucopian theme?" Anyway, it will have to do. We couldn't think up anything else.

287

I hang back a bit. I came for this moment, yet I am ambivalent. A part of me wishes I were dead – but dead and reincarnated as a fly on the wall. Because the elements of this traditional landscape painting are small compared, say, to the canvas-filling figures of Martin Luther King and Henry Kissinger in a work of monumental scale, and because the idyllic composition, though continually mined by artists for the past two hundred years, is un-famous specifically (not a Last Supper), its content is hard to read from a distance. But Kahn recognizes it immediately. Actually, he jumps. He jumps toward it. But he immediately restrains himself. He realizes, I presume, in an instant, that nothing he can do can make it go away. And he knows that anything he might try to do toward that end would be counterproductive; would attract greater attention. His persona, as always, must be Mr. Cool. Mr. Detachment, Mr. Irony. Any show of emotion, any appearance that the exhibition was not within his control, would look bad. Kevin and I had discussed this likelihood. Though we would be fools to have counted on anything, we foolishly counted on this. It seemed our only way of surviving – surviving the evening anyway. As with the title card, it was all we had.

But there is also Dalmore. Dalmore is another story. A man not cool; emotional, in spite of himself. I quickly get the feeling that he is familiar with this manifestation of Kahn's oeuvre. His gaze has followed Kahn's, and his own reaction comes just two seconds later. He does a double take, bringing his elbows up sharply behind him. I now guess this pained gesture of his – I'll call it "the Funky Chicken reflex" – which I first beheld and captured on film on board the *Laura T* – may be more chronic than acute. Dalmore's facial features are working through maneuvers that would do credit to gold medal winning Olympic gymnasts' arms and legs. Kahn, cautioning him, grabs the Dalmore elbow that almost struck him. Dalmore moans.

But this is all subtle. People standing closest look perplexed. A few patrons exchange glances. Something may have happened – or it may not. Nobody's sure. Rebecca studies Kahn quizzically, frowning with incomprehension. Oggelvy looks alert. Apparently *he* thinks something may have happened. David and Bollard still float one room back – David seems to be giving Justin his private take on one or the other work of art. Avrum, perhaps feeling if-you-can't-beat-em-join-em, lingers on their periphery; contemplating David close up. Christopher Vine from *The Times*, is out-of-step too – taking time taking notes. Lucinda, so intent on Kahn, seems sensitive to the change that just came over him. Watching him proprietarily, she registered his eyes going to the small alcove the moment before he took his funny little jump. But not even she has assimilated the canned-sour-kraut-at-a-banquet implications of the *"German"* Kahn. And no one has any reason for guessing the artist and curator may be half out of their minds with anger and humiliation. Lucinda , though, is thinking.

Kahn's grasp steadies Dalmore – and seems to convey the "be cool" message intended. They share a glance, then separate. Both try to corral and herd individuals near them toward officially intended, highly accomplished exhibition pieces – pretending at a necessity that they require closer inspection.

I allow myself the luxury of exhaling. A moment of relief. Then I notice Lucinda. She stands before *German Lake*. She looks at Kahn. Then looks at the painting. Then she looks at Kahn again. And then she looks at *me*. Lucinda has not acknowledged my presence yet. But now she does. She strides toward me.

*"You!"* she calls out. "You did this. – This and that 'birthday suit picture' of me in your crumby little pretend newspaper. Just cause I slept with him."

Apparently, no one knows what she is talking about. Even the pronoun, "him," doesn't necessarily refer to Kahn any more disclosively than to any one of the about one hundred seventy-five other men here tonight. But Rebecca is looking from the painting to Kahn to Lucinda, starting to put two and two and two together.

Roger moves toward Lucinda in support – or restraint – or supportive restraint.

"No," I say. " I mean 'no' to the paper. I didn't do the paper. I

289

recused myself."

"You what?" I think she says this as much from not knowing the definition of the word as from disbelief. But she hurtles on. "You took the fucking picture, didn't you?"

"A lot of people took that picture. It's part of your portfolio – and your criminal record."

Just when Lucinda begins to lunge at me Roger's arm comes out in front of her. I see Avrum pushing through the crowd. He gets to Lucinda and says, "Hey, kid – it's cool. It's cool."

Lucinda immediately realizes that she is a focus of art world attention of a character different from what she craves.

Kevin, nonplussed, but feeling responsible, moves forward. Dalmore, realizing that this scene is perhaps more destructive to his gala than the renegade painting, thrusts himself between Lucinda and me. Lucinda's white skin is red. Kevin comes to my side.

Dalmore says, "Perkins and Perkins...? Kevin Perkins get a rolling partition to block that alcove..." As he looks in that direction he sees that the critic, Christopher Vine, apparently impervious to the mêlée, has come to stand in front of *German Lake*. He studies it intently. Kahn, a few feet away, appears to be dancing: two steps toward Vine and the painting, one step back. One step toward, two steps back. His knees sag a little as he does. He is oblivious to Rebecca. But she's riveted on him.

"Oh, no," Dalmore says softly as he sees where Vine is positioned. He looks at *his* ceiling and then *his* floor. Then he looks at me. "Alex Perkins," he says, "please leave my museum."

It seems I can't stand my ground to back up Kevin. My support would only make his situation worse. Probably Dalmore can't toss him out with me. He has to put on the museum's best face. And ejecting an assistant curator in the middle of a gala would not be good form.

I'm embarrassed though. There is no excuse I might put together that wouldn't involve mostly inexcusable parts. While I know that most men use truculence as a substitute for apology, I, more enlightened, instead muster humor.

"And to think I changed my underwear just to come here tonight," I say, shaking my head. "However, if – even in spite of that – you still insist, I will go." It's unfortunate that nothing seems to bring out bad behavior as effectively as being confronted about having behaved badly.

After waiting two seconds to see if the crowd will burst into cheers, or even just  applaud politely, I pivot and weave my way outward – to where I almost bump into Steve. He is five feet to one side of my exit path, still in the company of Oggelvy and Deborah. He blocks their view and leans into me.

"What've you got yourself into? What's going on? Was that the performance nudist? Who was she cursing out? Not you?"

"She cursed me out because of you," I say. But I know that is only half the story. More pot and kettle. I remind myself of Dimitri Karamazov, "I may be a murderer, but I'm not a thief."

"Yeah, well, I'll tell her it was my fault. I think I'd enjoy having her take off on me that way."

Behind Steve, I see Rebecca, drawn and pale – pausing barely two seconds to nod to  Oggelvy and Deborah – moving hurriedly – and alone –  toward the exit. She stops at the payphones and picks up a receiver.

"I've got to go," I say to my boss.

I make a stab at guessing what is happening and approach Rebecca as she digs into her tiny handbag. I assume she is looking for phone change.

"I'm leaving, too," I say, "if you need a ride."

"No. No – I…I" She seems on the verge of tears. "Thank you," she says, and adds, as if in apology, "I don't think I'd enjoy waiting in here for a cab."

# 24

I don't normally open car doors – or any doors – for women anymore. I was sort of taught "chivalry" by my mother. But having been castigated for chauvinism – and having even feared *assault* as a torrent of abuse came down upon me when I'd been door deferential at the height of feminist grievance redressing in about 1972 – I gave it up. So now I try to repress the reflex. But tonight I open my Karmann Ghia's door for Rebecca Sharma. And she says, "Thank you."

"Where to?" I ask.

"I have a place – I mean I'm renting one, a summer rental – at Blue Heron Beach. I guess you know where that is?"

"Yes, that's where I live, too."

"Oh? Yes – you live there with your grandmother?"

My mind races. The night of the whale. When I brought up Fred, I'd said he lived next door to my grandmother. I thought I'd caught myself before self-incriminating further.

"Yes," I say. "How did you know that?"

"Kevin told me."

Innocent, honest Kevin likely had no guess that I would have preferred to not look like a guy who lives with his grandmother to the loveliest woman I've ever seen not on television.

But she continues, "He said that you do a great job with her, and that everyone in the family is so grateful. It sounded very sweet."

"She's a champ," is all I can think to say.

We swing out of the museum lot and wind through the acres of green lawns and ornamental trees that surround it. It's twilight now. Wisps of pink and peach vapor still float overhead. A twisted apple tree appears almost black against the low horizon. I'm transported to a John Hulton painting. – Or I would be if I were not as thrown by the scene just left behind, and by the presence of this woman – who challenges my usually complacent self-image.

"I love convertibles," she says. I steal a glance at her. I need to, to believe that she is really here. She looks serene as always, despite that "scene." But she doesn't smile. For the first time I realize she is probably a few years older than me. Her black tresses that fall loose over her right cheek slap her face lightly in the automotive breeze.

"It's less of a buffeting if you roll up the window," I say.

"No, a buffeting is nice. It's a buffeting that I can handle. It's like a firm caress. Buffeting…" She trails off then says, "I guess we're both in the same boat."

"Same boat?" I say too quickly. I could easily have understood that she meant, *we have both been cuckolded by the same actors.* Perhaps male pride makes me want a distinction made between my losing a silly and inconsequential game I'd been playing for only a little more than a week, and Rebecca's suffering a deeper wound. I kick myself as I realize making this distinction expresses vanity more than empathy. So I quickly try to correct. "Same boat – yes, I guess we are in the same boat."

"Are you in love with her? Or were you?"

I don't want to seem cold – like the male flesh-consumer I guess I have pretty much been vis-à-vis Lucinda. I say, "Well, everything seemed to happen so fast. I only met her – what? – a little more than a week ago." I guess I got in my disclaimer anyway.

"Yes. I guess she's fast. As fast as he is."

"Does that mean that something like this has happened with him before? – I mean, I don't mean to pry. I mean, you said we were in the same boat. – I ask as one shipmate to another."

"Oh, yes – that's William. But he told me that he was through with that. Turning over a new leaf at forty. He said he would 'for me.' I suppose it's hard to blame him. She does *exude*. You all love that, don't you? I certainly never could have done what she did Sunday on the boat. I guess my background makes me too...*prim*. And, of course, I'm too old to start now."

This statement stuns me. My feeling is that Lucinda is not nearly in Rebecca's class. But maybe that doesn't contradict what she's saying. Haven't I mused that what I feel for Rebecca – or imagine I feel – isn't sexual? But a film clip of her with fingers in caviar does a quick cut across my memory circuit. *That* was sexy. But I can't tell her that. She's putting me on the spot. I can hardly "reassure" her that I find her sexy. I mean, I'm giving her a ride that I would have given to any three-hundred-pound man with a head like a potato, who needed to be away from a cheating wife. But she comes to my aid.

"I'm sorry," she says, "I guess that wasn't very nice. I'm blaming her. Probably if Lucinda hadn't been on the boat he'd have been sizing up Deborah. Oh, maybe not. She's probably too much like me."

Were I a true warrior male I could use the name of Deborah to deal Kahn's chances of reconciliation a lethal blow. Certainly Deborah was also a straw on the camel's back. Kevin would never have participated in the embarrassing painting caper without that straw. But, for some reason, I bite my competitive tongue. And I decide in favor of modified candor.

"What you say we all like *is* why I was with her. But it is also why I haven't been sure I should even have been with her at all." I venture a bit further. "And why – except that someone like you got hurt by it –

I don't much care what she does. I decided that before I knew she went off with William." This is pretty much true except for the word *decided*. The completely honest word would be *considered*.

"Well, then why did you try to get revenge? I mean, *that painting!*" She does smile now. She slides down a bit in her seat and placing her hands over her eyes, rocks her head from side to side. I find this intensely charming to watch. But I must remember I'm driving. "Was she right? Did you do that? I haven't considered how you could have."

She's again putting me in a tough spot. Since I have not been honest about the difference between *decided* and *considered*, I am making myself out so vengeful that I would destroy the reputation of a man who has done harm only to my pride. But she is right to wonder at my limited resources vis-à-vis the museum.

"I had people working for me on the inside," I say out of the corner of my mouth – taking advantage of her humorous gesture to contribute one of my own.

"Yes, of course – Kevin. But why would he help you? He might have risked his job. What has he got against William?

I can feel the wheels turning.

She straightens up in her seat. "Not Deborah *too?*"

I don't answer. She notices this, I think. Then I divert. I don't know why I do, but I do.

"Kevin and I are fond of old John Hulton. We didn't think William showed him much respect."

"That's true. That bothered me too. He's a sweet old man. And his work was wonderful."

This is music to my ears. That Rebecca could prefer cheap art like Kahn's to the real thing would be parallel to Lucinda's offering only image in the place of reality. If we can like the same thing, perhaps she is not from so different a world. But liking Hulton's painting doesn't mean that she doesn't like Kahn's. Well, it isn't the time to clarify this. Besides, she isn't through.

"But all successful artists bad-mouth. Even when they compliment

295

each other."

"Well," I say, "Hulton doesn't. Perhaps it was something about the contrast."

"And nothing about Deborah?"

I don't reply. For some reason, I feel I can't be the one to have told her. Why? She should know this. Is it male solidarity? No. I'm not enough of a *guy* for that.

"It's about justice – I don't like his work. I think it's shallow."

"Oh," she says.

"And you like it?" I ask this even though I had decided that this wasn't the right time. I guess that's another discrepancy between decided and considered.

"Yes, of course," Rebecca says. But I sense – or project – that there is less conviction in her tone than usually is associated with 'of course.' "But where did you find that awful one? Is it really his?"

"You've never seen work from his time in Germany?"

"No."

"If I might ask, how long have you two been going together?"

"The gallery I work for wooed him away from Correlli last fall. It started shortly after that." (Eight or nine months, I'm thinking. Neither insignificant nor *too* significant.) "But you're not telling me, how you did get that painting?"

"It was an accident."

"An accident?"

"The assistants grabbed a wrong crate when they picked up his show. Kevin told me about it on the boat Sunday."

"And you thought it was a necessary piece of the William Kahn biography."

"Hulton did."

"Hulton did? I thought you said he isn't competitive?"

"He isn't. He was defending Kahn. He said he hadn't seen his work, so how could he judge it. – Imagine someone today thinking he couldn't give an opinion about something he didn't know anything about?" The dashboard glow barely lights the left side of her face –

296

but enough so for me to see pleasure on her cheek at my explanation. So I told him about *The Lake*. And he said, "what a shame that won't be in his show.' But he wasn't serious. — I don't know. Perhaps he could be a little competitive."

We stay quiet for a while. Her smile fades and she looks tired. I surmise she has been putting on a courageous face, adequate for accepting a favor from a stranger in a moment of distress. I ask her how to get to her house and she tells me in a perfunctory way. We pull into her driveway and she doesn't give me the chance this time to open her door. She reaches around with her left hand for the handle and pushes out. With her right she reaches to shake mine, politely mouthing the words, "Thank you."

This is the first time a handshake has ever felt like a kick. I foolishly go for broke and ask, "Can I call you?"

She takes this with a little bit of a shudder. Then she gives what I could only call a forlorn smile and says, "It seems everyone in this little town is faster than I'd guess." And she turns away.

# 25

"Alex – wake up. It's Kevin. He's on the telephone."

"Okay, Gram. I've got it."

I look at my watch. Seven fifty-five. I finally drifted off as daylight started seeping semi-effectually into the dark. Since I left Rebecca Sharma at her door, I'd been replaying the Kahn opening and its aftermath – on the beach at the end of my childhood ritual road, where with a half-pint bottle of coffee brandy, I swatted mosquitoes until about one, then here in this sweaty bed.

"Hi, Kevin," I say. "You still in one piece?"

"Did you see today's *Times*?" Kevin asks as if that is the answer to my question.

"No, they don't sell it here in my bedroom."

"Let me read you some of it."

Normally I'd insist on having a cup of coffee in my hand – and one under my belt – to anyone wanting my attention at 8:00 in the morning. But since I'd been thinking: Kevin – Rebecca; Rebecca –

Kevin, all night, I'm primed to hear anything one or the other of them might have to say. But there was only a possibility of hearing from Kevin. I assume that the only thing Rebecca has to say is *nothing*.

"Sure. Go ahead." I don't have the foggiest what he is on to.

"I'll go right to what you'll like best. After he both praises and questions some of the underlying architectural assumptions behind the new contemporary wing of the Northport Modern and, as you might expect, raves about the new "Donald Duck's Favorite Hits," critic Christopher Vine writes: 'The star of the show and harbinger of things to be anticipated with considerable relish, is the lusciously ironic *German Lake with Deer and Eagles*. In the *Donald Duck Looks Back at the Masters* series, Kahn walked us to the edge of delicious slander of the canons of western art. But he actually pulls us along with him over that edge into a brave new world where all standards of the past are demolished – not like ducks in a row, but like clay pigeons. He coolly, but with unquestionable authority, demonstrates that these "standards" are as contextual as they are taste-relative and culturally manipulate-able. Kahn is confronting us with a revolutionary reality. Speaking in the sweet vernacular of a postmodern street mime, he is saying 'This painting that would be kitsch in a gallery on the Zimmerstrasse, will yet become *Art* when its context is an American museum.' Therefore, the obverse must also be true: our *masterpieces* will become merely kitsch when divested of the stamp of canonical authority conferred by the bitch goddess, Tradition. This insight is true creative maturity. Art, Kahn is saying, is anything the truly audacious artist says it is. Art isn't about aesthetics. It is about audacity."

Kevin waits a minute for it to sink in, then asks, "What do you think of that?"

"I thought the 'bitch goddess' was 'Success'."

"Is that all you have to say?"

"Well, I'm stunned. I mean, it's only been twelve hours. That's in *The New York Times*. What did he do, dictate it on the phone?"

"Who knows? Maybe he did. Probably faxed it," says Kevin.

"Who cares? Don't you see what this means?"

"It means that instead of making Kahn into a laughing stock, we've made him an even bigger hero. We've failed."

"Well, that may be true. But it also means that I can probably keep my job."

"When did you start worrying about that?"

"As soon as people in fancy clothes started coming through the doors last night."

"I wouldn't have figured you cared about fancy clothes."

"I don't care about the fancy clothes. It just made me realize that you need money to live, and I like working in the field I'm already in. If I got canned, what museum would hire a guy who intentionally sabotaged his own exhibition? That's not just fear of fear."

"You didn't think of that when you were putting that stupid painting over that window?"

"I don't know. Maybe I didn't. I was feeling *giddy*. It was like a practical joke. I wasn't thinking of consequences."

First throwing himself into the sea after a philosopher and now into practical jokes on a famous artist. My older cousin has more parts than they list in the Boy Scout handbook.

"Well, it's a crime against truth and justice," I say.

"You know," says Kevin, "it wasn't a complete failure. For one thing, didn't I see you going out the door with Rebecca Sharma?"

"Yes. I took her home."

"Wow."

"Well, that's what *I* thought. She was nice – at first. Even told me the good word you had put in for me – you know, about my taking care of Gram. But then I said something wrong. Or she started missing him or something. And she shut down. Anyway, no kiss good night."

"Gee, you expect a lot."

"I'm not serious."

"Well, that's too bad. You made a good looking couple."

"Don't be sarcastic. I'm completely crushed."

"Sorry."

"But, you know," I say, "maybe you're right and we didn't fail completely. Maybe it was worth it for that look on Kahn's face. And Dalmore's too. Can you imagine being an artist and doing a painting so bad that you panic if you think someone will see it? I wonder why he kept it. Even paid for having it shipped from Berlin. Maybe he really likes it."

"Well, if he doesn't he'd better learn to, because *The New York Times* is staking his reputation on it. This is just like 'The Emperor's New Clothes.'"

"It's all like the 'Emperor's New Clothes'. I just thought we'd end up being the little boys in the crowd saying, 'Hey, look – he's naked.' And everyone would say, 'Hey, they're right.'"

"Well, that's the difference between fairy tales and real life," Kevin says.

"Yeah – they're not the same thing at all, but people think they are. What's that guy's name, Joseph Campbell? 'If it's a myth, it has to be true.' People wanna believe in fairy tales."

"Hey – I like Joseph Campbell," Kevin says.

"Well, that's probably why you'd throw yourself into the cold, raging sea to rescue a philosopher – and I wouldn't."

"He turned out to be an alright guy, though – Bollard I mean, Not Joseph Campbell."

"Yeah, I kind of like him now too. And *he* likes *my* philosophy. So I guess together the Perkins boys converted him."

"What's your philosophy?"

"Just that relief is the greatest sensation there is."

"Relief?"

"Relief. – Like you felt when you learned you wouldn't be losing your job."

"Hum. Interesting," Kevin says. "But I'm not sure. You may be taking in too much territory."

"Me? Never! – You really think so?"

"I don't know. I'll have to think about it."

301

"You think about it. I have to take a shower."

"Wait – one more indication we didn't completely fail."

"What?"

"Oggelvy – Deborah's uncle. He thought *German Lake* was funny as hell."

"Good"

"And Deborah – She's pretty much a team player at the museum. I think at first she was down on my free-lancing, hanging an unapproved piece. But it seems her uncle changed her mind. He even put his arm around me. Said doing that was real curating – not being enslaved to the artist's self-promotion. Honesty before career.

"So we didn't fail."

"No. So I'm pretty happy."

"Relieved."

"All right, relieved. – And guess what? Oggelvy asked for *your* phone number – I mean Gram's. Said he didn't want to call you at *Currents.* I guess I seemed perplexed about his asking. So he mentioned that he wanted to compliment you on your Hulton piece. That's nice too, huh?"

"It is," I say. "Getting wealthy, powerful people to step up to the plate for me is something I've been really lazy about for a long time. I was just telling Gram I thought we should cultivate a wealthier class of friends."

"Right. Well, I've got to get to the museum. Have to act as normal as I can. Nothing to fear but Dalmore himself. But with this *Times* review and a few wealthy and powerful people stepping up to the plate for *me,* I'm not too afraid of him."

"Well, good luck anyway. I still feel bad about that Funky Chicken photo. I didn't mean to humiliate him. I'm sure all the good will and all his quotes I put into the article itself will be right out the window. That article wasn't half-bad. Right? Okay, maybe that is going a little too far. But if my name comes up, tell him… Well, I was going to say, tell him the picture wasn't my fault. But I guess that's just a technicality. And after *German Lake* I probably don't have much credibility as a compassionate guy."

"He doesn't know you had anything to do with that."

"What about Lucinda accusing me publicly?"

"After he ordered you out. I told him she was wrong. The painting was just my doing."

I feel a stab of deep tenderness.

"You didn't need to do that. Hell, the repercussions were likely to be a lot worse for you. You should have said it was just me."

"Well, that would have been breaking and entering. And then we couldn't chalk it all up to curatorial incompetence."

"He's going to believe that's what it was?"

"Not with me having hung a piece over a window. No curator's that incompetent."

"So what's he think?"

"I *think* he thinks Oggelvy put me up to it. Dalmore did see him having such a good time with the whole *German Lake* thing. And my guess is he's worried – now that he knows Deborah and Oggelvy are related; and maybe even thinks she's on my side – that Deborah – his own assistant – will need finessing too. But that's all moot since *The New York Times* labeled *German Lake* 'a fucking masterpiece.'"

"Language, Kevin!" I reprimand. "What about the Boy Scout oath?"

"Oh yeah, that," he says. "…Well, I've got to run."

I put down the phone and gather an armful of clothes, heading for the shower. I don't turn the hot all the way up, after my sweaty night. Luke-warm feels pretty good right now. Things really aren't so bad. It's been an odd week or so. But I think of what Steve would say: "At least you got laid." And instead of disaster for Kevin, things look pretty good. And about Kevin and me, as Rick Blaine put it, "This looks like the beginning of a beautiful friendship."

Rosebud, seeing me exiting the bathroom, wriggles into paroxysms of joy, almost tying herself in a knot. Maybe dog love is the best love. Nice dog. And nice cousin, I guess. Nice grandmother, too. What more could a guy in my position reasonably want?

As I enter the kitchen I smell burnt butter and perceive dark wisps rising from an unattended pan. Gram is on the wall phone. I dash to turn off the burner.

"Alex," she says. "Quick – take the phone. I think I smell something burning. I couldn't tell who it is. My hearing aid is on the other ear."

Frank Oggelvy springs to the forefront of my consciousness. Something else to feel good about. Someone with money likes something that I did. Gram goes and relights the stove. Whether she thinks she's in fact turning it off by following the twist of least resistance, I can't tell. But when she reaches for the eggs, I decide she's adequately attentive.

"Hello?"

"Alex?

"Yes?"

"This is Rebecca Sharma."

I'm stunned. "Yes," is all I can say.

"Good morning."

"Good morning."

"Well, I found a 'Perkins, G.' on the beach road you mentioned, and I guess I guessed right. The 'G' doesn't stand for 'grandmother' does it?"

"No – Gram…I mean 'Georgia'."

"I wanted to thank you for the ride last night."

"Sure," I say.

"And I wanted to apologize because I may have been a bit rude."

"No, no – you weren't rude."

"Well, I think I may have been." Pause. "I guess I was upset at men, and you were one. And, of course, I should have been just as upset at women. I'm sorry – do you understand what I am saying?"

This woman has *diction*. I'm in love with her diction. "Sure," I say again. And for want, at this moment, of much thought dexterity, I blandly add, "I understand."

"Well, that's all. I don't want to keep you from your grandmother right now…"

My grandmother! Who cares about my grandmother?

"No, no – she's fine," I insist, trying to get some traction. I must keep this woman on the phone. But what good is that if I can't think of anything *interesting* to say. "Look, maybe I was a jerk bringing it up last night. I thought it might be my only chance to ask. But – really – can we get together sometime…and talk? I'm really a much slower person than you might think." That's what I, very interestingly, come up with. Not too good, huh?

Pause. "I don't know." Pause again. "I have a number of things to…think about these days."

"How about the week after next?"

She laughs. Thank god she laughs. It's a melodious sound. I can picture her with caviar on her fingers.

"I…don't…know…" There's a long pause. Then she says, "But I might tell you that a boy on a bicycle threw your newspaper onto my porch this morning. And I saw your… *review*…of conceptual art. I guess you're quite opinionated. With that and the freelance curating I saw last night, I'm afraid you may be a more mischievous fellow than you seem. Not as slow as you protest. – I mean, I guess there's more to you than meets the eye."

Her tone is neutral for what she's saying, but I can feel there's laughing still in there. Ladies love outlaws. Or so I hope. So I won't tell her Steve's the real outlaw. And I decide to ignore the downside implications of "more to you than meets the eye." Of course, I know I'm no Tom Berenger.

"That's true," I say. "At Halloween I like to dress up as Clark Kent. You know – 'mildly manic reporter for a great metropolitan newspaper.' Only it's not really such a great newspaper."

"Did you make that up just now?" I detect muffled buoyancy in the way she asks this.

"No. But I did *make it up* – last Halloween."

"So you really did go as Clark Kent?"

305

"I said I did. I never lie. Well, that's not true."

"What did you wear?"

"One of my father's old suits. And his glasses. And I Vaselined my hair."

There's a barely audible sound. Perhaps a stifled snort. Then nothing.

"Hello?" I say.

"I'm here."

"So?"

Pause. Then: "Well, maybe in a few weeks we could...oh?... perhaps...have a cup of coffee. You know – some afternoon. How do you feel about that?"

How do I feel about that? How do I feel about that?

"How do I feel about that? Well, I'd have to say I feel ...*relieved.*"

"*Relieved?*"

"*Very,*" I say.

"That's it? I mean, is that's *all?* 'Relieved?'"

"'Is that all? Is that all?' Listen Rebecca," – I guess I'm saying her name aloud for the first time ever. Saying it, and hearing it, too, sounds wondrous in this childhood kitchen on the open-windowed morning of a fine summer day. "In my book," I proclaim, godlike to this goddess of the summer morning telephone lines – "'relief' *is the greatest sensation there is."*

# 26

"I don't think your blue trench coat is going to be warm enough, Gram. There were some snow flurries this morning. I think your wool coat would be better."

"Snow on Thanksgiving! What's the world coming to? What time is Steve expecting us?"

"Not Steve, Gram. Steve was my old boss. This is Frank. Remember Kevin's going to be there too. Remember he's engaged to Frank's niece." I'm looking forward to this. Boss or not, Frank really is an all right guy. And, John Hulton will be at Thanksgiving dinner. I could listen to that guy's stories all day.

"Of course I remember. I was thinking about something else. Mr. Oggelvy, I mean."

"You can call him Frank."

"Alex – don't make trouble. *Steve – Frank*, what time is he expecting us?"

"Four o'clock."

"That seems pretty late for Thanksgiving dinner. Maybe rich people do it like that. I'm hungry now. It's only 2:30. Why are we leaving now if we don't have to be there until four? Where does he live, Boston?"

"No, he lives here in Northport. We're going by Rebecca's place first – to show it to you. Remember? You can have a bite there."

"Yes, I remember. With the little boy. What's his name again?"

"Dev."

"Dave?"

"No. With an 'e'. D-e-v.

"Oh that's right. The Indian boy."

"Gram, we talked about that. He was born in New York and his father is Norwegian. It's just an Indian name. People don't call you an English woman. And you're English on both sides."

"That's because my people came here a long time ago."

"What difference does that make?"

"Alex – I asked you not to argue with me. It's cold out here. And my panty hose are down around my knees."

"Well, let's go back inside so you can fix them."

"Never mind. It's hard enough for me to get out of the house once. We're almost to the car."

"Well, it's going to be harder to fix them in the car."

"They're okay."

"But if they're down around your knees, you're going to need to pull them up."

"They're not *that* far down. You take the things I say too seriously."

Right, I don't say. Except when you think I don't take them seriously enough.

I feel kind of bad that I'm here a lot less since I started seeing Rebecca. I began staying a few nights a week at her rental a half-mile away around the middle of July. But I seldom do that two nights in a row. And Gram hasn't complained about my being out all night because she knows where I am, seems to approve, and can always get me on the phone. And Kevin, and his mother, my aunt, Sylvia, have taken up the slack by stopping in a lot more. Our only concern – since we believe Gram's insistence that she doesn't have any reason to go upstairs when I'm not here – is her using the stove.

Oddly, that concern was mitigated a bit by what happened at the NoMMA in the aftermath of the William Kahn opening in June. When Arthur Dalmore's taste in contemporary art – though well reviewed from New York – had, by the time of the annual August board meeting, failed to ignite widespread excitement in Northport, the members, when voting on a permanent successor to the deceased director Jonathan Cutts, chose to put the overall operation of the museum in more conservative hands. Kevin's hands were the most obvious around. Most obvious, that is, to Frank Oggelvy – who had demurred, yet deferred, on Dalmore previously. Scattered grumblings about nepotism were emphatically dispelled by iteration of Kevin's eight years of competent service to the museum *before he even met* Oggelvy's lovely niece. Somehow *German Lake* never entered the discussion. A wash is a wash. Dalmore did not publicly resist being passed over. I assume he believes the *German Lake* caper was the first step in his being over-thrown. And that the Funky Chicken photo in the paper, for which I, Kevin's cousin, was the source, was arranged by me as insurance that he proffer a lower profile, at least for a while. But I am not smart or effectual enough to move and shake worlds – even little worlds – that way. Do I wish I were? No comment. Dalmore remains curator of the contemporary wing; it's still his sanctum sanctorum. He probably has at least a few years grace period to continue trying to bring religion to the natives of these parts – and to enjoy entertaining New York notables at his seaside retreat and on his wonderful yacht. Perhaps someday, when any lingering hard feelings are long past, I'll volunteer to crew for him again. (Love that boat.) I'll promise not to bring my camera.

Anyway the first thing Kevin did when he got his promotion, replete with a big raise, was buy Gram an electric stove. And I leaned on Fred Avery to wire a smoke detector that activates a buzzer in his house next door. Of course, Fred's not always home to hear it. But every little layer of protection helps some. Gram's sense of smell is about as good as ever. So she usually detects a burnt pot even before the alarm does. The big worry with her gas range was bathrobe sleeves tempting the flame.

So I'm not too worried about Gram at present. And after all she was living totally alone until about a year ago. And she doesn't seem any less capable at 91 than she was at 90. Of course, that's probably hard to tell. – That *lab frog on slow boil* thing. Can you really see small changes while they are happening in front of you? A problem may come in the spring when my new house is ready for occupancy. It's going up on the land about ten miles into the countryside that had been just sitting since I bought it five years ago. Kevin wasn't the only one who got a pretty hefty raise when his employment picture evolved. In working for Oggelvy, I report to the offices of the *Beacon*. But my reviews are syndicated and regularly appear in more than one of his newspapers – hence my being able to afford a building loan. I'm on the road a lot of the time now – covering further flung events – so I'll probably need a better winter car than the Karman Ghia. The top has a tear, the heater sucks, and the road salt will eat up that frameless body in no time. And I can't put that kind of work miles on Rebecca's car.

I am excited about the house, though. I've designed it and it will be, considering my budget, pretty much what I want. However, my dream of building it myself will not come to pass. To the contractor's consternation, I go by and do some slam-banging on weekends. But I don't have enough free time for more than that. Writing for real newspapers requires me to know what I'm writing about. So I've got to study up on many subjects, the kind I used to just wing it on, writing for *Currents*.

I'm not naïve enough to think that I am building the house for Rebecca and me – and Dev, who is five. The relationship is too new to bank on. Rebecca says she loves Northport, but I know she misses the *pace* of New York – sometimes anyway. But the plan as of now –

310

almost the six-month point in our being together – is for us to move in as a couple – dare I say *family* – when the winter lease runs out on her place here at Blue Heron. It will be a bit of a test. I try hard with Dev but he's slow at accepting me as a substitute for William Kahn – let alone his actual dad. Lars and Rebecca parted company only less than two years ago. And Dev demands a lot of attention. He seems to take after William more than Lars, who is a lawyer. Like last night. I'd wanted to get some quiet time with Rebecca, so I brought Dev an Etch-A-Sketch, thinking it would take him a while to get tired of it. In about five minutes he was all over us on the couch, waving the thing. "Look! Look!" he said, showing us something that appeared to be a cat or a small dog. "Can you believe it," he entreated us incredulously, "I'm only five years old and already I can draw a deer that good?" Lars lives nearby in Boston. It turns out having her son able to see his father was as much of the reason for Rebecca's taking the Northport gallery job, as following Kahn.

So Kevin, Sylvia, and I are discussing whether Gram can go on living alone here when I move completely out and am ten miles away. Maybe we can find someone to live with her. It's hard to imagine her being very willing to leave this old house. But I intend to bring up soon to Rebecca that I want Gram to move in with us when the new house is ready. My "writing room", with a curving bank of windows facing the pond, is on the first floor. I don't really need a writing room for the small amount I do away from the office. So I'd be happy to give it up for Gram for a few years or however long she's got. I figure a five-year-old boy and a ninety year old woman just about cancel each other out as burdens on your partner. But I guess that's truer in other countries. In the U.S. we are much more sympathetic to the next generation than we are to the last. But Rebecca is very good with Gram. And I think she is "old country" enough that she may go along with the idea. We'll see.

Basically, Rebecca and I get along fine. She wasn't exactly lying when she called herself "prim". She's not very, but she is a little. Perhaps I was saying something not just about me when I mentioned

I didn't *lust* after her when we first met. – I said I could be happy just pushing her on a swing for a while. I assumed the lust would come along in about two days. There is some of that now, of course, but less than I'd guessed. But I had vowed "no more difficult women," and I seem to have gotten my wish. "Fortune favors the lucky," they say. Or maybe they don't. But I do. – Goes with my belief that the thing we can count on most is the law of averages. Though Angela and Lucinda were much more hot and cold – and the hot was pretty exciting; and, be honest, the cold kept me on my toes – Rebecca is never either extreme. Mostly she's pretty warm and that feels good.

But when I think about that week or so in June that rearranged my life, I can get a just bit wistful. I don't mean that I miss Lucinda, or anything like that. I just didn't know that that manic interlude with her and her friends was going to be the storm before the calm. But that's okay. It was peace I said I was looking for – though I'm a little too busy for this to be that. I do wonder though, was I ever really fair to Lucinda? Was I too judgmental about her beliefs and opinions? (She certainly had a point about *contexts*.) And Rebecca seems to believe the same stuff about finding parking spaces by harnessing cosmic – or karmic – radiation, and other magical things like that. But I've yet to give her a hard time about it. – No, I did once. When she had a cold and speculated that she got it because she *needed to be sick*. That was over the top, and when I howled, she gave it up gracefully. But I think that was the only time. I wonder if the reason I don't bug her – the way I did Lucinda – is because Rebecca's spiritual beliefs come from deep in her ethnic heritage, and aren't just things she read in some new age magazine about a week ago. Still I can't take even that too far. I remember my projections about Rebecca's Eastern serenity or equanimity that day on *Pure Conception*. She's really not much less an American girl than Deborah or Lucinda – or Angela for that matter. So maybe I don't bug her because I learned a lesson about tolerance from having that guilt about Lucinda. I don't know. It's hard to think of myself as enlightened enough for that. Maybe it's just that Rebecca is beautiful enough for a beauty addict to cut her more slack. I imagine, though, a *tits addict* might be quite tolerant of Lucinda's spiritual beliefs where I wasn't. Who knows? – Maybe it was the coke talking that night. I haven't had a nose-full since. I know Rebecca wouldn't put up with cocaine. And I wouldn't want to do it behind her back. Rebecca even hassles me for the amount I drink. She's right. I should cut down. I guess. I think it's possible that I drift off into beauty less far, and maybe less often, the more I drink.

So I think I wonder about Lucinda more for what it might tell me about myself. I'd have to admit she was too much for a guy like me. – And also admit that she isn't too much for a William Kahn. But I never set out to compete with him anyway. Well, I mean, I didn't at first. But what *do* I mean by *at first?* Within two weeks of my meeting him, we'd traded girlfriends. That could mean that I'd remained uncompetitive for the first 100 yards of a thousand yard race. By the way, I hear, when he went back to New York, Lucinda went too. (The NoMMA never offered her a show.) I even saw a picture of them arm and arm in one of the arts mags that I have to spend more time reading these days to be up to my job. So maybe they've become a real couple – like Rebecca and me. And that may mean that Kahn's going after Lucinda wasn't just ego and random horniness – and opportunism on her part. How should I know? One picture in a magazine.

There's another piece of news from New York. It seems David Player is riding the decline to dizzying heights. He has a solo show scheduled for May at Sunderland. Sunderland is one of Soho's prestige galleries of the moment. So it's beyond question that his sculpture has merit. They've already sold several pieces out of the back room, each for about the price of a fishing boat. But he can't quite yet afford a studio loft big enough to use dynamite in, so he'll have to come back here to produce the work he'll need for the spring. It will be good to see him.

The thing that ten days or so in June fostered in me, about which I feel most truly grateful – and it is Thanksgiving, after all – is my recognizing what a terrific person Kevin is. Kevin, who was there all the time. Kevin, whom I'd hardly ever noticed. So I'm really happy for him getting that top job – and getting Deborah. Deborah just seems great too. No "there are no coincidences"-type stuff for her. When I remember that day on *Pure Conception*, with her at the helm, competent and dignified, in the face of just being passed over for Rebecca by Kahn, it strikes me odd now that – like with Kevin – I'd hardly noticed her quality. I mean when I was weighing the charms of the women on board, I considered only Lucinda, the siren and Rebecca, the goddess. I never guessed that Deborah might be the pick of the three. I shouldn't put it that way, I know. What if Rebecca knew I said that? Of course, I'm not jealous. I'm truly glad that Kevin – probably a better man than I am – has her.

And I do love Rebecca. I wouldn't want to take her on a camping trip, but I'm not complaining about how things turned out. It's just that what little edge I started gaining in June may have gotten a bit duller by now. Rebecca enjoys my attempts at humor; tells me I'm funny. But she does emit seriousness. Eating caviar with fingers fell about as far outside her daily routine as mine. And embracing step-fatherhood runs very high in my seriousness book. I also now fill a serious job position and am mortgaged in a serious way. I feel I could just use a bit of relief. Not the capitol "R" kind – like when it turns out the firing squad was really using blanks for a joke. "Relief" as in things almost stopping and the world getting really quiet now and then – like it did more often before. But it's a lot harder to float away on sunlit rippling water in November than it was in June.

Still, if anything haunts me from that week back then, it is that poem by Baudelaire I read on Lucinda's wall, *Be Drunken*. "If you would not be martyred slaves of time; be drunken continually! With wine, with poetry or with virtue, as you will." Actually, I have cut down on the wine – spirits, I mean – as I now, as I said, wonder if it inhibits getting "drunk on beauty" – washes the last micrograms of LSD from my mind or imagination. And I am still a teetotaler when it comes to virtue. So I wonder about poetry in my life. And for poetry I could substitute art – or just beauty itself. Am I drunken with

Rebecca's beauty? Sure sometimes. But, as we do with relief, we get used, even, to beauty. Everything is most precious when we don't exactly have it yet – and sadly, of course, after it's gone. A song I like on the radio might envelope me in excitement or a romantic or haunted mood. If I never own it – buy it or tape it – the emotion will come back each time I hear it played. But if I own it, the magic starts to fade after I've replayed it only a few times. I fear we drift toward boredom; toward taking things for granted. – That is until the well runs dry. Should we live as though the well might run dry any minute? I don't know. Depends on your temperament. It could make you *appreciate*. Or just make you a bigger worrier.

I did go out and buy a book of Baudelaire and found, even he, could have some reservations about overdoing things. A poem called, *Which Is True*, gives me pause about my beauty addiction. It goes:

*I knew one Benedicta who filled earth and air with the ideal; and from whose eyes men learnt the desire of greatness, of glory, and of all whereby we believe in immortality.*

*But this miraculous child was too beautiful to live long; and she died only a few days after I had come to know her, and I buried her with my own hands, one day when Spring shook out her censer in the graveyards. I buried her in my own hands, shut down into a coffin of wood, perfumed and incorruptible like Indian caskets.*

*And as I still gazed at the place where I had laid away my treasure, I saw all at once a little person singularly like the deceased, who trampled on the fresh soil with a strange and hysterical violence, and said, shrieking with laughter: 'Look at me! I am the real Benedicta! a pretty sort of baggage I am! And to punish you for your folly you shall love me just as I am!'*

*But I was furious, and I answered: 'No! no! no!' And to add more emphasis to my refusal I stamped on the ground so violently with my foot that my leg sank up to the knee in the earth of the new grave; and now, like a wolf caught in a trap, I remain fastened, perhaps forever, to the grave of the ideal.*

I memorized it to recite at Thanksgiving dinner at the Oggelvy manse today. Well, no, I didn't. I memorized it, but just for myself. Along with *Be Drunken*, I've now committed a total of two and a half poems, over the course of my life, to memory. Edgar Allen Poe's, *Annabel Lee*, I learned shortly after my mother's death. But I realize that *Annabel Lee* is mostly gone now. *Which Is True?* makes me see how hard it would be to really "Be Drunken". I guess the trick is to be drunken with what's actually here, and not with an ideal.

So I've learned that even for a beauty addict, beauty isn't salvation. And maybe somehow I did know that all along. I like to think I'm enchanted by the ideal version of something – like I am by a lilac being a lilac being a lilac – but not imprisoned by it. Beauty – whether in sunlight on water, in art, or in your girlfriend's face – can be a pretty big help. But it can't be all.

By twists and turns, I've settled Gram into to the passenger seat of Rebecca's Toyota for the short drive to her/our house.

"Alex, you aren't wearing a seat belt."

"I know, Gram. We're only going a half mile."

"That isn't any excuse. I saw it on television just the other day. A man was only going out for cigarettes and he didn't put his belt on. Out of the blue his car was dilapidated and he was killed. If he didn't smoke he'd be alive today."

I suppress a laugh. "Or if he smoked," I say, "*and* had a seatbelt on too."

I am trying her patience.

"Alex! You know what I mean. Stop arguing with me and put it on before you drive another five feet."

"Yes, Gram," I say, pleasantly enough. Then I buckle-up my seatbelt and put the car in gear.

# About the Author:

Peter Agrafiotis dropped out of college at 19 to work as a reporter for a Maine weekly newspaper. While still in his twenties he created his own publication, *CLUE, America's Only Vacation Magazine That's Sarcastic.* His satiric tales earned *CLUE* a coast-to-coast following, financial success, and the praise of a wide range of authors and comedic storytellers of national repute. The *Anthology of Maine Humor* called Agrafiotis "Maine's Least Traditional Humorist."

Agrafiotis also is a painter with a dozen solo shows to date in major cities, including New York and Boston. His canvases hang in over 100 public, private, and corporate collections. He has been nominated four times for awards at the American Academy of Arts and Letters. (See website: peteragrafiotis.com.)

In this his first novel, *This Is Not My Bathing Suit,* Agrafiotis distills the experience of these dual careers and his years as a Gulf of Maine sailor, into a sly and comic swipe at the contemporary New York art world, caught off-guard on its summer vacation.

Agrafiotis lives with his wife, Janice Plourde, in an eccentric house on the Maine coast he has been building for decades. As a child he wanted to grow up to be Bret Maverick, but after puberty that changed to Marcello Mastroianni. In more recent years Agrafiotis has become an avid exponent of the law of averages. He also believes in having a good dog.

www.ingramcontent.com/pod-product-compliance
Lightning Source LLC
Chambersburg PA
CBHW021305250626
47155CB00002B/390